BOOKS BY OAKLEY HALL

The Children of the Sun 1983
Lullaby 1982
The Bad Lands 1978
The Adelita 1975
Report from Beau Harbor 1972
A Game for Eagles 1970
The Pleasure Garden 1966
The Downhill Racers 1962
Warlock 1958
Mardios Beach 1955
Corpus of Joe Bailey 1953
So Many Doors 1950

The Children of the Sun

———————————

Oakley Hall

THE CHILDREN OF THE SUN

Atheneum   New York

1983

LIBRARY OF CONGRESS CATALOGING IN PUBLICATION DATA

Hall, Oakley M.
The children of the sun.

1. Núñez Cabeza de Vaca, Álvar, 16th cent.—
Fiction. 2. America—Discovery and exploration—
Spanish—Fiction. I. Title.
PS3558.A373C5 1983   813'.54   82-73039
ISBN 0-689-11348-X

Published simultaneously in Canada by McClelland and Stewart Ltd.
Composed by Maryland Linotype Composition Company, Baltimore, Maryland
Manufactured by Fairfield Graphics, Fairfield, Pennsylvania
Designed by Mary Cregan
FIRST EDITION

This book is for Barbara,
without whom . . .

"My companions were a timorous man, a sensual man, and a competent man."

ÁLVAR NÚÑEZ CABEZA DE VACA

Contents

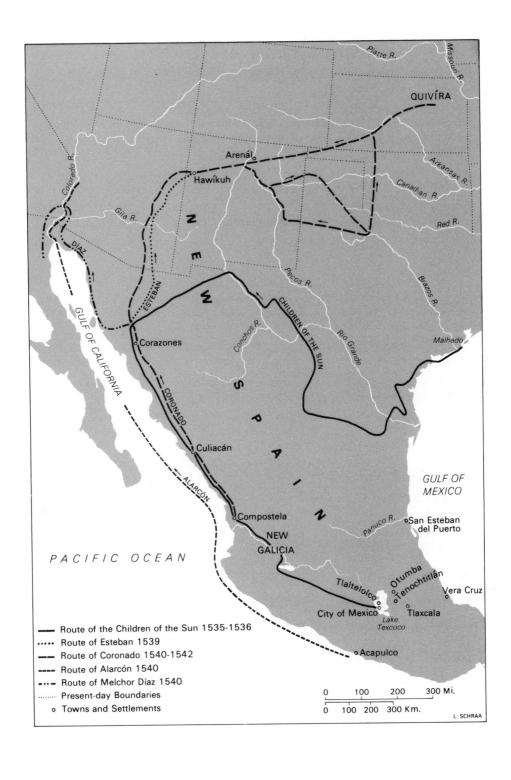

Platte R.

Missouri R.

QUIVÍRA

Arkansas R.

Canadian R.

Arenal

Hawíkuh

Red R.

Colorado R.

Gila R.

N

DÍAZ

E

Brazos R.

ESTEBAN

W

Pecos R.

CHILDREN OF THE SUN

Rio Grande

GULF OF CALIFORNIA

Conchos R.

Corazones

Malhado

S

CORONADO

P

A

Culiacán

I

ALARCÓN

N

GULF OF MEXICO

Compostela

Panuco R.

San Esteban del Puerto

NEW GALICIA

PACIFIC OCEAN

Tlaltelolco

Otumba
Tenochtitlán

Vera Cruz

City of Mexico

Tlaxcala

Lake Texcoco

———— Route of the Children of the Sun 1535–1536
••••• Route of Esteban 1539
— — Route of Coronado 1540–1542
- - - - Route of Alarcón 1540
-•-•- Route of Melchor Díaz 1540
•••••••• Present-day Boundaries
o Towns and Settlements

Acapulco

0   100   200   300 Mi.

0   100 200   300 Km.

L. SCHRAA

❀

Prologue

Two Virgins dominate the history of Mexico.

During the Conquest, after the terrible retreat from Tenochtitlán called the "Night of Sorrows," the Virgin of the Remedies appeared to the shattered band of Spaniards who had survived, to restore their courage, heal their wounds, and dazzle the Aztec hordes that harried them. Her image still resides in a shrine in a chapel on the Cerro de Toltepec in Mexico City, blonde, blue-eyed, and sumptuously gowned in the sixteenth-century Castilian manner.

This Lady exercised her power once again for those who loved her, when Hidalgo's revolutionary army swept all before it in its advance on the capitol in 1810. The viceroy, Vanegas, led a procession of Europeans to the cathedral and laid his baton at her feet, proclaiming her captain-general of the viceregal army and reinvoking Hernán Cortés' war against the Indians.

With nothing between his eighty thousand and the capital, Hidalgo paused and veered off to Queretaro, and the city of Mexico was saved for the Spaniards by the intercession of the Virgin of the Remedies.

The other Virgin is known as La Morenita, the Dark Virgin, Nuestra Señora de Guadalupe, Our Lady of Guadalupe. In 1531 Christianity in Mexico made an enormous breakthrough with her appearance, so much so that Bishop Zumárraga has been accused of conniving in a useful miracle.

A poor Indian baptized Juan Diego encountered this Lady at a place called Tepeyac. She spoke to him in his native tongue, commanding him to go to the bishop and ask that a chapel be built in this place, where she might give solace to the Indian people in their sorrows.

When Juan Diego was turned away from the bishop's palace, the Lady appeared to him again. He was instructed to climb the hill of

Tepeyac, a place of weeds and cactus, and gather the flowers he found there as a sign for the bishop. He found Castilian roses growing in profusion, and wrapped some blooms in his cape to take to Zumárraga's palace. When he spread out his cloak before the bishop, imprinted upon it was the image of a radiant, dark-complexioned Virgin. The shrine was quickly built, with the cloak displayed within it. Miracles were immediately attributed to La Morenita.

In the next fifteen years, nine million Indians were baptized.

An intense mysticism accompanied the growing popularity of the cult of the Dark Virgin. The army of revolution in the War of Independence flourished prints of her image as it marched behind its leaders, and a hundred years later the soldiers of Emiliano Zapata fought with her icons pinned to their sombreros.

The two Virgins faced each other in many battles, with the darker Lady ultimately victorious, and La Guadalupana has also come to symbolize Mexico's racial integration and unity. The fair Castiliana, however, retains her adherents.

The Conquest of Mexico:
A Gallery of Conquerors

MONTEZUMA

He had the misfortune to be the Great Speaker, the Emperor of the Aztecs, when the Spaniards arrived in force on the mainland in 1519.

The Aztecs themselves were relative newcomers to the Valley of Mexico, having arrived from the north in the twelfth century, a poor, nomadic tribe. Their capitol, Tenochtitlán, was founded on the islands of Lake Texcoco about 1325. By alliance, treachery, and conquest, they came to dominate an expanding area. They claimed to be the legitimate heirs of the noble Toltecs, the ancient inhabitants of the valley. Toltecs were civilized, Chichimecs barbarians; a wound in the Aztec psyche was the knowledge that they were Chichimecs pretending to be Toltecs. The god of the Toltecs had been Quetzalcoatl, a benevolent deity who had been tricked by the Aztec god, Tezcatlipoca, into drunkenness and incest. Quetzalcoatl in his shame departed from Mexico, vowing, however, to return.

The empire of the Aztecs was based literally on blood. It was their belief that they were the chosen instruments in the task of maintaining the gods who ordered the cosmos. Their deities demanded human blood for ensuring the rising of the sun each morning. Failure of this supply would result in final darkness and a surge of monsters from the vasts of night. Slaves and prisoners of war were sacrificed, and, when these proved insufficient, the "Flower Wars" were devised, mock wars in which real prisoners were taken. When the Spaniards came and their victories seemed to signify the disfavor of the gods, sacrifice became more and more wholesale. The demands of the Aztec sacrificial machinery created such hatred in their neighboring, and victim, states, that it may be said that the sufferers from the Aztec tyranny, with Spanish leadership, overthrew the empire.

Aztec time was circular rather than straight-line, recurring in 52-year cycles. Quetzalcoatl was born in the year 1-Acatl. In 1-Acatl, again, he sailed away from Mexico. It was supposed, then, that he would return in another 1-Acatl. The "floating islands" of the Spaniards were reported off the coast by Montezuma's spies in 1-Acatl. Montezuma was faced with the return of Quetzalcoatl in these fair-complexioned men debarking. They were the true heirs of the Toltecs, the Aztecs impostors.

The emperor sent bribes in hopes that these newcomers would desist and depart. When they persisted he devised, at Cholula, a massacre that backfired. His sorcerers failed to deflect them. Finally he could only invite them to Tenochtitlán. His welcoming speech to Cortés is significant:

"My lord, you have come back to your land. You have arrived in your city. You have come to sit on your throne, under its canopy. Brief was the time they held it for you, preserved it for you, those who have gone before, your substitutes."

Hernán Cortés was not one to fail to take advantage of this religious confusion, and the Emperor of the Aztecs became subservient to the Spaniards' will, ultimately as a hostage. This prevented any Aztec rebellion against the invaders, until, in a riot, Montezuma was killed—whether by his own people or his captors is not known—and the Spaniards were bloodily expelled from Tenochtitlán.

CORTÉS

The voyages of Córdoba and Grijalva to the mainland of what is now Mexico had brought back to the Antilles a few gold trinkets and tales of temples and palaces of stone and mortar. Hernán Cortés was the second choice of the governor of Cuba, Diego Velásquez, to command a military expedition, and so little trusted that Velásquez tried to call him back—too late, for Cortés was already bound for glory, throwing off Velásquez' authority to claim that of the Crown itself.

En route to Tenochtitlán, he first defeated the Tlaxcalans, fierce enemies of the Aztecs, who then became his always-faithful allies. When the Spaniards were driven out of Tenochtitlán on the Night of Sorrows, it was in Tlaxcala that they recuperated, gathered new recruits and military stores, and planned the Reconquest. Tenochtitlán-Tlatelolco was laid siege to; the new Emperor of the Aztecs, Cuitláhuac, fell victim to the Spanish smallpox that swept the land; the last emperor, Cuauhtémoc, surrendered after the final defeat at Tlatelolco, and the Spaniards had conquered Mexico. Cortés, who three years before had been secretary to the governor of Cuba, an intriguer, ne'er-do-well, and participant in sleazy adulteries, had become one of the most powerful men in the world.

In another three years he had thrown a good part of it away on his disastrous expedition to Honduras. The government of Mexico fell into the hands of his enemies, and he was never to regain power. Although on a triumphal journey to Spain he was made Marqués del Valle de Oaxaca, and married the niece of the powerful Duke of Béjar, the Crown withheld from him Cortés' dream, which was to rule New Spain as a virtually independent prince. The Conde de Tendilla was named viceroy, and the power and wealth of Cortés steadily declined, though not his ambitions.

An apocryphal story has the aged conqueror still striving for the favor of the monarch he had served so well, clutching at the steps of the emperor's carriage and begging for a word with him.

"But who are you?" Charles demanded, who had not recognized the ruin of his old captain-general.

"Sire," Cortés said. "I am the man who has given Your Majesty more provinces than he had cities."

MALINCHE

Shortly after the Spaniards landed in Yucatán in 1519, the Mayans of Tabasco presented them with tribute consisting of nubile girls. One of these was named Malinali Tenepal, the daughter of a Nahua noble whose step-mother had sold her into slavery. When Cortés learned of her attributes as a linguist he appropriated her for himself. She was baptized Marina, and, as she was of the nobility, the Spaniards referred to her as Doña Marina—the prefix "Doña" being roughly the equivalent of the Nahuatl suffix "tzin." Thus Doña Marina, Malintzin, Malinche.

Cortés had also freed a Spanish priest who had been a captive of the Mayans and had learned their tongue. Between them Jerónimo de Aguilar and Doña Marina could communicate with the Spaniards and with speakers of Nahuatl, the dominant tongue on the mainland. Doña Marina presently learned Castilian herself, and, as Cortés' translator, was at his side throughout the Conquest; so much so that both were known to the Aztecs by the same name: "Malintzin."

In Cholula, en route to Tenochtitlán, she learned from the Cholulan women of Montezuma's plot to massacre the Spaniards. The Cholulans were massacred instead, with the enthusiastic participation of Cortés' Tlaxcalan allies. Malinche thus becomes the villainess of Mexican history, an ethnic temptress, but it is hard to think what call for loyalty, other than racial, she had to the tyrants of Tenochtitlán. She had been freed from slavery and endowed by the Spaniards, and, as the mistress of the conqueror, enjoyed more power, prestige, and consideration than any other Mexican woman ever had. From Cholula on she was present at most of the policy-making assemblies of the Spanish captains, and in all the dealings with the Aztecs she wielded power not only as the linguistic intermediary, but as Cortés' advisor on Indian matters.

Her sway continued until 1524, and coincided exactly with the years of Cortés' "luck," during which time it seemed that he could make no wrong move.

But on the Honduran expedition, which was to prove Cortés undoing, he committed two betrayals which displeased even his most loyal soldiers: he ordered the murder of Cuauhtémoc and he rid himself of Doña Marina in order to enjoy a younger concubine, one of the daughters of Montezuma. Passing through Malinche's native country in the Isthmus of Tehuantepec, he endowed her with a large estate and married her to Juan de Jaramillo. History has little to say of her thereafter.

However, in the abortive creole rebellion of 1563, when Martín Cortés, the legitimate son of the conqueror, was banished to Spain, the only man who conducted himself with dignity and honor, even under torture, was the other, the mestizo, Martín Cortés, son of Cortés and Malinali Tenepal.

NARVÁEZ

This blunderer figures twice in the annals of the Conquest.

When Cortés disobeyed his charter from the governor of Cuba and pronounced himself, on shaky legal grounds, directly answerable only to the Crown, Velásquez sent Pánfilo de Narváez, with an army twice the size of Cortés', to bring the mutineer back to Cuba in chains.

To meet this threat, Cortés left Alvarado in charge in Tenochtitlán, where Montezuma was a Spanish hostage, and marched to the coast with a force of seventy men. He collected a couple of hundred more from garrisons along the route, and attacked Narváez' army of eight hundred and fifty in Cempoala, where they had set up camp. Cortés' good luck held, while Narváez' bad luck never failed. One of Narváez' eyes was dashed out by a pike in the defeat of the Spaniards of Cuba by the Spaniards of New Spain.

With his remaining eye he watched his soldiers pledging their loyalty to the traitor he had come to arrest, impressed by Cortés' charm and the Aztec gold he and his veterans displayed, as well as by his victory. Thus Cortés trebled his army, obtaining also necessary arms and supplies, and marched back to Tenochtitlán in time to relieve Alvarado, whose impetuosities led to the death of Montezuma and the assault of the Aztecs in overwhelming numbers. In the flight from Tenochtitlán Cortés lost two-thirds of his army, including most of the soldiers of Narváez.

While Cortés returned from his defeat to conquer the largest city of the known world, Narváez and Diego Velásquez stewed in black envy in Santiago de Cuba. Ponce de León's settlement of Florida had failed, and now, fifteen years later, Velásquez planned a new entrada to expand his domain and block the expansion of Cortés'. Pánfilo de Narváez was named captain-general.

Spanish cartographers gave the name "Florida" not only to the peninsula and its panhandle, but to the entire coast of the Gulf of Mexico, to where it met Panuco, the northeastern province of New Spain. Narváez fitted out four ships and gathered under his banner four hundred and eighty men and eighty horses, the soldiers to turn into colonists as their chargers became draft horses. The flotilla landed at Tampa Bay on Good Friday, April 10, 1528, and the army marched north, drawn on by tales of the great city, Apalachen. This proved to be a settlement of forty mud huts, and the Indians were so formidable that the Spaniards fled back to the gulf coast in the hopes of intercepting the ships. They found themselves deserted. Constructing rafts, they coasted west, contriving to keep together until their captain-general informed them that he was abandoning his command, and it was every vessel for itself. That of Pánfilo de Narváez disappeared into the night, others foundered and were lost, one by one. Those of the king's treasurer, Álvar Núñez Cabeza de Vaca, and the captains Alonso del Castillo and Andrés Dorantes, were wrecked on the gulf island beaches. The castaways who survived were enslaved by the Indians, and their seven years of captivity began.

❀

Book One

THE JOURNEY

(1535-1536)

Chapter One

The naked, starving Spaniard squatted on a mound of oyster shells on the low shore of this island of misfortune somewhere between Florida and Panuco. The shells crackled beneath his feet as he adjusted himself to sight across the two stakes toward the lightening eastern sky.

The pink glow that stained the horizon was centered on the stakes, as it had been these last two mornings. It was the spring equinox when those Christians left alive were sworn to rendezvous here. His slave, the Moor Esteban, and Alonso del Castillo had gone trading to the mainland, and his cousin Diego Dorantes exploring to the south with Hernando Esquivel. He, Andrés Dorantes, had finally come to accept the fact that their ships would never come—that longed-for vision of one day the little fleet's standing offshore in the gray water, barnacle-encrusted hulls and dirty sails with the heraldry of Spain upon them, the flash of gilt from an after-castle as they swung at anchor, and a small boat pulling for shore with its eight oars like the legs of a waterbug—

Now if they came they came too late, for Andrés thought he must be the last of the Spaniards, so weak he was no longer able to carry firewood or fresh water, pull canoes over marshy ground, grub for roots with bleeding fingers, and soon his masters the Marímnes, the Indians of this island, would kill him for his uselessness, or, less mercifully, simply let him die. A guttural voice whispered, "In nomine Patris et Filii et Spiritus Sancti—"

He heard, from the direction of the village, thin barking and the approaching shouts of the band of half-grown boys who were his most frequent tormentors. Steadying himself with a hand pressed into the oyster shells, he watched them zigzagging toward him through the clumps of salt-caked seagrass. Behind them on the creek bank crouched huts of woven reed. Men in animal skins moved around a smoking fire.

Coming up, the four boys began to pelt him with handfuls of mud. A small stone struck him on the cheek, and he was angered only at his instinctive flinching. A larger stone was threatened; he watched the hand that held it jerking back and forth. One of the boys kicked down the stakes by which he had been sighting sunrise and sunset. Then they all ran on, two of the bony yellow dogs barking after them. He watched them go, scraping the mud from his face and rubbing his chilled wrists for circulation. If he did not respond the boys soon tired of tormenting him. Not so their fathers.

Andrés no longer bothered to curse his captors, saving his curses for greater matters. They were a people beneath contempt. During the winters on this inhospitable shore they subsisted upon anteggs, roots, worms, lizards, salamanders, and the stringy flesh of their yellow dogs. He had seen them feasting upon the pulverized bones of fish, the dung of deer, on dirt. Thus they sustained themselves while the more discriminating Spaniards starved. Now at this chilly equinox he wakened each morning so weak he thought his body must have perished while his brain lived on to torture him with litanies of sorrow and remorse.

Two of his masters now strolled toward him, one of them Kiphalu, the Toad, the other the Toad's crony the Christians called Shitface. Both had perforated lower lips and left nipples, straws stuck horizontally through the nipples, bodies decorated with red ochre and stained with filth. Kiphalu's upper lip was bunched with his sneer to reveal stumpy yellow teeth. He held out a small, black-bound book, swollen with an old soaking; the prayer book that had once been the property of the priest Asturiano, passing on his death to Hernando Esquivel. A rosary hung around Kiphalu's neck. His cousin Diego's, the rosary.

Andrés reached for the book but restrained himself when he saw that the gesture pleased the Toad. Grinning, his master drew the edge of his hand sharply across his throat. He pronounced the Han word that meant dead.

Diego Dorantes, eight years his junior, had come to the New World to make his fortune just as Andrés had ten years earlier. Diego had never tired of hearing of the gold, the glory, and the girls of Mexico, the close calls, defeats, and victories; but most of all those golden-in-memory girls, bemoaning his young age that he could not have been present at the destruction of the Aztec empire, and the spoils thereof. Diego had joined the expedition of Pánfilo de Narváez to Florida in company with his cousin, one of the captains—who had joined Don Pánfilo twice, and should have known better after the first time.

4

He said the Han word that meant "who."

Shaking the fat little book, the Toad said, "Young brother, useless one!"

He touched his throat in imitation of the gesture Kiphalu had made, and repeated, "Who?"

"Quevénes! Quevénes!" Shitface shouted at him.

Dorantes was able to make out that a woman of the Quevénes had had a dream in which Diego and Hernando were Bad Things, an expression that seemed to mean monsters from a nightmare. So the two had been murdered. Shitface carried an arrow, with which he made jabbing motions.

Diego had been obsessed with escape to the south, where surely it could not be many leagues to Panuco, the northeastern corner of New Spain—although there were known to be fierce tribes in that direction. It had been decided that escape could only be attempted in the summer, when the crop of cactus fruit ripened, the one time of the year when there was plenty to eat and their strength returned. But Diego had been impatient, and so Andrés had given his cousin permission to explore, with Hernando, the south end of Malhado and the island beyond it. Esteban and Alonso, with his permission and that of their masters, had crossed over to the mainland to trade with the inland tribes, and to see if escape might lie in that direction. But they must be dead also, who were to have returned by the solstice. He was alone, squatting on frozen feet on the hillock of oyster shells where he had planted his aiming stakes, with his masters standing over him, the useless one.

Kiphalu held the prayer book and twisted the rosary around his neck, grinning, and Shitface grinned and stabbed the arrow at him. They loved to threaten their captives with arrows, to beat them with sticks, to throw mud or dung into their faces, to pull the hairs of their beards. They were not very terrifying demons compared with the Aztecs of the Night of Sorrows, or the invisible bowmen of Apalachen. Shitface jabbed the arrow close to his eyes.

"You next, Useless One!"

Panting with the exertion, he rose. The arrowhead jabbed at him. He caught the shaft, twisted it from the Marímne's grasp, broke it over his knee, and flung down the two pieces. Shitface had stepped back a pace. He folded his arms, jerked his chin up, slitted his eyes, and clucked deep in his throat. Then he sucked air noisily through his teeth.

The Toad broke into speech too rapid for Dorantes to understand, but the gist was comprehensible. Andrés must fight Shitface before the assembled village tomorrow for this insult. He had seen a number of these fights, and although weapons other than fists were rarely used, they were savage enough. He had barely the strength to stand with dignity before his masters, much less defend himself.

When the two had gone he sank to his knees with his head jerking forward as though it would snap loose from his body. He covered his face with his hands, too despairing even to pray, the last man of the expedition which had set out from Cuba to settle Florida; last of the terrified and starving remnant of that four hundred that had coasted east from Tampa Bay in crudely-built barges with clothing strung up for sails, boys crying for their mothers as they died, and the barges foundering one by one, until the last had dropped its castaways on this island called Malhado; ten, and eight, and five, and now one single dying man, Andrés Dorantes de Carranza of Béjar del Castenar, of Extremadura, of Castile, of Spain; the crossbowman Andrés Dorantes of the Conquest of Mexico, Captain Dorantes of the lost army of Pánfilo de Narváez; the last.

He dreamed that night of Extremadura, high plains stretching into a clarity of distance, with the sierra floating on the horizon like islands, between them forest islands of dark green oaks, castles rising from the heights of land; the town of old walls, twisting alleys, gray stone bridges, and the stone cottages along the streets; his plump, frightened mother, his dour father, the chill of the walls of the little house in winter, the painful pretense that there was a living as well as gnarled honor in that place.

He dreamed, this morning that he was to die, of the excitement of sailing down the Guadalquivir from Seville on the *Santa María de Luz*, he and his friend Bernardo laughing out loud in their excitement and pounding each other on the back. And of the dazzle of Santiago de Cuba; gaping at a dandy strolling by with a diamond rose in his hatband and a black slave padding behind him, flowers in his frizzy hair, thick lips grinning over white teeth. He had vowed to Bernardo that he would have a Moor of his own! And the ladies at the levees, gold and silver lace adorning their rustling silks, topazes and pearls on pale fingers, throats, and ears, and high jeweled haircombs; the men in silk over silk, pinked and slashed; the gold glittering on the gambling tables, and the tales of banquets where the meats were salted with gold dust. The wealth of the Indies! And the promises of the Indies; those of the governor, and those of Don Pánfilo, followed so quickly and confusingly by those of Hernán Cortés. For so long the promises of Cortés, but finally those of Narváez again, and, come full circle, the promises had run out.

Shivering on his stinking pallet of brown leaves, back to the woven reed panel that failed to cut the wind from the sea, in this waking dream he seemed to see his own slave, Esteban, approaching at his jaunty walk, red feathers nodding in his kinky hair, white teeth grinning, bangles clicking at his ankles above bare feet. The jingling came louder. The figure raised an arm in greeting, with a shout of, "Master!"

It was not a dream. There he came, hide pack slung from a black shoulder. Ten steps behind him appeared a skinny, breech-clouted, balding, bearded white man, also with a pack, also raising an arm in greeting—Alonso del Castillo! The two of them looked so cheery and healthy compared to his own miserable state that he burst into tears.

Esteban loped toward him, to drop to one knee before him. Strong arms raised him. "Andrés!" Alonso called, limping. His naked shoulders were scarred with sun sores.

Then he was wrenching a lump of dried venison between his teeth, with the sweet juice trickling down his throat, weeping still while Alonso showed him a palmful of small pearls from his pack and Esteban chattered.

"Quevénes have killed Diego and Hernando," he said.

"Mother of God!" Alonso said, hiding the pearls in his fist and crossing himself. Esteban drew an elaborate cross in the air.

"Ah, those poor cavaliers! When has this sad thing happened, Master?"

He shook his head, uncertain suddenly how much time had passed since he had heard this news from the Toad, since Diego and Hernando had set off south, since Esteban and Alonso had gone to the mainland, since they had been castaway here even. But he remembered that he was to fight Shitface today.

"I thought I was the last, you see," he said.

"We are here, Andrés; we have returned!" Alonso said. "And, moreover, we have heard that there are also two hairy-faced men alive to the north. Ah, but our poor Diego! So young! The devils!"

"Who could these two Christians be?"

"One very tall, they say," Esteban said, illustrating with a raised arm.

"Perhaps Álvar Núñez, we have thought," said Alonso.

His brain revolved slowly on the possibility that two more Spaniards still lived, one of them perhaps Álvar Núñez Cabeza de Vaca, King's Treasurer of the Florida expedition. Why did he feel responsible for them, as well as for Esteban and Alonso? Now it was too late for responsibilities.

A dozen Marímnes, men and women, had gathered in a half circle to observe the newcomers, and he saw the Moor wink, flex his shoulders languorously, and make a gesture of scrubbing his right forefinger in his left palm for the benefit of a maiden with pouchy little breasts, a moss girdle, and a face like a mud tart. She showed her teeth in a grimace of a smile.

Alonso ignored the audience, bringing other items from his pack to exhibit for Dorantes' admiration. "We are traders of great success! We carried inland reeds for arrow shafts and shells for knives. We should have taken more of the long ones they use to cut beans! In return we have received venison, flints, and red ochre. I am a wealthy man, but Estebánico has wasted his goods buying women for his pleasure. Of course, being a Moor, he finds attraction in these females with breasts like rocks who stink of fish. Those inland do not smell so rank, Andrés!"

Smiling toothily, Esteban said, "My master remembers too well the pretty girls of Tenochtitlán! Of Tlatelolco! And the beautiful one of Texcoco to whom he speaks in the night!"

Dorantes' mouth felt like a scar when he tried to smile; his eyes were leaking again. Alonso regarded him worriedly.

"How the little birds of one's youth are more beautiful than those of present time," Esteban prattled on. He laughed and signaled again to the watching maiden. "One must remember this truth, or in future he will have nothing to look back upon with pleasure!"

"Estebánico leaves no stone unturned in this regard," Alonso said.

"Nor moss either," he managed, and his two friends shouted with laughter.

Alonso bowed his head close and said in a low voice, "We believe our escape from this damnable captivity lies to the west, Andrés. The barbarians inland are more amiable. There is more food also. I believe we can trade our way west to rejoin our fellow Christians in New Spain! How often did you and I warn Diego there was no safe route to Panuco? Quevénes! And fiercer devils beyond, as you yourself can attest. After all, the land between the seas may be as narrow here as at Panama!"

"I think I could not walk half a league," he said.

"We will buy and roast one of these dogs! We will fatten you up, my friend! And of course we must await the season of the cactus fruit, when we will be already traveling inland with our masters. We will see that you regain your strength, Andrés!"

He ground the dried venison between his teeth, jaw aching, and swallowed the sweet juice. "I must fight Shitface today."

He explained, while Esteban gaped at him and Alonso's monkey face twisted into a comical anxiety. Laughter jerked in spasms in his throat.

"But Master, this must not be!"

"Can you even stand, Andrés?"

His hand braced on the black man's shoulder, he endeavored to rise. Esteban lifted him by the armpits. He stood.

"Estebánico will fight in your place, Don Andrés," the Moor said.

He shook his head. His knees were quivering with strain. He wrenched off another bite of the venison.

"Honor is unneccessary among these filthy Marímnes, Andrés. No, you will not be such a fool!"

He was reminded of his father's crotchety and pretentious honor, and of his own tangled contempt and admiration for it. "Honor is necessary between man and his Redeemer," he said. His voice sounded so solemn to his own ears that the jerking laughter shook him again. Beyond Esteban and Alonso the Marímnes stood silently watching. He did not see Shitface nor Kiphalu among them.

Later in the morning the boys ran toward him, one of them yelling, "You die, Useless One!" Esteban shouted and shook his fist at them, and they ran off.

"Listen!" Alonso said, squatting beside him. In the village women were wailing. It was the sound of death. These Indians died swiftly, seeming to know their time had come and to accept it, curling up knees to chest and giving up their spirit without a struggle. It occurred to Dorantes that he had accepted his own end as readily, except that as a Castilian he would surrender his spirit in hopeless combat.

As the wailing continued he began to wonder if there were not a chance in this duel to come. He had wrestled as a youth in Béjar. Once he had been strong, one of the strongest of the remnant of the army that had escaped in the barges. Once hope, confidence, and faith had sustained him through trials greater than this one. Remembering his strength and health, his faith, his throat thickened and his eyes smarted and as though out of that very ache of tears he remembered so clearly the beautiful one of Texcoco, and his son. Or was it the wailing of the Marímne women that brought back that old death and loss? He slapped at the needle prick of a mosquito.

Esteban loomed over him, to whisper, "Master, that one is *dead*!"

The Moor's hands flashed elaborately. He reenforced his words with the weaving of his hands, twisting of shoulders, contortions of his face. He had not even bothered to learn Han, so clever was he at making himself understood, while his master had methodically collected the words for actions, the names of things, and noted the many cognates from the Nahuatl he had learned in Mexico. The words for dead were very similar. Shitface was dead.

"Curled up in a ball as they do, these barbarians! Hear the birds chirping so sadly for him, that bad man!"

"Praise God, Andrés!" Alonso said.

He raised himself on an elbow, squinting up at the gray glare of the sky. He remembered Fray Cristóbal telling the boy Andrés Dorantes, beneath an illuminated tent of stars, that each one of those innumerable stars was numbered, and the intensity of each one decreed by God. And each event in a man's life was similarly decreed; for him, on this day, life instead of death, for Shitface death instead of life. When Martín was born the Aztec book of auguries had shown bad signs, so they had simply changed the day of his birth; God decreed, but the Redeemer interceded, and the Mother looked down in pity. He gave thanks, his fellow Christians crouching beside him.

He said, "Estebánico, you must travel north to see if Álvar Núñez and another still live. They must come with us if we are to escape inland at the time of the cactus fruit."

"Yes, Master, that I will do!"

From Shitface's hut the women continued their wailing. Soon they would tear down and burn the habitation of the dead. He stared up at the gray clouds as though he might discover in their formations what had been decreed for him. It seemed he was not yet to die.

"I have purchased a dog to eat, Andrés," Alonso said.

After Esteban had departed, he and Alonso were sitting together when the Toad appeared, to stand silently before him with hands clasped at his crotch, the horizontal straw adorning his nipple, a vertical one piercing his lower lip. Other Marímnes came up, carrying bows and arrows, faces smeared with ochre. The men were small, with short, powerful legs, very dirty, hair matted and ribs showing from the privations of winter. Two yellow dogs squatted among them. The women had stopped wailing.

An old man came forward. He halted before Dorantes, holding his head and groaning. He peered out from under an eyebrow with a wily expression, and spoke in a lisping mutter. There was a Bad Thing in his head.

"He wants you to cure him, I believe, Andrés," Alonso whispered.

He understood that it was considered that he had caused Shitface's death, therefore he must also have the power to heal. Once before, his master had shouted that, as he was useless otherwise, he should be a healer.

The old man beckoned to Kiphalu in the stiff-wristed Marímne manner, and the Toad nodded like a chicken pecking and waved a hand in command at Dorantes. The old man was one of the village elders.

"The beads of the young brother," Dorantes said in Han.

The Toad stripped off the rosary as though it were scalding hot, and handed it to him.

"The other thing as well." There was no word for "book."

The Toad trotted off, to return with the prayer book. Alonso helped Dorantes to his feet, steadying him as he faced the sick man on trembling legs, the bunched rough beads in his right hand, the fat little book in his left. A confidence like a warm draft seemed to settle in his forearms and hands.

"In Nomine Patris et Filii et Spiritus Sancti," he intoned. He touched the man's left temple with the beads, his right with the book.

The patient pressed the flat of his hands to his temples, spread them out as though his head were double-size, finally dropped them. He nodded vigorously, grinning. The other men stood staring, all with hands crossed guarding their genitals.

"Aheu!" the patient cried. He smoothed his temples, slapped his thighs, and turned away, to be surrounded by the other men, all chattering.

He heard Alonso blow out his breath in a cautious whistle. He let himself slump down onto the sour leaves again, watching the men moving in a tight group toward the village. Presently a boy hurried up with a bit of venison the size of a walnut. He took it, nodding in a dignified way, and set it aside until the boy had gone. Then he scraped the mold from the gobbet using his front teeth; devouring it, his jaws ached from disuse.

"One must be cautious, Andrés—" Alonso began, but broke off to say, "Ah, see what comes!"

A woman sidled toward him in her best finery, wads of moss protecting her modesty, shell beads around her neck, smile twitching on and off. She stank of fish, sweat, smoke, and fear, one of the wives of the elder he had cured of a Bad Thing in the head, come to his bed for his pleasure.

So long since he had known lust, or even interest; he called to mind Timultzin dancing, slim buttocks and small breasts protruding, dark, high-looped hair swaying, gleam of candlelight on golden flesh, mysterious dark of her crotch, her eyes sliding sideways to watch him watching her, never a hint of fear in them. Her clean smell. He sent this gift away, indicating a Bad Thing in his genitals.

"Andrés, how have you healed that barbarian?" Alonso said in a stifled voice.

"With the holy book and the rosary, as you observed. In fact, he decided to be healed, as he had decided to have a Bad Thing in his head in order that I might heal him."

Alonso sighed deeply. "Among the inland peoples, it was often demanded of Estebánico and me that we heal Bad Things. Always I said
no, no, no, always no, and instructed the Moor the same. They believe
that because we are of a different color, and strange to them, that we
can heal ills. But Andrés, as you know, they have healers of their
own, and when these fellows fail they are killed. Yes, killed!"

"They are as often driven away, Alonso."

"Yes, that is true. But one must be very cautious!"

"That one had faith I had killed Shitface, so he had faith I could cure
his Bad Thing. Faith is not only the portion of Christians, Alonso."

"Their healers I have seen on the mainland," Alonso said, "make
little cuts where the pain is located and suck the blood that comes.
Some will only breathe on the place. They believe that certain objects
have strong virtue. Such as the book and the rosary! But their healers
have shown me simple stones from the fields they believe to have a
power of healing. They will heat these stones and apply them to the
place of pain.

"They also cauterize wounds with great heat, although I have not
seen them using boiling oil as we Christians do." Alonso slapped at a
mosquito.

"After the Night of Sorrows the wounds were so multitudinous that
the oil became merely warm," Dorantes said. "The little Italian physician stroked this oil on us, and the wounds healed in a day. But there
was much prayer to Our Lady of the Remedies. Much faith."

"One has heard that during the Conquest, when there was no oil
available, the Castilians boiled up fat Indians for grease to cauterize the
wounds of the horses. Did you see such a thing?"

"No," he said.

"Such a horrible thing cannot be true," Alonso said, slapping again.

"I only say I did not see such a thing. But there was much evil,
Alonso. There are many sins upon the souls of those who followed
Hernán Cortés." Both slapped together.

"The mosquitoes have come," Dorantes continued. "And the time
of the cactus fruit comes after them. How long from now, Alonso?"

"Two months, no more. Certainly the time of the mosquitoes is
terrible, but meanwhile there are oysters to eat, and then the black-
berries. Meanwhile Estebánico and I will accumulate goods for our
journey."

"Did you find inland the evidences of minerals you sought?"

"I am no miner to know what to look for in the cracks of rocks. But
I am certain minerals are to be found in these lands we will traverse!
Gold, silver—"

"Have you seen gold and silver in the villages you visited, Alonso?"

"None," Alonso del Castillo Maldonado said sourly. "No more than we found in Apalachen."

In three days Esteban returned, striding proudly with his knapsack slung over one shoulder, red hairfeathers lifting with his steps, black skin gleaming, bangles clicking. Dorantes had effected a second cure, this one a young man with belly spasms—as though an animal were kicking inside him. The healed Marímne had produced rewards of venison and the hard, pitchy tubers that were a winter subsistence item. Now he was feeling stronger, and he rose to embrace the black.

It was indeed Álvar Núñez, Esteban said. "Also Don Lope, who is very ill. The Christians are slaves of barbarians called Deagúnes, an ignorant and shit-eating people. They were of the barge of Don Álvar, and all but these two drowned or have died since. Don Álvar is ready to escape, but cannot leave his sad companion. I think that that poor cavalier cannot live for very long, Master.

"And what is this, please?" Esteban said. Two young men were approaching, patting their bellies, faces contorted with agony.

"Your master has become a great physician," Alonso said. "He claims he only pretends to heal those who pretend illness, but his successes have become famous."

Esteban frowned worriedly, watching him reach for the rosary and the book. He no longer entered into this process of healing so lightly as he had done at first. Although he had made a joke of his cures, it bore upon him that this power, or luck, was another sign that Heaven was interested in him, as in the death of Shitface.

And there had been another occasion also, during the terrible retreat from Tenochtitlán, when some had been saved and so many were lost, and he was one the finger of Providence plucked from death.

His first vision of Tenochtitlán had been from the pass on the Day of John the Baptist, June 24, 1520, when he was just twenty years of age. The army of Hernán Cortés swung along to the brave music of fifes and trumpets, and the beat of kettledrums, with banners flapping in the wind that blew through the pass, to halt, and gasp, at the first sight of the Valley of Anahuac in its great beauty: the sunny glistening of the lakes, dark clumps of woodland against tan fields, and greener fields—yellowish patches of maize, gray-green of maguey, brilliant squares of flowers—all of it vivid and close in the high, thin air, color and outline like a feast for the eyes. The shores of the lake in the center of the great basin were studded with gleaming white towns, and, central to all this vision, was the magical city, the Venice of the Aztecs.

"It is paradise!" his friend Bernardo said hoarsely. The two of them had been recruited in Santiago de Cuba, for that other doomed expedition of Pánfilo de Narváez, which had been dispatched to the mainland to bring the mutineer Hernán Cortés back to Cuba in chains. Instead the mutineer had surprised and defeated them, and with his silver tongue and golden promises beguiled them into joining his little army. Now Cortés' veterans grinned proprietorially at the amazement of the new recruits, as they began their descent into the green valley.

Carried across his shoulders was the crossbow, which he had yet to fire in anger, cranequin and quiver of bolts slapping against his thigh. He grinned back at Bernardo's grin as they marched down hill with the army, the captain-general riding ahead, a broad-shouldered figure in a shining corselet, black velvet sleeves and cap, a feather in his cap, and across his shoulders the heavy golden chain, booty of Tenochtitlán that had so impressed him and the other soldiers of Narváez.

Following Cortés were more than a thousand Spaniards, infantry and cavalry, crossbowmen, arquebusiers, and pikemen, morions gleaming like silver melons, some wearing breastplates or chain mail, but most of the veterans in the quilted cotton they had appropriated from the indigene warriors, legs swinging in thick hose, soft leather boots pulled up tight on thighs or thickly folded around calves, cloaks embroidered with gold and silver hanging above scabbarded swords, pennons fluttering, music shrilling and drumbeats keeping the step. Behind them marched some eight thousand Tlaxcalan allies with their plumed helmets and their own banners.

So they came to one of the great causeways that led across the lake to the island city, a solid structure of stone and lime that was, in parts, wide enough for eight horsemen abreast, and always at least a lance in breadth. A few canoes dotted the shimmer of the lake. Lean clouds sailed west. On one of the bridges of the causeway a horse caught a hoof in a crack in the planking and fell. The rider was unhurt, but the horse had broken a leg and had to be destroyed. There was muttering that this was a bad omen, the mood was changed, and the army marched in silence now, scuff of boots, clink of steel, and rattle of hoofs, with, at intervals, the drawbridges echoing beneath their tread—a league across the lake to Tenochtitlán.

There began a distant mournful tolling of a great drum. He and Bernardo glanced sideways at each other, no longer grinning. "What is that?" Bernardo asked.

"That's the drum on the cu," the corporal said, a heavyset soldier limping behind them. His name was Botello and he was called Caballo, the horse. He winked at Andrés with a creasing of his whiskered cheek. "They say it's made of the skins of giant lizards, big as churches, that they find down in the hot lands. You can hear it all around the lake. Means there's meat for sacrifice coming up the pyramid."

They marched on, sweating in the sun, finally entering the outskirts of the city between low, windowless, flat-roofed structures. They crossed a canal on another rumbling bridge. A few children peered out at them from doorways. The great drum had ceased, but now the quiet seemed even more ominous. The bridge over the next canal had been removed, and they were forced to circle a block of buildings. Now men and women watched from the rooftops. The men wore white robes, and some had carmined their faces so they looked like demons. The women wore short blouses, and their black hair done up in two high loops that flexed pleasantly when they moved. Caballo pointed up past the roofs to the top of the great pyramid where two painted wooden houses stood. They had already been told of the sacrifices that took place there, the hearts of the victims snatched out of opened breasts and held up steaming, bodies flung down the steep steps to the cooking pots below, where the meat was eaten in a stew of squash and chiles. Three black-clad priests were visible atop the cu, filing into one of the buildings there.

When the great drum beat again, Cortés ordered music, and their own instruments began to play a merry tune. From ahead came a crash of artillery, a salute from the garrison that had been left under the command of the captain Pedro de Alvarado. A cheer was raised, and answered by cheers. The red faces of the Aztecs glared down from the rooftops.

"*Malintzin!*" a voice shouted. "*Malintzin!*" The booming of the great drum rolled out. "*Malintzin!*" Cortés paid no attention to the voice calling his Aztec name. Andrés had never known such a man as this one, so certain of himself in this fearful and beautiful place, so charming at one instance, so soldier-stern at another, so calm at others. It was as though the halos of the frescos of the saints in the cathedral at Béjar had been diffused into a golden haze that seemed to encase the mounted figure leading the army. What a man was there, then! Taking confidence from their commander, they marched on into the capital of the Aztecs to join their comrades.

But within two weeks, during which they were all but imprisoned in their quarters, great Montezuma, their hostage, was dead, and they were fighting their way out of the magic city on a rainswept night, along the causeway where the drawbridges had been removed. Warriors with red-painted devil faces surrounded them, both on the causeway and in canoes alongside it, screeching and whistling in a hail of javelins, darts, and stones. The warriors hurling their missles and swinging their obsidian-toothed maces, and, most terrifying, their nets for captives, were arrayed as jaguars and eagles, and each waterway the Spaniards had to cross was a disaster of pushing, half-swimming, through chest-deep water, and fighting up the far abutment against the press of warriors there. All the while, over the shrill din and the shouts of dying men, came the booming of the drum on the cu.

So many of them drowned or were taken at the canal at Tolteca, where the lake was deepest. The soldiers carrying the treasure, the king's fifth, and Cortés' and the captains' fifths, and those who had been most greedy with their own booty, sank under the weight of their gold. The rear guard and the center took the brunt of the Aztec attacks, he and Bernardo in the center with no more bolts for their crossbows, his cranequin discarded and the bow itself snatched away, and half blinded by the driving rain besides. In the night and the black water the two of them managed to thrash across the canal and, panting and gasping, clamber up the far side in the face of the screaming jaguar knights there.

A canoe shot in out of the darkness. Dorantes was seized; there was no strength left to resist. Bernardo cried out as he struggled against his own captors, swarming out of a second canoe. But all at once the corporal was sliding down the slippery stones of the abutment, shouting their names in a brass voice, sword slashing right and left. Caballo grasped his arm and jerked him free. "*Get on, man!*" The two of them stumbled out of range of the canoes, as Bernardo was hauled away screaming for help. Instantly the canoe that had taken him shot away into the darkness, and the screams were shut off as if a door had slammed.

They made their way to shore, those who were left, and there he saw Cortés with his bleeding head and hand kneeling sobbing beneath the gnarled tree. Yet the Virgin of the Remedies, whose image they carried, had hovered very close on that Night of Sorrows when they had escaped from Tenochtitlán, and saved many of the wounded afterwards, for the next day the little Italian physician rubbed lukewarm oil on their wounds that seemed to heal like miracles. But why had some been saved, and others killed or taken to be sacrificed on the great cu, with their living hearts snatched from their chests and held up before their horrified eyes? Surely Bernardo had possessed a cleaner soul than he, certainly Bernardo had been more pious and God-fearing.

Much later he had mentioned this to Caballo over cups of wine, who had made the choice between the two of them at the Tolteca canal.

"That's an easy one," Caballo said in his gravelly voice. "You were closer. Couldn't reach him." Then he grinned and said, "I'd've taken you anyway, for a better soldier."

Chapter Two

In the spring the coastal tribes moved inland to await the ripening of the cactus fruit. Meanwhile there were acorns, hackberries, persimmons, and the green fruit itself, with its bitter juice. Bodies began to fill out, padding over sharp ribs, swelling of shrunken haunches. It was a time of truce between enemies, of feasts, and orgies of dancing. Against the intolerable mosquitoes great fires of damp wood were built.

In the cactus groves, where thickets of thorny paddles rose higher than a man's head, the Marímnes and their slaves camped in the open spaces. The three half-naked Christians crouched weeping in the smoke from the fires, watching their masters dancing. The Marímnes hopped and swayed, circling the central fire to the tootling of a one-note wooden flute and the beat of drums made of deer hide stretched over hollow logs. Their black silhouettes leaped against the flames and smoke, sweating breasts and buttocks gleaming in the light. Sometimes Esteban whistled along with the monotonous music.

"I believe I will join these pleasures, Masters," the Moor said, rising, stretching, and jingling as he strode out to become a part of the circle of dancers. His taller figure could be seen leaping among his other masters.

"How long will we wait for the other Christians?" Alonso asked.

"Until the cactus fruit is full ripe," Dorantes said. "Another half a month."

"Then we must move swiftly, for our masters will not wish to lose a healer of so many successes."

Dorantes still considered that his successes came from curing Marímnes who pretended illness out of boredom, or to gain the envy of their fellows or the admiration of women, by employing him with his rosary, prayer book, and Latin prayers. When he suspected real illness he would disengage himself with the deep cluck in his throat that was the Han negative.

He watched the silhouettes circling to the tootling and thumping, and the couples moving out into the darkness. It was a time of great concupiscence among the Indians. His eyes ran continually, from the harsh smoke and old memories.

Watching Esteban accompany a ridiculously shorter figure away from the firelight, he recalled his own compulsions among those slim, proud, frightened girls of the cities around the lakes of Mexico through which they had fought their way in the Reconquest. So much Castilian seed had been sown that surely the lighter brown race about which they had so often laughed was by now well established. Older soldiers had collected gold, jewels, and portable curiosities, but he had preferred the pretty girls of Mexico to its other treasures. There had come a time, after Texcoco, when it had begun to seem to him that, through these casual rapes, he was accumulating a vast debt which ultimately he would be called upon to repay. Then, as his friend Caballo Botello had said, he had become old before his time.

He found himself shivering. "It is turning cold, Alonso."

"Which will subdue the mosquitoes, it is to be hoped. Still, these cursed fires will be needed for warmth."

Unseasonable cold settled in. Water froze in the puddles, and a crust of ice formed along the edges of the little creek. The Marímnes wrapped themselves in deerskins, and Dorantes was tempted to chancy cures by the necessity of skins to cover his own nakedness, for the cold here was harsher than it had ever been on Malhado. These nights the three Christians huddled together and talked of nothing but the means of their escape, and how pursuit might be ensured against. No one mentioned that Pedro de Escobar and the priest Asturiano had been murdered for just such an attempt. The impatience of awaiting Álvar Núñez, with or without Lope de Oviedo, was very great.

One night they saw a tree light up like a candleflame a half league away, flames spiraling upward so that the tree seemed to be spinning as it burned. The Marímne women were moaning in fear, the wailing chorus rising as more and more joined in, and all the Indians huddled around the fire watching the blaze across the cactus plains. Dogs howled.

A delegation came to where he and Alonso sat shivering together with a deerhide draped over their shoulders. The men's faces glinted like copper in the firelight, they wore deerskin shawls; several carried bows and arrows, while others clasped hands before their crotches.

The Toad wore his complicated expression of pride of proprietorship combined with respect for the healer.

"It is Bad Thing!" Kiphalu said, gesturing toward the burning tree. "You will make Bad Thing go away!" he said, folding his arms.

He heard Alonso's low whistle of dismay. He said to the Toad, "What is Bad Thing?"

Kiphalu seemed pleased by the question, puffing himself up into the stance of an orator, as, with gestures, he explained that Bad Thing came in strange ways, in lightning from the sky, in the earth shaking, in whirlwinds. He caused objects to burn inexplicably. Many had seen him, a small man, with a knife of flint. He would appear beside a victim and, with the knife, cut a gash in the man's side, thrust a hand into the wound, pull out the entrails, cut off a piece, and throw this in the fire. Sometimes the man would die, other times he would be healed. Or Bad Thing would cut the victim's elbow in such a way that the arm would be twisted and crippled, although that man might also be cured. Many times he had been known to appear during the dancing, sometimes in the dress of a woman, and if a man were to possess that woman his genitals would disappear, leaving nothing between his legs. Bad Thing lived in a deep crevice in the earth.

It was the healer's task to make Bad Thing go away.

Perhaps it was his contempt and hatred of the Toad that made him do it. "The burning tree is not Bad Thing!"

Alonso hissed a caution. The Marímnes stared at him with white-rimmed eyes that jerked aside to stare at the burning tree.

"It is Bad Thing!" Kiphalu said.

Dorantes rose, pulling away from Alonso's hand that grasped his arm. He crossed himself. The motion seemed to take excessive effort, as though his hand had been weakened by the cut of Bad Thing's knife. "It is Good Thing!" he said.

This time several of them yelled at him. "What is Good Thing? There is no Good Thing!"

"Good Thing is the son of the sun!" He gestured. "The son of the sky! Good Thing can heal all things." He had never had such control of Han; the words seemed to leap to his lips. "Good Thing breaks the knife of Bad Thing! Good Thing comes in burning trees!"

"Andrés, what are you *saying*?" Alonso whispered.

The Marímne men gaped at him. They pressed their hands to their genitals, they made jerky motions with their heads, they whispered among themselves. The Toad was glaring.

"Does Good Thing come here?"

He shrugged. "Sometimes Good Thing will come. Other times he will not. But Bad Thing will not come."

Some of the women had collected behind the men. They had stopped their moaning. The tree on the horizon continued to burn as though it were not consuming itself.

Folding his arms on his chest, the Toad said, "The healer will keep Good Thing from coming here!"

It pleased him that the Marímnes were as frightened of Good Thing as of Bad Thing, but he told Kiphalu he was stupid, Good Thing, if he came, would bring great good. After a long silence the Marímnes moved back to the fire in a troubled manner. There was a muted jingle as Esteban came to crouch beside him.

"They are frightened of the tree that burns, these ignorant people," the Moor whispered. "These foolish women believe it is a thing that turns their wombs inside out like cactus fruit laid to dry in the sun."

"Our Andrés preaches the Holy Faith to them," Alonso said in a dry voice. "It is Good Thing who inhabits the burning tree!"

He stood between the Moor and his comrade watching the tree flare. Upper limbs glowed red, and one fell in a shower of sparks.

"It is a pretty thing, anyhow, Masters," Esteban said, squatting beside them. "The burning tree."

The next day they were gathering the green fruit from their spiny beds with numb fingers when Alonso cried out. A tall, bearded, naked white man shuffled on a twisting, hesitating course through the clumps of cactus, sometimes disappearing behind higher growth, but always reappearing, closer. He was thin as a lance, hair and beard matted, one hand raised high as he saw them. Far behind him stood the black skeleton of the burnt tree. It was Álvar Núñez Cabeza de Vaca, alone.

The three of them ran to meet him while the Marímnes watched in a congealed motionlessness. One of the women began tentatively to moan. When Dorantes pointed a finger at her she ceased her noise.

"—dead," Álvar Núñez was saying, one hand on Esteban's shoulder and one on Alonso's when Dorantes joined them. "A blessed relief from his long misery, praise be to God! And so I have come. Ah, Andrés, my good fellow!"

Dorantes embraced the skinny frame. "Álvar, it affects the eyes to see you! You will give us strength for our journey."

"God will give us strength: Esteban Dorantes; and Andrés Dorantes; and Alonso del Castillo Maldonado. So we all at least still live. And will be reunited with our fellow Christians again, I know it!"

The Marímnes had approached cautiously, men with hands covering their genitals, women with arms crossed over their bellies.

Esteban offered Álvar a nearly-ripe cactus fruit. Pale juice stained the newcomer's beard as he bit into it. His thighs and forearms were hatched with savage cactus scratches and caked with blood. His mouth full, he gestured in a serene way, a forefinger raised, other fingers folded into the palm. Dorantes could not understand why meeting the other's blue, curiously unfocused eyes should make his own eyes ache.

"I was reminded of our Redeemer's sufferings as I wandered through the cactus patches last night," Álvar said, wiping his mouth. "And the cold was so severe I thought I would perish of it. Then before me a tree began to burn. I survived by its heat."

"We saw the burning tree, Álvar," he said.

"It frightened these our masters to distraction," Alonso said. "For they did not know whether it was Good Thing or Bad Thing."

When Álvar turned toward the Indians, Dorantes saw them fall back before his gaze, all but the Toad, who stood spread-legged with his assertive glare.

"Is this Good Thing?" he shouted at Dorantes.

"This is the messenger of Good Thing," he replied. "He comes from the burnt tree." He waved toward the black skeleton.

Eyes fixed on Álvar, the Toad retreated reluctantly with the rest. The Marímnes collected together, whispering.

"Soon we will go," Alonso whispered, as the four Christians stood together under the gaze of their captors. "Soon! *Soon!*"

"We must have faith that the proper moment will be revealed to us," Álvar said.

Early the next day a delegation of Marímnes approached Dorantes, the Toad with four of the elders, and the old chief, Sombé, a gnarled, toothless fellow with gray hair drawn tightly back into a pigtail, the customary perforated lip and nipple, a short arrow drawn through the nipple. The other Christians watched from nearby, and a group of Marímne men squatted observing from a cactus thicket.

After a bout of the chicken-pecking nodding, Sombé enquired if the healer was well. He replied that he was well. The Toad looked proprietorial and smug, glancing frequently toward Álvar.

"Charruco good friend to Marímne," the chief said.

"All are good friends during the time of the cactus fruit."

Sombé scowled ferociously. "Charruco good friend! Good friend!" He smiled and spread his arms. "Charruco chief sick."

He felt a wave of apprehension like nausea.

"Healer go with Charruco!"

"Charrucos have their own healer."

"Charruco healer no good!"

Now he saw the group of strangers standing half hidden behind a clump of cactus. The Charrucos were leaner and taller than the Marímnes, with white feathers braided into their long hair.

He clucked a no.

One of the elders said, "Charruco give Marímne gifts."

He clucked again, wondering what had become of the no-good Charruco healer.

"Messenger of Good Thing heals Charruco," the Toad said, folding his arms on his chest.

Dorantes imitated his master's stance, shook his head, and strode off to join the other Christians. "Master," Esteban whispered. "This village is to the west!" The three clustered around him.

"If these Charrucos have come like this, their chief is truly sick," he said.

"It would be a start, Andrés," Alonso said.

He continued to shake his head. "I can only heal men who pretend to be sick," he said. He met Álvar's eyes. "For I can only pretend to heal."

"We have seen you heal, Andrés," Alonso said.

"No," he said. "No, I have insufficient faith. No, I will not do it." Álvar's blue eyes were fixed on his disturbingly.

"Listen," he said to the treasurer. "I know that men sometimes have the power to heal. I believe they are men of powerful prayer. I remember the little Italian physician, after the Night of Sorrows, with his vial of oil—he had this power. But I do not have it, Álvar."

"You have healed, Andrés," Alonso said stubbornly. "I did not wish to believe that you had that power, but I have come to believe it."

He turned angrily on the smaller man, whose carbuncled shoulders never healed. "You treat this Charruco. You have as much qualification as I!"

"Ah, no, Andrés; for I hate these dogs every one. I would see them all dead. That is no qualification for a healer."

"Estebánico, then!"

"I have only some tricks, Master!"

"What else do I have, with my rosary and holy book and some Latin?"

"Certainly you must not attempt this, if your faith is insufficient," Álvar said at last. The force of his eyes suffused his beautiful skull of a face. "Would it be possible that I replace you, as the one fellow has requested? For my faith is very strong."

Dorantes inclined his head and closed his eyes. The sense of a weight removed from his shoulders was so powerful it seemed he might drift loose from the earth he stood upon. He found himself nodding.

He led Álvar back to where the chief, the elders, and Kiphalu stood waiting. The other Marímne men watched. The Charrucos pretended to be uninterested in the proceedings.

"The messenger of Good Thing will heal the chief of the Charrucos."

Sombé nodded vigorously. "It is well!"

"All the Christians will accompany the messenger of Good Thing to the Charrucos," he said.

The Toad clucked. The elders chattered. Kiphalu gestured at the chief, protesting and clucking.

Sombé silenced him with a slashing gesture, and beckoned to the Charrucos.

Their party consisted of the five Charrucos and about a dozen Marímnes, men and women, including Kiphalu but not the chief. So they set out westward on what all of them knew was the beginning of their great journey, to encounter New Spain and their countrymen along the Southern Sea. Women carried the packsacks of Esteban and Alonso, with their stock of hard canes for arrow shafts, shell knives, bows, three deerskins Dorantes had earned by healing, a bundle of dried cactus fruit, and Alonso's little pouch of pearls.

Esteban strode out in the lead with one of the Charrucos, his bush of black hair adorned with red feathers, his ankle bangles clicking cheerfully. The language of the Charrucos was enough different from the Han of the Marímnes to give Dorantes trouble, but Esteban's big, pink-palmed hands flew in monologues, and he seemed to understand well enough the Charruco guide's half-spoken, half-sign responses.

Alonso lagged behind from time to time, stooping to examine pebbles and crevices in the rocks. Dorantes and Alvar Núñez marched in a cluster of Indians, Álvar's eyes fixed on distant mountains sailing in the west. Dorantes found his own limbs responding in a kind of effortless rhythm so that he seemed almost to glide, as though they knew instinctively to gear themselves to a farther destination than merely this one day's journey.

The village of the Charrucos lay along a steep-sided creek in which a trickle of water connected a chain of sandy pools. Huts were constructed of woven matting over a frame of poles, in the same manner as those of the Marímnes. As they descended a long slope to the creek they could hear the wailing, and Dorantes felt relieved in a complicated way, for if the Charruco chief was already dead Álvar's great faith was not to be tested.

Across the creek they passed through a crowd of Indians. The corpse had been covered with a freshly woven grass mat, and women were already tearing down the chief's hut, ceasing their labors when the Christians appeared. They set up a wail, and men muttered angrily when Álvar flung the mat aside. The eyes of the chief were covered with two pebbles; the face was gray and lined, the body wrapped in a deerskin. Álvar knelt to uncover the wrist and feel for the pulse. His calm eyes encountered Dorantes', then turned to heaven as he began to pray aloud. Rosary in one hand, prayer book in the other, Dorantes knelt to pray with him. Alonso gazed down at them with pure terror in his face, then knelt also, and Esteban joined them as well.

A woman brought the chief's bow and presented it to Álvar, who laid it on the cadaver. An elder proffered a packet of dried, flattened cactus fruit, which Álvar also placed there. He said a Paternoster and a Hail Mary, then rose, crossing himself, and finished the motion by shaking his finger at a young man who started to cover the body with the mat again.

With the Charruco guide beckoning, they retreated through the crowd, Indians plucking at their arms and indicating sickness in heads, bellies, limbs. They accompanied the most importunate of these into a smoky hut, where a man lay groaning. Like a sleepwalker Dorantes touched the man's head with the beads and the book, while Álvar knelt to pray and dirty faces watched from the doorway. He found that his own fear was tempered by Alonso's terror.

"Andrés, that man was *dead* and so are we!" Alonso whispered, and gasped as there was a shout from outside.

The patient's eyes glittered in the smoky light, and he no longer groaned. Dorantes let his hands with their queer warmth and heavy burdens drop to his knees. Álvar continued to intone Latin. Esteban wormed his way through the Charrucos crowding the doorway with their stench of sickness, fear, and hope.

"Masters! That one has risen and called for food to eat!"

"Ah, praise God!" Alonso whispered.

"Praise be to God!" Álvar said, and blew his breath out in a sigh.

They had no chance to observe the miracle immediately, for many other Charrucos were suffering from maladies Dorantes felt competent to heal, although Álvar prayed earnestly over each one. When Dorantes had time to think, he found he felt no surprise that a man had been dead and now, apparently, was not.

The Christians watched as the Charrucos presented the Marímnes with baskets of dried fruits, venison, and a great robe that seemed to be highly valued—very heavy, with thick, black curly hair. Alonso gaped in amazement as the Marímne women were laden with these goods and departed with the unencumbered men, Kiphalu without a backward glance. "What, have we new masters now?"

"It appears we are free of the old ones," Dorantes said. "I believe our journey has truly begun."

That night at a great fire Dorantes sat between Álvar and Alonso, watching their hosts dancing, their rejoicing, bare-breasted women revolving sedately while the men leaped and postured among them, Esteban dancing with them. The Lazarus was seated like an idol surrounded by his women, a blanket of skins covering his head like a cowl so that his face was invisible in shadow. From time to time one of the women knelt before him to push some tidbit into the oval shadow. Dorantes strained his eyes to make out if these disappeared, and they seemed to do so.

"Álvar, you have made us free!" Alonso said. "It is impossible to believe, it was so easy. I confess I had not your faith, my good friend!"

Álvar smiled gently, nodding, watching the chief on the other side of the dancers.

"These people have given the Marímnes many gifts," Dorantes said. "And must be convinced that they will receive gifts also if they escort us to the west. I believe it is a means we may count on for our progress."

"Our trust in God is what will preserve us, Andrés."

"But God will be most pleased if we help Him to preserve ourselves."

Alonso said, "Andrés, perhaps you who speak best these unspeakable tongues can best assure these people of the advantages the messenger of Good Thing can bring them when we are guided to the west."

He shook his head. "I think it will be better for Estebánico to do so. Better if Álvar and I do not fumble with these tongues, nor concern ourselves with gross matters of bargaining."

"It is well thought, Andrés!"

Álvar laid a hand on his knee. "You must be our captain, Andrés."

"And you the healer. But I will assist you."

"I will be the trader!" Alonso said excitedly. "And collect the things that will show the riches of the lands through which we pass when we have returned to New Spain!"

"Each will do what he can do," Álvar said, nodding.

"Regard the Moor doing what he can do!" he said, and laughed; he felt that same bubbling excitement he had heard in Alonso's voice.

They watched Esteban, a head taller than any of the Charruco men, dancing close to one of the women and fondling her breasts.

That night lying on a hard, woven mat next to Álvar, Dorantes listened to the healer stirring and murmuring, soft sounds of delight, perhaps like those out of his own dreams of his Timultzin, about which his slave would sometimes slyly tease him. Grimacing with jealousy for Álvar's hot dreams of pleasure and fullfillment, he strained to hear the endearments his bedmate was whispering:

"Ah, my God! My *God*!"

He remembered Timultzin, baptized in the Holy Faith as Juana, describing the presence of her Aztec god as she danced. That god had not been terrible to her as he was to the Spaniards, nor were the priests with their blood fetor, their torn ears and blood-matted hair, as they prowled among the dancing virgins with obsidian knives. They could behead a girl with one stroke of those knives, but she had felt no fear, only an excitement of the nerves, pleasurable prickling of the skin in the proximity of the god. Death meant joining him, a hummingbird sipping honey and darting in the sunlight of his pleasure forever. She had been able to feel the pulse of the god's attention and interest, of his love for her, washing over her like fluid, like liquid sunlight, as she danced. Yes, he had spoken to her, but not in words; what words would a god speak? That love, that interest, that attention, that nearness and communication of which she had spoken so longingly, she had never felt as a Christian—until it had come to her so terribly at last.

And so he lay awake weeping for Timultzin, as he listened to Álvar communing with his god.

Chapter Three

The Charrucos surrounded them, their bare-breasted women clad in deerskin skirts of long panels front and rear, dirty legs revealed at the sides. These people seemed good-natured, and were certainly grateful to the Christians; did Dorantes find himself capable of liking them because they were not his captors, or because he had done something to incur that gratitude? Esteban's hands wove before them, wiping left, wiping right, pointing west, pointing to the setting sun, as he explained to them that the Christians must depart in that direction, and that the Charrucos would receive great benefit by accompanying them to the next village. Dorantes could not keep his eyes from the returned-from-the-dead chief, whose aged face was visible now, not gray but a muddy brown. His hooded eyes regarded the Moor without particular interest; from time to time he pursed his lips, or turned to speak to one of his wives. Álvar stood with his arms folded within the deerskin they had presented to him, gazing west toward the mountains.

Alonso nudged Dorantes and jerked his chin to indicate the old chief; Alonso found it difficult to believe the man really lived.

"It was said in Béjar that the old duke died as a child and was raised by the intervention of Saint Vincent," Dorantes said.

"Certainly one has heard of the many miracles of the Redeemer and the saints of the Holy Church," Alonso said. He frowned toward Álvar, who was not a saint, not a priest nor even a lay brother; only a soldier like the rest of them, who had brought a man back to life and breath who had been dead. Dorantes had found that his only surprise was that he was not surprised.

Álvar glanced toward him and said, as though he was aware of what they were thinking, "The grace of God is as powerful as need be, Alonso, Andrés. Nor can it be easily explained."

"I have been thinking, if by His grace we join our fellow Christians again, how this matter is to be explained," Dorantes said. "I think the Holy Church will not look with enthusiasm upon miracles performed by soldiers and castaways."

Alonso snickered, while Álvar pondered, frowning.

"See how the linguist-of-hands persuades these Charrucos," Alonso said, for the Moor seemed to have succeeded. The Charrucos were laughing, slapping their thighs and nodding and smiling at the Christians. Women brought them cups of the purple juice of the cactus fruit, which was very sweet but also tasted of the earthen pots in which it had been stored.

"You were King's Treasurer," Alonso said to Álvar. "Not so much a soldier as the rest of us, on the expedition to Florida. And so not so great a sinner."

"A very great sinner, my friend," Álvar said, smiling.

"I believe you were only a common sinner. I do not believe that the grace of God would be vouchsafed to a very great sinner."

"What of Saul of Tarsus, who became the Holy Paul? All sinners may be redeemed, Alonso. All may share heavenly grace."

"I knew one who will not be forgiven," Dorantes said suddenly. He cleared his throat to rid his voice of its thickening. "Julian de Alderete, who in his arrogance and impetuosity lost sixty good men to the knives of the Aztec priests. And who forced Hernán Cortés to torture the emperor Cuauhtémoc so that he was crippled until he died."

Certainly the church taught that forgiveness was continuous and uncontingent, and yet, as Alonso had suggested, there must be degrees. Was there forgiveness for those who did not forgive themselves?

"All may be forgiven, Andrés," Álvar said reprovingly.

"You were there, were you not, when they burned the Aztec devil's feet?" Alonso asked.

He nodded.

"And when he was garroted, on the road to Honduras? He conspired to murder the conqueror, to whom he had sworn allegiance, is it not so?"

He said carefully, "I believe it is what Hernán Cortés believed."

Esteban trotted toward them, stuffing dried cactus fruit into his mouth. "Masters! We will depart at sun-up. They say there are people called Cuchendádo who will give them many gifts in exchange for healings. These fellows will accompany us, as the Marímnes have done."

"And so we proceed," Álvar said. "By the grace of God."

It seemed strange to him that the Charrucos had so easily been persuaded to speed them on their way, for they had paid the Marímnes well, and repayment by the Cuchendádos was hypothetical. But glancing at the old chief surrounded by his women, it occurred to him that the chief, for political reasons, wished them to be gone.

The village of the Cuchendádos was the largest they had yet encountered. Dorantes estimated forty lodgings, conical structures with smoke rising from some of the peaks. There was a wait in sight of these while Esteban and three of the Charruco men went ahead to announce the advent of the healers, and to bargain for their services. Seated on a rock, Alonso poked into a little deerskin bag filled with some glittering mineral none of the Christians had been able to identify, which he had received in trade from a Charruco.

Their reception was loud and cheerful, the entire village turning out, and the Cuchendádo men leaping and shouting, and slapping their hands loudly against their thighs.

"They say they must carry the healers into their village, Masters," Esteban explained, and the three of them were swept off their feet and borne on the shoulders of the Cuchendádos to a clearing in the center of the conical huts. Here they were set down while their new hosts crowded around them, smoothing hands down their bodies and in turn down their own, conversing in their rapid, high-pitched tongue. Glancing around him for the ill of this place, Dorantes saw examples that disturbed him—a man with great sores on his face, another with a withered leg and a crutch, a gray-faced, big-eyed child in his mother's arms.

"Tell them we must have a hut to ourselves, and those to be treated are to enter one by one," he told the Moor, who whooped for silence. His hands performed their dance. They were led to a large hut by a woman wearing a rabbitskin cape and skirts decorated with shells and beans that rattled as she walked, in dull accompaniment to Esteban's clicking jingle.

The hut was dense with smoke from a small fire smoldering in the center, surrounding which were pallets covered with skins. Esteban evicted the occupants and their guide, and barred the entrance against the Cuchendádos who would have entered behind them. Álvar knelt to pray, Alonso crossed himself, and Dorantes felt a queer, hard laughter bubbling in his throat like hiccoughs. He began to sing, Alonso joining them, then Álvar; their voices swelling together on the refrain:

> "*Fonte frida, fonte frida,*
> *fonte frida y con amor.*"

His eyes watered in the smoky room with the song of old Castile. When they had sung the many verses Álvar began a Te Deum; this finished, they knelt in a congealed silence.

"Let one of them come in now," he said to Esteban.

Entering first was one who was clearly a notable person of the village, from the red and yellow decorations painted on his torso. While Álvar prayed, Dorantes touched the man on his indicated painful chest with the rosary and prayer book. Immediately the man was slapping his thighs and grinning. He departed, and another entered to be cured. Esteban joined in the healing, laying on his pink palms with great flair, raising his face to the peak of the hut and intoning meaningless sounds, sometimes leaning forward to blow upon the place of pain. Only Alonso did not participate in these ceremonies, collecting from the patients, however, what tribute he could. This included several decorated gourds that rattled cheerfully when shaken.

"They say there is great virtue in these gourds, Masters," the Moor said. "Perhaps they will assist us in the healing. I cannot understand where they say they come from. Some may say heaven, but others the river in flood." He rattled a gourd close to his ear, grinning at the sound.

Two men entered, one holding his arm against his chest, bent with weakness and coughing. His friend explained his affliction to Esteban, and Dorantes knew from the Moor's expression as well as the patient's posture that here was no imaginary ill.

"Very sick, Masters," Esteban whispered, his eyes rolling whitely. "He carries an arrowhead here!" He touched his chest between the paps. Álvar rose, so tall he had to bend his head beneath the slant of the roof.

"Tell him to remove his shirt."

Esteban and the friend helped the invalid off with his rabbitskin cape. Carefully the man lowered his protective arm. Dorantes could see the lump in his bony chest that was not a bone, beside a healed scar that palpitated when he breathed. When Álvar touched the lump the man winced and wheezed. The friend was speaking with many gestures to Esteban, whose face was contorted melodramatically.

"It has been eight moons, Masters," he said. "The pain is great. He is less than a man with his women. He is very sad. What can be done?"

"Alonso, the sharpest of the knives—"

"Álvar—" Dorantes started, but halted as Alonso spoke: "Álvar, let us pray merely! This one is *very* sick, Álvar!"

It seemed to him that, as captain, he must order Álvar to leave this man alone and pray for him merely; but when he met the healer's eyes he only nodded. Alonso rummaged in his pack. Esteban stood with his big hands working together as though they carried on their own dialogue. The friend leaned outside the entrance to speak to someone there.

"Have him lie down," Álvar said.

After protests from the patient and peremptory orders from Esteban, the sick man carefully lowered himself to one of the pallets, staring straight above him in resignation.

Dorantes bundled deerskins into a pad and helped the patient to arrange himself with this beneath his back so that his chest was curved up to Álvar's knife, like a victim on an Aztec sacrificial stone. Álvar murmured a Paternoster, and crossed himself.

With a swift motion the man's chest was laid open. Blood flowed. Dorantes watched Álvar's fingers palping within the wound. He cut again. The Cuchendádo groaned. The arrowhead was revealed. The fingers worked at it. Gradually the bit of stone was loosened. Dorantes handed Álvar a deerskin with which to mop away the blood. The friend took the arrowhead from Álvar.

"Alonso, a needle and cording," Dorantes said.

These were produced from Alonso's pack, Dorantes threading the needle and passing it to Álvar. The Cuchendádo's eyes were still locked on the peak of the cone above him. Álvar had put down the bloody knife to receive the needle, and took four stitches, grimacing for the first time. Sweat and smoke smarted in Dorantes' eyes. The silence around them had bulk.

The friend murmured something, and Esteban said, "He asks if he may show the accursed arrowhead to the others."

Álvar grunted assent, and the arrowhead was passed outside, where a muffled chatter rose. Dorantes mopped blood from the patient's chest with the deerskin, sweat from his forehead with the back of his hand.

"Tell the others that this one can return to his lodging now," Álvar said.

Esteban signaled. They helped the patient to his feet. With his friend's arm around him he passed slowly outside, where the muttering rose in pitch.

"I believe he will live, Andrés," Álvar said.

"Let us pray, Álvar."

Alonso made the sign of the cross.

"There are more who must be served, friends," Álvar said, and the Moor leaned out the entrance to beckon to the next patient. Dorantes had a glimpse of long shadows, fading light; time had passed as though the removal of the arrowhead had taken hours instead of minutes. Another Cuchendádo stepped inside.

"This one has much pain in his head," Esteban said contemptuously.

Álvar had remained kneeling, eyes turned upward like those of a kneeling saint in an old fresco. Dorantes rose, taking up the rosary and prayer book. He touched one side of the patient's head with the beads, the other with the book. "Hail, Mary, full of grace—"

It sufficed.

That night the Cuchendádos danced. Dressed in their finery, faces striped with red ochre, they pranced around the fire. Dorantes, with Álvar and Alonso, watched them in solemn boredom. One of the men brought the Christians the small cactus buttons the Cuchendádos used as intoxicants, which Dorantes and Álvar refused, but Alonso appropriated for his pack. Esteban had joined the circle, hopping, belly to rump, between two of the women with their swaying, rattling skirts. Couples retreated to the shadows, where firelight flickered on laboring knees, backs, and buttocks.

Alonso stretched. "These skirts are more taking than the garments of moss of the Marímnes," he said. "I believe I will fuck one of these women, since I have no need to preserve myself in order to perform great healings." He sauntered off to join the dancing and was presently to be observed escorting one of the skirted Cuchendádos away from the fire. Esteban had already disappeared.

"Are you married, Andrés?" Álvar enquired.

He said he was not. "And you?"

"Yes." Sticks whacked rhythmically on a hollow log, the skirts of the women rattled provocatively. Firelight caught the heaving flesh in the shadows. "Do these skirts stir you also, my friend?" Álvar asked.

"The ear is stirred more than the eye."

Álvar laughed. "Perhaps it is as Alonso says."

"Celibacy for the sake of the grace that heals?"

Álvar laughed again, and did not reply. Esteban appeared out of the darkness and squatted with them. His smell was not of celibacy.

"Estebánico," Andrés said. "It may be that we will encounter indigenes who view their women in a different light than these we have so far encountered. They may not be pleased by your attentions. They may decide to kill you for a Bad Thing."

Esteban shook his new gourd until the pebbles inside rattled furiously. "This will preserve me, Master. They are sacred to these barbarians, these rattles. Also I have discovered that when this is shaken in the ear of the bird beneath one, she becomes very active."

"It is written in Holy Scripture that a man may not serve two masters," he said severely. "Yet you have a master whom you serve besides me."

The Moor was giggling nervously before he finished. Alonso also returned and joined them, squatting with his back turned to the dancers.

Esteban rattled his gourd again, his teeth gleaming in the firelight. "My masters, there is only one life, and after it a long time will be spent dead. And although the angels of heaven are beautiful, and smell so sweet, and sing sweetly, one understands that they are chaste. Still, if heaven is the reward of good Christian men, perhaps the angels are not so chaste as one has heard. Think of it, to lie among the clouds with good meat and wine, and beautiful, sweet-smelling angels singing, and—"

"I believe that is the heaven of the Mussulman, Estebánico," Andrés said, and thought of the heaven of Timultzin, transformed into a hummingbird swooping in the sunlight of the pleasure of Huitzilopochtli. "Have a care for blasphemy," he said, as Alonso whooped with laughter.

"Yes, Masters, yes; always careful. I do not say that such a rare thing could be true, only that—"

"And have a care also for the favorite wives of jealous chiefs."

"Yes, yes, Estebánico will have a special care for them." The Moor rattled his gourd noisily. "But there is an old saying among my people. If one is too careful to take the first bite from the apple, the fruit will spoil while he starves. So I do not count on the unchaste angels of the Mussulman heaven, but accept the birds that alight upon my branch. For I tell you, Masters, a Moor would rather pass eternity regretting those things done than left undone."

"We are of different races, truly," he said, grinning at his slave in the darkness. "For Castilians it is the other way."

The next morning the Charrucos set off for their own village, well pleased with their rewards for bringing the healers to the Cuchendádos, their women laden with baskets of pine and mesquite nuts, rabbit and deerskins, and other treasures. More of the Cuchendádos had discovered ailments, and the crowd outside the hut of the Christians was as great as it had been on the first day. On the third day the patient of the arrowhead appeared, still on the arm of his friend but standing straighter and not so pale of face.

Álvar drew out the stitches he had made, and Dorantes examined the wound. It had become a scar hardly more noticeable than a crease in the hand, still slightly inflamed and with a drop of pinkish fluid oozing from one of the stitches. After the Night of Sorrows the wounds that had healed this quickly had been considered miracles of the Virgin of the Remedies. He rocked back on his heels, squatting to gaze into Álvar's serene face.

"Ask him if he feels pain," Álvar said.

Esteban had hardly begun to gesture when the patient spoke lengthily, twice slapping his thighs in a restrained manner.

"There is no more pain, Masters," The Moor said.

That night he lay listening to the low snores of Alonso and the louder but less frequent ones of Esteban. He was recalling the King's Treasurer he had known in Florida, before the barges, where Álvar had been stern and fretful, a stiff stick of a man no one had liked.

"Álvar," he whispered. "Has the state of your faith always been so strong?"

For a moment he thought the healer also slept, but after a moment Álvar said, "Not as a young man. But in the years of our captivity always stronger."

"How did this come to be?"

"I think it was our abject state, with death always very close. When I carried the mats of my masters from one place to another, when I pried for roots in salt water with bleeding fingers, when I devoured the spiders and lizards I had begged from my captors, I was purged of my pride, which had formerly been very great. Pride had been my great sin as a young man. I was very proud of my mother's name of Cabeza de Vaca, which is an honored one.

"I remember that I would begin to tremble if one of the Deagúnes even looked in my direction. Their favorite joke was to press an arrow to my breast, or my crotch, nock it with the string stretched, scowling frightfully—then to relent and ask if I had been frightened. I was always frightened, though I never said so, until one day a voice spoke in my ear, to say, 'Be not frightened, my son. All will be well.' And I was never frightened again."

He listened to the snores of Esteban, and Alonso making a wet blowing sound. He felt the slow, hard beat of his heart as he thought of that reassuring voice in Álvar's ear.

"You have doubts?" Álvar asked gently.

He nodded until he realized that this could not be seen in the darkness. "Yes."

"But think of the miracles that have been granted us that we survive."

"Ah, Álvar, I have had no voice in my ear, and no vision of the Redeemer, or Our Lady." But he was caught up short thinking not only of the death of Shitface, but of Caballo snatching him, instead of Bernardo, from the grasp of the warriors at the Tolteca Canal.

Álvar was asking how he had lost his faith.

"I remember when I first came to Santiago de Cuba, how the cavaliers there used to brag for the benefit of newcomers. I remember one boasting that he could behead an Indian with one blow of his sword. How in fact that very day he had beheaded three indigenes with three blows, while another required five blows for the same number. And these same countrymen of ours bragged of their dogs that had been raised upon human flesh to make them good slavehunters. How Ponce de León's great mastiff Berecillo did such execution that he received a crossbowman's pay. I think that when I listened to these men, and pretended that their stories were not horrors beyond comprehension but matters for laughter, that I began to doubt."

And after that the Conquest—Tenochtitlán, Tlatelolco, Panuco, Honduras; and before that, of course, with his father in the Plaza del Triunfo, in Seville, where the heretics and apostates were burned in iron cages shaped like the prophets.

"May God have mercy on them," Álvar said, stirring and drawing up his knees.

"Yes," he said. "We thought the Aztecs animals, but I have seen Christians *worse* than animals. I think it was when I began to turn against my own kind that I questioned our Maker's purposes." He halted for a long moment before he said, "And I have done things and seen things done for which I can never forgive myself. So how can I accept the forgiveness of Heaven? As myself, as a Castilian; as a man! I cannot! I think I can never recover my faith, Álvar, despite these miracles of our escape."

"Yet here you are alive when so many others have perished."

"Who should have been saved more than I. Diego, for one. The priest." He lay with his eyes closed, tears burning in them not for Diego and the priest, but for his sins. Esteban muttered in his sleep.

"I pray that your faith will be restored," Álvar whispered.

He said, "I believe this. That our presumptious dreams of wealth and honors in Florida and Apalachen were properly smashed. That properly we were stripped of our weapons, our horses and fine armor —all our worldly goods. And of our great pride. And that we were cast away upon a barren island to show us there the tortures of purgatory. Enslavement by savages, and moment by moment fear for our lives. All that is a proper lesson. But for what, this lesson? For we will all die, one by one, after this lesson, so that it will have been for nothing." He had not meant to speak with such passion.

Álvar sighed. "But Andrés, this despair is a greater sin than any of those you hesitate even to describe. We four are not to die. I know that in my heart."

"Sooner or later, Álvar."

"Yet I have been told that all those held captive by the Marímnes would have died the sooner, but for the strength of Andrés Dorantes."

"They only died the later, except those of us here. Listen: we know how these peoples kill the deer. They build great fires which hem in all the other life as well. So everything is killed, and the hunters feast on venison for a little while. This waste of life is done by men, and men are what we know them to be. But the great pox, which is the ruin of children, is done by heaven. And what is the heavenly purpose of the smallpox that—" His voice choked, and he could not go on.

"It is not for us to ask, Andrés."

Still unable to speak, he did not say, "I ask." He lay between the warm bodies of the healer and the Moor, remembering the first time he had asked, the first time his faith had been shaken, in the Plaza del Triunfo in Seville, when he was just eighteen.

He and his father had come to Seville for Holy Week, where they were guests in the household of the Conde de Aguilar, his father grizzle-bearded, bald and stiff-backed, and skinny as a child's stick figure. The conde was plump and smiling, with a tricorn mustache and beard, slapping his father on the shoulder and calling him "old comrade," while the son of the old comrade bowed low as he had been instructed to do, and muttered the flowery greetings with which he had been ordered to speak up strongly. He was awed by the palace with the marble coat of arms displayed over the great gate, and impressed that his father was greeted so warmly by nobility, although the Dorantes were of hidalgo stock and could claim the Marqués Dávila Fuente as kin. But he was all too well aware that Old Castile was populated by impecunious but well-connected small nobility like his father, with sons like him they sought to place in the service of a grandee.

They were seated in a high-ceilinged room with dark beams separated by narrow strips of plaster, and high windows letting in a dusty sun ray that illumined heavy furniture and fabrics in dark red and blue. Wine was brought in heavy goblets. The conde, in his green doublet, was serene and deliberate in all his motions, while the elder Dorantes slopped wine on his sleeve in his nervousness.

"And how old is your fine son?" the conde enquired.

"Just eighteen this month, Álvaro."

Nodding to this, the conde said, "He has a breadth of shoulder to him, Luis."

He felt like a prize calf at the Béjar fair as he resisted moving his shoulders in embarrassment.

"Very strong," his father said gruffly, who was unused to praising his son. "And quick. Good-natured as well." There was a pause in which Luis Dorantes evidently decided not to mention his son's quick temper. "A good son!" He coughed. "I have seen that he is well trained."

The conde smiled his cool smile and continued to nod. "So you would like to come to our service, my son."

"Yes, sire!"

"We will find a place for you. Your father's son could be no other than honorable and valorous, and such we are proud to have in our service!"

"Thank you, sire," he managed, watching the high hectic flush on his father's cheeks.

The conde reached across the table to clasp his father's hand in his two hands. "I know he will never disappoint me, old comrade!"

"Never, Álvaro!" his father said, glaring at him. "The blood is pure in sire and dam! Never, on my life!"

His father remained in residence for that week while he, Andrés, trained with Agustín, the master-at-arms who had served with the Great Captain, Gonzalo de Córdoba, in Italy and had the scars, limp, and temper to prove it. They traded blows and parries with broadsword and rapier. He bestrode Campañero, the enormous, heavy-footed sorrel who responded to a whisper, not even the touch of a spur necessary to send him surging down the rutted course toward the swinging target, lance leveled, with Agustín bellowing, "Hold it tighter! I tell you hold it like your cock that will fall off if you don't hold it tight, hidalgo!"

Agustín seemed pleased that he had had no training with the crossbow, and after the first day they drilled each afternoon with that weapon, aiming at the battered target, letting the bolt fly with the savage whack of string against metal, then jamming the tiller to the ground with his boot while he snatched the cranequin from his belt, caught the string, and spun the winder to attach it to the nut; aiming again, releasing again. Agustín did not concern himself at first with accuracy, but attended the speed of loading, his hourglass gauging how many bolts were released as the grains ran out; five, then, sweating and cranking, six, finally seven. Then there was a complicated method of scoring with scratches made in the beaten earth, values given the concentric rings of the target, little by little the score better and better, until Agustín, scowling and scratching his fingers through his graying beard, was satisfied.

During the festivities of Holy Week he and his father strolled among the crowds in the Plaza del Triunfo, beneath the Giralda. In the broad aisles of the cathedral, gentry and commonality jostled together, admiring the splendid high screens, the multitudinous flames of the candles, the gigantic font for consecrated oil, the illuminated books on their stands, the iron-bound chests for contributions. A sluggish movement outside began as a sound of chanting was heard, nearer and louder. He thrust a passage for his father through the press of bodies, clutching his purse against the basket of his rapier.

In the square the constables held back the crowd while the chanting penitents in their hooded gowns with red crosses on the breast paraded past. The sound, low and hard, with a driving imperative to it, made his stomach squirm, and his father's grip tightened on his arm. Constables, carrying torches, preceded a cart with tall decorated cornerposts drawn by a team of horses. From its grillwork gray faces peered out, ghastly by the torchlight. His father muttered and crossed himself.

Following the cart were floats of scenes from scripture, men immobilized into statues borne on the hundreds of bare feet that were visible beneath the skirts of the floats. A drum beat steadily, and from time to time the trumpets brayed. On a high platform past the facade of the cathedral curious iron cages had been placed, shaped, he realized, like huge men. They were the prophets, this one with iron strut arms raised characteristically to heaven, that one cradling what must be a lamb. Heaped around the feet of each of these iron-cage prophets were short lengths of faggots.

The cart with its barber-pole cornerposts halted before the platform, and its occupants, in black sanbenito, were half-helped, half-carried by the constables to the cages, whose fronts hinged open. Into these the victims the Holy Office had released to the Secular Arm were stuffed, one by one, and the fronts of the cages swung shut.

"Who are they?" he asked, lips close to his father's good ear.

"Witches, heretics, apostates—" His father cleared his throat. "Those of corrupt blood."

Corrupt blood was Moorish, or Jewish, and its tendency to apostasy was pursued by the Inquisition. On the platform now, an official of the Holy Office, in a black robe, rope girdle, and wooden beads that swung from his neck when he gestured, was speaking, the words lost in the chanting of the penitents. The floats had halted, sinking down as the porters rested. From one of the cages a steady, high, thin screaming began. His father crossed himself, muttering.

"Sire?"

"You saw the greeting of the conde, my old comrade. And how he accepted you readily to his service. Clean blood in sire and dam! You heard me vow it to him, my son!"

He could not make out what so troubled his father, who still clung to his arm.

"Perceive the fate of those whose blood is contaminated!" His father's voice was so thick he could hardly understand it. The exhausted screaming continued. The torches of the constables flickered in the breeze off the river.

"You will maintain the pure blood that has been bequeathed to you, Andrés! Swear it!"

"I swear it, Father!"

He could hear his father's heavy breathing as a hooded figure with a brand knelt to ignite the first heap of faggots. His heart was beating as though it would bruise his chest. Inside the cages some of the condemned moved, but some appeared already dead. He saw that a constable was passing behind the cages with a garrote. A weakening sickness seemed to flow in his blood as his father continued to babble about its purity. He had never heard Luis Dorantes sound frightened before.

His father's words were lost in the rising clamor of the crowd as the flames spiraled upward. The clothing of one of the dead men flared. All at once he smelled the stench of burning meat.

"Father, we must go from here."

"Yes," his father said, leaning heavily on him. "Yes."

They were five days with the Cuchendádos, and each night there were feasts, the taking of the cactus buds, dancing, and bouts of copulation. One night by a full moon the chief, a tall man with scarred features, presided over a different ceremony. A brew of tender shoots of an evergreen plant was set over live coals in a fat clay pot. The chief tended this carefully, skimming off a yellow froth. Others of the elders joined him where he squatted watching the pot, and soon all the men had assembled at the fire. A chant began: "Hai-yah, hai-i-yah; hai-yah, hai-i-yah." The men shook their sacred gourds in rhythm to the words and partook of cups of the brew offered them by the chief.

Dorantes, observing from the shadows, could not see what effect the liquor was having, but wondered if the Truce of the Cactus Fruit might be over and the Cuchendádos preparing for war, with the brew to change the procreative mood to the martial.

The next day was devoted to the making of arrows. But in the midst of these preparations four women arrived, emissaries from a tribe to the west petitioning for the healers. After a noisy conference among the elders, this course was decided upon and the warlike preparations called off.

They set out parallel to a dragonback of blue peaks raised against the southern horizon. The land was sandy, with clumps of low brush, and they must keep watch for poisonous serpents. The Cuchendádos killed one of these, its fat, triangularly-marked body tossing this way and that and its yellow rattle still making a disquieting sound.

Within a band of Cuchendádos they followed Esteban and the four Avaváre women. Once the Moor waited beside the trail to join the three other Christians. "Masters, have you heard what our friends the Cuchendádos call us to these Avaváres? They call us 'the Children of the Sun'!"

"Ah, we are no longer the 'messengers of Good Thing,'" Álvar said.

"They are telling these women we are *gods*," Esteban said excitedly. "Of course, they would make much of our powers to give us the more value. We are gods who will travel only in the direction of the setting sun, you see."

Alonso laughed, rubbing a hand over his bald head. Dorantes laughed with him. Yes, their destination was the setting sun! He saw that Álvar looked worried, but the infection caught him and he began laughing also. All laughed together, in their great optimism.

"Children of the Sun, Masters!" Esteban cried. "Black and white alike!"

The village of the Avaváres was smaller than that of the Cuchendádos, the huts constructed of branches woven together and plastered with mud. The Cuchendádos surrounded the Children of the Sun protectively while three of the Avaváre chiefs gesticulated and clucked in a blurred and staccato tongue from which Dorantes could make no sense, although he guessed that the Cuchendádos were withholding the services of the healers until some terms were met. The scar-faced chief stood with arms folded on his chest, scowling at the protests of the Avaváres.

"What is it, Estebánico?" Alonso whispered.

"I think Cuchendádos ask more than Avaváres can pay, Masters."

There was a new disturbance as an Avaváre was brought forward between two others. The man was blind, Dorantes realized; a cautious shuffle, deepset eyes invisible beneath shelves of brows. The blind man grumbled in the clucking way as the angry parley continued. Esteban joined in, gesticulating with his hands flung right and left, and his chin jutted. He swung back toward them.

"Masters, the Avaváres demand that this blind one is healed before they will give what the Cuchendádos require."

"No!" he said quickly.

"I will try, Andrés," Álvar said.

"Not on those terms, not on demand. The Cuchendádos are trying to rob these people."

"It is true, Master! They demand all their goods. Also women. So the Avaváres demand proof that the Children of the Sun are gods."

"We will not be used in that way," he said.

"But what of this unfortunate one?" Álvar said.

Brown faces were shouting at each other. As the blind man turned from side to side, Dorantes had a glimpse of dead white eye.

"Andrés!" Alonso whispered. "This is very bad for us!"

The scar-faced Cuchendádo chief was haranguing Esteban furiously, bow and arrows gripped in one fist and jerking up and down. Álvar prayed with his eyes closed, the Latin phrases scraping at Dorantes' nerves. He called to the Moor.

"Tell them this: the healers have not the power to heal on command. The healing must be freely given. Afterwards the Avaváres are welcome to give gifts to the Cuchendádos if they are grateful. That is the way it must be."

Esteban's lips drooped open to show his fat pink tongue. He drew himself up tall and addressed the infuriated Cuchendádo chief, hands flying, voice sing-songing, the other shouting back at him. All at once the chief thrust him aside, and nocked an arrow. He jabbed the arrow's head at Álvar in a sudden, frozen silence.

"Masters!" Esteban whispered. "They will kill us if the blind one is not healed!"

With a sweep of his hand Dorantes jerked the bow and arrow away from the chief. He flung the bow humming over the heads of the Avaváres and broke the reed shaft of the arrow over his knee. He flung the pieces into the chief's face. Surrounding them other Cuchendádos had nocked arrows.

The chief stared into his face. Dorantes felt a queer chill in his eyes, upon which the other's eyes were fixed. The chief retreated a step, the other men giving way behind him. Fear had come across his face like a deeper scarring. Suddenly he squatted in the dirt. He gestured once to Esteban and bowed his head.

"He begs that you will not take his life, Master!"

"Tell him that it must be as I have said." Dorantes was shaken and confused by what he had felt in himself.

Esteban explained. The chief remained squatting with his head bowed. He made a gesture of capitulation and rose to stand with his back turned. The others had let their bows drop. Dorantes' jaw was aching. Álvar prayed.

"In nomine Patris, Filii, et Spiritus Sancti—"

They were almost two weeks with the Avaváres before arrangements were made for their progress to the next village, that of the

Anaquas. The blind man had not been produced again, and Dorantes was aware that this was out of fear of his anger. Nor had Álvar pursued the matter. The route led northwest, toward floating blue peaks, along a broad riverbed, where water trickled along a chain of pools in the sandy bottom. The small, brown, smiling men and women of their escort flocked around them, carrying their goods and often patting and stroking the healers. As they walked Dorantes reflected upon the pleasures of the floating gait his limbs seemed to know how to fall into, and the pleasure of his companions, Esteban, as always, traveling at the head of the troop, while Álvar walked on his right and Alonso on his left—the one God-possessed, whose every thought seemed to turn upon faith, grace, healing; the other fearful and suspicious and still professing to be a hater of the indigenes, although he indefatigably collected their artifacts and searched the earth for evidence of minerals that would make these desert lands valuable.

Alonso wore a small grass mat tied over his bald pate as protection from the sun, which, however, was not so powerful these days. As they walked he shook his pearls from their pouch and rolled them in his palm.

"One day we will have pearls from the Southern Sea also, Andrés! Still, these are not such bad ones."

"We have no fine ladies to decorate with them, Alonso!"

Alonso flipped his other hand at one of the smiling Avaváre ladies walking beside him. "Pah! I could buy any one of these for one pearl. Three for two! What a fortune we could gather if we had only the means of drilling holes in these pearls to make a necklace! If we only had one sliver of hard metal!"

"How burdensome this journey would be if we had to carry a fortune with us," Álvar said. He had stepped on a cactus thorn and was limping.

Dorantes touched his arm. "Álvar, I see that your foot hurts, but I do not believe a Child of the Sun should be seen limping. May this not cause a loss of faith in those who observe it?"

Álvar nodded, with a flash of his bland blue gaze; he endeavored not to limp and did well enough.

"As for me," Dorantes continued, "I have some understanding of the tongue the Avaváres and Anaquas share, and might parley with them—though not so well as Estebánico, certainly. But I believe it best that the healers do not converse with these people if they cannot do so perfectly. So; silent and unlimping."

Alonso was squinting at his pearls as he carefully funneled them back into their pouch. "But what of the natural functions, Andrés? Is it thinkable that gods have these?"

42

"Unthinkable. Privacy must be sought."

"What of the lusts of the flesh, Captain Dorantes? What of the overpowering lusts of Estebánico?"

"It is thinkable that the herald of the Children of the Sun might have overpowering lusts." In the lead the Moor paced proudly among three Anaqua women, his black frizzy head far taller than the small indigenes who scampered along beside him with their loads.

"When we have come safe to New Spain," Álvar said, "I will petition to return as governor to these lands we cross. My family is related to the Bishop of Burgos, who has a strong voice at court. Will you return with me as captain, Andrés?"

"Yes," he said, and did not realize that he had made a solemn vow.

"This land will be conquered with gentleness and not with slaughter," Álvar said. He walked naked, no longer limping.

"Do we not come with soldiers then?"

"With soldiers who shall be under strict orders."

He shook his head, feeling a testing of the serenity that had come to possess him on this journey. "They will still rape the women in their lust and kill the men in their greed."

"I would prevent this, Andrés. And I know you would."

"Then they would kill us. What if instead of soldiers you came with an army of friars? Franciscans, perhaps."

"I would fear they would not listen to me, but to their superiors. I have not much faith in Franciscans."

"I have more faith in friars than in soldiers," Dorantes said, and, turning to Alonso, "and what will you do when we return to New Spain, Alonso? Will you also return with us to help to gently settle this country?"

"I will look for a wealthy widow well-furnished with lands and indigenes to work them, and walk no more. Perhaps my legs will fall off from disuse, but not from overuse. If one returned as a trader he would need no soldiers nor friars either. Only his own shrewd sense." He tapped his forehead beneath his sunshade. "Still, it is my desire never to be frightened again."

"My foot no longer hurts," Álvar observed. "You have healed it, Andrés, by our command."

He laughed.

"Perhaps I should remain among these people as a healer," Álvar continued. "If I thought that was the desire of my God, I would do so. I have prayed for enlightenment. Yet I see it is you, Andrés, who should be captain of such an expedition, for you possess an authority with these people that is very strong."

"They fear him when he is angry," Alonso said.

The serenity of the slow approach to those distant peaks crumbled further as that fear he engendered troubled him. It was as though heaven's power through him, because of his sins, was exactly the opposite of Álvar's, of death rather than life, and indigenes such as the Cuchendádo chief recognized it in him. He said, "Álvar, I take nothing away from the healings we know you have performed—certainly they must be miracles. But it seems to me that many of our successes are due to their faith as much as yours, and to our novelty to them. Perhaps it is our history as much as our faith. That our ancestors were united in fighting the Moors, that generation after generation they tilled the same fields and inhabited the same dwellings, and each Castilian has his place, as a farmer, alcalde, nobleman, and thief. Perhaps it is all this that they discern in us."

"No, I do not agree with you, Andrés," Álvar said. "For all that I have known in my life has had to be discarded, history and experience and knowledge, until all I retain is what I knew as a babe in my mother's arms."

"And what did you know then?" he asked. His voice sounded rusty.

"I knew that she would not let me drop," Álvar said, his smile suffused with the bland, blue stare of his eyes.

Before nightfall they came to the village of the Anaquas, for another leaping, thigh-slapping welcome. Dorantes examined the faces before him for evidences of severe illness while Esteban made eyes at the women with their bare breasts and decorated skirts, and Alonso no doubt took stock of the goods on display. Some of the Anaquas stood in small groups outside the circle of the greeting. He noticed the milky film on the eyes of one of these, then another. These were groups of the blind. There were many blind, smiling blank faces directed toward the newcomers.

"Andrés!" Alonso whispered, gripping his arm. "This is very bad! It is a village of the blind!" Esteban was gazing around him with an expression of almost comical dismay.

"We must pray for these people," Álvar said. He began to recite a Paternoster in a loud, clear voice, palms of his hands pressed flat together before his face. The Anaquas retreated at first from his voice, then approached closer, and Dorantes saw the sighted attendants of the blind herding their charges closer also. He joined Álvar in his prayers, but he knew, as captain, he must command them all to hurry onward, away from this village of the blind.

But he allowed them to be led to the usual smoky hut, where the ill were to be brought in one by one, for Álvar to pray over and him to touch with his beads and prayer book, which process today seemed a mockery.

Each time another patient appeared stooping through the doorway his heart beat harder. The truly blind must be assembling outside the hut, and soon the first of them would enter. But each new patient exhibited only the familiar complaints of headache, chest or belly pain, boils, infection, earache—nothing serious. So they continued to await the first of the blind Anaquas, Álvar apparently serene in his faith, Dorantes and Alonso not even looking at one another in their dread.

Then Esteban came, panting as though he had run a long way, to kneel among them. He whispered, "Masters! The blind ones are sacred to these ignorant people. They believe they have been touched by God! They believe great good fortune comes from them. Masters, they do not wish that the Children of the Sun heal these blind ones!"

He felt laughter jerking in his throat. "Ah, praise God!" Alonso said in a thick voice. Álvar bowed his head over his hands in prayer.

Chapter Four

Some days they walked as many as ten leagues. They did not tire, nor did they require much in the way of food and drink. The days were sometimes very hot, but became colder as they moved north and west along a river broad as the Guadalquivir at Seville. They passed from village to village—Malicónes, Coáyos, Susólas. On each exchange their former hosts collected gifts from their new ones, but the system whereby each new village was plundered by those who brought the healers to it gradually changed. The gifts were offered to the Children of the Sun, who, wanting nothing for themselves, passed them along to their former hosts.

In some villages the indigenes would be so fearful of the Children that they were unable to look at them directly, fixing their eyes instead upon the ground, or upon the sky, or covering them with a hand. But little by little they would gather the courage to present their sick and hurt, and to discover more and more ailments urgently in need of attention. Word of the healers would also spread to outlying settlements, and these people trudged into the village with their diarrhea and ague, blisters, indigestion, constipation, wens and boils, headaches and mental depressions, to crowd around the lodge in which the healers held their clinic.

The Susólas guided them many leagues across the desert, mountains behind and ahead now, high, cold country, dry and without game. Esteban and Alonso grumbled with hunger, but Álvar seemed never to notice hunger, thirst, or cold, still traveling naked. Wondering at his companion's fortitude, Dorantes realized that he had few needs himself, although he did wrap himself in a deerskin. He gnawed at a bit of venison when one was given him and drank when they came to a spring. Was he following Álvar's example, of his own command that

46

the healers not appear too human in their necessities? Or, during the years of their captivity, had his needs gone so long unassuaged that they had diminished until he was hardly aware of them? Was he, in his own way, possessed if not of God's grace, like Álvar, of His *interest*?

Often, these nights in the desert, Alonso would ask him for tales of the Conquest, of which he had a store. One night he told of the Battle of Otumba, which had been much on his mind, for great faith had also been present there.

After the Night of Sorrows they made their way around the lakes of the valley, hoping to gain the safety of Tlaxcala before the Aztecs mounted another attack. There was hunger and thirst, and although their wounds healed with what seemed supernatural quickness, there was great fear, and sorrow and horror for the comrades who had died and who had been taken.

The turkey buzzards of Mexico floated in circles overhead as they trailed north, away from Tenochtitlán, and then east, toward Tlaxcala, Hernán Cortés and four hundred and sixty men, including a dozen crossbowmen, seven arquebusiers, twenty horsemen, three captains— all that remained of an army of thirteen hundred who had marched so bravely into the island city on the Day of John the Baptist. Always, as they marched within sight of the lakes they could hear the booming of the great drum on the cu.

Following them were the Tlaxcalans, still loyal in their great hatred of Tenochtitlán, and bedeviling them always the Aztecs in their fantastical uniforms as jaguars, ocelots, and eagles, screeching, whistling, and blowing on their conch-shell horns. They kept out of range of the arquebusiers and crossbows, although there was no powder left, and few bolts. From time to time the horsemen would mount a charge and scatter them, but the whistling, jeering Aztecs were never for long out of sight.

Cortés rode up and down the column with his bandaged hand and head, and gave what cheer he could, but something was lost that the captain-general had been wounded like the common soldiers. Perhaps his veterans had come to think of themselves as invincible, but the recruits from Narváez' force had never had occasion for much confidence, and now it had been proven to enemy and ally alike that the teules could be defeated. They subsisted on the wild cherries they found in quantity and a few ears of maize yielded by the stripped fields they passed through.

On the third day when the column halted for a rest, Andrés realized that his leg was no longer stiff. The wound the dart had made, which once had gaped open, had healed to no more than a wrinkle, slightly pink with new skin and all its angry red vanished. And when he glanced at Caballo Botello, who was popping cherries from his pouch into his mouth, he saw that the corporal's torn cheek had also healed.

That day they came in sight of two great pyramids. Around their skirts low stone structures were arranged in some mathematical order that was based on measurements of the stars—so said Fray Rufino, who was interested in the mysterious ways of the enemy. This place was deserted, but they circled well away from the pyramids in a silence that threw a pall over everyone.

Beyond these pyramids they began to mount the heights that still separated them from Tlaxcala. The cavaliers were sent out on scouting sweeps, and the army halted to watch the captains conferring, Cortés, seated upon a stone, settling his helmet and working his shoulders as though to throw off some mood. Then he rose to jump up on the rock, drawing his sword and directing Gonzalo de Sandoval and the advance guard onward toward the pass. Sandoval's division trudged on up the narrow trail, and, on the ridge line, each man paused in turn before moving aside along the ridge. When Andrés, with Caballo Botello's square, came up to the pass, he halted as Blas de Garay before him had done. He could hardly catch his breath for the sight that lay before him.

The valley was filled with warriors, the vastest crowd of men he had ever seen. Their spears spiked up through the carpeting of red, purple, and yellow plumes. Their red-painted faces were all turned in silence to the Spaniards appearing one by one at the pass, to range along the ridge line. They seemed to Andrés as multitudinous as ants beneath a rotted log, or fallen leaves in an autumnal forest. The mountains of Tlaxcala floated in the clear air, very near but beyond this valley filled with the warriors of Tenochtitlán.

There was a low groan from the next square of soldiers toiling over the pass to join them. Beyond Andrés a pikeman dropped to one knee, helmet gripped in the crook of his arm and his pike held perfectly upright. Fray Bartolomé had knelt in prayer. Grouped around Cortés, Alvarado, Olid, and Sandoval gazed from their horses down on the Aztec horde calmly enough.

After that one groan there was no sound but the pad of hoofs and the clatter of metal as the army spread out along the heights. The Tlaxcalans gazed expressionlessly down upon their ancient foe. The bearers dropped their loads. Fray Rufino supported himself upon the shoulder of one of these as he limped along the line, holding a sword hilt up for a cross of blessing.

Nor was there any sound from the multitude below. Their cacique was visible, reclining on a palanquin with a purple sun-cloth held over him by his guard of eagle knights. Other chiefs were also to be seen, all on their decorated litters.

Beside Andrés, Caballo stood with his thick legs apart and hands on hips, scowling down on the sea of warriors. Blas de Garay was on one knee, helmet under his arm. Gil de Herrera stood with arms folded on his chest, grinning like a skull, beyond him Toribio Sánchez in similar stance. Fray Rufino, supported by his bearer, passed by again, holding the sword hilt high. Men crossed themselves.

Sandoval turned his brown charger, Motilla, away from the other captains and trotted along the line of his division, halting before Caballo's square. His eyes were set so close together that he appeared always to be frowning, as though with a headache. Pedro de Alvarado, red beard blown over his shoulder by the wind that swept along the ridge, rode past and through the Tlaxcalans to the rear guard. Olid remained with Cortés, who sat his horse very erect among the cavaliers, gazing along the Spanish line with a severe expression. The corporals began to straighten their squares.

"Do we fight them, Gonzalito?" Caballo demanded.

Sandoval nodded. "These instructions from the captain-general, fellow Christians. Cavaliers to thrust for the face, the lance gripped tightly, always tightly. These barbarians will seek to pull away the lance that has wounded them. Pikemen the same. Arquebusiers—"

There was laughter when he halted. All knew there was neither powder not shot. "Crossbowmen!" he said. José Figueras flourished his bow, one of the few still in working order. "Crossbowmen will leave their weapons with the bearers," Sandoval said.

"Swordsmen will thrust rather than slash. This cannot be repeated too many times, Christians! A slashing weapon can be more easily snatched away. Rodrigo Botello, your square is to fight through to that cacique and kill him." He drew his sword and rose in his stirrups to point. Andrés marveled that the extended hand, and sword, were perfectly steady.

"Pedro de Uhurquez, your square—" The captain continued to give orders in his cool, boyishly high voice. The booming instructions of Alvarado could also be heard. Cortés rode out before the army to speak.

"Castilians! We will supplicate Our Lady for victory on this day!" All knelt while he offered a prayer for victory, then rose to don helmets, the cavaliers and captains snapping down their vizers.

"Santiago and at them!"

As the army started forward in its squares, hanging close together, the Aztec horde began all to shriek at once, that bone-chilling sound,

THE CHILDREN OF THE SUN

full of triumph. And the plain of colored feathers and lances agitated itself like a bird of prey stirring.

Cortés shouted, "Cavaliers! With me!"

The army raised a shout as the little wedge of horsemen, lances leveled, hoofs flying, hurtled down toward the Aztecs, whose first ranks parted before it. The army broke into a run in the wake of the cavaliers. Andrés fended off the thrust of a javelin and plunged his sword into the breast of a carmine-faced jaguar knight. He had one glimpse of the horsemen breasting their way through the mass of warriors toward the prince on his palanquin. Then they were engaged so heavily, thrusting with swords and jamming bucklers forward, that no one knew how the other squares and the horsemen were progressing.

When they had won through to the lesser chieftain Sandoval had pointed out, and Gil de Herrera had crushed the man's head, already that vast, brilliantly-garbed horde was milling in defeat. Later they were to learn that Cortés himself had lanced the Aztec prince, and Juan de Salamanca had despatched him.

After the Miracle of Otumba, with that great army of Tenochtitlán put to flight, the way was clear to Tlaxcala, where the Spaniards could give thanks to the Virgin, rest, receive supplies, arms, and reinforcements from Villa Rica de Veracruz, and plan the Reconquest. All were now veterans, who had proved their invincibility against odds of five hundred to one.

Beyond the desert they came to the village of the Arbadáos, who brought forth their pitiful worldly goods as offerings to the healers, and squatted glumly among them as they were picked over by the Susólas.

It was to the Arbadáos that Álvar preached for the first time, the old familiar story of the Son of God, the redemption of mankind, the hope of Heaven and the fear of Hell, preaching in rough terms and without theological niceties, but effectively enough. The sermon was translated into sign language by Esteban, who seemed to swell in size as he gesticulated for the benefit of the indigenes who surrounded him, gaping at his red hair feathers and ankle bangles and the sweeping gestures of his hands as he expostulated in this language Dorantes also found himself able to understand, for it was closer to Nahuatl than any they had encountered before.

After his sermon Álvar prayed, and the sick were brought forward, and Dorantes realized that this was to be the procedure from now on.

The next village, two days journey up the river, that of the Adáyes, stood on a promontory. The Arbadáos returned to their own village considerably richer than they had been before the advent of the Susólas, for the Adáyes were a wealthier and more civilized tribe. As well as deerskin skirts, the women wore short blouses of the same material, decorated with embroidery of colored yarns. Here the chief was desperately ill, and, after preaching the True Faith, Álvar had him borne outside into the sunlight, where he prayed and invoked the aid of heaven while Dorantes performed his increasingly distasteful ritual with the rosary and swollen little book, Esteban and Alonso squatting watching. And the chief claimed to be cured, sitting up grinning, nodding, and patting his belly, and offering the choice of his wives to the Children of the Sun.

Later they sat on the beaten earth floor of the house that had been given them. A pine knot blazed in the corner, smoke sucking up through a hole in the roof. Alonso squatted before his bulging pack, with its continually changing contents. He brought out an object that gleamed in the firelight. It clinked metallically as he passed it to Dorantes.

"Observe the gift of this grateful cacique," he said.

It was a crude, metal figurine, a bird. A clapper suspended inside made it into a bell. The metal was copper, cool in his hand. He passed it on to Álvar and watched his comrade's calm, disinterested face as he examined the bell, rang it, smiling, and passed it back to Alonso.

"It comes from the north," Alonso said. "Estebánico has enquired if there are other metals there also, but either there are not or these people do not understand him." He held the bell so that the metal gleamed red. "It is a hawk. Not badly made."

In silence they all considered the fact that worked copper implied a foundry, crafts, fixed habitations.

"It is not very well made," Alonso admitted. "They say that whence this comes there is much copper, which is highly esteemed. Plates are made of it. But this is in hollow form, and so there must be means for the molding of metals. If they can mold copper they can also mold gold, eh?"

He said, "Ah, Alonso, remember how we sought the city of Apalachen, where it was said there was much gold? And found a village of mud huts less than this place, and, instead of gold, arrows that could pierce the body of a horse and the rider's leg on the other side?"

"I remember very well," Alonso said. "But surely the possibility of gold must be explored!"

"Our task is not to search for gold," Álvar said.

"Surely it is not a sin to search for gold!" Alonso said in an exas-

perated voice. "Gold is treasure, is it not? A man who possesses sufficient treasure may do as he desires in the world."

"A man should endeavor to change his desires instead of his fortunes," Álvar said.

"A man may do great good with his wealth!" Alonso tucked the
copper bell back into his pack. "For me, I would rather change my
fortunes. I say that the Lord God Himself does not disdain treasure,
much less the Holy Church. It is well known that sufficient treasure
can pave a man's path to paradise. I see you are smiling, Andrés; so all
this is a joke to you."

"I suspect that all life is a joke," he said. "On the other hand I
remember well when a bit of deer suet which sustained life just a
little longer was no joke."

"I tell you this bell of copper is no joke," Alonso said. He dug
within his pack and brought out a painted gourd that rattled when
shaken. "Nor are these, which also come from the cities of the north. I
can tell you that these Arbadáos do not consider these a joke." He
shook the gourd.

"Cities?" Dorantes said.

"They speak of the tall houses of the north. What are towns of tall
houses if they are not cities?"

Esteban entered, to squat with his back against the wall and a self-
satisfied air. He had been sampling the chief's gratitude. Alonso
glanced at Dorantes with a sly expression.

"What do you know of Cibola, Andrés?"

"When all the peninsula was lost to the Moors in centuries past, the
Bishop of Oporto and six other bishops, and many people, set sail for
the west. There each of the bishops built a fine city. It is a story for
children."

"Seven cities, Andrés! Álvar! And they would be people like ourselves!"

All gazed at the excited little man in silence.

"We had thought we must turn south toward the Southern Sea to
encounter Christians. But perhaps we must turn north, eh?"

Dorantes and Álvar glanced at each other. Dorantes said, "I think we
must follow the course we have set, Alonso. We will find out what we
can about these tall houses, but I believe it is our task to rejoin our
countrymen in New Spain."

"It is true these Arbadáos tell of tall houses, Masters," Esteban said.
"They point to a house and stack their hands, one on top of another.
Six, seven, eight."

"We might discover a new Tenochtitlán! If there are tall houses and

foundries, there are treasures! We will be renowned! We will be ennobled for our discoveries!"

"It is what Hernán Cortés assured us, Alonso. That we would all of
us sleep beneath escutcheoned marble."

Alonso made an angry face. "What do you say, Álvar?"

"I do not desire gold nor a new Tenochtitlán, my friend. I have
healed these people. I would not turn conquerors loose upon them."

"Pah!" Alonso said, and folded his arms and sulked.

They were seventeen days with the Arbadáos in cold weather. They
had not inhabited houses for so long that these seemed luxurious.
Esteban and Alonso questioned their hosts about the tall houses of the
north, the copper rattle, and the sacred gourds, of which the Moor had
collected a supply, but little more was learned.

The Arbadáos harvested mesquite beans. These Dorantes found to
be bitter, like carob, but the Arbadáos had discovered a means of making the meal palatable. A hole was dug, and with a wooden pestle the
clay dirt was mixed with the flour. The indigenes squatted around the
hole, dipping in hands to sample the mix, to which more handfuls of
clay were added. This became a grand banquet in which the Children
of the Sun declined to share, although Esteban sampled the mixture
and pronounced it very sweet. The Arbadáos' bellies swelled from their
gorging, and the next day a dozen of them petitioned the healers, stroking their middles and grimacing. Dorantes touched their bellies with the
book and the beads, and Esteban shook a gourd rattle over them, which
also proved effective. Álvar had fashioned a crude cross out of two
sticks fitted together, which he wore on a thong around his neck. He
held this up to bless his patients, and also to bless his listeners when he
preached.

Alonso said grouchily, "If we had some gold to show these people,
they could tell if there was such a substance in the seven cities."

With an escort of upwards of a hundred Arbadáos, they marched
westering through brown meadowlands. On tireless legs and feet as
hard as horn, wrapped in a deerskin, Dorantes' head seemed to float
above the movement of his body in anticipation of those distant snow-
capped peaks and the next village that marked their progress like the
beads upon the string of a rosary, and a calm of mind that was exhilaration also. Was it total content with where he *was*? So that it was not
the achievement of that next village, or passing that peak, but the
process of the journey itself? He knew that it was also love of these
people they moved among, and that love was always stronger. He

strode between his two companions, Alonso also deerskin clad, with his sunshade and his fat packsack slung from his shoulder, Álvar naked, skeleton-thin and tall, fingering his wooden cross. The healer resembled a hermit from one of the mystery plays presented upon the steps of the cathedral of Béjar on the Day of the Holy Kings, chanting to the music of pipes, drums, little bells, and the tapping of staves. Far ahead the Moor might have been another exotic orient king, marching high-headed among the indigenes who surrounded him.

Flooding over him came the memory of the Day of the Kings in Coyoacán, in those few years of felicity there. Martín was nine months old, and Fray Rufino had organized the mystery play, in which both Timultzin and Martín had their parts.

For weeks he had been hearing the preparations. Timultzin was often called away, sometimes with the child. At home she was serious and preoccupied, sometimes softly singing the words of the choruses. At night he could hear the chantings, frail with distance as the actors practiced in the little hall behind the church, a sound like the talking of the coyotes in the hills. Gradually the singing came louder and clearer, and it was so like the same seasonal sound from his youth that it brought back those crisp January days with their anticipation of the play, as though the Holy Kings from distant lands were in fact following their star toward Extremadura, to the cradle in the manger in Béjar.

Once he went to watch their rehearsals, the little hall utterly strange by night with candlelight picking up glints of gold and embroidery, and making inky pits of Rufino's eyes as he limped up and down giving commands. He stood with the Nahua girls, the baptized concubines of the conquerors, ranged in a half circle around him, two shepherds standing by tapping their belled staves with a concentrated rhythm behind the singing, while Timultzin stood apart with her face shrouded in her shawl, tallest of the young women and the most beautiful, with her delicate features and eyes cast down. The dark, intent faces of the chorus, the dense tinny beat, and the words of the ancient songs made the hairs at the back of his neck crawl, and tears sprang to his eyes when Timultzin sang alone in her high, clear voice.

On the Day of the Kings the procession made its way through narrow streets toward the church, the crucifix and the banner of Castile leading the way, following them the sumptuously dressed and crowned kings on their mules, waving regally to the assembled crowds of Spaniards and Indians. After them paraded the bearded hermits, shepherds with their staves, black-faced Moors, helmeted Romans, shepherdesses in virginal white with flowered headdresses, and all the company of the play itself. The troupe chanted in plainsong as it marched, and, when the voices ceased, the chinking beat of the belled staves, and the pipes and echoing drumbeat continued, until the voices took up their chant again.

At nightfall the play was performed in the atrium of the church, with torches of pitch-pine flaring and white curtains of cotton decorated with embroidered sacred symbols closing off one corner of the walls. A silent audience of Spaniards in doublet and hose faced the curtains, four soldiers with pikes to keep order, and a few Castilian women. Behind these was a dense crowd of Indians come to observe the religious ceremony of the teules, some of them baptized but most not, and the baptized with little understanding of the faith they had accepted, with its ideas of love, the redemption of sins, and a God who died so that they might live, instead of the other way around.

After what seemed endless minutes of provocative movements behind the curtain, of shuffling, whispers, the clink of weapons, some stifled laughter among the Spaniards, fits of coughing, and the hushed wailing of children, the curtain parted. Rufino appeared in the rippling orange light of the torches, to cross himself and bow, seeming awed by the numbers of eyes fixed upon him. Limping, he turned to pull the rope that drew the curtains aside in a hush of expectation.

Revealed stood Lucifer, a slim, proud-headed girl, a marvel in red, red helmet decorated with blossoms, red breastplate encrusted with tiny mirrors that gleamed and winked in the smoky light, red greaves, red sandals. Her sword flashed in her hand as she advanced three precise steps and declaimed:

> *"I am light, as my name proclaims,*
> *But because I would not humble myself—"*

There was a great sigh from the Spaniards, because it was enunciated in creditable Castilian—good enough to stir Dorantes with jealousy, for she was not only pretty but spoke almost as well as Timultzin. The ranks of Indians stirred with awe at the splendor of the spectacle, for behind Lucifer was arrayed the entire company, shepherds and shepherdesses, Moors with purple turbans and scimitars, Romans, hermits in brown robes with wild hair, and the masked devils. These immediately began to prance, advancing, the others all advancing with them, although there were hitches and delays. The shepherdesses bore ropes of flowers, which they raised high as they sang. Soon the piercing voices of the girls were joined by the deeper rumble of the men.

Then the slow, so familiar, so satisfying progress of the play to the birth of the Child, all gathering around the manger, and, dramatically, in a great burst of song, the ponderous arrival of the Three Kings in their lavish, gold-embroidered robes and glittering crowns. All now joined in a chorus of praise of the Child, the Word Divine made human flesh, born this day in Bethlehem for the ransom of mankind, while the Child was held up by the Mother, with her crown of flowers, her face like a brown jewel in her white silks and laces, not merely pretty but beautiful, transfigured with reverence and self-absorption as serenely she exhibited to the Holy Kings the Holy Infant, and they, kneeling, presented their gifts and their adoration to Timultzin and the child Martín.

The village of the Aguénes was on a high flat beside the river, mud-walled cubes of huts struggling along a single street to a grove of leafless trees. Álvar preached the Holy Faith and the healing began, in a preempted hut. Possessions of the Aguénes were presented to the healers, who passed them on to the departing Arbadáos.

That night the Christians politely attended the dancing and festivities around a fire before retiring, leaving Estebánico participating.

Rolled into his deerskin in the cube of darkness, Dorantes stared up into the black night above him that seemed to whirl as though it would suck him up. He sat up as the chanting and drumbeat ceased abruptly.

Álvar whispered, "Andrés! I think you must go to see!"

"What is it?" Alonso said.

"I think it is Estebánico!"

He blundered outside. Firelight flickered on brown bodies and one black one congealed in a tight and ominous grouping. A voice was raised. Hurrying toward the tableau he roused a dog to hysterical yelping.

Esteban's taller figure loomed motionless at the center of the group of Aguéne men. He saw no women. *"Master!"* the Moor called in a choked voice.

He halted and clapped his hands together. "Come!"

Esteban broke free of the indigenes to kneel panting before him. The Aguénes approached slowly, and the Moor's shell bangles clicked as he drew himself into a tighter ball. The faces of the Aguéne men were black ovals with the firelight behind them. Several carried spears, one or two bows. The yelping of the dog died away.

"What was it?" he said to his slave, crouched at his feet. "Women?" he asked, and the frizzy head nodded convulsively. "Go in with the others," he said.

Esteban rose slowly. His eyewhites flashed, as, his back to the

Aguénes, he stalked toward the house of the healers. Dorantes remained confronting the Indians. The chief was a small, broad-shouldered man with beads on a leather thong around his forehead. He stood a step in front of the others, carrying a bow with an arrow nocked but the string not drawn.

Dorantes spoke in Han, saying that the Children of the Sun did not understand the ways of the Aguénes, having come from the east where the peoples had different ways. He saw no comprehension in the faces staring at him.

He repeated his statement in Nahuatl. This time the chief responded perhaps not so angrily. He traced a cross in the air and recited a Paternoster. The faces remained blank, but the chief had let his bow drop to his side.

As he made his way back inside the pit darkness of the healers' house he could hear Esteban sobbing. "Master! You have saved Estebánico!"

"They are still discussing the matter," he said cruelly. "Tell me what caused this."

"But Master, I did nothing! One of the birdies of this place has made round eyes at me and I made round eyes in return. Then I stroked her hand and shook my gourd a little. Suddenly these barbarians are very angry! I do not understand, Masters!"

"You must rest your hand from stroking and shaking gourds among these barbarians, Estebánico," Alonso said, with a nervous laugh.

"There is more," Dorantes said.

"Master, there is nothing more! I scarcely touched this plump little bird!"

"I warned you that in time we would come to a village where the men did not wish their women making the two-backed beast with strangers."

"Master, it is to the contrary! They treasure very much the seed of the Children of the Sun, black or white! It is very tiring to satisfy these little birds! Only Don Alonso will help."

He snorted.

"Andrés, I believe this is a serious matter," Álvar said.

"The rest of the story, Estebánico."

"There is one other little thing," the Moor said. "It is greatly to the comfort of these birdies if I shake over them the gourd rattle I have had from the Cuchendádos, which all these ignorant barbarians set great store by." He laughed fatly.

"And you shook your gourd over this one?"

"I did, Master!"

"The time for shaking the gourd is after making round eyes and stroking hands?"

THE CHILDREN OF THE SUN

"It will entice those who are a little reluctant, you understand, Masters."

"How is it they are reluctant when they are so eager for the seed of the Children of the Sun?"

"They are women, after all!"

It was Alonso's turn to snort.

"It was very strange, Masters," Esteban continued, a dimly visible squatting shape. "I shook the gourd in the usual manner, which I have done many times. But this time the gourd was snatched from me and hurled away to smash!"

"By the woman?"

"By the men who were nearby! They do not like this gourd, they say it is the gourd of the enemy! They say Estebánico is Bad Thing because of his gourd!"

He remembered the designs on the gourds in Alonso's pack, one with a wash of vermilion in which designs had been scratched, others of other colors.

"Good Estebánico," Álvar said quietly, "there may come a time when your master cannot save you from the results of your heedlessness."

In the morning sunlight that streamed through the doorway, he, Esteban, and Alonso examined the ten gourds Alonso had accumulated. Another was identified as similar to Esteban's which had been smashed by the angry Aguénes. Three were of a kind, a girdle of interlocking triangles scratched into the hard surface of the gourd-rattle and tinted with red. Another was stained a pale purple, very handworn. One had been very precisely engraved with what appeared to be a fat cow with short, hooked horns and a curly fleece.

The day of healing was left to Álvar, Esteban remaining with him. Dorantes arranged a meeting with the little chief, he and Alonso squatting on the hard-packed earth facing the unfriendly man in his grimy deerhide suit and forehead thong, and four of the village elders. Eagle feathers were braided into their hair in different formations which, he supposed, indicated rank. He was eager to learn what the markings and colors of the gourds signified. Alonso carefully removed from his pack the gourd with the cow etched upon it. He set this on the ground before the chief.

"Passaguete," the chief said, prodding the gourd until it rolled and rattled.

"From where?" he said in Nahuatl.

The chief grunted and pointed north. "Passaguete," one of the others said, nodding. The chief called out a word, and a woman in skins, points of her skirt dragging fore and aft, brought a pipe and an ember held between two sticks to light it. The chief sucked contentedly on the pipe and gestured to the north. Then he scratched with a twig in the dirt, many scratches; many Passaguetes.

Alonso produced a second gourd. This the chief passed to the elders, each man examining its decorations closely. The pipe was also passed. He sucked a little harsh smoke and expelled it, nodding his approval in what seemed to be the proper manner. "Shocorro," one of the elders said. Others agreed. The gourd was passed back. Alonso looked questioningly at Dorantes.

"Not that one yet."

Alonso set the purple gourd before the chief. After some argument it was agreed that this one was of the Comos'. The pipe continued to pass, its bit running with spittle. He nodded to Alonso, who worriedly brought out the gourd similar to the one that had caused last night's trouble.

The chief snatched it up and flung it away from him. The faces of the others turned to stone. One clapped his hands, and the woman hurried up to take away the pipe. They sat in silence.

"From where?" he asked.

The corners of the chief's mouth drew down savagely. He jerked his hand to the west. Two of the others made similar gestures.

"Very bad," the chief said.

"Huh!" another said.

The youngest of the elders rose, flinging his deerskin over his shoulder, stalked to where the offending gourd lay, and, crying, "Huh!" crushed it with his foot. Alonso brought out the copper bell and set it before the chief.

He regarded it without interest, shrugging. He was more interested in the gourd with the belt of triangles. There was disagreement whether this was "Iumano" or "Yeguaz," both to the north.

Alonso produced the last of the gourds, this one lightly scratched with circles and triangles, and tinted with vermilion and pale green. The chief stared at this so fiercely Dorantes thought he would fling it away like the other. But he made no move, only nodding agreement when one of the others said, "Hawíkuh!"

"Hawíkuh! Hawíkuh!" the chief said. He pointed to the nearest of the houses, and, with the flat of his hand, made motions of stacking.

"Tall houses," Dorantes said.

"Cíbola!" Alonso said. He urged Dorantes to question the chief as to how many stories, three, four, five. But the chief was not interested, nor did he respond when Alonso, making scratches in the dirt, tried to find out if there were many houses. Finally the chief covered his face with the crook of his elbow, as though he wanted to sleep. But they had the information that a place of tall houses was located to the north of the village of the Aguénes and was called Hawíkuh.

The next day they were surprised to find no patients waiting upon them, and the village of the Aguénes was very quiet. A howling dog was silenced so suddenly it might have been killed. They remained during the morning in the dim room that stank of smoke and badly tanned hides. Dorantes watched the Moor's expression switching from fear to confidence and back. Outside there was the commotion of many men gathering.

Dorantes ducked through the doorway, to straighten blinking in the brilliant sunlight. Four naked warriors supported a fifth. His head was slumped forward and blood had drained from his mouth and caked on his chin. Beneath his ribs a clutch of gray feathers showed. The arrow had ranged upward through his body. The stone head and a palm's width of shaft protruded from his chest, close to his shoulder. The wounded Aguéne sagged in the arms of his fellows with only a little moving shine of blood at the corner of his mouth to show that he lived.

The chief appeared, bow in hand and a coronet of white feathers on his head, a beaded quiver slung from his shoulder. He shouted at Dorantes, indicating the dying man. Others shouted also. He felt the old knee-weakening hopelessness.

But he beckoned them inside, and they eased the wounded man through the doorway. Álvar was standing, his naked body gleaming like old silver in the light from the doorway. When he saw the arrow he pressed his hands together in prayer. More warriors crowded inside, Esteban huddling against the far wall, Alonso guarding his pack like a mother hen. Álvar inspected the arrow, touching each end. The chief shouted at him. There was war.

Esteban whispered, "Doguénes have done this, Masters!"

"Doguénes! Doguénes!" several shouted at once.

"Andrés, this arrow must be drawn," Álvar said. "Have you the strength?"

"He will die of it."

"Trust God."

Sweat and smoke stung in his eyes as he examined the protruding ends. The Aguénes supporting the dying man stank of something sour, like rotted milk and pepper. With the shell knife Alonso held out to him, Dorantes stripped off the feathers, scraping carefully. The man groaned. Álvar was praying. "Stand back!" Dorantes said in Nahuatl to the chief who crowded close to him.

He grasped the shaft with a hand covering the arrowhead, and pulled. The man groaned again, deep in his chest. The shaft did not budge. He thought his strength insufficient, but he managed to get both hands on the slippery shaft. Surely that was a death groan as the arrow moved. It seemed endlessly long. When he had it out he signaled that the limp body was to be laid on one of the pallets. He squatted, watching the man's chest heaving in spasms, and felt his own breathing attune itself to that rhythmic heaving. A little blood had welled from the dark mouth in the man's chest.

Álvar knelt, and Alonso beside him. Esteban scuttled forward to join them. Álvar prayed aloud. The spasms slowed. He watched the rise and fall of the gaudily painted chest. The slowing, even whisper of breath was audible.

"He lives," Álvar said, dropping his hands to his thighs. He knelt against the sunlight that streamed in the doorway past the Aguénes crowded there. It was as though his sharp-edged profile caught the shards of light like a magnet iron shavings. Eyes aching, Dorantes remembered when Hernán Cortés in the fullness of his health and powers, in his embossed and engraved breastplate, black velvet sleeves, and gold chain, had glowed like Álvar now.

"He will live," the healer said.

That afternoon the Aguénes prepared for war. Esteban, restored to favor, reported that they expected an attack from the Doguénes.

Some of the Aguéne men had been set to clearing ditches on the side of the village from which the attack was expected; others had gone to try to recover arrows from the site of yesterday's ambush. Dorantes observed that the Aguénes always moved in a crouching position, bow in hand, like cats on the prowl, which accounted for the angle of the arrow in the wounded man's chest. That night they could hear parties of men running past their house, but no action seemed to have taken place.

The next morning the chief, wearing his coronet of feathers, and a dozen of his warriors came in a delegation. The Children of the Sun met them outside their house, where, following the chief's example, they squatted facing each other. A woman hurried up with a lit pipe. The chief sucked on it, groaned with appreciation, and passed it to Dorantes. Álvar squatted with hands spread on his thighs, staring straight ahead with his mild blue gaze. The chief began to speak, gesturing toward the other side of the river. Dorantes understood well enough, but Esteban translated for the benefit of the others:

"The Doguénes will attack. Perhaps tonight, perhaps another night. They may also attack by day. These people have prepared the ditches as we have seen, covering them with branches and with earth so that they appear to be solid ground. Instead warriors are hidden there. They will kill all the Doguéne warriors. Then the Aguénes will possess all the goods of the Doguénes. Bows and arrows, knives, skins, baskets. Their food, venison, and other meats. The meat and robes of the hairy cows. Also the Doguéne women. All of this, when the Doguénes have been killed."

The chief sat blinking and smiling in the sun, until the pipe returned to him. He sucked smoke and held it in his mouth for a long time, savoring already, Dorantes thought, the fruits of victory. Finally he blew smoke and spoke again.

"The Children of the Sun will cause this to happen," Esteban said unhappily.

Dorantes said in Nahuatl, "It cannot be."

The chief shouted, "It must be!"

"He says it must be, Masters!"

"Tell him the Children of the Sun have no powers for killing," he said.

Esteban translated and the chief made a furious slashing gesture. "Huh! *Huh!*"

"Master, it must be done or they will kill us!"

He shook his head again.

The chief began to shout. He foamed at the mouth. He rolled on the ground, kicking his heels and pounding his fists. The other warriors squatted watching him expressionlessly. The chief rose to his knees, drew an arrow, and shook it before Dorantes' face. Then he stamped away, the Aguénes rising to follow him.

"He dreams of the spoils of victory," Dorantes said. "Wealth, glory, and many women. He would be disappointed in any case."

"So speaks the soldier of Cortés," Alonso said. "But Andrés, this fool can do us great ill."

"He is very fierce, Masters!"

"You were steadfast, Andrés," Álvar said. "I believe we need have no fear."

And later that day a party of Doguéne women, painted and be-feathered, appeared across the river, and, with elaborate solicitations of permission, crossed the ankle-deep stream to sue for peace.

Their triumphant hosts invited the Children of the Sun to a hunt in preparation for a great feast. Some of the Aguénes, with bows and arrows, dispersed in ridges of wooded land south of the village, in Doguéne territory, to hunt for deer, while the Christians accompanied other Indians who carried short clubs in search of rabbits. These, when flushed, were controlled by the Aguénes hurling their clubs, working the animals back and forth until they arrived, panting and quivering, in the hands of the Children of the Sun, who understood that this was a ceremony of gratitude and honor. The rabbits and the deer were broiled that night, and men and women gorged themselves upon steaming meat. The Doguéne women had remained in the village and joined in the dancing, over which the Christians must preside like deities, with women to bring them tidbits of meat, cups of a bitter, frothing intoxicant, and the pipe. It seemed to Dorantes that they were disappointing their hosts in some way he could not fathom, though they made a show of swallowing the liquor bitter as gall and imbibing the smoke that made their heads spin.

Esteban capered among the dancing Aguénes, whooping with pleasure in concert to their drunken whooping, sometimes bounding straight up in the air to clap his hands and feet together with a clatter of his bangles, encouraged by shrieks from the Aguéne and Doguéne women. Finally Dorantes saw him escorting one of these into the shadows. When the Moor reappeared, he beckoned to him.

"You are serving your other master again. Would you like a beating with one of these little rabbit clubs?"

Esteban widened his eyes to show rims of white. "But Master, these women of the Doguénes have presented themselves for the pleasure of the Aguénes—who cannot partake until the Children of the Sun have had their satisfaction. Since none of my masters have chosen, it was left to Estebánico!"

It was true. All the Doguéne women had disappeared into the shadows with Aguéne men.

When, to amuse each other and pass the nights, the Children of the Sun told each other tales, Dorantes related how he had first come to the New World, for his voyage had been more romantically instigated than any of the others'.

As soon as he had begun his service with the Conde de Aguilar in Seville, he began seeing the dwarfs and midgets of the count's court, always at a distance until one afternoon in the courtyard outside the chapel he encountered the gaily chattering, skipping pack of them, accompanied by an old, white-muzzled greyhound. He realized that one of this company of tiny people was a normal little girl. In her black lace mantilla, bright spots of color in her cheeks, she halted facing him with her fan sweeping up and opening. The straightness of her back, the set of her head, the roundness of her forehead, the white knot of her hand gripping the fan affected him like a tremor of his heart. Her companions, one a grotesquely big-haunched dwarf, ranged themselves in an expectant half-circle around their mistress, while the greyhound casually interposed his body before her, seating himself with a lolling tongue.

She said in her rather shrill voice, "So this is the crossbowman from Béjar one hears of everywhere."

He bowed. "And who may the crossbowman have the honor of addressing, my lady?"

"My name is Doña Juana de Aguilar y Zúñiga, and I am the daughter of my father, your master, sir." She spoke proudly but perhaps not arrogantly, adjusting her fan.

"And how may I serve my lady?"

She giggled delightedly. Then she composed herself into a great lady, folding her fan with a slap and touching it to his shoulder.

"You must tell me your name, señor."

"I am Andrés Dorantes de Carranza, of your father's service, and yours."

She giggled again. He thought he had never seen flesh so white, almost luminous, eyes so blue, a mouth so prettily pink, hair so fair and fine. She said, "I think you are not so handsome as they say, but handsome enough, señor!"

"Handsome enough for what, my lady?"

"Why, to capture ladies' hearts, señor!" In delight at her cleverness she swung around in a dance step, while all her tiny troupe laughed with her, spinning and circling in their bright silks and velvets on the black and white tiles. The dog remained seated.

He bowed low and said, "And will my lady give me a token of her favor?"

She halted, to suck in her breath, eyes rounding. A great lady again, she extracted a wisp of handkerchief from her sleeve and presented it to him. He had lost it with the rest of his possessions on the Night of Sorrows.

"And will you take this to the Indies with you, señor?" she asked.

The words shocked him, as though she had read his thoughts. That very day he had walked along the river to see the vessels from the Indies at anchor there, and walked for the tenth time past the Casa de Contratación, where arrangements for passage were made, and had met there another like himself, Bernardo Fuentes. Together they had talked of the fame and fortune to be had across the ocean, two young hidalgos of good blood and no prospects.

"And would you like to sail to the Indies, my lady?" he countered.

"If I were a cavalier I would! I would sail for the Indies and become very rich there. And then I would come back and marry a great lady. That is what I would do!"

She covered her face to the eyes with her fan, but not soon enough to conceal the flush that had risen in her cheeks. One of the tiny people grasped her hand.

"Come along, Doña Juana! We will be late for nones!"

"Goodbye, Don Andrés!" she said, and was swept off by her courtiers, the greyhound hobbling after them.

And when he sailed for the Indies on the *Santa María de Luz* within three months time, with the conde's blessing but without his father's, at the back of his mind was the conviction that, when he had made his fortune in the New World, he would return to Seville and ask the Conde Álvaro for the hand of his daughter, she by then come of age and a great lady, and he a wealthy planter—though he did not tell his comrades, the other Children of the Sun, of these foolish aspirations of his youth.

They were many days with the Aguénes, a season of cold nights and clear, cold days, steam rising from the river so that the village seemed cut off from the surrounding countryside by a barrier of cotton, and sometimes a skim of ice on the water jars. But it was time to resume their journey.

They squatted facing the squatting chief and his elders, passing the pipe and groaning with satisfaction until Esteban rose, towering over the Aguéne men, and, with gestures, announced that the Children of the Sun must depart for the sunset.

The chief responded animatedly, at length, and negatively.

"He says it is very far, Masters! And the people are their enemies, and are the enemies of the Children of the Sun also. These people have no name."

"Hawíkuh," he said, at which the chief and one of the elders gestured vigorously to the north.

"Tell them we will travel north, then," Alonso said.

"They say it is the same, Don Alonso. Many, many leagues, and only the hairy cows whose herds cover the earth and trample everything before them. Besides there is no water. All will die who venture in that direction, they say."

"Do not these hairy cows need water?" Alonso said. "These indigenes lie to you."

"They have become overfond of our presence," Dorantes said. "We must go to the west, Estebánico. Not to the north, or the northwest, Alonso. We return to New Spain."

Nodding, Álvar gazed west past the houses of the Aguénes. Esteban spoke, with sweeping gestures, and the chief harangued him in return with the many reasons why the Children of the Sun should not depart at this time.

"There is no more healing needed here," Álvar said. "They will not seek to stop us if we leave them."

"We must have bearers for food and water and our possessions," he said. He rose and turned his back on the Aguénes. Álvar and Alonso also rose. He said to Esteban, "Tell them that if they will not guide us, the Children of the Sun will go alone. But they will have no rewards." Leaving the Moor to communicate this they walked back to their house to prepare to leave.

It seemed that every man, woman, child, and dog of the Aguénes stood on the bank watching them wade across the river, Alonso and Esteban heavily laden with their packsacks, Dorantes with the pouch containing his prayer book and rosary slung over his shoulder and a sealed water jar in the crook of his arm, the healer by his order unencumbered, and naked except for his wooden cross. Beyond the river they camped for the night in a grove of evergreens, and, seated beside their fire after a supper of dried venison, they sang the songs of Castile with their endless verses. Dorantes was aware of stealthy movements outside the circle of firelight, birdcalls, even whispering, but, watching Álvar's calm face, who must be aware of those same sounds, felt no fear. They slept close to the embers of the fire, wrapped in deerskins; it was very cold.

In the morning he wakened to a circle of Aguéne warriors with painted bodies and faces, and feathered hair, and arrows nocked; the indigenes as insubstantial in the misty air as a bad dream out of the past. Wrapped in his deerskin, he rose to confront them, Álvar and Alonso also rising, with Esteban crouching at their feet. The chief, with his crown of feathers and down-slashed mouth, stepped forward threateningly.

Dorantes spoke in Nahuatl, in anger: God had ordained that the Children of the Sun follow the sun to the west. Those who aided them in this would be rewarded, as the Arbadáos had been rewarded by the Aguénes. Those who did not aid them would not be rewarded. Those who interfered with their journey would suffer. Those who threatened them would have their threats turned upon them, and those who harmed them would die.

As he spoke the little man wilted before him. He hid his face in the crook of his elbow. He removed his feather headdress and fingered his long hair forward until it covered his face. He spoke through his hair in a low voice.

"What does he say?" Alonso whispered.

"He begs Don Andrés not to be angry," Esteban said.

He turned his back on the chief and said to the Moor, "Tell him we will wait here until they have decided to guide us to the west."

Esteban sprang up, hands flashing. The chief and the Aguéne warriors faded back into the mists from the river. Álvar said, "We can continue without them, Andrés."

The anger rose in him again, but he only said, "I know it is possible, Álvar, but if it is far it will be useful to have guides and bearers."

Álvar only shrugged and smiled. And of course he was right. They proceeded by the grace of God, which had brought them safely this far, who could have perished in a hundred different ways, as the others of the Florida expedition had done. Álvar had faith that food, water, shelter, and guidance would be provided, and perhaps by now Dorantes had it also, but there were practicalities a captain must consider. Besides, he had taken an extreme dislike to the Aguéne chief and was determined that his will would prevail over that ugly, arrogant little man.

Before nightfall they heard the women wailing across the river. The sound froze his bowels, for it could only be his murderous power proven again—who had claimed to these very people that the Children of the Sun had no such power. He prayed that it was not the little chief who had perished.

A naked figure appeared through the trees, head and shoulders caked with mud so that only the raw eyes showed through the mask. The man squatted before them, scraping up dirt and stuffing it into his mouth. It was the chief, who muttered and combed his muddy hair over his face as he spoke. Many in the village of the Aguénes were sick and dying.

"He begs us to return, Masters. Four are very ill. They will die! Afterwards they will guide us where we wish."

So they waded back through the freezing waters to the village filled with the wailing of women and a sympathetic howling of dogs. Álvar prayed over the ill as they were brought before him, holding his cross over each one. Dorantes, with his own ritual, watched the hands of the true healer, as expressive in their way as Esteban's; the cross raised, the sign of the cross made, right hand held up with thumb and little finger tucked into the palm, while the left hand let the wooden cross fall to his chest; then both hands clapped flat together in prayer. The ill were brought before him, some supported by their wives, some by friends, all with faces contorted with agony and hands pressed to bellies, and all relieved of their pain by the healers.

Alonso whispered to him, "Are these not miracles, Andrés? And yet they do not seem like the miracles of the Holy Scriptures one has learned in his youth."

"Perhaps those also did not seem so rare when they occurred."

"Do you believe these Aguénes are really sick to death, Andrés?"

"Yes," he said. "I believe they would die without Álvar to heal them. However, it would be well if they were instructed not to excrete themselves upstream of where they take their cooking water."

Alonso's hand rose to cross himself. He said nervously, "Ah, Andrés, it is well for us that one may still make a joke of these great matters."

He crossed himself also.

"Now we will continue our journey," Alonso said. "And I pray we will hear more of the cities of tall houses." He fingered the copper bell, which he wore on a cord around his neck as Álvar wore his cross. It gave off its unmelodious clink.

The next day all the sick were well, and a throng of Aguénes accompanied them across the river, following the direction of the sun's track. The women carried venison and dried cactus fruit, jugs of water, and grass mats and skins for shelter and warmth. It was the largest procession that had accompanied them so far, winding through the ravine country west of the river and then heading across a plain dotted with clumps of cactus and scrub brush, toward those distant peaks gleaming white out of a lower haze. At nightfall the women propped up the mats for shelter. Dorantes lay wrapped in his deerskin, watching his breath steaming before his face and wondering that he was not merely inured to cold and exhaustion, but took pleasure in them.

After five days the snowy peaks were no nearer and it was clear the Aguénes were suffering from hunger, which was an ill the healers could not cure. It seemed also that their guides were increasingly fearful of encountering the indigenes they knew lived somewhere this side of the mountains, who had proven enemies in the past. There was a halt while Esteban and Alonso set out with packs of trade goods that included the sacred gourds. Other Aguénes spread out to search for food and water, and a muddy spring was found.

At the end of three days Alonso returned with five Indians called Guayacónes, well-built people taller than the Aguénes. He and Esteban had come upon the fixed dwellings of civilization, houses of two stories, and inhabitants who cultivated beans, pumpkins, and maize! The Moor was approaching with a larger band of Guayacónes to welcome the Children of the Sun. The Aguénes, Dorantes noticed, kept carefully out of the way of the Guayacóne men, and that night he listened to the stealthy sounds of their withdrawal. In the morning all had disappeared.

Soon they encountered Esteban, leaping and waving to them from a height of land. With him were hundreds of Guayacónes, the men naked, the women clad in decorated deerskins. Older men also wore skins. These people had brought supplies of beans and calabashes of water, and, as gifts, heavy robes of the hides of the hairy cattle, thick, dark brown or black fleeces which they presented with great ceremony to the Christians.

"They have heard of the Children of the Sun, Masters!" Esteban told them, standing tall and gleaming black with folded arms and the red feathers of his hair decoration moving in the cool breeze. "They were awaiting our coming, which had been foretold. There are tales of the white healers, and the black herald who comes before!"

The town of the Guayacónes consisted of two-story mud brick houses with rafter ends protruding from the walls. From a distance it resembled a village in Extremadura, and it was set among cultivated fields in a cup of hills, although the fields were very dry, with a leaning funnel of dust blowing across them in the afternoon wind.

"They have maize but they no longer plant it," Esteban told the others. "They say to put seed into the ground is only to lose it, for the rains have failed for two years. They will not venture to plant again until the rains return. And so they eat their seed instead of planting it, and soon must starve, they say, Masters."

"Estebánico!" Alonso said worriedly. "Can it be that they believe the Children of the Sun can cause the rains to return?"

"Yes, Masters, that is what they believe."

Chapter Five

They were hardly established in a smoky, sunless room in one of the substantial Guayacóne houses, when they were summoned outside by a great drumming. Although the surrounding hills were still visible, the evening star was centered in the sky above two peaks like a Spanish saddle. Men were drumming and women dancing, clad in rabbitskins, with hide slippers on their feet, carrying pine boughs arched above their heads. They danced with great concentration, placing their feet precisely, the boughs shifting rhythmically. From time to time the clatter of the drums would sink to a mutter, then bang out like a thunderclap. Now men appeared, with painted wooden masks, prancing through the ranks of women, straightening to gesture commandingly at the evening sky. They danced to a faster beat than the women, slapping their feet down, jerking arms toward the sky, while the women maintained their more sedate movements with such unanimity and decorum that Dorantes was reminded of the Nahua maidens dancing at Coyoacán, and the orgies there, after Tenochtitlán-Tlatelolco had fallen.

He stood with Álvar, watching in the fading light the dancers advancing and retreating, boughs swaying. Alonso and Esteban were squatting with one of the village elders, Esteban indicating with his hands the two-story houses, then pointing north and stacking his hands, questioning, while Alonso exhibited the copper hawk bell he wore like Álvar's cross. Dorantes had found he could understand the tongue of the Guayacónes, as though the strain of Nahuatl grew stronger the closer they approached to New Spain.

The drums banged out another thunderclap. The masked men commanded, the pine boughs swayed like a moving forest. A girl in the second rank reminded him of Timultzin, taller than those on either side of her, smooth bare arms raised from her rabbitskin garment, a gentle pride in her face—not that Aztec pride that was so often arrogance.

He asked the Guayacóne elder to explain this rain ceremony, and they conversed haltingly, but with comprehension. The drums were the thunder that preceded rain, the pine boughs were the rainbows that followed it, as well as green growth. The masked men commanded rain to fall, the women accepted it.

"Tell him that tomorrow at dawn the Children of the Sun will pray for rain," Álvar said.

To this the elder nodded and smiled. His fingers touched Dorantes' arm. The Guayacónes would dance all night in honor of the Children, he said, and at dawn all would pray together.

And throughout the night, during which he slept little, he heard the drumming slam out at intervals in thunderclaps, supplicating and commanding inattentive gods.

Before sunrise Álvar preached, in Castilian, from the high roof of one of the houses, a stick figure against the green glow of the promise of dawn, which the Aztecs had believed would not come unless the gods were kept satiated with human blood. He seemed a potent figure there, gaunt and bearded, with his wooden cross held out in blessing to the Guayacónes in their hundreds gathered beneath him. Then he raised the cross to heaven in the gathering brightness of the east, in supplication or perhaps command, and in faith. Dorantes concentrated on how to translate Álvar's message into Nahuatl, the complexities of the relationships of God to man, His Son as the Redeemer of all mankind, Our Lady in her infinite and unqualified mercies, the forgiveness of sins and the necessity of faith. At least the intricacies of the Trinity need not be attempted. Still it was too much for him, the abstract words escaped the clutch of his mind like quicksilver. He prayed.

When Álvar had finished the sun was well up. All prayed together to the cloudless sky. Afterwards the Guayacónes faded into their houses, and the old men of the council—for there seemed to be no single chief—came to console the Children of the Sun for their failure. That day they healed, Álvar as serene and confident as ever, and as successful with these more sophisticated indigenes as he had been with the others.

That night they danced the rain ceremony again, and once more he found himself watching the tall girl in the second rank. At dawn Álvar preached and prayed as the sun rose in the clear pale blue of the sky, and again Dorantes searched his mind for the Nahuatl words to explain the message of the Christians.

On the third dawn, when Álvar preached, Dorantes stood beside him on the rooftop and translated the words into Nahuatl, sentence by sentence, halting at first, but with gathering confidence as he realized from the murmuring of the Guayacónes and the expression on their brown faces raised to him that there was comprehension. That afternoon it rained.

All that night and the next day it rained steadily. Clouds drifted over the bowl of the valley, sending down gray skeins that connected earth and heaven. Now the Guayacónes danced in thanksgiving, and the elders of the council brought the Children of the Sun gifts, robes of the curly, black-haired hides for Alonso and Esteban, and of a dark brown fur as soft as marten for him and Álvar, which Álvar politely refused, but he accepted. There were also five green stones, perhaps low-grade emeralds, which Alonso appropriated, a feast of roast meats and a sweet, thick drink made from maize.

Dorantes saw that it was satisfying to the elders that their gifts were appreciated by the healers, and, when women were proffered, he enquired of the tall girl who had reminded him of Timultzin. She appeared, in her rabbitskin dress, and lay with him that night in a room of their own. But although she was acquiescent and mild and clean, she did not smell right. Her hands, stroking his back rather fearfully, were not right. He could not think whether she regarded him as a god or a man.

The next day he could feel Álvar's disapproval like a chill, and he knew Álvar also disapproved of his wearing the very warm, soft, glossy fur coat he had been given. The healer remained naked, and seemed impervious to the cold, for the rain was chill and changed to swirling snow.

Indians came from the nearby smaller villages to view the Children of the Sun who had successfully invoked the rain, and were healers besides. Álvar was petitioned to visit their villages, while Dorantes remained with the other Christians, attending the ceremonies of the Guayacónes, the rituals of planting and the harvest ceremonies, men dancers rhythmically rattling their sacred gourds, naked legs churning and foxtails flapping from their rumps. During one of these sessions a child near him began sobbing.

The mother, her face a mask of humiliation, produced a little stick with a rodent tooth implanted at the end. With this she scratched the child from the shoulder down his body to his leg. The sobbing subsided to a stifled choking, and the boy's dark, fearful eyes swam at him.

He snatched the child from the mother and pressed the warm, straining little body to the martenskin coat, the wet face into his shoulder.

"Why do you do this?" he demanded of the mother, who crouched before him.

She stammered that the child had been punished because he had disturbed one of the Children of the Sun. As he admonished her his instant anger was instantly disarmed, and he returned the small body to the arms of its mother. Once the child Martín had been punished in just this way.

That night in their sleeping room, Alonso said, "I do not believe these green stones are emeralds, Andrés. They are too dull." He heard the dull clink of the copper bell when Alonso changed position in the darkness. "Álvar does not approve that you wear your fine fur coat, does he? Nor of the fine fucking we have had in this place. Even you, one observes, Andrés."

"One appreciates the fact that he does not give voice to his disapprovals. As for my fine fur coat, no doubt I would be a better healer if I had the faith Álvar has that our Maker will keep us warm. But I do not wish to trouble Him with such trifling matters."

Alonso snickered. Then he said, "These people agree that the great city of Hawíkuh lies to the north. And more and bigger cities beyond it. Can these cities be Cibola?"

"I do not think Cibola lies in the north, I think it lies in the imagination merely."

"Pah!" Alonso said, but not angrily.

"I think to the north are more villages like this one, only of houses of more stories. I do not think the children there play with dolls with heads of gold, as we were informed they did in Apalachen. Nor that the fishermen weight their nets with gold nuggets, as we were informed they did in Honduras."

"If Hernán Cortés had listened to you he would not have marched to Honduras," Alonso said. There was a muffled clink of his bell. "Or to Mexico either."

He was wakened by a hand shaking his shoulder and Esteban whispering, "Master, it is a woman come for you. She says her child is very sick, and you know this child. And Don Álvar is not yet back from across the valley."

He rose and donned robe and deerhide slippers. He fumbled for the pouch that held his prayer book and rosary, but decided against taking them with him. He should have realized that the child was burning with fever. Outside the woman was waiting, bundled in rabbitskins. He accompanied her silently through the silent village, snow blowing in sharp bits against his face and into his eyes. The woman touched his arm to turn him into a doorway. A sliver of burning pitch-pine gave a flickering light. The boy lay on a pile of skins, moving his head restlessly. He knelt beside the pallet to touch a hand to the forehead of the child, whose eyes seemed to have sunk into his head, gleam of his pupils gazing up.

The woman spoke softly, but he did not understand her. Three other shrouded forms watched from a far corner. He was conscious of their faith in him. Leaving his hand on the hot little forehead he said a Paternoster, a Hail Mary; he closed his eyes and bowed his head. "Dear Lady," he said within himself, "please have mercy on this child. For the sake of my son Martín. For the sake of your own Son, dear Lady!" He tried to focus all the intensity of his mind upon the prayer. He felt heavy and exhausted, but, as time passed, lighter. He strained to feel the warmth in his arms, moving down into his hands, flowing into the feverish child. Instead it was as though the fever was absorbed into his hands, rising in his arms. The hot flesh seemed to have cooled. He felt, first, exaltation, then fear; then relief and exhaustion. He rose.

"He will be well," he said, and passed outside where blown snow peppered his face, gathering in his eyelids when he raised his face to give thanks, tasting curiously sweet upon his lips.

In his prayers the old sorrow had intruded, twisting into remorse. Where was his own son? Was he dead of smallpox, or saved from it? How did he fare, that mestizo child of a Castilian soldier and his Nahua love?

Back with Alonso and Esteban, he slept, and dreamed he still wandered through the silent town of the Guayacónes. In his dream dawn lightened the storm in a nacreous gleam. In his fine fur coat and deerskin slippers he came to the empty fields beyond the town, approaching a low, more solid shape than the trees, as though drawn to it. Nor was he surprised to see that it was a woman. She held a child in her arms, not to her breast but as though extended in entreaty toward him, this small Indian mother with her hair in braids falling inside either shoulder, and the glint of her eyes fixed upon him. No snow adhered to her hair, nor to the brown bare flesh of her arms, or the naked flesh of the child.

He halted before her. It seemed to him that these two must be very cold, and he removed his fine coat and held it out. She was unable to accept it because of the child, and, moving closer, he draped the coat over her shoulders. Instantly the child disappeared within its folds and she drew it closed. He turned away to retrace his steps over the ovals of his footprints in the thin mantle of snow, back toward the village of the Guayacónes. For a time he resisted looking behind him, but at last he glanced over his shoulder to mark the double row of footprints, and, at the end of their track, the insubstantial shape in the falling snow.

He wakened again to Alonso whispering, "Andrés, why do you weep? Did you not save the child as you thought?" It seemed to him that he had been weeping with Timultzin's lament that the Christian God did not speak to her, know her, find her. He put out a hand to feel the deep, soft fur of the coat.

He never wore the martenskin coat again, but from that day went naked, as Álvar did, thankful at least that their course lay to the south and day by day it would become warmer. He carved his own cross, and hung it around his neck on a thong, and wore it thereafter.

One year after that solstice when he had crouched on the mound of oyster shells, sighting across two sticks at the rising sun, when his fortitude had failed him and he had prepared to die, they were making their way down a long valley of civilized peoples and had not slept in other than fixed habitations for some months. They had seen no tall houses, and the rumors of them faded as their route led south. A jagged range of mountains paralleled their course to the east, a lower range to the west. They traveled no more than a few leagues a day, for there were many villages in this long valley, many sick to be healed. Often whole villages accompanied them for days, numbering as many as a thousand men, women, and children. There was great gaiety, singing and dancing nightly, and plenty of food in these settled places. The spring was bountiful. The Moor pranced ahead with the van-guard, jingling, shaking his magic gourds, and performing prodigies of seed-scattering, so that Dorantes and Alonso joked of the darker-tinged generations to be born, as once the soldiers of Cortés had boasted of lighter ones. Alonso collected samples of the gifts offered the Children of the Sun that seemed of value. There were pearls from the Southern Sea now, which must not be far off, kept separate from those brought from Malhado Island, fine blue turquoises, the green stones that might be emeralds, samples of minerals, and the sacred gourds. His copper bell was still the only example of worked metal they had seen. As they progressed to the south Alonso began to speak more and more of New Spain, and less of Cibola.

Alonso and Esteban had become the heralds of the healer, one white, one black. Traveling well behind them, in the midst of the crowds of indigenes, came Dorantes and Álvar, naked, bearded scarecrow Christians wearing crude wooden crosses on their breasts. They spoke little to each other in some kind of inner understanding, tirelessly striding through these fertile lands and cultivated fields, eating and drinking

75

sparingly even at the feasts laid out for them, Álvar preaching, Dorantes translating; healing. All these peoples spoke a tongue they called Primahaitu, closely related to Nahuatl.

As the relationships among the four of them had changed, two now the heralds and two the healers, one the preacher, two the linguists, one the trader—so also had he and Álvar changed. It seemed to him the healer had become almost pure spirit, the flesh that thinly covered his bones a kind of fabric with a glow radiating visibly through it, pure spirit visible also in his strange, intense gaze. It was to Álvar the Indians knew to look in their faith in the healing magic of the Children of the Sun. Yet he knew he himself was often indistinguishable in their eyes from Álvar, as Doña Marina, the linguist of Hernán Cortés, had been indistinguishable from the conqueror to the Aztecs, who had called them both "Malintzin."

The inhabitants of the villages to which they came now wore cotton garments, a shirt that fell as low as the knee, and, over it, a half-sleeved jacket. The women wore long skirts, the men short breeches. In each village the procedures were the same. The people assembled, and in Castilian and Primahaitu were informed that in heaven was a man called God, who had created the sky and the earth, and all things upon the earth, and all the peoples on it. The Children of the Sun did as he commanded, for from Him came all that was good upon earth. And they should do the same, and then all would be well with them.

Then the healers touched and blessed the sick, and also the well who wished their benediction, especially pregnant women and those who had just given birth, for their children. Álvar prayed over the more seriously ill, sometimes performing surgeries, while Dorantes treated the less serious with his beads and prayer book. Alonso added to his collection, and Esteban to his.

One day as the healers rested after hours spent touching and blessing, Esteban swung into the door of the mud-brick house, breathing hard.

"Masters, there is a little bird here who is from another place where they have seen men like the Children!" He made gestures of pulling at a beard. "*Christians,* Masters!"

Dorantes' heart swelled with a complex of emotions, triumph that they had almost reached their goal, pain of their great journey ending, dread of encountering their countrymen mixed with the pleasure. He saw a similar mix of emotions play also upon Esteban's black face, for in New Spain the Moor would become only a black slave again, who had been a herald of the Children of the Sun. And what of himself, Álvar, and Alonso; what would they become?

"She says they are like us but not like us, Masters!" Esteban continued. "They kill the people, and carry others away with them. They do not heal, like the Children."

He watched Álvar's face as he watched the Moor. Their fellow Christians, the first of their countrymen they were to encounter, were slave-hunters. Was it for this that they had crossed a continent, preaching the goodness of God, the Passion of Christ, the mercy of Mary?

Alonso hurried out with Esteban to interview the woman who had seen the Spaniards, while he remained with Álvar.

"Andrés, I believe it is God's will that I return to this country I have traversed. Do you feel anything of this?"

He nodded. On Malhado Island he had been poisoned by hatred of his masters, the Marímnes; but on the journey to the west it seemed to him that his soul had been cleansed by the love of these gentle people for the Children of the Sun, and so his gratitude was like that of those they had healed, for *he* had been healed.

"I believe it is God's will that these peoples be brought to His Word as tenderly as possible," Álvar continued. "And become the vassals of His Holy Catholic Majesty the same. That must be our cause, Andrés."

He nodded again.

"Then you will be my captain?"

"Yes," he said, and this time it was a vow.

In the next, very large, town to the south, they preached and healed and awaited the inevitable festivities. These did not transpire, however, nor the next morning either, although all that day there was a smell of broiling meat. In the afternoon drums began to throb.

They waited outside their quarters as the drumming approached. The chief, a silver-haired, gentle old man named Petaín, was leading a procession toward them, carrying a platter upon which were four gobbets of broiled meat. These were the hearts of deer, Petaín informed them; for their health and long life. As Dorantes understood him, the lives of the deer for the lives of the Children of the Sun.

The chief stood aside as the elders of the town, in their white, belted, cotton shirts came up, each bearing his platter of deer hearts. Behind them it seemed that all the men of the village were bringing platters of broiled hearts to the Children of the Sun, the smell of cooked meat overpowering, the platters set before them with reverence.

As he stood with Álvar, Alonso, and Esteban, trying to appear pleased and grateful for this excessive tribute, in a powerful bursting rush of realization it came to him that these hearts were being presented to gods just as the Aztecs had flung living men down upon the sacrificial stone to snatch out their hearts in this same offering. As these Pímas spoke a simpler form of Nahuatl and were gentle by nature, so they were a simpler people than the Aztecs, who had changed this ceremony of presenting the hearts of deer into the offering of human hearts to baleful gods. And this queer mingling of satisfaction and gratitude, awe in it too, even the horror of the realization, and with it all the love of those who made the offering—was it what the god felt?

It was with difficulty that, holding one of the warm, heavy rounds of meat in his hand, and inhaling the over-rich smell under the eyes of the multitude of indigenes who had made this great tribute, he began to eat.

"Andrés!" Alonso cried. He was holding out something that Dorantes could not distinguish in the dimness of their house, except that it appeared to be another piece of worked metal. Then Alonso's hand moved it into the wedge of light from the doorway and he saw that it was a Spanish buckle.

Alonso was accompanied by one of the Píma elders, whose property this belt buckle was, a plump, smiling little man with hair in twin braids. The buckle had come from heaven, he said. Certain men with beards like those of the Children of the Sun, who came from heaven, had arrived at the sea. The little man waved a hand to the west. These men rode great deer and carried long, pointed sticks with which they had killed two Indians. Then they went into the sea. He described their lances going into the water, then the horses, finally the men themselves with the fine plumes on their heads. Afterwards they were seen on the surface, riding toward the south, in the direction in which the Children of the Sun were now traveling.

In the days that followed, accompanied by a great band of Pímas and the old chief's son, Natsá, they found deserted villages, although the land was fertile and well watered, and crops were still in the fields. Then they came upon a burned village, and two Indians, long-dead and stinking, hanged in the branches of a tree. Sometimes indigenes would appear from hiding, encouraged by the sight of the troop of Pímas who followed the Children of the Sun. They related that the man-monsters with lances had passed this way, burning villages and carrying away the crops, carrying away also half the men and many women and boys. Those who had escaped had hidden in the mountains.

Always in these parts now buzzards were to be seen circling.

Alonso was frightened that these Indians, who had been so mistreated by Christians, would seek revenge upon the Children of the Sun, but Dorantes assured them in Primahaitu, and Esteban in sign language, that the Children searched for the man-monsters in order to tell them not to kill or enslave the Indians, take from them their food, and burn their villages.

And so, at the time, they believed they had the faith and the power to do.

"Our destiny becomes more clear, Andrés," Álvar said. "We must bring these indigenes to be Christians and subjects of His Catholic Majesty, but by kindness and by faith. Soldiers must be controlled very severely."

"Yes," he said thoughtfully, whose part that would be as captain. He sent Esteban and Alonso on ahead to announce the coming of the Children of the Sun, but as they followed with the army of trusting Pímas, they met Esteban returning.

"Masters, everyone has fled! And we have seen traces of the Christians—where they have slept and kept their horses. Masters, these people say they carry them away in chains!"

"What must we do, Álvar?" Dorantes asked. "These Pímas belong a hundred leagues behind us. Should we tell them they must go home?"

"They would go hungry, Andrés."

"There are worse things than hunger."

"We must have faith."

They continued their way south and west, encountering, for awhile, no more signs of their countrymen, although still buzzards circled, very high, above this dry, semidesert country. But one day they marked a smudge of smoke on the horizon and came to a burned village and traces of Christians again. And finally from the top of a hill they saw four horsemen, strange figures in gleaming metal holding their lances upright like tall needles against the sky. From the tip of one a small banner drooped. All of them remained perfectly motionless as the Children of the Sun and the horde of Indians came over the top of the ridge, halting there.

Esteban began to run toward them, his tall black figure bounding through the brush. He rattled his gourds furiously, bellowing, "Christian men! Christian men!"

Alonso began to run also, pack banging on his back, his rabbitskin cap flying off. Álvar hurried after them, although more slowly. Something pulled at his own feet also, and all the Children of the Sun were running toward the waiting soldiers, with the host of Pímas sweeping down the ridge after them, as the man-monsters dismounted from their great deer to embrace the castaways.

Chapter Six

The corporal was Lázaro de Cebreros, a man of Hispaniola, and two of the soldiers with him were also Hispaniola born. They were part of a detachment of cavalry commanded by a Lieutenant Alcaráz, who was exploring this northern frontier of New Galicia, whose governor, Beltrán Nuño de Guzmán, resided in Campostela. Nearer was Captain Melchor Díaz, alcalde in Culiacán, on the coast.

In a shabby hut in a deserted village, Alcaráz embraced the three white Children of the Sun. Dorantes was struck by the smell of him, old salt sweat mingled with a sour odor, and he saw Alonso's nose wrinkle in puzzlement also. Stools were produced, and the three of them sat across a low table from the lieutenant and Cebreros. Esteban squatted uncomfortably just inside the doorway.

"What can I offer you, far-travelers?" Diego de Alcaráz asked, spreading his hands. "We have wine, but it is poor stuff."

"We have not tasted wine for eight years," Dorantes said.

Alcaráz produced a bottle, and Cebreros cups which he wiped out with the tail of his shirt, a stocky, dour, heavily bearded man, lame in one leg. Alcaráz was younger, with a weedy beard and an affectedly aristocratic manner of waving a hand to emphasize his words.

"Eight years!" he said, with this flourish. "Why, that long ago I was no more than a schoolboy! Imagine! Certainly one has heard of the lost expedition of Pánfilo de Narváez. There was a great storm, as I remember the tale."

"A great storm, yes," Alonso said. "Many were lost in the storm in Trinidad, before we had truly set out. Bad luck all the way."

"But in the end we have had good luck," Dorantes said, and Alonso nodded vigorously, with a false smile. Álvar perched emaciated and naked upon his stool, holding his cross in his hand. Dorantes saw that he was shivering, although it was very warm here.

"You have walked a thousand leagues," Alcaráz said, watching the corporal pour the wine. "Imagine it! And we have no clothing to give you to cover your nakedness."

"It is unimportant," Dorantes said. "Perhaps our nakedness and our good luck can persist a little longer." The cups were passed, none for Esteban, whose lower lip protruded sulkily. The unfamiliar liquor tasted like vinegar. He held a dollop in his mouth and let it trickle down his throat.

"I can tell you of ill luck!" Alcaráz said. "The indigenes of these lands have fled to the mountains where it is impossible to follow. They hide from us."

"And why do they do that, Lieutenant Alcaráz?" Álvar enquired.

Dorantes watched the play of expression on Alcaráz' face as he glanced at Álvar; amusement, contempt, distaste. Indeed they were four strange looking specimens, but Álvar the strangest, a sticklike insect perched on the stool, with his innocent, bearded face and blue stare.

"They do not wish to be taken to the mines of the Antilles," Cebreros said, showing dirty teeth in a grin. He tossed off his wine.

"You are slavers," Dorantes said.

"Those who are in rebellion may be enslaved, by orders of the governor," Alcaráz said. "Those who flee from us may be said to be in rebellion."

Dorantes watched Álvar Núñez shivering.

"They seem to us gentle people, but frightened," said Alonso, once the hater of all indigenes.

"Runners and hiders," Cebreros said.

"Sodomites and cowards," Alcaráz said, rubbing his hands together as though washing them. "To the north they are more warlike, we have heard."

Dorantes said that they had not found this to be true, but the Spaniard only gazed at him without interest.

"It is said that those of the dry lands to the north poison their arrows. It is said to be a terrible death." Alcaráz shuddered delicately and waved a hand before his face as though to dispel this unpleasant subject. He said, "These cowardly monkeys flee us, burning their maize or bearing it away with them. We have had little to eat. Nor does the governor enjoy these tales of ill luck."

Dorantes questioned him about the affairs of New Spain. Cortés had gone to Spain, where he had been ennobled as the Marqués del Valle de Oaxaca and married the niece of a duke. When he returned he was no longer governor, however. There was now a viceroy, Don Antonio de Mendoza, who had been sent from Spain to trim the sails of Cortés and the conquerors. Guzmán had been governor of Panuco, then president of the First Audiencia which had ruled while Cortés was in Spain, quitting the capital for the conquest of New Galicia, which consisted of Michoacan, Jalisco, and the coast. The Tarascans and Zacatécans had long been subdued, and now these small detachments were exploring to the north. Cortés was also building ships and sending them north to explore the coast.

"Those must have been men of Cortés of whom we heard in the town of the deer hearts, Andrés," Alonso said.

Alcaráz leaned toward Dorantes with a smile that revealed pale gums. "These indigenes who accompany you believe you to be gods and follow your bidding in everything. Tell me, what will you bid them do now that you have rejoined your countrymen?"

"We will bid them return to their country. They may or may not believe we are gods, but we could not have survived without their help."

Cebreros poured more wine. Esteban scowled with the swollen lower lip, shifting position in the doorway. Alcaráz was frowning and nodding.

"Tell me, Andrés Dorantes, you speak the language of the barbarians, do you?"

"I learned Nahuatl in Mexico. Their tongue is not very different."

"The black one converses with his hands," Cebreros said. "Eh, Moor?"

"Yes," Esteban said.

"They understand what we have to tell them," Álvar said suddenly. "Which is the Passion of Our Lord, and the virtues of the Christians."

The two Spaniards burst into laughter, Alcaráz breaking off when he realized that Álvar was serious. "Praise God!" he said, and crossed himself.

He said to Dorantes, "Perhaps you can send a message to ask the villagers of this place to return. We will not harm them. But they must bring food."

"To enslave them is to harm them," Álvar said.

"I tell you we will not harm them!"

Dorantes said, "I believe first we must have words with your captain, the alcalde at Culiacán.

Alcaráz shrugged and waved a languid hand. "As you wish. Lázaro will guide you to Culiacán. I warn you that it is a journey of many days."

"We have already traveled so long that days are as nothing to us," Alonso said.

"Tell me, travelers," Alcaráz said, leaning his elbows on the table with his cup held before his lips. "Have you found many treasures on your long journey?"

Dorantes stretched a foot out toward the Moor in the doorway and glanced sharply at Alonso.

"A few pearls, some turquoise, and some green stones merely," Alonso said. He managed a laugh. "And many indigenes!"

"And are the women pretty?" Cebreros asked.

"Some pretty, some not, as everywhere."

"Tell me, do these indigenes with whom you converse so well speak of the seven cities of Cibola?" Alcaráz asked casually, "which Beltrán Nuño de Guzmán dreams of discovering, and Hernán Cortés also."

"No," Dorantes said. "We have heard nothing of that."

The two naked Children of the Sun strolled apart from Alonso and Esteban through the deserted village where the Spaniards had quartered themselves, back toward the encampment of the three hundred Pímas.

"I do not trust that man," Álvar said.

"I know his kind very well. He would consider it virtuous to break vows made to Indians."

"One must trust that his captain is a better man."

"But beyond the captain is Guzmán, who was always the slaver in Panuco." He cleared his throat of its thickness. "I have seen the mines of the Antilles. The mines can be located by the buzzards circling. It seems that the buzzards follow the Christians."

Álvar's eyes blazed palely at him from the almost translucent flesh of his face. "They have not followed us, Andrés! We must continue to have the faith that has brought us safely here."

Álvar preached to the Pímas from a hill beyond the village of the Spaniards. As they listened to him some of the Indians held up wooden crosses they had made in imitation of Dorantes' and Álvar's, and others stood with their arms spread wide simulating crosses with their bodies. Dorantes translated, and, in mime-show, Esteban acted Álvar's words. To the north two trios of buzzards circled, very high.

When Álvar had finished and blessed the Indians, drawing the sign of the cross in the air, Dorantes announced to them that this was the end of the journey. They must return to their homes.

All eyes were fixed upon him, the men in their long cotton blouses, the women in long skirts and shirts, many with children on their hips or strapped into flat baskets on their backs, all with their long black braided hair. The young chief, Natsá, was conferring with three of his elders. These four came forward together, and Natsá, with folded arms, addressed the Children of the Sun.

It was impossible that they return to their villages until they had delivered the Children into the safekeeping of other Indians, and those of this place were hiding in the mountains. This delivery of the Children was essential to all those who had accompanied them on their journey, and the Pímas were afraid, Natsá said, that if they returned to their homes without accomplishing this, they would die.

Moreover, the young chief continued, the Pímas were fearful for the Children among these other Christians. They had come to understand that, as there were different tribes of Indians, some of which were peaceable and others warlike, so there were also different tribes of Christians. It was well known that these other Christians lied, which the Children had never done, that although both the Children and these other Christians came from the direction of the sunrise, the Children traveled naked and barefoot while the others had clothing, armor, swords, lances, and the great deer to carry them; that the Children were not covetous of anything, except for the few things collected by the white herald. But the others were great robbers, and moreover stole women and children, and carried men away in chains.

Dorantes gazed helplessly at Álvar, whose eyes were closed in prayer, hands placed flat together before his face. Alonso still knelt, face hidden; the Indian-hater was weeping. The Moor glowered.

"You must obey without question," he replied to Natsá. "The Children have come to the end of their journey. Their work with the Indians is done. They have returned to their fellow Christians, where they have other work to do. Now their faithful servants must return to their homes and fields. And they must not forget the Children, who will never forget them."

He waited for Esteban to reinforce his words, but the Moor made no move. There was no sound from the great crowd of Pímas, but the intensity of their waiting had a palpable force. Finally Natsá bowed, and, with the three elders, returned to the ranks. But still the Pímas remained gazing up at the four on the hillock.

Alonso rose. In a shaky voice he began singing a song of the star of Bethlehem they had often sung together, and the Pímas had often gathered to hear:

> "Cuando, brillando en la celeste bóveda,
> El sidral ejército se vé,
> Una estrella tan solo las miradas
> Puede del pecador á sí atraer—"

Álvar joined in, in his toneless voice.

"Dance!" Dorantes called to the Moor, who gave him a startled glance. As Dorantes sang with the others, Esteban postured, leaping once, tentatively, with a jingle of ankle bangles. The three sang, verse after verse, the song repeated and repeated, and Esteban danced before them. The Pímas also began to dance, in their own way, men and women separating into two ranks facing one another, the women shuffling with bowed heads, the men filing through them, sometimes leaping and calling out in unison. The dancing was ragged and uncertain at first, but gathered precision as the Children bellowed their endless song and Esteban capered, his black body glistening with sweat.

At the edge of the deserted village Dorantes could see Alcaráz, Cebreros, and the three soldiers standing watching in a tight grouping, breastplates gleaming in the sun, Cebreros wearing his helmet, Alcaráz with his carried in the crook of his arm, one of the soldiers with his lance braced upright.

When they ended the song the dancing also ceased. The Pímas formed into a long line, Natsá leading them, and filed past the Children of the Sun on their hill, while Álvar, with tears on his cheeks, blessed them one by one.

In the morning, with Cebreros and two mounted soldiers to guide them, and eighteen Indian bearers, the Children of the Sun set out for Culiacán.

Five days later it became clear that they were lost in the desert. There was no water, no food, and the Children as well as the bearers were suffering. Moreover, the old lightness and exhilaration was gone. Dorantes could also tell by Alonso's feverish eye that the herald was very low. Esteban complained frequently and dramatically. Only the soldiers seemed unaffected, and it was suspected that they had food and water secreted. Cebreros and the others rode well ahead, rarely glancing back at them, although sometimes they walked leading their horses, which suffered more than the men. Last of all trailed the Indian bearers. At night the three groups huddled separately, here the soldiers with their starved horses, there the silent, miserable Indians, and apart from them both Dorantes, Álvar, Alonso, and the Moor.

"They have been in my pack," Alonso whispered one night. "I cannot think when. The emeralds are gone."

"These Christians are bad men, Masters," Esteban whispered.

Dorantes did not speak of his suspicion that they had been purposely brought to this pass. Álvar joined the conversation to say that they must have faith.

The next day many of the Indians had deserted. The procession moved very slowly, under a terrible sun. One of the horses fell and could not rise. The soldiers walked leading the others, far enough ahead to be out of sight sometimes beyond a rise of ground. Dorantes placed one foot before the other, moved himself.

That afternoon they came to a village on the edge of a river, huts of palm thatch and a dark, silent, suspicious people. But there was water, and boiled tubers, and fruit to eat. The four Children of the Sun lay exhausted in the heat of one of the huts, Alonso shivering with chills. The small, half-naked women brought them food. Cebreros stamped in, shifty-eyed, helmet in the crook of his arm, to say that the soldiers would continue on to Culiacán, a day's journey further down the river, and would bring aid from there.

Esteban crouched in the doorway to report that the corporal, with one soldier riding and the other afoot, had passed out of sight headed down the river.

"Will they return?" Alonso asked, shivering.

"We are not badly off here," Dorantes said. He drew himself to a seated position on his pallet of palm leaves. "If they do not return we can make our own way to Culiacán when Alonso is well."

"They are bad men, Masters!" Esteban said.

Álvar had also sat up, face covered with his hands, murmuring but not as though he were praying. His voice rose to a broken cry.

"What is it, Álvar?"

The healer's voice was choked through his hands. "I see it! Those—those—those *devils*! They have brought us this long way so we would not know what has happened, Andrés!"

He had also come to understand the betrayal.

"But what is it?" Alonso demanded.

"They have taken our faithful servants into slavery! Oh, the *devils*! Andrés, what can be done?"

In silence the Children of the Sun stared at each other, Alonso with his bright feverish eyes. One of the women came to the door of the hut, bearing a hand of yellow bananas. Esteban sent her away. Dorantes saw that the other three were staring at him. Álvar's face glistened with tears.

"We must have faith, Álvar," he said.

"My life, Lord!" the other whispered. "I will give my life to save those innocents from these evil men. My life, my Lord!"

The next afternoon, after a clamor of voices and barking dogs, a Spaniard swung off his horse outside their hut, others with him. He bustled inside, a short, stiffbacked, balding young man with a close-cropped beard on a chin thrust out like the ram of a galley. Spurs clanked on his boots. "Christians!" he cried, kneeling beside Alonso. He grasped Dorantes' hand where he lay. "What is this, Christians? How are you treated here? I am shamed in my own district. Captain Melchor Díaz at your service, Castilian gentlemen!

"Where have you come from, please? Can it be true you have walked from Florida? From the Río de las Palmas, indeed. Tell me if it is true?"

He squatted with them while the tale was told, sometimes springing up to pace the floor, Dorantes and Álvar sitting up and Esteban crouching nodding, but Alonso remaining supine on his pallet. Dorantes wept unashamedly as he told of their long captivity on Malhado Island, Alonso taking up the tale of their journey, wetting his parched lips with his tongue as he spoke. It seemed to Dorantes that this energetic little man radiated an energy which strengthened them all.

"It is a miracle!" Melchor Díaz cried. "I welcome you on behalf of the governor. I welcome you on behalf of the viceroy! Tell me how I may give you comfort. I see you are very weak still, and this one feverish. Can you come to Culiacán by horse? A litter! I will have a litter made! You will be carried with the greatest care, Alonso del Castillo."

He halted as Álvar said, "We will not move from here until justice is done!"

When the captain was silent there was an intensity as though of silence solidifying. "What is that, my friend?" he asked.

"We have told you how we have made our journey," Álvar said. "From place to place we have been accompanied by indigenes, sometimes very many, who fed us and cared for us and guided us. Those who were with us at the last are called Pímas, from more than a hundred leagues north of here. These three hundred souls have been enslaved by Lieutenant Alcaráz.

"And we have been brought to this place roundaboutly, by Corporal Cebreros, so we would not know of this monstrousness. And have almost died. I tell you that we were closest to death in all our long journey when we were in the hands of our fellow Christians!"

Díaz stood straddle-legged, hands on his hips and jaw jutted, staring at Álvar. "But how do you know that this is true, Álvar Núñez?"

"I know," Álvar said.

Dorantes said, "On this journey we have become very close to God, Captain. Álvar has been the closest."

Díaz remained in the congealed silence, scratching his fingers through his beard. A little light came through the interstices of the thatch, to play in flecks upon his freckled bald head.

He strode outside with a chinking of spurs, and they could hear him issuing orders in his high, rapid voice. He bustled back inside, slapped his gauntlets against his booted leg, and squatted with them again.

"I knew there was something wrong in the way that toad Lázaro told me of your presence here. He is fearful of justice, let me assure you. One word that all is suspected and he will bleat like a goat of the fault of his master."

"But slaves are taken at the command of the governor," Dorantes said. "And one knows the history of Beltrán Nuño de Guzmán."

Díaz grimaced. "The governor has issued an order that slaves may only be taken who are rebels, conspirators, and disturbers of the peace."

"Alcaráz spoke of this order with laughter," Álvar said.

"Listen, my friends," Díaz said. "The Council of the Indies has forbidden enslavement. Well, New Galicia is far from the Council of the Indies. The second Audiencia of New Spain, six years past—ah, you would not know of that!—has issued very strict orders against enslavement. Well, New Galicia is far also from the capital, and the governor would have it that New Galicia is under his orders only. But I will tell you this. I am new in this district. And why? Because my predecessor has been tried and condemned to death—although they say that in the end he will be pardoned. And why condemned? For chaining, branding, and selling slaves!"

Álvar was serenely smiling. Alonso gaped up at Captain Díaz as though he had never seen such a man before.

"I speak freely here," Díaz continued, "to those who have been close to God. Certainly I am a soldier and obey my orders as a soldier, but I am not a blind follower of orders."

"One sees that Alcaráz has a good man for a master," Dorantes said. "But the governor is *your* master, Captain."

"Who also has a master," Díaz said, with a flashing grin. "For one hears that any day a Judge of Examination will arrive in Campostela. Don Antonio de Mendoza is not called 'the good' for nothing, my friends! Have we not learned from the teachers of the Holy Church that the mills of God grind slowly, but in the end grind fine? So also with the viceroy.

"One can only await the actions of this Judge of Examination," he went on. "But these things are known. Beltrán Nuño de Guzmán has had Indians hanged because they failed to sweep a path before his horse. He has had the toes burnt from the feet of his translators when they did not tell him what he wished to hear. He dragged the chief of the Tarascans behind his horse to make him reveal where his treasure was hidden, before burning him alive. This is a man like few others, praise God! He fled the capital one step ahead of the Second Audiencia, to found New Galicia. And I believe he will flee here one step ahead of justice again, to find Cibola!"

"Cibola!" Alonso murmured.

"Those who roam the north, like our friend Diego de Alcaráz, are to bring back reports of Cibola as well as slaves. The governor has great fear that Cortés will find Cibola before him!"

One of the women brought them a platter of shredded meat wrapped in thin cakes of maize flour. "Good!" Melchor Díaz said, stuffing one of these into his mouth. "Good! Eat!" During the meal he plied them with questions, crying out, "Praise God!" and "It is a miracle!" at intervals, although Dorantes had the sense that he was preoccupied with other matters. Still it was impossible not to like this bustling, fast-talking little alcalde.

"I am not one of the those who believes we must pamper these indigenes," Díaz said, wiping his hands on his breeches. "I leave that to the holy brothers. Conquest is conquest, after all! Nevertheless, one sees immediately that an uninhabited country is of no value to its conquerors. These people must be tempted back from the mountains where they have hidden themselves, and you must trust Melchor Díaz, my friends."

"We will trust you," Álvar said.

"When we have been convinced that Alcaráz has released his captives," Dorantes said.

"Consider it done!" Díaz said. "Tell me, Christians, shall I hang the dissembler?"

"No," Álvar said.

"And what of the dog Lázaro Cebreros, who has led you into the desert to the point of death? Death for him?"

"No," Álvar said, sighing. "For in the end he has directed you to us."

"Ah, you are truly good Christian men!" Díaz said, and clasped hands with each of the whites in turn, while the Moor squatted sulkily by the door.

Dorantes said to Álvar, "How far may we trust the alcalde, do you think?"

"I would trust him very far."

"Alonso?"

"I also."

"Estebánico?"

"What Estebánico thinks does not matter anymore," the Moor said in an offended tone.

"You will tell me your opinion anyhow."

"Perhaps this man is trustworthy, Master. He is not like the other Christians we have met in New Galicia."

"If we send to the Indians in the mountain and tell them the Christians will not harm them if they return to their villages, can we trust that they will not be harmed?"

"Yes," Álvar said.

"Why would they take our word in the matter? They do not know us."

"The Cháhtas know the Children of the Sun, Master," Esteban said. "Those few we have seen have told me so. They know of the black herald, and the white, and the healers."

Alonso had opened his pack and, raised on an elbow, searched through it. With a pebbly rattling he brought out the sacred gourds they had collected in the north. "This is how they will trust our word," he said. "We will send these gourds as tokens. If Álvar will pray that none of these are the gourds of their enemies, as happened when it seemed the Aguénes would kill Estebánico."

"I will pray," Álvar said, smiling.

"We will send the Pímas, when they have been freed, to the mountains with the gourds," Dorantes said. "And the Cháhtas are to be instructed that each one is to make himself a cross of wood, like these of Álvar's and mine. When they return they will carry these in their hands to show the Christians they encounter that they trust in God and the word of Melchor Díaz." He began to laugh at the spectacle of the fugitives in the mountains returning to their villages bearing their crosses, and the soldiers watching them as they had watched the Pímas and the Children of the Sun dancing. Alonso laughed with him.

"And we will see that the alcalde has a church built in which these peoples can worship God!" Álvar said.

"Ah, Álvar, if only one could believe that all will befall as we have planned it here!"

"I believe," Álvar said.

They walked to Culiacán, all but Alonso, who was borne on a litter, very weak still, although his fever had passed. In this tropical town with its palms and lush growth, the dark-skinned Indians assembled to hear Álvar preach. Dorantes' translation was not effective, for these people did not seem to understand Primahaitu, but they understood Esteban's inspired mime dance of sign language well enough—the flourishes of his big hands, melodramatic outreachings, body swayings, advances and retreats, leers, smiles, and expressions of agony and bliss as he illustrated the Passion and the Resurrection, the love of the Father and the mercy of the Mother, Heaven and Hell.

Melchor Díaz and his soldiers knelt listening, after the sermon kissing their thumbs and making other gestures of appreciation and reverence. They shouldered the Indians aside to beg confession and communion from Álvar, who was troubled that he could not indulge the needs of these priest-starved Spaniards.

Messengers came from Natsá that the Pímas had been freed, and these were now sent with the tokens of the magic gourds to the dispossessed Cháhtas, with assurances that they could return in safety.

On the fifteenth of May, with Alonso recovered, they set out to the south again, toward Compostela and the governor of New Galicia, with an escort of twenty mounted soldiers, on the next to last leg of their great journey. Still the Children of the Sun were afoot, and still the healers walked naked as well as barefoot, although Melchor Díaz had offered them clothing. It was, Dorantes knew, that he and Álvar did not wish to feel that their journey was done quite yet, although, as the Moor was faced with the fact that he was a black slave and no longer the boon companion of hidalgos, so he himself was beginning to feel uncomfortable under the curious and amused gaze of his countrymen.

"Think of it!" Alonso said, as they walked through these tropical lands south of Culiacán, "the pork meat we will find in the capital! The hams of Granada! And the wine! Think of it!"

"We will have to learn again to wear clothing and sleep in beds," Dorantes said. "Even you, Álvar."

Álvar nodded and smiled, his gaze fixed on the horizon, confident in his faith, perhaps framing his petition to the court that he be granted the governorship of the northern lands. Dorantes was preoccupied not with the hams of Granada, the pretty girls of the capital, or royal petitions, but with the memories that swarmed upon him as they neared Mexico. The boy Martín would be, would have been, fourteen years of age this very month, for it was fifteen years since the fall of Tenochtitlán.

On the fourth day their track intersected that of a train of slaves also bound for Compostela, all men, all naked and chained together at the wrists. They were guarded by six heavily armed horsemen, whose booty they were. The slow line shuffled through low brush, while the Children, with their own escort, watched from a rocky outcrop, the four of them standing close together. The captives were small and dark, long hair knotted into loose wads behind their bowed heads and fettered arms swinging together. The Spaniards were burly, bearded men except their leader, who was slight of build with a cleanshaven, pockmarked face. He saluted as he passed, and his soldiers called out greetings, staring at the nakedness of the healers. Álvar was weeping.

"We must stop them, Andrés!"

"It would be like trying to take away a man's gold."

"They will fight, Álvar," Alonso said.

"But would not these soldiers fight upon our command? Or do they merely guard us as those poor innocents are guarded, although we wear no chains!" He dropped to his knees to pray.

Dorantes remembered that Alcaráz had been, as many soldiers in this New Galicia of Guzmán seemed to be, from Hispaniola and Cuba. He knew the attitude toward the indigenes of those places very well from the years he had spent in the Antilles. The natives were suffered to live only for the benefit of their owners, less valuable than dogs and with the same lack of rights, by some mysterious providence placed upon earth for the particular profit and glory of Spaniards. He was aware of the Crown's predicament in the matter, for if the urging of the great mendicant orders was followed and the terrible exploitation modified, the colonists would face bankruptcy, the Crown loss of revenue and possible rebellion. The Council of the Indies and the Second Audiencia had issued their edicts, but Spaniards were expert at the art of obeying without complying.

He stood beside his kneeling friend as the line of slaves passed from sight behind a low ridge, where the helmets of the mounted horsemen remained visible. Once he thought he saw the flicker of a whip. Esteban and Alonso stood close to him, watching also, while their escort waited a little apart, dismounted and gossiping idly.

"Andrés," Álvar said in a low voice, rising. "My journey is not over when we come to the capital. I will go to Spain. You will come with me, Andrés, to court. Surely these people can be ruled with honor and justice."

"Yes," he said.

Álvar sighed deeply. "I know it is a dream," he said, barely aloud, and Dorantes did not know what to say to comfort his companion other than to remind him of the need for faith.

Chapter Seven

Beltrán Nuño de Guzmán strode toward them with arms outstretched, an elegant man with a neatly barbered triangle of beard, a handsome, petulant face, and a silk handkerchief flourished in one hand. He wore black velvet and hose, fine leather high-heeled shoes, and a heavy golden chain. The reek of perfume assaulted Dorantes' nostrils as he was embraced, and the governor embraced in turn Alonso and Álvar. Attending him was a retinue of young dandies, three soldiers in breast-plates and mail hose, and four young Indian girls wearing gleaming white shifts decorated with gay embroidery. They surrounded a carved throne of a chair. On a table before this was a bowl heaped with fruits. The polished tiles of the floor were cold underfoot.

"How you resemble the hermits of the caves of Old Castile!" Guzmán said in his lisping Castilian. "These are the travelers who have traversed a continent!" he continued, extending a white hand as though offering the Children of the Sun to those grouped around his throne. "Manuel, bring them clothing to cover their nakedness! How inhospitable that Melchor Díaz has not clothed you, travelers!"

"We were not anxious to be clothed, Excellency," Dorantes said. "Who have been naked for many years."

A servant brought cotton shirts, which the three donned. The Moor had not been summoned with them to this audience with the governor.

Guzmán called for chairs, and they seated themselves under the gaze of the handsome young men and stolid Indian girls. Guzmán reestablished himself among these, elbow braced on the chair arm, chin on the white knot of his fist, other hand swinging the handkerchief from side to side beneath his nose, smiling.

93

"And now you must tell us of the marvels you have seen on your journey, travelers."

With a glance of permission at Dorantes, Alonso began the tale, while Álvar stared steadily at the governor. They had agreed not to mention the tall houses of the north, but, at Guzmán's urging, Alonso opened his pack to exhibit the square of fleecy black cowskin, the remaining sacred gourds, the crumbling silver mineral, and the pearls. These Guzmán examined, frowning delicately, and passed along to the other Spaniards. One of the girls stood by the arm of his chair, hardly taller there than he was, seated, and from time to time he fondled her breasts, once pinching a nipple until she winced.

He lingered longest over the copper hawk bell, shaking his hand that enclosed it until the clapper sounded dully. "Men of some skill have made this," he said.

Dorantes moved his shoulders uncomfortably in the confinement of the shirt.

"Ah, the great north!" the governor said with a sigh. "And what have you learned of the north, travelers? Are there new Tenochtitláns awaiting discovery there?"

Alonso's eyes flickered toward Dorantes. "We found none of those, Excellency," Dorantes said. "There are many villages, very poor, although they are more prosperous in the west. The little bell you hold is the only worked metal that we came upon."

Guzmán's hooded eyes fixed on his face for a long moment, then swung toward Álvar, who stood with his cross gripped in his right hand as though confronting a demon who would try his faith.

"And this one is the great healer-of-Indians. Can you heal Castilians also, Don Álvar? There is much sickness in Compostela, and little arborvitae to heal it."

The men laughed, and one said, "If he could cure the woman's disease he would become rich as a duke!" Guzmán smiled as he twisted the girl's nipple again. Álvar did not respond.

Guzmán leaned his chin on his hand, studying him. Dorantes could feel a force the governor projected, a demand, an aggression, and a bitterness.

"There is a disease of which I would like to see Christians cured," Álvar said suddenly. "And I will cure it if I can, by prayer, or appeal to the emperor if need be."

"And what disease might that be, my good physician?" Guzmán asked.

"Enslavement, Excellency."

"Slaves are not taken in New Galicia," Guzmán said, still pleasantly.

He slid his hand over the girl's breast, then flattened it on the arm of his chair as he leaned forward. Dorantes heard the warning little suck of Alonso's breath.

"We have seen enslaved indigenes yesterday," Álvar said. "More than a hundred, I think. In chains, and guarded by soldiers with whips."

"They were prisoners of war," Guzmán said. "There is much rebellion in the northeast. The only way to subdue these willful peoples is to treat them with steel in their disorders against us."

"We have observed much taking of slaves between here and the frontier," Dorantes said, and heard Alonso hiss again.

The hooded eyes examined him. "You are the captain of this band, Don Andrés? Who have discovered so little of interest in the great north. Tell me, do you speak the tongue of these barbarians?"

"I can make myself understood."

"And you, Alonso del Castillo?"

"Very little, Excellency. Estebánico—" Alonso stopped as though he had bitten his tongue.

"Ah, the black speaks their language?"

"In signs only," Dorantes said, but he knew that they were caught.

Guzmán nodded, tucking his handkerchief into his sleeve. "García, you will show these weary travelers to their quarters." He beckoned to one of the young men, who knelt on one knee beside him. Guzmán spoke to him in a low voice, flipping a languid forefinger from side to side.

They followed García through patios where fountains cooled the air with their spray to a distant wing of Guzmán's sprawling, ramshackle palace. Alonso was allotted quarters, then Álvar and Dorantes were led through corridors until Álvar was shown his apartment. Dorantes was then led further along. Finally García opened a door and lit a candle to illuminate a room with a bed, chair, and low table. Over the bed was a crudely carved crucifix, the Christ with a tiny silver crown on His inclined and suffering head. Beyond the bed was a black doorway leading to other rooms. His guide put the lighted candle down on the table and stood facing him.

"Melchor has sent me word of your coming," he said. "He is my friend. You may trust me."

"Are we in danger here?"

"Anyone is in danger who has something the governor wants."

"What do we have that he wants?"

"Information of Cibola. Seven years ago he came here to escape his fate. Now his fate closes upon him again. His only hope is Cibola."

Hernán Cortés also sought Cibola. Dorantes had a sense of the pressures that would be exerted upon them when they came to New Spain.

García grinned at him, not so young as he had seemed at first, shadows pooling in his eyes. He said, "You are not to fear the governor, however. If need be, there is a protection that can be invoked."

García only shook his head to his questions about this safeguard, and said again that the travelers were to trust him. Dorantes asked of his slave and García promised to bring word.

"Tell me if I should advise my companion not to be so outspoken."

García grinned again. "I believe the governor finds him formidable."

When the other had gone, he removed his shirt and lay naked on the cot in the dim light, staring up at the plastered ceiling and beams of peeled logs. His mind told him that he should fear Guzmán despite the assurances of García; instead he felt only dread at reencountering Hernán Cortés, now the Marqués del Valle, who also sought Cibola.

He was summoned by an Indian servant, and, donning the shirt again, was led through the corridors and patios. In the great sala was the same assemblage, with the addition of a young Indian dressed in an exact copy of the governor's clothing, hose, black velvet doublet, and gold chain, although all much smaller. He stood at Guzmán's right hand where the girl had stood. Álvar and Alonso had also been summoned, but Esteban still did not appear.

"Tell me, Don Alonso," the governor said, leaning forward, "where are the emeralds you brought from the north?"

Alonso gaped. Dorantes silently cursed the Moor.

"Gone, Excellency!" Alonso stammered. "Lost or stolen from us as we approached Culiacán!"

The hooded eyes with their reddish glint fixed upon Dorantes. "Tell me, Captain, whence came these emeralds?"

"I do not believe they were emeralds, Excellency. Only green stones of no brilliance."

A twitch of anger creased Guzmán's face, instantly gone. "But from whence in the great north, Captain Dorantes?"

"From towns that were there, of which I have spoken."

"What kind of towns, if you please?"

He frowned, pretending not to understand, and Guzmán leaned forward again. "Towns of tall houses, perhaps? Towns of four- and five-story houses, where men work metal and possess precious jewels?"

He could truthfully say, "I do not know that, Excellency." It infuriated him to feel the chill of sweat on his forehead that must be visible.

"It is like picking maize from beans!" Guzmán said with a sigh. His entourage laughed. "It is like pulling the hairs of a beard one by one!" He patted the shoulder of the Indian boy. "This is my Tejo. He is of the north. See if this talkative captain speaks your tongue, Tejo."

The boy said in Primahaitu that he was from a people known as Tejos, from north of the great river to the east of the mountains.

He pretended not to understand all, but spoke the name of the river.

"Yes!" the boy said in Castilian, with a flash of white teeth.

"Tell these travelers of the towns of tall houses they have not seen, my son."

"When I was a little one, with my father I went to see these places," Tejo said, in glib, heavily accented Castilian, indicating with the palm of his hand a hip-tall child. "There are seven of these towns, each one more rich than the one before it. With my father I visited only the least of these seven towns." He declaimed the words as though reciting a dramatic poem, clenched fist held to his chest, then jerking out with the fingers extended.

"In this town there are streets of gold workers, many streets of them—so that these streets gleam with gold! And other streets—" he made motions indicating a terraced hillside—"of the workers of silver. These streets gleam with silver. There are precious jewels also, and these people are very cunning setting them into gold and silver rings, and bracelets, and neck-pieces. And the kings of this place wear golden crowns set with jewels upon their heads.

"My father had come there with the feathers of white birds, with which these people were also very clever in their use. For the less rich, you understand, sirs, who could not have gold and silver embroidered into their clothing. My father traded these feathers for copper metal made for the tips of arrows, which these people make also. They are very skillful in many things. These things I have seen as a child." He folded his arms on his chest and gazed arrogantly at the Children of the Sun.

"And what do you think of this tale, Captain?" Guzmán asked.

"Very interesting," he said, and thought it best not to enquire of Tejo if the fishermen had weighted their nets with gold nuggets.

"Physician?"

Álvar said nothing, holding his cross.

"And there are seven of these cities?" Alonso asked quickly.

The Indian boy nodded.

"Have these cities names?" Dorantes asked.

"The greatest and richest one, which I did not see, is called Cibola," Tejo said. "Although sometimes all together are called by that name. I saw only the least of them, which was called Hawíkuh."

He felt a chill of uncertainty to remember that name, and saw from Alonso's frightened glance that he did also. But the stories of the fabled cities were always the same, and always their seekers, after terrible suffering, would find the mud villages of Honduras and Apalachen.

"And how many days journey from here, my son?" Guzmán asked.

"No more than fifty," Tejo said glibly. "Twenty days to the north to the desert country, through which ten days. Ten days more through rich country of fields and trees. After that ten days through mountains, with snows, high passes, and rushing rivers. To the first of the seven cities!"

"What of that?" Guzmán asked.

"We have traveled from the north for more than fifty days, Excellency, but have not seen these cities."

"García!" the governor called. García knelt beside his chair to listen. Out the corner of his eye Dorantes could see the sweat on Alonso's face as it must glisten also on his own. Álvar, holding his cross, stared steadily at the governor.

García disappeared, to return with a tray upon which silver coins were piled in profusion, both hands supporting its weight. He presented this to Dorantes.

"In exchange for your black slave, Captain," Guzmán explained.

"The slave is not for sale, Excellency."

"It is a good price. You have counted the coins carefully, García?"

"Yes, sire." García stood holding the heavy tray and gazing expressionlessly at Dorantes.

"Five hundred silver pesos are better than nothing, Captain," Guzmán said.

He said carefully, "The viceroy will be expecting the four of us who have made this journey to come to him all together to tell him of it, Excellency. No doubt he has already been informed of our coming."

He caught the red glint of fury in the hooded eyes again. Guzmán turned lazily toward one of the soldiers. "Remind me, Corporal, of the disposition of the crossbowman Pérez, for I have forgotten how we dealt with him."

"Nailed to a post by his tongue, sire," the soldier said.

There was a silence. Guzmán leaned back in his chair with his hands clasped on the arms. "Tell me, Captain, will you have the same tale for Don Antonio as you have had for us here?"

"The viceroy shall also be told the truth, Excellency."

"García, you will see that these truthful travelers receive their supper," Guzmán said. He lifted himself from his chair and sauntered from the sala, trailed by the young Indian in the velvet doublet and beckoning to Álvar to follow. Dorantes anxiously watched these three disappear together. García handed the tray heaped with coins to one of the other young men and led Dorantes and Alonso to the dining hall.

They sat at long tables among Guzmán's courtiers. The governor himself did not appear, but presently Álvar rejoined them and Esteban came to wait upon them, rolling his eyes excessively when they encountered Dorantes'. He brought them heaping plates of red meat and kept their goblets brimming with wine.

"The governor would exchange one hundred slaves for one slave, Andrés," Álvar said quietly. "It was the substance of our conversation."

He shook his head.

"So I told him."

"I would give Estebánico and much besides to keep the governor from the lands through which we have passed," he said. And Hernán Cortés also. He glanced down the table to see how many of Guzmán's young men were watching them. Two at least.

Álvar was nodding silently. "More wine, Masters?" Esteban said, coming up behind them.

After supper the Moor came to his quarters, sinking to his knees before him. "Oh, Master, Estebánico has been so frightened!"

Dorantes cuffed him on the side of the head, and Esteban toppled melodramatically to the floor, where he lay with his knees drawn up, like a Marímne accepting death. "Master!"

"You have placed us in more danger than we have been in since Malhado Island with your gossiping about emeralds and tall houses! You were told to keep your mouth sealed!"

"Oh, Master, Estebánico could not help himself! There was this Indian fellow in velvet clothes giving himself airs!"

"The governor has offered me five hundred silver pesos for you. Evidently you have made yourself worth it to him."

"You would not do that, Master!" The Moor sat up with hands clasped in prayer.

"He would dress you in fine velvet like Tejo. Between you, you could lead him to Cibola of the tall houses."

"Master, the governor is a very bad man!"

"I was prepared to give you your freedom, as I have told you, when we have reached the capital. I have thought of you as a companion and not a slave, and possessing a slave is no longer a pleasure to me. But if I gave you your freedom you would have your head in a noose within a week."

"Please, Master!" Esteban moaned, hands thrust out beseechingly as through prison bars. "Estebánico wishes only to be Don Andrés' faithful servant!"

99

"Then you will not speak of the tall houses. There are powerful men who would perform great evil to discover the tall houses. And you will remember that we know little of them."

"Yes, Master, but Don Alonso—"

"Knows to keep his mouth sealed also!"

Esteban rose to his feet, dusting his hands together and looking cheerful. "Estebánico may sleep here tonight, Master? I do not wish to see that prideful fellow Tejo anymore."

The next day Guzmán was not in evidence, and Dorantes said to García, who seemed to be the governor's chamberlain, "Please inform the governor that we must begin our journey to the capital. The viceroy will be expecting us."

But the next day there were still no arrangements for their departure. Moreover, Esteban had disappeared again and now soldiers patrolled the patios between the wings of the palace. The Children of the Sun could not make out if they were being restrained or not, but that night after supper the three of them gathered in Álvar's quarters.

"But we cannot just set out on the Western Road!" Alonso said. "We will need an escort—bearers, supplies for the journey—"

"We must do without, it seems," Álvar said calmly.

"But I believe he will prohibit our departure!" Alonso said. "These soldiers are not here for nothing! And Estebánico! We cannot leave the Moor behind!"

Álvar's blue gaze rested upon Dorantes. "Are you also fearful, Andrés?"

"For Estebánico."

"It may be we must leave without him. And have faith in the viceroy."

A servant boy knocked at the door, mumbled, "The captain," and handed a bowl of fruit to Dorantes. He set aside the fruit until he found, in the bottom of the bowl, a rolled parchment tied with a red cord. He unrolled this and stared at the cursive. It had been so long since he had seen Castilian script that the curling lines were meaningless. He passed the document to Álvar, who was an educated man.

After studying it for a long time, Álvar said, "It is a copy of the governor's order for the taking of slaves, with the testimony of the notary that it is a true copy."

"It is a trap!" Alonso whispered.

Álvar shook his head and handed the document back to Dorantes. He smiled. "From whom does this come?"

"From a friend of Melchor Díaz, with whom I have spoken. I think we must trust him. I believe this document is to be exchanged for our freedom and Estebánico's."

"It would be valuable to bring it to the viceroy," Álvar said.

Alonso was grimacing. "Andrés, you would not threaten him with this? He will *kill* you! He—"

"No," Álvar said. "But we may also demand the freedom of those we have seen enslaved. Or—"

"You must trust my judgment," Dorantes said, rolling the parchment and retying the cord. "And that of the friend who has given us this gift."

Guzmán received him alone, seated in a small chamber writing at a table. A large green and yellow parrot sidled in an intricate cage on a stand beside him.

"Excellency, we must depart for the capital tomorrow, and I request that you make appropriate arrangements."

"I have no objection to your two companions proceeding, Captain," Guzmán said, laying down his pen and knitting his fingers together. "But I wish to discuss with you a plan I have for an expedition to Cibola. You would be my guide and captain."

He bowed and said, "I could not guide you to Cibola for I do not believe such a place exists."

The flush mounted in Guzmán's cheeks, but the governor said lightly, "I have enough faith in Cibola to suffice the both of us, Captain. But I will excuse you from this duty to me."

The parrot flexed his wings in his cage, opening his beak to expose a gray wad of tongue.

"Then the four of us will depart from Compostela tomorrow."

The governor shook his head very slightly.

He told Guzmán of the document he possessed, of which there were other copies also. The flush darkened, and the governor picked up the pen and bent the quill between his fingers.

"I will speed you on your way if you will tell me how you obtained this forgery."

"I found it in my room."

Guzmán sighed. "Fortunately for you, I believe you are a truthful man, Captain. Also a fool, like your companion the praying fool. The other is simply a fool. Cibola, Captain Dorantes! *Cibola!*"

He produced the rolled parchment from within his shirt. Guzmán frowned down at his white fingers unknotting the cord. He glanced at the document, but did not read it.

"How it drains the life from a man to discover a viper in his bosom," he said. "How lions are hemmed in by the nets of tiny men, as my enemy Hernán Cortés has also discovered. I hope, Captain, that you will have an uneventful journey to Mexico and discover there whatever it is your heart desires."

The next day, with an escort of the same twenty mounted soldiers who had brought them to Compostela and a pack train of mules and Indian bearers, the four Children of the Sun set out on the last leg of their journey, to the Valley of Anahuac and the Very Noble, Notable, and Most Loyal City of Mexico.

Book Two

TENOCHTITLÁN

(1520-1526)

Chapter One

Sixteen years before, the army of Hernán Cortés, which had lost two-thirds of its force on the Night of Sorrows but had been victorious on the plain of Otumba, trailed east to the safety of their ever-loyal ally, Tlaxcala, Andrés marching with the square of Caballo Botello in the division of Gonzalo de Sandoval. Their confidence, which had touched the depths during their retreat, had returned to the heights. The soldiers who had joined the army after Cortés' defeat of Narváez had had time to realize that the eight hundred who had been lost on that rain swept night had been chiefly from their ranks, and they were never to trust Cortés as fully as his veterans. But now they were veterans also, for new recruits were flocking into Tlaxcala from the Antilles.

Before the end of the year the Reconquest of Tenochtitlán had begun, and they were back in the valley of Anahuac, taking, one after another, the lakeside cities, some without a fight, others after sharp little engagements in which the crossbowmen and arquebusiers engaged warriors foolish enough to dispute their progress until the cavaliers with their lances swept in from the flank. This never failed to rout the indigenes, for they could not stand against horsemen. Then the sword and pike men would hack their way through to the cacique, always now since Otumba their quarry, for when the Aztec captain had been slaughtered the enemy fled. Victory followed victory as they fought back toward the shining vision of Tenochtitlán on its islands in the lake, playing the exalting and exciting game of their lives staked against glory, gold, and girls, and never forgetting their leader's promise that one day they all would be ennobled.

In one of those lakeside towns, in a room in the temple always to be found atop the cu, they discovered the flayed skin of a Spaniard. The thing hung from a peg on the wall, in folds more like thick cloth than tanned leather, the face a white mask with the open round of the mouth, gaping eyeholes, another hole where the sex had been, toed feet dangling. Into the plaster of the wall had been scraped the words: PITY JUAN JUSTE WHO HERE AWAITS HIS FATE.

Andrés gingerly ran a hand down the soft skin. He had never seen leather so beautifully cured. In many ways these people were cleverer than the Spaniards. He tried to recall Juan Juste in his life, a serious man not given to laughter or idle talk, older than most of the other soldiers. When he thought of Bernardo Fuentes in some other captivity, awaiting his fate, the black-clad priests with their bloody knives, he could feel the snakes and toads of hate in his blood—more and more hate, but less fear now since Otumba and the subsequent victories.

How had poor Juan Juste come to this place, who had been taken on the causeway? No doubt all these towns had furnished warriors to man those canoes that had so persecuted them in their retreat.

"Kept his cock," Caballo said. "That much can be said for him, poor bastard."

"What kind of people are these hounds of hell?" said Gil de Herrera.

"Never have I seen such things!" Blas de Garay said, staring at the skin with his teeth showing in his beard. Like Andrés, both were twenty and had come to New Spain with Narváez, as Juan Juste had also, enlisting with Cortés after Don Pánfilo had been defeated at Cempoala.

"Perhaps you have never seen the burning of the heretics in Old Spain," Caballo said. "What kind of people are those? Only Christians."

"But heretics, Caballo!"

"Come, take Juan Juste down from his peg and fold him up."

"Do not ask it!" Blas said.

"Andrés," Caballo said, and he was the one who folded the skin. The legs kept slipping free of the little bundle. Blas and Gil had passed out of the gloomy cell into the sunlight, where screeching could be heard from the plaza and once the crackle of musketry. As Andrés carried the bundle outside Gil crossed himself.

Caballo grinned and winked. "And what do you say of your precious whore of Joseph now, my young friends? Who permits such things? This Juan Juste was a very pious fellow."

No one responded to the blasphemer, who loved to shock them, for he was a good soldier and comrade.

They trotted through the sprawling palace in the silent city, through arcades in and out of the sun's glare, warmth turning to chill in the shadows, and back to warmth again in sunny patios, through gardens of red and yellow flowers that climbed into low, spreading trees whose red berries mingled a spicy smell with the aroma of the blossoms. Purple flowered vines cascaded from stone walls. Within small patios opening off the larger ones, birds chirruped in elaborate wooden cages, and water splashed into pools from terra cotta pipes.

Searching for the girls they knew they must find here, they trotted in and out of the verdant courtyards and through the arcades, wondering how people who could create such beauty could be such bloodthirsty devils. All at once two girls were flushed like pheasants, running before them slim and brown-legged in their white shifts, black hair done up in two high loops that bounced above their foreheads, big-eyed faces turning to glance over their shoulders. Then there were four, and five, and six, all running in silence except for the patting of their feet and the scuff of pursuing boots, weaving in and out of the raised flowerbeds like water washing through rocks, hardly more than children these girls who must be of the harem of the prince of this town.

Two of them collided, one spinning off balance. With one swift step, laughing, Gil caught her by the hair, jerking her around to face him. The others ran on, Andrés and Blas laughing after the girls like children in a game of tag, like Doña Juana de Aguilar y Zúñiga and her tiny retinue spinning and chasing through her father's palace. Caballo Botello limped far behind the rest of them, occasionally bellowing blasphemies in his pain and frustration.

When Blas cornered one, Andrés loped on after two girls who ran together, one plump and bouncing, the other tall for an indigene, her black hair shaken loose from its loops and streaming down her back. His breath whistled through his lips as, sweating in the sun, he chased them past flowerbeds and pools. In the distance there was screaming, where the Tlaxcalans were slaughtering the people of this town. Both girls' faces jerked toward the sound.

The plump one stumbled and went down, rolling herself into a ball with her face buried in her arms. He leaped over her and ran on after her companion, who cut in and out, feet patting, arms carried high, elbows out. When he was almost on her, she dodged aside. He skidded to a halt, swinging around as she dodged again, almost lazily reaching out to catch her hair as it floated past him. Instantly she stood motionless, chin strained upward and head back from his grasp. He laughed into her face. Her lips were tightly closed, nostrils whitening and relaxing as she breathed, dark eyes gazing fearlessly into his. They were a proud race, that could be said for them also.

He flexed his thumb and forefinger into the arc they called "the

Hook of Extremadura," to reach up beneath her shift, but something in her face halted him. He bent forward to kiss her nose, her eyes widening as he did so, although she did not flinch. He fingered his beard and twirled a point of his moustache, smiling at her. "How old are you, pretty one?" he asked.

She said nothing, not understanding. Her nostrils whitened and relaxed. When he moved closer she retreated a step. He continued to advance until she was forced to seat herself on the stone wall of a flowerbed. Grinning, he pushed her back until she lay among the flowers. She flinched for the first time as he flipped up her shift to reveal thin legs and a flat belly with a delicate curl of a button. He bent down to kiss her belly, whispering, "Very pretty, señorita!" He inhaled her clean smell. These barbarians bathed themselves daily; in Extremadura it was considered excessive to wash more than once a year.

He loosened his breeches, spat on his hand for damp, and was in her. This one did not squirm, but lay quiet. Her eyes stared straight into his. He spent quickly, controlling his panting; it seemed important to reveal no weakness of pleasure to this silent girl. He rolled off, imprisoning her arm beneath his back, to lie staring up through tangled branches at white clouds sailing over like galleons in the Mexican blue. The screaming had ceased. He listened to his heartbeat slowing. After a time he raised his head to see if there was virgin's blood, but the girl had covered herself with her shift.

He sat up to gaze into her face, which still stared straight back into his. She sat up also, catching her hair over her shoulder with fingers loosely plaiting it, lips closed. Her complexion was lighter than his, burned as he was from the sun. When she turned aside, the curve of her cheek was as childish as Doña Juana's, so for a moment he was ashamed.

"Good," he said in Nahuatl.

In a small murmur she made some reply. She did not turn back to face him. Caballo was waddling toward them across the courtyard, grimacing and cursing at the torture of the syphilitic lesions in his groin.

"Go!" he whispered, poking a finger into the girl's side. She understood this well enough, for instantly she was loping off between the flowerbeds in the complicated shadows of the branches of the trees. Caballo bellowed, "Stop that cunt, Andrés!"

He made a show of lurching after the girl, encumbered by his unfastened breeches. He raised his hands helplessly as she disappeared between stone columns. It did not occur to him that he would ever see this one again.

"Ah, Caballo, the knees are too weak!"

The corporal slumped panting against the wall where the girl had lain, wincing as he adjusted his diseased member in his breeches. "One ran swiftly enough on the Night of Sorrows," he said philosophically. "But not enough to catch these low-flying birds. Do you know what they have done, some of the birds here? Smeared mud on their faces so one cannot discern if they are pretty or not!" His sword clanked against the rock wall.

Blas and Gil came toward them, arm in arm, boots folded in loose folds to their calves. Their girls had disappeared also.

"See how cheerful they are!" Caballo said. "What cheer is there when the great beast of lust has fled his lair!"

"Not for me," Andrés said. "That is the time when sorrows circle my head."

"Have a care not to grow old before your time, my friend," Caballo said, squinting at him. "Next you will become a blasphemer like your corporal."

"Ah, but the fear of hellfire is one of the sorrows!"

Caballo snorted. "Let me tell you the sorrows you will feel if you are not careful where you sheathe your cock. How the women we have violated take their revenge upon us!"

Blas was pointing; the four of them watched the flames climbing the wooden temple atop the cu. Striding between the flowerbeds, Gonzalo de Sandoval appeared. With him was Fray Bartolomé Olmedo, in his black, much-patched cloak and rusty helmet.

"You know the captain-general's orders against rape," the captain said sternly. "One day we will see if a little bastinado will not cause these lusts to subside." Sandoval's burnished breastplate gleamed in a shaft of sun through the branches. "It is hoped that these people will become our allies," he added.

"Our other allies will not leave enough alive to be of much use," Blas said, nodding toward the burning oratory.

"We choose to impregnate the girls rather than hack apart their brothers, Captain," Gil said. "It is our great duty to produce a lighter race than these mud-colored people."

"God forgive you, my son," Fray Bartolomé said grimly.

"The prince of this place, whose women these are, has consented to be baptized," Sandoval said.

"After which they removed his feet from the coals," Caballo said. "Ah, cunt of Joseph!" he growled, wincing with another spasm of pain.

"One day there must come an accounting for your blasphemies, my son," Fray Bartolomé said.

Caballo farted lengthily, shaking a leg.

"It would seem that the prince of this place has more women than he can make use of, Captain," Andrés said.

"Their ways are different from ours," Sandoval said.

He found himself thinking of the tall girl staring back at him as he mounted her. The differentness she saw must be as great as that he did. Perhaps she had not been displeased to be taken by a teule, and one who had been considered handsome by a count's daughter. The curve of her cheek when she had turned away had touched him. What was her life to be? But who could understand such a people, who flayed men alive, snatched out their hearts, ate human meat, and were great sodomites, it was said, besides? Hounds of hell indeed, as Gil had said.

Chapter Two

For days the unbroken line of Tlaxcalan bearers, wound down the long slope toward the lake, against the backdrop of the volcanoes. Singly, in pairs and gangs, they carried the arches of the joinings, the adzed planking, the iron fittings in nets supported by tumplines—these all the way from Villa Rica de Veracruz. The brigantines had been manufactured in Tlaxcala under the direction of the shipbuilder Martín Lopéz, disassembled and sent forward to Texcoco, where eight thousand Texcocans had been set to digging a canal to the lake from a launching basin protected from the attack of Aztec canoes.

On the eighth of April the thirteen assembled brigantines, brave with new paint, were afloat in the completed canal, to the marvel and pride of the army. A review was held in the shadow of the pyramid, which now supported a Christian shrine; eighty-six horsemen, one hundred and eighteen crossbowmen and arquebusiers, five hundred infantry with swords and bucklers, three heavy and fifteen small bronze fieldpieces, all paraded to the music of drums, fifes, and trumpets. Afterwards the army was drawn up in divisions, and Cortés and the captains rode along the ranks, plumes and banners blowing, to a steady roll of the kettledrums. Then the captain-general, in his burnished breastplate and helmet, the gold chain of the treasure of Montezuma arrayed across his shoulders, addressed his army.

"Comrades, I have done my part. I have brought you back to the gates of Mexico, the capital from which we were driven broken and dispirited. We now go forward under the smiles of Heaven. If any man doubt it, let him compare our present position to that of the Night of Sorrows, or the terrible encounter at Otumba, to our sheltering within the walls of Tlaxcala—even to but a few months ago, when we took up quarters here. Since that time alone our strength has doubled.

"Comrades, we will fight for the True Faith! For wealth, for revenge, and for our Castilian honor! I have brought you face to face with the foe, now you must do the rest!"

They cheered him in roaring waves of sound: "Cortés! Cortés! Castile! Castile!" Tomorrow they would set out for the causeways to Tenochtitlán.

After mass the square of Caballo Botello lounged on their grass mats in the palace of the local lord, in which they were quartered, Andrés, half-dozing with his head propped on his packsack. Juan de Solís, one of the new men, a beardless boy with a face much marked by smallpox, said, "What a fine figure of a captain is Pedro de Alvarado! He gleams like gold in the sun."

"That asshole," Caballo growled.

"He is the right hand of Cortés. I have heard it!"

"Listen, pipsqueak boy. If it were possible by grinding up Pedro de Alvarado, Christóbal de Olid, and even the left arm of Gonzalito de Sandoval, to thus bring back Juan Velásquez de León, I would get myself a meatgrinder. For there was a true captain."

Andrés roused himself to say that Sandoval was a true captain.

"You see I would preserve the good right arm of Gonzalito," Caballo said. "But Pedro de Alvarado! Without *that* right arm of Cortés we'd've had no Night of Sorrows. For when the captain-general was away subduing you fine lads of Don Pánfilo's, the Aztec nobility got to dancing and chanting in some celebration for their nasty idols, which made Pedrito so nervous he massacred them. From then on we were doomed.

"Then on the Night of Sorrows he deserted his men, two hundred and fifty of them of the rear guard," Caballo continued, pointing a finger at Juan de Solís. "Not to speak of the others that might be with us still if Pedrito hadn't run like a rabbit. Juan Velásquez de León for one."

"It is well known that his men deserted him," Gil said. "Left him bleeding for dead."

"Oh, yes, it is easier for two hundred and fifty to desert one than one two hundred and fifty! But who do we have with us here? Not the two hundred and fifty! The great leap of Alvarado! Leaped right up behind the nearest horseman and never looked back!"

"Tell us about first coming to Tenochtitlán," Andrés said. The corporal loved to tell the story, and they who had been with him for a year now still loved to hear it. It perfected itself with each telling.

Caballo stretched happily. "We were quartered in one of Montezuma's palaces, one that belonged to his father, I forget his heathen name. It wasn't yet the fort and junkyard you lads of Don Pánfilo's marched into; made this palace here look like a sidestreet wineshop. Great halls and canopied parlors for the captains, and the royal suite for Cortés and Doña Marina. Oratories for their heathen idols which the Mercedarian father couldn't wait to convert into oratories for *ours*. In this land the first thing you do is tear down the local temples and set up your own. Anyway, each of us had a bed with a canopy over it and pretty girls sent in by squads. Beautiful girls! And young boys available too, if any had that preference, though no one would admit it."

He winked at Andrés and glanced slyly around to see who had been shocked.

"They'd send in that brown chocolatl drink that's supposed to restore your energy after being too much with women, and by the great whore we had need of it!

"Then after we'd made Montezuma hostage, didn't we see some things! At mealtimes he'd be served by ugly hunchbacks. Jesters, they were, and others like mountebanks saying witty things to amuse the emperor and his lords there. Others that sang. Always there was music. And dancers! Naked girls that would dance with little butts stuck out to give a man a boner you could sling a fieldpiece from. And men that danced on stilts and others that flew through the air. All these with nothing to do but amuse great Montezuma.

"Four comely women would bring his supper, removing cloths from platters of those little maize cakes and pouring chocolatl while the emperor conferred with his lords. They'd be brought pipes, very fancy, painted and inlaid with gold. They'd smoke with great reverence. Then the others'd leave, and if Montezuma was going to fuck one of the dancing girls they'd slide a screen in front of his pillows for privacy."

"You mean right in front of you?" Juan said.

"He hadn't much choice. The captain-general wouldn't let him out of his sight." Caballo sighed hugely. "Ah, those girls of Tenochtitlán! These Texcocan wenches are pretty enough, but nothing like those."

Andrés said, "What I remember is the fort and junkyard, and the noise. Always that screeching and whistling."

"By that time your fine Alvarado had us in the soup," Caballo said. "Next thing you know they'd stoned Montezuma—their own emperor! After he died we were never without arms again, swords always in reach and guards everywhere. Yes, and the *noise*. That damnable big drum. Ah, but friends, that first time we came to Tenochtitlán we thought it was heaven for certain!"

"Tell us about finding the treasure," Blas said, seated cross-legged with his chin resting on his knitted fingers.

"It was behind a walled-up place, not even a solid wall. We were three days just sorting through it, and half-blind from the glitter! Montezuma sent out for goldsmiths to melt it down into bars. There were great heaps of gold ornaments alone they said weighed six hundred thousand pesos, not to speak of gold and silver plate, and grains straight from the mines. And heaps of jewels. Pearls, and pictures of birds done in feathers and mother-of-pearl. They are great craftsmen, these heathens. I say they are not to blame for their bloodthirsty priests. There are priests the same in Spain, where they burn the meat instead of eating it."

Andrés crossed himself and watched the others do the same. He and Blas grinned at each other, indulgent of the corporal's extravagant blasphemies.

"And you had to leave all that behind?" Juan asked.

" 'Take what you will,' Cortés told us. Well, he who travels lightest travels fastest, and there are a good many souls in hell who wish they'd traveled lighter."

He squinted around at his audience. "No, friends, the only one who will get rich from all this, except Cortés and the captains, is that new fat padre with a pocketful of indulgences for sale to sinners. He'll sail back to Spain rich as a duke!"

"And the barbarians kept their treasure," Juan said.

"What's not sunk in the lake."

"They are devils from hell," Blas said thickly.

Devils who lived in a paradise, Andrés thought. Fray Rufino said they were great architects. Also poets and astronomers, besides being skilled tanners. And that it was their religion that the sun would fail to rise if their gods were not kept surfeited with the bloody hearts of men.

"And now we return, comrades," Caballo said. "For the True Faith, our Castilian honor, and Montezuma's treasure, which we lost."

Alvarado, with two hundred horse and foot, set out for the Tacuba Causeway, Olid, with the same numbers, for the Coyoacán, and Sandoval for Ixtapalapa, at the foot of the causeway that led north to Tenochtitlán. Cortés took personal command of the thirteen brigantines, each one containing twenty-five men, including captain, pilot, six musketeers and crossbowmen, and one fieldpiece.

With Sandoval's division, Caballo Botello's square fought hard, burning the lakeside city and the shrines atop the pyramid; no time for chasing girls on this day. Cortés brought the fleet into action, pounding at the flank of the Ixtapalapan warriors until they broke and fled, pursued by the Tlaxcalans.

They rested after the fight on a hill on the edge of the town, gazing out at the little brigantines becalmed in Lake Texcoco offshore. Caballo rose to his feet with a low whistle, to lean on his sword, staring.

Out of the mists of the north, the direction of Tenochtitlán, Andrés saw the shapes congealing, a great "V" of canoes like water-snakes, a multitude so vast that he gasped for breath as he got to his feet to stand beside the corporal. Others around them rose one by one. The fear from the Night of Sorrows, which had been almost forgotten, beat behind his eyes again. Cortés' little flotilla must be over-whelmed by sheer numbers, as well as the maneuverability of the Aztec canoes filled with plumed warriors. And then the little army on the shore would be devoured as well.

They watched in silence from the hill as the canoes swept silently down the lake, the formation shifting into a broad arc to surround the brigantines, which lay dead in the water, sails slack. A single cannon boomed in pathetic bravado.

"Andrés!" Gil whispered, and pointed behind them. The ensign, Cristóbal de Corral, supported the staff from which hung the banner of Castile. The pennon moved like a sleeping animal flexing its limbs. It flapped, and he felt that same breath of cooling air on his face. Ripples showed in the gray lake. The sails of the brigantines writhed, half-filled, fell slack, bellied. There were shouts from the Spaniards on the hill as the thirteen fat little boats began to move toward the host of canoes. With the wind in his face Andrés felt that faith of Otumba return. "Praise God!" Caballo said hoarsely.

The cannonading began as the brigantines bore down upon the canoes, which now proved unmaneuverable in their sheer numbers, which at first had so awed him. There was a popping of musketry. So rapidly changed the fortunes of war! A shout was torn from his throat, joining the shouting of the Spaniards as the first canoes were crushed beneath the bows of the brigantines. Feathered warriors could be seen thrashing in the water.

"Castile! Castile!" the men of Sandoval's division were shouting. "Cortés! Cortés!" And their allies, with the flying crane ensign raised beside the one that Corral held aloft, shouted, "Tlaxcala! Tlaxcala!"

The canoes fled back into the northern mists with the brigantines in pursuit, the ships sailing right over the smaller craft, which were crowded together too tightly to dodge aside. The fieldpieces boomed dully. From the town behind the hill there were screams, where the Tlaxcalans were murdering Ixtapalapans, and Sandoval on Motilla and the ensign with his flapping banner rode around the hill to see if the women and children, at least, could be spared. The Tlaxcalans hated the Aztecs so much that no task was too dangerous or onerous for them to undertake if it might lead to the downfall of the tyrants of Mexico, but the savagery of their vengeance shocked the Spaniards.

Seated among the others watching the spectacle on the lake, holding his crossbow upright between his knees, Andrés nodded off and jerked awake. He was very sleepy. They had fought hard, had won, and now there was nothing to do but watch a scene that, like so much in war, was dull and repetitious. The brigantines were tiny in the distance now, and the canoes had disappeared; the cannon were still audible, as, a deeper note, was the great drum.

"He possesses the grace of God, the captain-general," Juan de Solís said, seated on the grassy hillside beside him. "The wind rises just as he requires it."

"And the new emperor has died opportunely also," Gil said. News had come that the emperor who had replaced Montezuma, a great warrior named Cuitláhuac, was dead of the smallpox brought from Cuba by the Spaniards, which had swept through the indigenes, ally and foe alike, until it had struck in the emperor's palace in Tenochtitlán. It was said that a new emperor had already been chosen, Cuauhtémoc, an eighteen-year-old, which was the age of Juan de Solís, the youngest among Caballo's soldiers.

There was another, prolonged outburst of screaming, which all of them, with taut lips, pretended to ignore. Now the brigantines were disappearing into the mist.

"I pray the captain-general is not sailing into a trap," Blas said, leaning forward with both hands on the half of his sword.

For a wind that came up so swiftly could just as swiftly die, Andrés thought, that grace Juan had named fail, as it had failed on the Night of Sorrows.

"I believe no harm can come to him!" Juan said.

In the weeks that followed, the ranks of the Spanish allies multiplied. Otomí and Chalcans, old enemies of the Aztecs, but also the warriors of Xochimilco, until recently vassals of Tenochtitlán, advanced behind the Spaniards in dense packs along the causeways. Each bridge had been removed, leaving water to cross and the far abutment to climb, these protected by breastworks topped by a hedgehog of spear tips. It was the reverse of the progress they had had to make on the terrible night of the retreat, but now Heaven supported them, as well as these armies of indigenes, and now there were the brigantines to cannonade the Aztecs and drive them back from their defensive breastworks. After each gap in the causeway had been crossed, the allies set to work bridging or filling in the breaches, not only so that the horsemen and supplies could be brought up, but to ensure a safe retreat.

At vespers each day they returned to the mainland, only to find the next morning that the Aztecs had swarmed out to tear out the rubble fill and rebuild their breastworks. But little by little, day by day, they moved closer to the shining city with its pyramids and temples, repairing the breaches more quickly and forging further ahead against the stubborn enemy.

There was a tower of idols at the edge of the city, and the usual destroyed bridge, with deep water in the gap. They stormed the far pier easily enough, for they were expert now, those who could swim crossing the murky water while the brigantines moved in close to bombard the defenders. Progress halted here, however, for it took the allies more than a day to fill in the deep canal, and it was Cortés' order that they not go forward without ensuring a line of retreat. Impatiently they gazed ahead down a broad avenue flanked by the low, whitewashed buildings to the central plaza, and the great cu with its steep sides, flat top, and painted wooden temples there. The rooftops along the avenue bristled with warriors screeching and brandishing weapons, and from time to time the drum would take up its tolling, which now seemed to be for the Aztecs rather than their foes.

The Tlaxcalans worked furiously, tumbling the cut stone blocks of the tower into the breach and then dumping in loads of rubble. When the roadbed was level with the avenue on the other side, the army forged ahead, preceded by the dogs—greyhounds and mastiffs trained to hunt down slaves in the Antilles, which the Aztecs feared as much as they did the horses. The Tlaxcalans were engaged in fighting along the rooftops, gradually forcing back the jaguar and eagle knights there, who rained down stones, javelins, arrows, and darts upon the raised shields of the Spaniards. And so it was that they entered Tenochtitlán, for the third time, some of them, and Andrés Dorantes entered it for the second, and they came into the square before the cu.

A heavy fieldpiece had been dragged forward with them, and this began to speak with a voice that drowned even that of the great drum. The square was quickly cleared of the enemy, the big dogs coursing along the far margins. On one side was the palace of Axayacatl, where the Spaniards had been quartered, on another that of Montezuma, and on a third the Wall of Serpents, which enclosed the city of the priests and the base of the pyramid, on whose terraces the priests in their black robes could be seen scampering. There was a shout of laughter as one of the greyhounds lifted a leg against the Serpent Wall.

Caballo Botello's square was one of the first into the plaza of the pyramid, where they halted, panting and exultant. In a clatter of hoofs

Cortés arrived, dismounted, and, vizer raised, shouldered his way through his soldiers. Flourishing his sword toward the cu, he set off across the paving stones without even looking back to see if anyone was following him.

"After the captain-general!" Caballo bellowed, and his square and that of Uhurquez broke into a following trot, Andrés and a dozen others mounting the stone steps after their leader. "The drum!" someone shouted, as it sounded above them and then fell silent. Blas and two others ran down one of the terraces in pursuit of a pair of the black-clad priests. One of these was cut down while the other fled around the corner, and the Spaniards were summoned back by their corporal.

Panting, Andrés mounted the steep steps following Cortés, while Caballo lagged further and further behind, puffing and groaning. At the top Cortés and Gil engaged three of the priests; another, wielding a javelin, bore down on him. Andrés stared fascinated into the insane face, reddened white-rimmed eyes, earlobes crusted with blood where they had been slashed, teeth shot out like a skull; then he knocked the javelin aside with his crossbow, and jammed the point of his sword straight into that face. The priest fell like a sack of grain, and he braced a boot on the bloody head to wrench free his sword. Another flew like a bat at him with an obsidian knife. As he lurched aside to dodge this, a sword point appeared out of the priest's breast. Gil was revealed behind his victim. Now all were dead like fallen crows on this high platform, and Cortés stood panting and sheathing his sword, gazing at the huge, round sacrificial stone, curiously carved and caked with blood.

Caballo appeared at the top of the steps, face streaming sweat. With him and Cortés, Andrés entered one of the brightly-painted housings, which contained a huge idol, hideous and stinking of rot. Blood was spattered in thick crusts everywhere. With a grunt of triumph Caballo stripped the golden mask from the idol's face and stuffed it inside his breastplate, as others, crowding inside, began prying loose the jewels embedded in the base of the idol. Three of them rocked it to dislodge it from its base, halting at Cortés command; then all crowded outside as there was a warning shout.

Below, the square was filled with warriors again and the rooftops were swarming with them. Fleeing down the steep steps and into the plaza, they were almost overwhelmed by a hundred screaming jaguar knights, but, bunching together, they managed to hack and stab themselves free and back toward the avenue. The drum, which they had not found in their greed for the gold and jewels of the idol, began its beat.

They joined the rear guard, Cortés shouting to make himself heard over the din, in a hail of missiles. The Tlaxcalans, laden with booty, caught the panic of the Spaniards. Andrés fought alongside Caballo and the captain-general, flailing and lunging at the feathered warriors who screeched and jabbed back at them. He stumbled over a dead mastiff bristling with arrows.

From a side street, horsemen appeared, their vizers lowered and lances leveled—Pedro de Alvarado and a charging squadron. Immediately the pressure was relaxed as the Aztecs fell back. The cavaliers spurred on across the square, the warriors in their thousands melting away before them, and suddenly those on the rooftops also disappeared, as though on a signal.

With a rattle of hoofs and a clinking of bit-chains the returning horsemen passed through the ranks of foot soldiers, their vizers raised now. Several of the horses had been wounded. Andrés saw Cortés grasp Alvarado's hand, Alvarado's red-gold beard bunched out of the chin-piece of his helmet and white teeth glinting.

"Thanks, Pedrito," Cortés said.

"Nothing, Hernán," said Pedro de Alvarado, whom the Aztecs called "Tonatio," the sun.

"And what of Tonatio now, Caballo?" Andrés said to the corporal as he leaned tiredly on his crossbow.

Caballo only grunted ill-naturedly, for he had lost the gold mask he had snatched from the face of the bloody idol.

"Mark my words, Andrés," he said. "The treasures of this place are not for the likes of you and me."

When they had finally secured the great plaza of Tenochtitlán, they burned the temples on top of the cu, where the Aztecs had removed the two huge idols from their housings. They burned the skull house, where the rotting heads of their comrades captured on the Night of Sorrows were among the hundred displayed, and burned the buildings behind the Serpent Wall. The Tlaxcalans threw themselves into demolishing the pyramid itself, rolling the stone blocks down the steep sides. The Aztecs had retreated to Tlatelolco, the sister city, and the great drum continued to sound from the pyramid there, although no longer so menacingly.

For the drive against Tlatelolco, Sandoval's division was combined with Alvarado's for a sweep down the north causeway, with Botello's square detached to serve with Cortés himself. The captain-general divided his force into three columns, each to push north along one of the three great avenues: one under his own command, one under Andrés de Tapia, and the third under the King's Treasurer, Julián de Alderete. All were under strict orders to proceed only when the breaches left by the burned bridges had been filled in, to ensure a line of retreat. The junction of Cortés' columns with Sandoval and Alvarado's at the plaza of Tlatelolco was to end the siege and complete the Reconquest.

Soon it was realized that Alderete was failing to keep his retreat route secure as the Aztecs gave way almost too easily before him. He quickly outdistanced the two other columns, sending back messages to Cortés that he had almost reached the plaza. When Cortés set out with a detachment to follow his track, he immediately discovered that the water passages had not been filled in.

At that moment the great horn of Cuauhtémoc howled over the din of the Aztecs and the Tlaxcalans, blown from the cu at Tlatelolco, from which the young emperor and his captains were viewing the battle. The horn rallied the warriors to their most valiant efforts, the Aztecs surged back to the attack, and Alderete's soldiers fled before a charge of jaguar and eagle knights in a deafening clamor of shrieks, whistles, and blown horns, and the beating of the great drum. In their panic Alderete's men mingled with those of Cortés, including the square of Caballo Botello, and all piled up at a water crossing that had not been filled in.

Warriors hurled themselves upon them from all directions, in a storm of missiles. Horses pitched and bucked in terror, and canoes filled with more Aztecs swept into the waterway. Cortés' horse slipped on the paving stones and went down. Immediately feathered eagle knights swarmed upon the captain-general.

With a yell Andrés leaped to his aid, along with a Tlaxcalan captain with a scarred face under a Spanish helmet. The eagle knights had jerked Cortés to his feet, two of them gripping his arms and a third snatching off his helmet, which clattered to the stones revealing a white face. Andrés swung his sword, leaving a feathered hand and forearm still clinging to Cortés' arm for a moment like a bloody spider. The Tlaxcalan crushed another warrior's helmet with a mighty blow of his mace, and, with a lurch, Cortés was free, with space enough to draw his own sword. But still another wave of warriors drove upon them, screaming, *"Malintzin!"*

Andrés drove his buckler into their faces, thrusting his sword into the breast of one. The warrior grasped the sword and tried to wrest it away even as it killed him, blood spurting like vomit from his mouth. Andrés jerked the sword free just in time to parry a macatl with its obsidian teeth swinging down. Caballo's brass voice was shouting for aid. Blas and Juan de Solís appeared with a knot of Tlaxcalans, shrieking to drown the shouts of "Malintzin!"

The chamberlain led up another horse and assisted Cortés to mount as jaguar knights battled past the Tlaxcalans. The horse reared, lashing out hoofs; the chamberlain was thrown into the arms of the jaguars, who swarmed upon him and bore him screaming away. Swinging their swords, Andrés and the others of Caballo's square cleared a space around the captain-general's horse. More Spaniards appeared, with them the ensign Corral bearing the standard of Castile.

Andrés saw the tattered banner tilting, Corral yelling as the press of the struggle forced him over the edge of the abutment, sliding down the slippery stones to where a canoe filled with warriors waited. The ensign's frantic face peered upward; he tilted the staff and Andrés grasped it. With Gil's help they pulled Corral to safety, and Blas scooped up one of the round stones that had been hurled at them and bowled it down into the canoe.

Andrés leaned on his sword hilt, panting as others battled the warriors back and the din subsided. He glanced up to meet Cortés' eyes beneath the brow of the helmet, which had been recovered; the captain-general nodded to him in recognition. Alderete, helmetless, his beard splashed with blood, appeared in a group of retreating soldiers. A line was formed at the water crossing, and the Spaniards began forcing back the Aztecs who assailed them. The Horn of Cuauhtémoc sounded again, and immediately the warriors melted away. Now the tumult was audible to the north, where Sandoval and Alvarado were engaged.

The Spaniards were too exhausted to push forward again. Many had been killed and wounded, and many captured. Andrés found he could not meet the eyes of his comrades, as though each one was ashamed personally of this defeat, and ashamed of the fear that had been rekindled. "*Alderete!*" Caballo said through his teeth.

Back in the plaza of Tenochtitlán, with its stink of burned wood and fabric, Cortés rode his gray horse through the ranks of his division. Andrés, sprawled against a stone wall with Blas de Garay, scrambled to his feet as the captain-general asked his name.

"Andrés Dorantes, Señor Captain-general."

"Crossbowman, is it not so? And of what place?"

"Of Béjar."

"My gratitude, Andrés Dorantes. And to these your companions also, who fought so bravely when I was in great danger. Tell me, would you know the Tlaxcalan lord to whom my thanks must also be given?"

"Perhaps, Captain-general. He was scarred on the face."

"Come with me, then," Cortés said, turning calmly as there was another burst of screeching approaching. Shell trumpets blew.

A shout went up: "Malintzin!" A delegation of ocelot knights had appeared in the central avenue that led toward Tlatelolco. Spaniards

rose to face them. Two of the ocelots moved forward carrying burdens. One bent to roll his a lance-length toward where Cortés sat the
gray horse; a head, Andrés saw, bearded, matted hair, bloody stump
of neck.

"Tonatio!" the Aztec leader cried, and the troop of them whistled
and screeched. The second bloody head was bowled toward Cortés.

"Sandoval!"

Cortés sat calmly facing them. His face, framed in his helmet,
showed nothing.

"That's not Gonzalito," Caballo said scornfully.

Ocelot knights ran out, gathered up the two heads, and all disappeared back up the avenue. There was silence in the square.

"That was not Pedro de Alvarado," another man said. Andrés
thought they had not been the two captains. They had, however, been
the heads of Spaniards.

Cortés beckoned a cavalier to him, they conferred, and the horsemen spurred toward the Tacuba Causeway. With a nod Cortés
commanded Andrés to follow him, as though there had been no interruption. He hurried after the gray horse through the ranks of the
Spaniards to where the Tlaxcalans rested. These greeted Cortés with
their salute the Spaniards called "eating dirt," squatting to touch the
ground with their fingers, then their fingers to their lips. Some called
out, "Malintzin!" Cortés saluted with his sword.

Their chief, Chichemecatl, was a squat, fierce-faced warrior in
cotton-quilt armor and a Spanish helmet. Cortés swung down from
his horse to embrace the Tlaxcalan, and a few awkward words were
exchanged before Doña Marina, who had been sent for, appeared. She
was very young, this mistress and "tongue" of Cortés, and swollen
with child in her black Spanish dress. Her dark, unremarkable face was
framed by black braids.

"My lord," she greeted him. At Cortés' order, Andrés tried to
describe to her the Tlaxcalan who had come to Cortés' aid, while her
obsidian eyes examined him. There had been a scar here, he said; the
man had black hair, dark skin, was short. This Doña Marina translated
to Chichemecatl, who listened without interest, shrugging. It occurred
to Andrés that the Spaniards with their fair skin and beards might be
equally undistinguishable to the indigenes.

When Doña Marina had finished, the Tlaxcalan spoke at length,
making motions with his left hand of slapping a fist to his breast, then
flinging the open hand out.

"He says it is very bad, my lord," Doña Marina said to Cortés. "He
says that many will depart because of this defeat. Back to their towns.
Otomí, he is certain. Chalco. Xochimilco."

"But not Tlaxcala," Cortés said, folding his arms.

She spoke in Nahuatl again, and the cacique's face twisted contemptuously. He smote his breast again, leaving his fist there. He replied with spitting vehemence.

"Not Tlaxcala," Doña Marina said.

"Castile and Tlaxcala!" Cortés said, smiling easily.

"Tlaxcala! Castile!" Chichemecatl shouted. Warriors around him took it up.

A horseman clattered up. His sorrel's flanks were bleeding and foam dripped from the bit. The cavalier jerked up his vizer.

"Captain-general! Thanks be to the Holy Mother! We had heard you were dead!"

"I live, Cano, as you see."

"The Aztec hounds rolled heads toward us, one they claimed was Malintzin!"

"So did they with us. Sandoval and Tonatio."

"They are well, my lord, though we are driven back with losses. Good men lost, captain-general! Gonzalito is thrice wounded, not badly."

"Thanks be to God!" Cortés said, crossing himself.

Alderete and two cavaliers joined them. Andrés saw the captain-general icily ignore the King's Treasurer, who was reponsible for this defeat, the loss of good men, and of many allies. He noticed also that the Tlaxcalans did not look at Alderete directly, nor did any of them eat dirt saluting him.

To Doña Marina, Cortés said, "Tell this lord that tomorrow we will attack again. This time we will level every house, every palace and building as we advance, and each canal will be filled with their rubble before we advance beyond it. And so we will progress, as slowly as need be, until the emperor has surrendered or is dead."

When this was translated, Chichemecatl gripped his fist to his chest. "Tlaxcala! Castile!" And the Tlaxcalans roared it out, "Tlaxcala! Castile! Malintzin!"

The chieftain who had come to the aid of Malintzin was never located, but Andrés Dorantes and the square of Rodrigo Botello became that day the bodyguard of Hernán Cortés.

"You and your companions shall be my Turks," the captain-general said to him, "and continue to preserve me from harm."

The next day they advanced slowly north along the avenues, with the allies filling in the water-crossings to street level before they passed over them, the square of Caballo grouping around Cortés' gray horse as they progressed. The Horn of Cuauhtémoc sounded, but differently, and the great drum tolled. The top of the cu on the plaza at Tlatelolco was visible, alive with black-clad figures. From the avenues the Spaniards watched a procession toiling up the steep steps to the priests. White skins were visible among the plumed warriors lining the steps, Spaniards stripped naked, daubed with blue and yellow paint and their heads gaudily decorated with plumes. They were prodded upward by warriors with trident spears. Some counted thirty-two of their fellows, others more. At the top the captives were harried into dancing before the sacrificial stone, then one by one flung down on it, a priest gripping each limb and a fifth plunging the black knife downward. The bleeding mass was jerked out, and held high to the gods. Then the body was flung down the steep side of the pyramid and the next victim, with a faint cry, flung down on the stone.

Some of the "Turks" who surrounded the captain-general's horse cursed. Some wept. Caballo cursed in a low mutter. Andrés Dorantes wept, in sorrow for his comrades, in anger at Julian de Alderete, but most of all in hatred of their enemy, whom he prayed to see dead, destroyed, stamped out utterly, every man, woman, and child of them. It seemed to him that he was not capable of enough hate for that deserved by these butchers and demons. He would never feel any mercy toward them.

And glancing up at the face of the captain-general, which was hidden by his vizer, he saw the gleam of the tears that trickled down Cortés' cheeks into his beard.

Chapter Three

Never again did they retreat, advancing house by house and street by street, fighting every day for ninety-three days, down the avenues that led to Tlatelolco with its famous marketplace beneath the cu where their comrades had been slaughtered after Alderete's defeat. Behind them, their allies leveled every building, until not one stone stood upon another, and filled in the canals with the rubble of the destruction of Tenochtitlán, that beautiful city that Andrés Dorantes had first seen from the pass between the volcanoes, twenty-two months ago.

There was no water for the Aztecs to drink but the polluted waters of the lake, and no food. Smallpox raged. As the Spaniards fought on, they found buildings filled with dead, dead of starvation and of the Spanish disease, covered with pustules so close together there was no healthy flesh between. The stench was so terrible the Spaniards covered their faces with dampened cloths. Nor did they pursue the women, the stench of blood, excretions, and the disease was so overpowering, and the girls who were not diseased had learned to smear themselves with mud and excrement so it appeared that they were. But the Spaniards never ceased searching for gold and jewels, and now the Hook of Extremadura was used to investigate beneath the skirts of the women for what might be other than naturally concealed there, and they searched also the mouths and breechclouts of the men, alive and dead. Undiseased men and women they took for slaves, but when the Tlaxcalans or the Otomí stormed a barrio they left no one alive. From the shores of the northern island city Aztecs fled into the lake, some by canoe but many simply wading out into the shallow waters, floundering when it deepened, many drowning in deep holes, many with children on their shoulders.

And so the Spaniards fought their way into the final plaza and stormed the pyramid of Tlatelolco, putting to the sword the priests and the warriors who still resisted. For the first time in ninety-three days there was silence, which now was almost as ominous as had been the battle din of the Aztecs when they first encountered it. They did not know it yet, but resistance had ended not only in Tenochtitlán-Tlatelolco but throughout the empire of the Aztecs, for the emperor, Cuauhtémoc, fleeing in a canoe to continue the war on the mainland, had been captured by the brigantine of García Holguín. It was August 13, 1521.

Caballo's square had grumbled throughout the seige because their bodybuard duties did not permit looting. Today they were freed while Cortés and his captains parleyed with the Aztec lords. Andrés returned to the plaza empty-handed, having found only death and ruin, and the overpowering stench.

The wooden buildings along the skirts of the pyramid were blazing, as were the temples at the top. He lounged in the shade of the arcades along the side of the square, watching the flames. Farther along the arcade was a charcoal fire, and a file of surrendered warriors wound between the columns of the arcade approaching it, guarded by cross-bowmen. Three sweating soldiers and a corporal were branding the prisoners.

For the most part it was a silent operation, for rarely did one of the Aztecs cry out in pain as the corporal pressed the red-hot prisoner-of-war "G" to his cheek or lips. The stink of burned flesh mingled with the fetor of death. The branded men then staggered across the square, where they were caged in a compound.

The men in the line were scarecrows, some in rags, others naked, some still with painted faces, for only yesterday many had been eagle, jaguar, and ocelot knights. He watched one in particular, who held himself straighter than the rest, gazing arrogantly around him—a nobleman, surely. At the fire he said to the corporal in understandable Castilian, "Who has given you the right to brand me upon the cheek?"

The corporal slowly straightened, staring at him. The other soldiers stared. As the corproal raised his iron to brain this prisoner instead of branding him, Andrés turned away. Later, handkerchief to his nose, he left the ruin of the island cities on the causeway for Coyoacán on the mainland. His purse contained a few gold ornaments and some stones that might be precious. Jubilant Spaniards and plumed, painted Indian allies jostled each other in friendly fashion. Most of his countrymen were more heavily laden with booty than he was, and several drew along strings of girls tied together at the wrists and some branded male slaves.

126

Francisco López passed him, leading a file of naked scarecrow girls with muddied faces, each one carrying a bundle of loot. "What a day, eh, hidalgo?" Francisco called to him. Behind came a quartet of horsemen, a troop of Tlaxcalans parting to let them pass, to hails and waves. All were heading for Coyoacán, on the mainland.

In a large sala in the palace were Cortés and Doña Marina, Julián de Alderete, the captains Alvarado, Sandoval, and Olid. The emperor and an Aztec prince were being tortured. Soldiers squatted to watch, leaned against the wall, or pressed close. Cuauhtémoc and the prince sat back to back on a wooden bench while a broad-backed soldier held a brazier of burning coals beneath the feet of one, then the other. Alderete, the King's Treasurer, paced up and down before them, slapping his velvet cap against his knee. Andrés watched from the rear of the spectators. He learned that no store of gold had been found at the fall of Tlatelolco.

"Ask them again!" Alderete said to Doña Marina. She spoke in Nahuatl while the soldier hunkered forward to hold the smoking brazier beneath the feet of the prince.

Grimacing, spitting with rapid speech, he replied. The word "Malintzin," by which the indigenes referred to both Cortés and his mistress, was repeated several times.

Doña Marina, thick-bodied with child and expressionless of face, said to the treasurer: "He says that all the gold that was in his palace was given to the lords in the time of Montezuma."

Then she addressed herself to the emperor, and the soldier hunched around to position the coals beneath the feet of Cuauhtémoc. The young emperor was naked except for a loincloth, with a rather square, stolid face. He gazed directly at Cortés as he responded.

In his breastplate, black velvet sleeves, and gold chain, hands on hips, Cortés nodded. "Yes, it is true. All the gold was melted down and stamped with a seal. But the bars were lost at the canal at Tolteca when we were surprised there. Tell him we must have it back."

"A bit closer with the coals, there!" a soldier near Andrés called out.

Doña Marina spoke, Cuauhtémoc replied, and she said, "He says that battle was fought by the Tlatelolca more than the Tenocha."

The other prince spoke and she translated: "This prince says that the Tenocha did not fight from the canoes, only the Tlatelolca. It is possible that they recovered the gold of the Castilians."

Cuauhtémoc added a statement: "They say they have brought all they have."

"This half-peso!" Alvarado growled.

"Somebody has it," the soldier next to Andrés said bitterly. "We dragged the canal a hundred times, but it was gone."

"Tell him," Cortés said, "that the Castilians suffer from a disease of the heart for which gold is the only remedy."

The treasurer glared at him, and there was a ripple of laughter from the others, and, Andrés thought, a lessening of tension; but the fact that the captain-general must defer to Alderete stuck in his throat like a dry wad. Doña Marina did not translate Cortés' joke.

Of course the disease required not so much gold as what it could buy: honor, position, independence, sleeping through eternity beneath marble arms. But the price was too high. Gold was too costly. Or perhaps he no longer suffered from the disease. For one was never autonomous, even the captain-general, even perhaps His Holy Catholic Majesty.

Alderete snapped his fingers, and the coals were placed beneath the prince's foot. There was a stink of scorched flesh, and the prince groaned.

Cortés said, "Bring oil for their feet. They will be lamed."

"Burn their feet off to the shoulder, I say!" a soldier called out.

Cuauhtémoc spoke: "He says mayhap some woman has hidden the gold beneath her skirts. But no doubt the lords have searched there also."

This time there was no laughter, and the soldier brought the brazier around to the emperor's foot. There was a stench again, and Andrés saw the sweat streaming down the impassive face. His own shirt was sweated to his back.

"Tell him we will have two hundred bars of gold if he is to keep his toes!" Alderete said.

Doña Marina did not translate this either, and there was a delay as a man appeared with a vial of oil. This was stroked onto the scorched feet of the two Aztecs. Cuauhtémoc's face never changed expression, but he turned his nose away from the blistered flesh of his soles to gaze steadily at Cortés.

"Tell him we must have two hundred bars!" Alderete cried, and this time Doña Marina translated the threat. Her hands were gripped together before her swollen belly.

The emperor did not reply. The soldier applied the brazier again, and the sala stank of singed meat. Andrés left, joining others also leaving. None of them spoke.

That night Cortés decreed a feast of victory. Many pipes of wine had arrived in Villa Rica on a ship from Spain. These had been hastened to Coyoacán on the backs of bearers, along with a herd of hogs from Cuba. There were also Spanish women in the palace that was the captain-general's headquarters on the mainland, whores with beauty spots and breasts spilling out of low-cut gowns, dancing and flirting with drunken soldiers still in their cotton-quilt armor. The press of bodies seemed to produce its own heat, and faces gleamed with sweat. Andrés found the stink of sweat, wine, and broiling pork, the smell of victory, almost as oppressive as had been the stench of defeat in Tlatelolco.

There were not enough tables for half those present but he found a place with his fellow Turks Caballo and Blas de Garay and half a dozen other soldiers, all of them Cortés' original veterans and cronies of Caballo's.

A bearded veteran with a scar that caused one eye to droop into a quizzical expression pounded the table until his cup tipped over, mingling spilled wine with the other stains. He proclaimed that he would buy a horse with golden harness. Another shouted that he would have only golden bolts for his crossbow. They had been discussing the spoils of Tenochtitlán and Tlatelolco.

Andrés did not say that it appeared to him there would be no spoils to divide.

"We are all rich! Rich!" the crossbowman of the golden bolts cried. "We are all dukes!"

"What ails my good Turk Andrés?" Blas demanded, leaning toward him grinning, spilled wine glistening in his beard.

He said he could not get the stink of Tlatelolco out of his nostrils.

"Drink wine!" the scarred soldier shouted, pounding the table. "Smell wine instead!"

"I will tell you what will be our share of the spoils of Tenochtitlán, friends," Caballo said. His pig-eyes squinted from one to another of them. "The least they can get by with giving us. Mark my words! First that asshole Alderete will have the king's fifth, and then Cortés his, and the captains theirs. The rest of us will sop the crumbs."

There was a silence at the table. The possibility had occurred to Andrés that the torture of the emperor and the prince had been staged to make the soldiers believe that there was no treasure of Tenochtitlán to be distributed.

A man in a red wool cap slapped a hand on the table. "I will have my share or throats will be slit!"

"We have our glory, friends!" Caballo said. He winked at Andrés; he seemed to be the only one not drunk. "Glory! And our Castilian honor! By the whore of Joseph, you will see them persuade us that it is enough!"

"And girls! Girls!"

"At least Julián de Alderete and the captains do not take their fifths in girls," Blas said. "Or there would be trouble, eh?"

"I say throats will be slit!" the man in the red cap cried.

Others laughed at his vehemence, and there were more jokes, but the mood seemed sour to Andrés, with jubilation forced and crabbed, and drunkenness an imperative.

It was as though the corporal had been thinking the same thing, for Caballo leaned on the table and glanced from face to face, and said, "I will tell you what victory is like, friends. Victory is like the morning after you have spilled your seed in a foul whore who stole your wallet while you slept."

The crossbowman of the golden bolts shouted that they would all be dukes and rich.

"No, friend," Caballo said. "We will only be soldiers who die so that others may be dukes and rich. But we have done one thing—we have stamped out this foul race of Tenochtitlán. And it is enough for Rodrigo Botello! And a toast to Hernán Cortés!"

They drank it in silence. Andrés watched the dancers. Soldiers danced with the whores from Cuba, and with each other. At a table on a raised dais like a parody of the Last Supper were Cortés and the captains, Doña Marina with them. Fray Bartolomé, in his black habit, stood beside the captain-general, frowning at the drunken soldiers. Sometimes he leaned down to speak into Cortés' ear, and Gonzalo de Sandoval was included in their conversation.

It was Sandoval who rose to quiet the crowd: a high mass was announced for the next morning, and all were urged to retire to their quarters in preparation. The captain's suggestion was ignored, the music, dancing, shouted conversations of quarreling and laughter rising in volume again. Andrés understood that Cortés had undertaken to comply with the complaints of the Mercedarian father but without any real effort to interfere with the celebration of his soldiers. It seemed another contrived scene, like the torture this afternoon.

He wandered alone back to his quarters.

In the apartment of the palace in which the Turks had installed themselves, there was music also. Two Indians were tootling on flutes while another tapped a drum. On cushions, like oriental potentates, Gil de Herrera and Juan de Solís lounged drinking wine and watching a dozen girls dancing, not the girls of Tlatelolco apparently, for these, although slender, were not starved. They were all naked, bodies gleaming with oil, most wearing a gold or silver cord knotted around their waists, black hair looped up into two horns that bobbed as they placed one foot before them, then the other, pushing their hands up and out as though against some fabric that encumbered them. They were all very young. Their feet patted in the rhythm of the drum, and their eyes glanced sideways at the Spaniards who watched them.

"Andrés!" Gil called. "Come and join us, man! We watch these charming children, and soon we will fuck them!"

"I say we should fuck them first, then they will dance better!" Juan said. He patted the lap of his breeches. The girls swayed, stepped, pressed out with their hands, circling slowly, eyewhites showing.

"No, Juanito, we must wait until the dance is completed. Are they not charming, Andrés?"

"A little thin for the Castilian taste."

"We'll fatten them up with good Castilian seed," Juan said. He caught the eye of one of the dancers, grinning and indicating his crotch.

"Andrés, have you heard that there were no births in Tenochtitlán, due to the privations of the siege? It is the duty of good hidalgos to replenish the population!"

"I see that we are duty-bound to create a new race," Andrés said. It would not be one of pure blood, and in his sour mood there came to him vividly the apostates of corrupt blood burning in the arms of the iron prophets in the Plaza del Triunfo.

"We will have a competition!" Gil said. "We will each fuck four of these birds, and in six months time we will see which one has planted his seed the best. By the plumpness that results. Eh?"

It seemed a better competition than that of those lordly planters of Santiago de Cuba, who had bragged of beheading their slaves.

"We will all be dead in six months," he said. "I have it on the good authority of Caballo. It is only death that awaits soldiers, not wealth nor the pleasures of many children."

"No more death!" Juan cried. "We will all live to fine old age! Grandfathers! Many times! Rich, ennobled, with our families around us, to whom we will tell tales of the Reconquest of Tenochtitlán."

"Come, Andrés, you must be cheerful," Gil said. "We give you the choice of these charming birds of mine and Juanito's. Choose and she is yours. Even two!"

"The tall one," he said. He had seen her before, in Texcoco, where she had submitted to him in the garden of the palace and fled the approach of Caballo Botello. She danced on the far side of the company of girls, but he knew she recognized him. She wore no cord around her waist.

"She is yours! We only require that you wait until the end of the dance, for thus our appetite is increased and with it our pleasures. Juanito, however, perishes of impatience."

"This one perishes of impatience," Juan said, indicating his lap.

Andrés seated himself with the others, watching the tall girl's movements. Candlelight flickered on her smooth tan flanks, and on the forming rounds of breasts. Gil passed him a glazed cup and a flagon of wine. The wine smelled like damp sawdust.

"Faster!" Juan cried. "Faster, musicians!" He jerked his goblet up and down to a faster tempo, and the frightened little drummer increased his beat.

When the music ceased the girls halted in their steps. Juan immediately leaped up to seize one and throw her down on the cushions. Gil rose more slowly, to catch one with the Hook while he bussed the lips of another. Andrés moved through them to the tall girl, who stood motionless with her arms crossed down the front of her body, hands folded together. She met his eyes as he took her arm, and, when he released it, followed him from the sala, soft patter of her feet on the tiled floor behind him.

In the darkness of his chamber he fumbled for flint and steel to light the candle. The white blade of flame flickered, shivered, and swelled. The plastered cell came into pale focus, his pallet on the floor in the corner, his few possessions in his packsack along with his crossbow and cranequin. The girl stood beside him in the same acquiescent attitude. Her waist was slender, hips just assuming feminine shape. Her nose was aquiline, eyebrows almost joining at the bridge. Her mouth was tucked into a thin line.

"Texcoco?" he said, indicating her and himself.

Her head jerked once, affirmatively. Her hands plucked at her girdle-less waist, and she made gestures he did not understand, nor try to, for he was feeling the impatience of Juan de Solís.

Holding the candle up he indicated her and himself again. Her nostrils whitened and relaxed. Her head again jerked affirmatively.

He indicated the pallet, and she quickly sat upon it, legs drawn up and knees together, hands pressed to her thighs and eyes fixed on his face. When she lay beneath him with legs spread for his pleasure, although she did not participate she did not merely submit either, like other girls who had been no more than warm brown meat beneath his lust.

The emperor Cuauhtémoc was given permission by Cortés to evacuate the island cities of their inhabitants, until Tlatelolco and Tenochtitlán could be purified. A pitiful procession streamed out the three causeways toward the mainland, men, women, and children so weak some could merely crawl or must be carried upon litters. Meanwhile, in Coyoacán, the army had assembled with banners, crucifixes, and the Virgin of the Remedies polished and gleaming in her sumptuous gown, borne in solemn procession to the beat of kettledrums. The litany was sung while Fray Bartolomé prayed. Thanks was given for the great victory. Communion was administered.

Afterwards Andrés found Fray Rufino seated in a sunny corner of the palace, his good leg bent up, crippled one stretched out before him, and a jug of wine close to his hand. His face was stubbled with beard.

"We have both supped of the Blood of the Redeemer, Andrés," Rufino said, as he squatted beside the drunken priest. "But yours was consecrated and mine was not. Have you properly confessed your sins as a victor?"

"There was little time for confession."

"What indulgences and treasuries of merit we will require! What were your special sins, Andrés?"

"Every sin, Rufino."

"Murder. Fornication. Sloth. Gluttony. The turning of people into beasts. Of course, that is a sin the Aztecs must share with us. Beware despair, Andrés, which is the compound of all the others. That is my contribution to theology!" Rufino seemed as oppressed by the destruction of Tenochtitlán as he was.

"And now what, my friend?" he said to the priest.

"Why, now the good Mercedarian father will confess, forgive, and bless us all."

"What of you?"

"I think my work lies with these sad people we have destroyed to the glory of the king and Holy Faith—if there are even any of them left alive after the twin catastrophes of the Spaniard and the smallpox. Maybe something can be preserved of what was good in their lives. For a great civilization has been reduced to rubble, Andrés."

"We were blessed and forgiven our sins this morning," he said. "By Fray Bartolomé. But what of Our Lady, to whom we pray? Does she forgive these sins, Rufino? I am troubled in my soul. Surely there comes a reckoning when all these things are accounted for."

"Ah, that dear Lady will forgive him who loves Her—even if he has slaughtered the helpless and raped the innocent. But can one who despairs, truly love her, Andrés? It is *that* that troubles my soul."

Rufino filled the cup and passed it, brimming, to him. He sipped from it and returned it as carefully as though it had been the sacrament.

"The plant of Noah is a known specific for the sin of despair," the priest commented.

"An aid to forgetfulness also."

"Bless you, my son," Rufino said. "Some of us grieve for our great victory."

He returned to his quarters, wondering if the girl would still be there. She was, seated on the pallet in the dim room with her legs drawn up to her chest. She had found a cotton shift to cover her nakedness.

He squatted beside her, surprised to find himself grinning, as though the sight of her was something of a specific against despair. He pointed to his chest. "Don Andrés."

She nodded once. He repeated his name.

"Donandrés," she said in her small voice, and pointed to her own breast. "Timultzin."

"Timultzin," he said, nodding and grinning down at her.

She returned his gaze, dark eyes examining his face. Then she pointed to her mouth, her throat, her belly, and spoke words in Nahuatl. He went to find her food.

Chapter Four

As alguacil mayor, Sandoval had the task of explaining to the soldiers that Montezuma's treasure had not been recovered, nor had any been found in Tlatelolco. It was rumored, however, that treasure had been secreted away by Cortés, and on the broad, whitewashed walls of his palace in Coyoacán libels against the captain-general began to appear, scribbled in charcoal. One of these was that his soldiers had conquered Mexico, but Cortés had conquered them. Another was that Cortés had taken one-fifth of the treasure as general and another fifth as king, and still another that Diego Velásquez had incurred the expense of the Conquest and Cortés had reaped the profit. Cortés prided himself on giving sharp answers and often responded to these graffiti, once writing, "A white wall is the paper of fools." To this someone added, "And of truths." After this soldiers were warned against defacing the wall under threat of punishment.

The soldiers of Pánfilo de Narváez were especially bitter in the matter of the lack of spoils. They considered that they had been badly treated throughout the Reconquest. All the soldiers had heavy debts. A crossbow cost fifty crowns, a musket one hundred, and a horse one thousand. Maestre Juan, the surgeon, charged high for his services, not to speak of the apothecary and the barber.

Next there was an announcement from the alguacil mayor that the women who had been taken by the soldiers as servants and concubines were to be returned to their fathers and husbands. This caused another spate of scribbling on the Wall of Cortés, despite the threats: that now Cortés was demanding three-fifths of the girls as his part, and with a fifth for the King's Treasurer and one for the captains, there was again to be nothing left for the soldiers. It was well known that Cortés had made pregnant many indigene women of rank besides

Doña Marina, and that he and the captains kept harems as had the Aztec nobility before them; as indeed did many of the soldiers, those who had the wherewithal to maintain these girls they kept for their pleasure.

It fell to Sandoval again to explain to the soldiers that not all the women were affected by this order, only those who had been the daughters and wives of Aztecs of rank, for the good will of these lords was necessary if the land was to be properly governed.

Still there was great grumbling, for it seemed that those of the enemy who had been the fiercest in the defense of Tenochtitlán and the cruelest in the murder of captured Spaniards, were now to be given precedence over their conquerors. There was anger at Fray Bartolomé in this matter, for it was well known that he had power over the captain-general in certain areas, as Julián de Alderete had in others, and the Mercedarian father had been preaching against the soldiers who maintained harems. There was such an outcry against this ruling that it was revised again. Those girls who did not wish to return to their fathers and husbands would not be required to do so, except in a few cases.

Fray Rufino came often to Andrés' quarters, a small house where an old woman cooked for him and Timultzin, and a lamed slave with the G-brand on his cheek fetched water and delved in the fields behind the dwellings. Rufino was endeavoring to learn Nahuatl and he had discovered that the girl was a good teacher. She could draw with marvelous accuracy, and covered the papers the priest brought with small, neat, square drawings that depicted the things of the lives of the Aztecs, Indians embroidering, making maize cakes, suckling babies; the activities of men also, cutting stone or wood, pumping bellows, goldsmithing, a drunken man, and a thief. Little curls, like tongues, before the faces of her figures denoted speech. She named the activities and objects in her drawings for Rufino, who transcribed her words into phonetic Castilian and wrote descriptions of her tiny scenes. And so the priest learned Nahuatl, Andrés learned it also, and Timultzin learned Castilian, for she was very clever and quick.

It was in mixed Castilian and Nahuatl, Rufino questioning her sometimes, and he, alone with her, at others, that he learned of her life. She was just sixteen. Her father and mother were long dead. She was the niece of a lord of Atzcapotzalco and had been married to a lord of Texcoco who was also an uncle. She had fled from Texcoco when the teules had come. The first time she had been with a man had been with Andrés, in the gardens of her husband's palace. Her husband, who was old, with many wives, had not yet visited her.

In their life together Andrés lived in a tumescent dream, for these days he had little to do but contemplate her body, which belonged to him, and take advantage of the subject of his contemplation. Where others might have four or five girls to accommodate their lusts, he was more than satisfied with the one who was his lot. One day when they rested flank to flank on their pallet, she said a word he did not understand and touched her belly in a different way than when she had explained to him that she was hungry. When he did not understand she took his hand and laid it there. She was with child.

She taught him to bathe daily, making a pleasing ceremony of it, the serving woman heating water and bringing it in clay pots and Timultzin sponging it over his body and rubbing him with a pad of rough fibres and the lather from a white root. She scrubbed him until his flesh glowed, until he drew her down on the pallet and they made love. She no longer dressed her hair in the two loops but in the Castilian manner, and she loved to wear the dress he had obtained from a trader from Santo Domingo, rich silks ornamented with braid, lace, and gilt thread, very heavy. Her breasts were maturing with her pregnancy, and the low bodice of her Spanish dress revealed a pleasing cleft. She wore no underclothing beneath the dress or her cotton shifts, which excited him, and he caressed her or summoned her to bed with a gentle Hook of Extremadura, until she began to guide his hand to her cheek instead of her crotch, and he understood that this crude affection offended her dignity.

In the night he would awaken to the touch of her hip or her toes pressed to his ankle, her face close to his and the light warm caress of her breath on his cheek. He would be aware of her dark eyes contemplating his face in the darkness and wonder what she was thinking. But it was impossible to put such a complicated question to her in their mixture of tongues, much less understand the reply.

But one night he heard her whisper, in a small rustling of Nahuatl: "My tuele."

Gonzalo de Sandoval, with a soldier, a wizened little Tlaxcalan translator, and two Aztec nobles entered the house without knocking. The two Aztecs wore white girdled robes knotted at the shoulder and different headdresses, one of blue and yellow feathers, the other a kind of crown of some stiff, painted material. They appeared very tall in these headdresses, both ducking their heads under the low lintel as they entered, although both were shorter than Andrés. The one with the feathered headdress was a sharp-faced old man, cheeks clawed by long wrinkles. His eyes slid toward Timultzin, who had risen from the table where she had been seated across from Rufino, and then took Andrés in with a little flare of intensity. Sandoval wore his dented breastplate, faded doublet, and high, soft boots. His short-cropped hair was neatly brushed and he carried his helmet underarm. Sandoval gazed severely at him.

"Don Andrés, the general has ordered that the women of these lords be returned to them. This one is the wife of this man." He indicated the old man.

In her clean white shift with her hair loose down her back, Timultzin looked like a big-eyed child. Rufino sprawled in the pigskin chair, with his stiff leg stretched out before him and his jar of wine and cup on the table with the papers on which the two of them had been working. "What thankless work is this, Gonzalito?" he said easily.

Facing his captain and the others Andrés felt as though he would choke on his hatred for these arrogant animals who had been defeated but had not been conquered. He could hardly trust his voice.

"Ask her if she wishes to return."

Timultzin seemed to vibrate, hands caught together at her waist, nostrils pale with tension. Her eyes were fixed on the older man.

He spoke. She replied. The younger man spoke. She shook her head. Her eyes evaded Andrés'. Rufino was pouring wine into his cup, squinting at Timultzin.

"She does not wish to return to her husband, Captain."

"It does not matter, Fray Rufino. Her husband is a lord of Texcoco and our ally. The women of such lords are to be returned to them."

He thought his head must burst. He stepped across the room and jerked his scabbarded sword from the corner where it had leaned for these months of inactivity. The soldier stolidly laid a hand on the hilt of his own sword.

"Don't be a fool," Sandoval said.

"Will you kill me to give this girl back to these dogs?"

"If need be, Andrés. The good will which the general seeks now is more important than a single life."

"Perhaps he will remember that this life saved his in the defeat of Alderete. Or is that another forgotten debt?"

Sandoval did not reply, gazing at him contemplatively. The two Indians watched with their stony expressions. The little Tlaxcalan looked embarrassed, the soldier uninterested.

He drew his sword and flung the scabbard down.

"One moment," Rufino said.

All eyes switched to the priest. "This girl has told us she was married to her uncle. Is this old man her uncle?"

The translator, on a nod from Sandoval, put the question. The husband replied lengthily, then the other Aztec more briefly. The translator said, "He says he has many nieces who are his wives. This is not the only one."

"The Holy Church does not recognize such a marriage," Rufino said. Purple wine gleamed in his beard. There was a long silence, Sandoval glaring down his nose at the priest. The translator and the two Aztecs conferred.

The eyes of the older one encountered his, to flare again. He felt a fool now, holding the naked sword. Rufino spoke in Nahuatl, too swiftly for him to follow. Timultzin's eyes were fixed on her husband's face.

The Tlaxcalan said, "This one, Don Carlos, says he has been baptized in a Christian church."

"Finished!" Rufino said, making a slashing motion with his hand. "An incestuous marriage is illegal in the eyes of the Holy Church. So is a bigamous marriage. A bigamous, incestuous marriage is unthinkable. This Christian Don Carlos will divest himself of his many nieces and many wives. The chaplain will be informed of this monstrousness. The captain-general has no authority in this matter of morals, Gonzalito."

Sandoval appeared to be sucking on a tooth as the translator explained the situation in Nahuatl. Now the husband's face was shuttered. The younger Axtec spoke to Timultzin, but she did not reply. The husband turned, and, ducking under the lintel, passed outside. The younger lord and the Tlaxcalan followed.

Sandoval said, "You would have lifted your weapon to your sorrow, Andrés."

"Perhaps to yours also, Gonzalo."

"There are many pretty girls in Mexico. Would you die for this one?"

"Would you die for these dogs who were our enemy?"

"If the general commanded it," Sandoval said, with a shrug. He bowed to Rufino. "You are a clever lawyer, bachelor." He left the house, the soldier following him.

Timultzin slipped quickly around the table to stand before the priest with her head bowed and her hands clasped together before her belly. Rufino patted her arm. Then she came to stand before Andrés in the same posture. He caressed her cheek. Rufino grinned drunkenly at him.

"I am in your debt, Rufino."

"Do not mention it, my friend. But tell me, would you in fact have died for our little artist?"

He drew a deep breath before he spoke. "There is a great anger in me that sometimes breaks loose. I believe I would have fought Gonzalito and the soldier, too."

"That is what I asked," Rufino said, nodding.

Sometimes he woke in the early morning to see her kneeling, heavy-bodied now, gazing out at the morning star which hung between the white heads of the volcanoes. But when she was baptized by Rufino, who had instructed her in the Holy Faith, he did not notice that she did this anymore. Juana now, she prayed to the pretty silver crucifix which he had bought for her and hung on the wall.

She was diligent in her work for Rufino, and Andrés knew that she had become more and more adept as the priest pushed her to recall details. She worked on a long series on the birth and raising of children, illustrating the punishments, the tears, the instructions, and the games. A boy's life she could only depict until it had been decided whether he was to become a priest or a warrior, when he was taken from his family, but a girl's was followed until she had given birth. She was unable to draw her people at war, but once she showed him a scene he remembered: cartoon Spaniards in doublets, breastplates, and helmets, running with legs apart and arms outstretched, chasing Indian girls in their white shifts with hair done up in twin horns.

The child was baptized Martín. The day after his baptism a little dark man arrived, his long hair worn over his ears, with smooth eroded features that looked as though they had been honed down by a rough stone. He brought a thick book of deerskin wrapped in a cotton cloth. Andrés observed that Timultzin treated the visitor with great deference. The book was the tonalamatl, the Book of Fate, she told Andrés; in it was to be found the boy's Aztec name and his future.

With great care the little man unfolded the book on the floor and knelt before it, Timultzin beside him. On the deerskin pages were painted one large square drawing of the kind that Timultzin had made for Rufino, only more fantastical—gods were depicted, Andrés realized—along with a number of smaller painted squares half-surrounding the large one. The old man turned the pages slowly, arranging each one so there were no wrinkles before turning the next. Andrés could sense the gathering tension as he peered over their shoulders at the meaningless figures or paced the room, sometimes looking into the basket at the tiny, sleeping tan face.

Finally, hands pressed to his thighs, the old man leaned forward. He pointed. Both he and Timultzin leaned back at the same moment. "Tlaloc," she said. "Water."

The old man spoke in Nahuatl too rapid and guttural for him to understand. He turned another page, Timultzin nodding in the bowed-head way that indicated subservience and gratitude. Another page was turned, and, as though reluctantly, another. Andrés peered down at the red depictions of stylized, warlike beings. This time he felt the relaxation of tension.

"One-reed," Timultzin said in Nahuatl. She smiled up at him. "Good fortune," she said in Castilian.

The old man, whom Andrés was certain was an Aztec priest, carefully turned one more page, then closed and refolded the book. He spoke at length again, Timultzin nodding with bowed head. Andrés could make out a repetition of the word "water," and the God's name, "Tlaloc."

When the priest had left with the wrapped book, Timultzin explained that the auguries of the day of Martín's birth had not been propitious. They had therefore postponed the birth day three days, which was permissible and common practice. Of course, it did not matter now that she was a Christian, and Martín had also been baptized, but there was no reason to offend the old gods. The birth day was One-reed, a day of good fortune, and that would be Martín's Aztec name. He knew by the hectic flush in her cheeks that she was afraid he would object to all this and that she was relieved when he did not. Afterwards, although One-reed had not made his small sounds of hunger, she fed him tenderly from her swollen breast.

The child had deepset watchful eyes. At first Andrés thought these might be blue, but they turned dark as the months passed. The skin of this child of impure blood was of a shade exactly between his own whiteness and Timultzin's golden duskiness. Rufino laughed at the child's resemblance to his father, and he himself often stood over the cradle, fashioned from a soft white wood by one of the clever craftsmen of the town, watching the little face that was his own face, only of a darker shade, as it turned from side to side, the hands with their marvels of tiny fingers reaching and clasping, the sucking motions of the minuscule slit of a mouth. He thought of his father's injunctions about the pure blood of the family, and of his vow; and thought also of those several other children, slightly older than this one, who must have begun their existence in the towns around the lake, and in Tlaxcala, who were also his.

When the dead had been burned or buried, the Aztecs who had dispersed upon the mainland were ordered to return, to clear the streets, fill in the canals, and restore the ruined aqueduct from Chapultepec. Cortés had ordered that a new city be constructed upon the wrecked buildings and pyramids of the empire. Armies of wood-

and stone-cutters and bearers were sent into the mountains to the forests and quarries, to drag back building stone and cedar logs for beams. The boundaries of Tenochtitlán were expanded onto filled land, and the Very Noble, Notable, and Most Loyal City of Mexico grew upon the foundations of the twin cities, on buried bones and broken spears and the lost treasure of Montezuma.

The Aztec square became a Spanish plaza and a cathedral was built where the great cu had been. On the site of Montezuma's palace rose that of Hernán Cortés, with cedar forests razed to furnish the seven thousand great beams for its construction. The Aztecs were urged to build their own homes in the suburbs of Poptla, and Tlatelolco, where the great native market was reestablished.

The tribute rolls of Montezuma had been found and examined to determine the sources of the empire's supply of gold and jewels. Expeditions were sent to these provinces, and others to search out the lands suitable for cultivation. Cortés requisitioned from Spain and the Antilles breeding stock, cattle, swine, goats, horses, and chickens, and seeds and cuttings of grain, fruit, nut, mulberry and olive trees, sugar cane, and grapevines.

Nor did he neglect the social and moral health of his army. Gambling was banned, as it often and ineffectually had been before, since all knew the general himself for an inveterate gambler. At the behest of the chaplain, church attendance was made compulsory. Proper dress was stipulated. It was known that his Catholic Majesty had issued laws against the granting of tracts of land with Indian serfs to work them, but Cortés announced that this policy was being renegotiated. Spaniards might be allotted land if they brought their wives from Spain or the Antilles. If unmarried, they must, within six months, import suitable mates or accept those the general had arranged to have imported. Marriage to Indian women was discouraged.

Cortés had been appointed governor, captain-general, and chief justice of New Spain, to the great rage of Diego Velásquez, the governor of Cuba and Cortés' mortal enemy. Clad in black velvet, wearing a black cap sporting a feather and his familiar golden chain, Cortés rode daily from his quarters in Coyoacán into his new city to observe the progress of the building. He was accompanied by Doña Marina and one or more of his captains, by Aztec nobles in their exotic finery, by a secretary, a valet, and a chaplain, and two soldiers armed with maces to clear the way along the causeway and the avenues. Now that there was peace he no longer had need of the Turks of his personal guard.

Andrés waited upon the new governor one misty morning in the palace in Coyoacán. Cortés received him in a sala filled with greenery,

soldiers, and secretaries, seated at a table in the far corner. He waved
Andrés into the chair opposite him and offered him nutmeats from a
polished wooden bowl.

"And how may I serve my crossbowman to whom I owe my life?"
Cortés asked, smiling.

He had practiced his speech. He said he wished to marry the indigene who was the mother of his child.

Cortés grimaced and moved his shoulders irritably in his short
cloak. A touch of gray had appeared in his beard, which did not
entirely conceal the scar on his chin, received, it was rumored, in a
brawl over a woman in Santiago de Cuba.

"You would have me make an exception in your case, then?"

"Yes, sire."

"This is an exemplary woman? She is of the pipiltin—of rank? Ah,
yes, Gonzalito has told me of her."

"She is baptized," he said. "She is very clever and is useful to Fray
Rufino in his researches into the ways of the Aztecs." He stopped as
Cortés' attention turned to the secretary, who had come up with a
document.

The secretary put down the paper and Cortés read it with an
expression of dismay. Then he dipped his quill into the inkpot and
signed with a flourish. He pushed the bowl of nutmeats toward
Andrés.

"Listen to me, my friend and good Turk," Cortés said when the
secretary had gone. "We have destroyed an empire here, you and I and
our brave comrades. We will build another on its ruins as this new City
of Mexico is building on the ruins of Tenochtitlán, for the glory of the
Holy Church and the hacienda royal. And of what men is this new
nation to be peopled? By the half-breed get of Castilian hidalgos and
native women? I do not believe you will argue with me, Andrés,
when I say this must not be."

The governor gazed at him severely. He thought of Doña Marina,
who had given birth to the governor's half-breed get, also named
Martín, and of the other concubines of Cortés, Indian women of
rank, in their various stages of pregnancy. He gazed steadily back at
Hernán Cortés.

"I have written His Majesty in this matter of the people of New
Spain," the other continued, lounging back in his chair. "I told him
that just now we should have no lawyers, and no scholars either, with
their books and their quibblings. No grand physicians, but simple sur-
geons. And no high prelates of the church, with their arrogance. Yes,
with their many faults that would deter the conversion of the indigenes! Only humble friars, holy men of good life and example. And I

have asked that he send me good Christian women, Catholic by descent rather than conversion. Women of clean blood—no Moorish or Jewish blood! These will be proper mates for my loyal and honorable soldiers, who deserve nothing less! These good women will be arriving in Villa Rica soon!"

There was a beating as of heavy wings in his head. It was as though Cortés, that cleverest of men, knew very well of the vow his father had extracted from him in the Plaza del Triunfo in Seville.

He said, "I ask this, sire, in order that I may be a loyal and honorable man."

With a nose-wrinkle of displeasure, Cortés popped nutmeats into his mouth, chewed, and pondered, his head cocked to one side. He leaned forward. "I tell you in confidence of other correspondence I have had with His Majesty. On the subject of encomiendas. As we all know, these have been forbidden due to the excesses of the encomenderos of the Antilles against the indigenes who are their care and responsibility."

"I know of those excesses, sire," he said.

"It has been decreed that there will be no more land and no more indigenes given in encomienda. I have informed His Majesty that this will work great hardships in New Spain. My soldiers cannot sustain themselves without such means of livelihood. Without their loyal— yes, their loyal and honorable!—assistance, New Spain cannot be defended against rebellious forces. You understand, my Turk, I seek to serve His Majesty and the Holy Church, but also the comrades who have fought so bravely at my side! I believe that my advice will prevail. Then all of my soldiers will become the possessors of building plots within the City of Mexico, and of encomiendas as well!"

Cortés leaned toward him confidentially, and, with a wink, said behind his hand, "And then I hope that those of you of the itchy hands will cease this scribbling of insults and bad poems on my walls!"

He felt a kind of weakening, as though he was soaking in some warm fluid that sapped his muscles and his will.

"Think of the future, man!" the governor continued. "Already one may say that all those of my army, commonality and hidalgos alike, have been endonned by their great service. In the fullness of time will come the coats of arms for their descendants to glory in, as I have promised. With these lands granted in encomienda these men will become the gentry of New Spain, progenitors of fine sons who will continue their line. With their clean blood, descended from conquerors and good Castilian wives. Andrés, those of soiled blood will curse their progenitors for the indulgence that has doomed them!"

Cortés gazed at him steadily. "Surely there is a pretty maiden in Béjar who awaits a conqueror?"

He shook his head. There was a count's daughter in Seville whom he had almost forgotten, and who had surely forgotten him.

"When these good women have married my soldiers," Cortés went on, "and others have, as I have said, indulged themselves to the sorrow of their heirs, there will come rankings and distinctions. For that is human nature, which you and I as serious men know well. Those who have married proper Castilian women will be favored over these others. As will be those proper wives and the children of those unions. It cannot be otherwise! Why, man, an hidalgo, with his responsibilities to his fathers and his sons, cannot in good conscience limit himself—" he held up a hand—"I do not say degrade himself!—limit himself in such a way!

"You may think me extraordinarily vehement in this matter," Cortés said, with a laugh. "It is a personal one for me. I have just received intelligence that my own wife has arrived in Villa Rica without invitation or prior announcement, and at this moment approaches Coyoacán! And so, my friend, my thoughts have turned much to the necessities for suitable instead of convenient marriages!"

He had nothing to reply, for he had lost his case.

"I believe my enemy Diego Velásquez has arranged this embarrassment. Well, so be it!" Cortés spread his hands, smiling. Then he leaned forward confidentially again. "I will tell you what else jealous men contrive. Francisco de Garay, the governor of Jamaica, has sent a force of settlers to the Panuco. The indigenes there, the Huastecos, are very fierce, and there has been much loss of life. But Garay will try again. And so, my Turk, we must don arms and armor once more and proceed to the pacification of Panuco. For the lands to the northeast belong within the boundaries of New Spain. Do you not agree?"

How could he not agree, even though it was not the point? One of the scribblings on the Wall of Cortés had been that the general's ambitions were only exceeded by those of the Archangel Lucifer.

"We will depart very soon, Gonzalito, Pedrito, and I!" said Hernán Cortés. "And you will accompany us as my chief of crossbowmen. What do you say to that, Andrés?"

So it was that he put off the matter of marriage to an indigene and accompanied Cortés with three hundred Spanish infantry, one hundred and fifty cavalry, and forty thousand Tlaxcalans, Texcocans, and Otomís, to Panuco, where the Huastecan hordes were defeated, and the territorial ambitions of Francisco de Garay as well.

The Spaniards were horrified to find in the temples of the Huastecos the tanned hides and recognizable bearded features of many fellow Christians of Garay's ill-fated settlers. And so, at San Esteban del Puerto, Sandoval, whom Cortés had left in charge of the army, questioned the captive Huastecos as to who had killed Spaniards. They responded truthfully, and for their honesty forty were bound to stakes and burned in the presence of their fellows and of the Spaniards.

Andrés stood on the grassy riverbank watching the doomed chieftains, who were not even to be garroted before they burned, writhing and twisting on the stakes as they tried to lift their legs away from the flames. Their screams rose in a throbbing chorus. As the flames whirled upward around their painted, brown bodies their breechclouts flared, and their hair, and the sweet stench of burning flesh drifted across the field to the ranks of the Spaniards.

Chapter Five

He was unable to call her Juana, for the name by which she had been baptized did not suit her. She called him by various names: "my lord," formally; semiseriously, "Donandrés"; and affectionately, "my tuele." She had become proficient in Castilian in her conversations with Rufino over drawings she had made for the priest's researches, her Castilian more expressive than Rufino's Nahuatl, which remained halting, even though they had worked together almost every day when Andrés was gone on the Panuco expedition.

In the darkness of their bed she spoke to her tuele lord in the mixed tongues by which they had always communicated.

"When does the Castiliana come, please, Donandrés?"

He said he did not know. "Two weeks. A month."

"Please tell me what she looks like. She has yellow hair?"

He did not know that either. "I have not seen her since she was a child—not much more than a child. She is a friend of my sister, who is younger than I."

"She will have how many years, please?"

He calculated. "I believe nineteen."

Timultzin herself was seventeen. She had drawn it for him once in connection with an ambitious series she had done for Rufino, depicting the stages of an Aztec girl's maturing. One scene had shown a man and woman in bed together, covered by a sheet and modestly separated from one another. "Timultzin," she had said, pointing to the girl. "The husband of Timultzin," she had said, pointing to the man. "My tuele!" she had said, giggling suddenly. The age of the girl was computed by large dots placed in the upper righthand corner of the drawing, two parallel rows of eight dots each. A further scene, which depicted a newborn child being washed by the midwife, showed an additional dot.

He had not even tried to explain to her the reasons that had caused him to send for Caterina de Duero, his sister's friend, upon his return from Panuco. He did not think she even felt the need of an explanation, merely accpeting whatever were the decisions of her lord, whether he was tuele or Indian.

"The Castiliana is more pretty than Timultzin?" she asked.

"No." She was pleased when he told her she herself was very pretty.

She palped his ankles with her toes, a sign of affection that he found very titillating. He stroked her breast, plump with milk, and felt the warm flow from the nipple. She moved his hand away.

"Castilianas are more pretty than Nahua girls."

"Not than this pretty Nahua girl." He kissed her cheek, and she giggled and scrubbed at the place. Her toes stroked his ankle, her fingers softly explored his arousal.

"You like your Timultzin?"

"Because you smell good," he said, pressing his nose to her neck. He licked the sweet milk from her nipple. "Even when you smell of milk."

It was her pleasure then that he mollify her by explaining that the smell of milk was not a bad smell. She asked if Castilian girls did not smell good.

"Not as good as Nahua girls."

"I will pray for my tuele that his Castiliana has yellow hair and smells good," she said, embracing him with her legs as he rolled to her. "Donandrés showed his captain his sword for Timultzin," she whispered; and later, "My tuele."

One day when he was playing with the child, tossing the warm, solid little body up, not quite releasing him and catching him again with a grunt, Martín laughing delightedly, he saw the long white scratch on the child's arm. The sight made his flesh crawl—the veteran of the Night of Sorrows, of Otumba, the Siege of Tenochtitlán, and of the horrors of Panuco. Anger beat in his head for the careless cruelty of these people he would never understand. This must have been some punishment of the serving woman, Obolte.

He showed the scratch to Timultzin. "Obolte has done this?" he demanded.

She shook her head silently.

"*You?*" He slapped her so hard she staggered. She knelt before him with her head bowed. "*Why?*" he demanded.

She explained that this was commonly done when a baby cried, so that he would become brave to pain and so the crying would not trouble his father. He had seen it depicted in one of her drawings, the crying child pricked with a maguey thorn.

"The scratch disturbs me more, do you understand? This is not the way of Castile!" He was nauseated with remorse that he had struck her, sick also at his hypocrisy, who had watched the burning of the Huasteco chiefs. He stroked her bowed sleek head and covered the child with his cotton mantle. He handed Martín to her.

"You must not do this. It is unnecessary for my sake."

She held the child against her breast, gazing up at him with a mask of a face. "We believe that the crying of children annoys warriors, my lord."

"No," he said. "No. No. No, pretty one." He stroked her cheek and she caught his hand and held it there.

Forty-two soldiers married their imported brides in the courtyard of the half-finished palace of Hernán Cortés. Fray Bartolomé performed the ceremony, with the general and the captains Gonzalo de Sandoval and Pedro de Alvarado as witnesses. The married couples were presented with houses in the Spanish sector of the City of Mexico. Most of them already possessed land in the Valley of Anahuac, and indigenes to work it.

Andrés Dorantes possessed a repartimiento in a place called Xicomilpa, planted in maize, beans, and long gray rows of maguey, and his Indians had already begun building a house there. He kept an indigene concubine and a son in a house in Coyoacán, an hour's walk from the plaza mayor. Now he possessed, in addition, a Castilian wife and an ugly little house in the city.

Caterina de Duero was a meager, terrified little thing, painfully thin. Her hair was not yellow but colorless, her eyes almost colorless also, and her mouth pinched and apprehensive of everything she encountered in New Spain. She smelled of perfume mingled with unwashed flesh as, dutifully, he relieved her of her virginity in an ugly, bloody little ceremony. She spent the rest of the night in tears and prayer. The next day he returned in relief to Coyoacán.

Along with Doña Caterina he inherited her kinsman, Nicolás de Cuéllar, a young dandy a year or two older than Andrés, a partisan of Diego Velásquez in the governor of Cuba's old quarrel with Cortés.

His double life functioned smoothly enough. He spent little time with his wife, most of his days in Coyoacán with Timultzin and Martín, and often Rufino; he made weekly trips to Xicomilpa to look over the fields and observe the slow progress of the building of the house there. Day by day supervision he left to Miguel, a baptized Indian slavishly solicitous of him and, he knew, a hard taskmaster to the indigenes of the repartimiento.

Although he usually attended Caterina on the Christian feast days,

Timultzin had become very devout in her new faith. She hated or feared Caballo Botello, although the Aztec-hater treated her politely if gruffly; he thought this was because of the old corporal's blasphemies against the Virgin, but it might also have been because she remembered Caballo's syphilitic advance in the garden of the palace in Texcoco. She had little to do with the other Indian concubines, except for Blas's Gualcoyotl, and he sensed a very rigid class structure. Rufino she had loved since even before the incident with Sandoval and her husband, and she was awed and exalted by her responsibilities when she was chosen to take the part of Mary in the mystery play at Coyoacán on the Night of the Three Kings. It was a Christian celebration he did not attend with Caterina.

That night he made love to Timultzin as to a queen, as though in worship of her still. Watching her in her role, beautiful face turned down to the child in her arms, he had loved her so much it had affected his breathing. She did not respond, and although he was irritated, he did not complain, for if the ceremony had been memorable for him, it must have been more so for her. Later he was aware that she was weeping. He wrapped her in his arms and asked her what was the matter.

"Your God does not speak to me," she whispered. "Does he know of me? Does he look for me? Will he find me?"

She wept at her lack, and he tried to comfort her but did not know the words.

He disliked the house on Salamanca Street in the City of Mexico, in which Doña Caterina was installed with a majordomo and six servants to attend her needs. Like all the houses in the Spanish quarter it resembled a fortress, with its solid front and small windows, and only the noon sun penetrated the patio. Caterina seemed always to be surrounded by a group of Castilians, friends of Nico's from the Antilles. It was a society in which Andrés felt clumsy and provincial. They dressed in the latest fashions and adopted the latest attitudes, one of which was contempt for Hernán Cortés and the Conquest. They ridiculed the exploits of the conquerors, and he knew that behind his back they ridiculed him. Caterina was distressed by arguments and contention, and in his sympathy for her he did not debate with these swaggering posturers whose company she enjoyed, but accepted the role of bluff old soldier and blind admirer of Cortés.

On the day he came to inform Caterina that he would accompany Cortés on the expedition to Honduras, she had just returned with Nico and his retinue from the funeral of Julián de Alderete. All were dressed, however, as for a levee, in their finest silks. Rafaelito and the serving women scurried through the rooms bringing wine and cakes on trays. He found himself with Caterina, Nico, Nico's friend Fernando Rodríguez, and a young woman with a cluster of moles on her cheek, Luisa Vásquez.

"So you march with Cortés to Honduras to punish Cristóbal de Olid, Andrés!" Nico said, with the fixed, three-cornered grin that seemed to be reserved for him, speaking in a loud voice as though to one who had been deafened by the roar of artillery. "The conquerors have fallen to contending among themselves."

Olid, with his rough voice and cleft lower lip, once the quartermaster of the army, was the only captain to have been disloyal to Cortés. In Honduras, he had declared himself an independent conqueror. It was said that Cortés, who had never been one to reveal his anger, was insane with fury.

"Ah, well, Nico," he said, "our Olid let his ear be caught by your Diego Velásquez."

Nico, Fernando, and the young woman, who was fresh from Cuba and was coiffed in the latest style and had rouged lips, laughed in a watchful way. Caterina was seated with her hands gripped together in her lap.

"But you must admit, my dear Andrés," Nico said, "that it is a delicious affair. Thus as Hernán Cortés was a traitor to Diego Velásquez, so Cristóbal de Olid has turned traitor to the traitor."

He managed to laugh with them, seated at pretended ease in the master's chair while the men stood straddle-legged before him and Luisa leaned to whisper to Caterina behind her fan.

"It would be well," Fernando said with his lisp, "if when your general meets his captain, Olid did not take breakfast with him."

This innuendo produced more laughter, in which he did not join. Cortés and Francisco de Garay, who had contended for the royal patent to settle the Panuco, had met in the capital to settle their differences. After attending Christmas matins, they had taken breakfast together. Garay had become ill and died a few days later. Cortés' enemies whispered that the breakfast eggs of the governor of Jamaica had been seasoned with something beside herbs.

"A stupid man, Don Francisco," Nico said, self-importantly, "but of fine family who will question this opportune death."

"We will see if the famous luck of Cortés still holds in Honduras," Nico said. He winked at Fernando with a smile of superior knowledge. "We will see what luck he has with these two fellows he leaves to govern in his absence."

He kept his peace. These occasions with Nico's friends made his shoulders ache. He said that if the famous luck still held they would find that the fishermen of Honduras truly weighted their nets with gold nuggets, as was rumored. This caused more merriment.

"Her mother vows that Catalina Juárez was strangled, not poisoned, as everyone believes," Luisa Vásquez said boldly.

It was another rumor against Cortés, that he had murdered his wife, and he held up his hands in token of surrender and said to Caterina, "Señora, these your friends force me to defend my general. I will not argue with them if they wish to hold he is less than virtuous as a man. But they will not argue with me when I claim he is a great general."

His wife smiled in a sickly way. The others gazed at him with an intensity he did not understand. Certainly they who were Caterina's friends knew he lived with a concubine, but such an arrangement was not even remarkable. Was it that he was known to bathe daily, while they all stank of perfumes and stale sweat? Was it simply that he refused to join in their condemnations of Cortés, who seemed to elicit animosity and loyalty in equal portions? He himself had been having bad dreams of this march to Honduras to punish Olid. His son was two, spoke more words every day, and was the pleasure of his life. He had moved this little family from Coyoacán to the newly completed house at Xicomilpa, where his lands were more extensive now, for he had purchased the adjoining property from an old comrade with gambling debts. His days at Xicomilpa were a kind of idyll, plagued only by nagging responsibilities to his wife, for he rode into the capital no more than once a week. He did not want to leave Xicomilpa; he thought he must settle Timultzin and the child in the city in his absence; and he dreaded this march south into country that was part unknown and part known to be very difficult.

"I believe, my good Andrés, that one could argue with you about the qualities of Cortés as a general," Fernando lisped. He regarded Andrés with his head tipped to one side. "For those qualities would seem to have consisted of powerful allies, guile, dishonor, and—"

"You will not speak of such dishonor in my presence, if you please, señor," he said, and must have assumed a threatening expression, for Fernando's cheeks burned as though he had been slapped and Caterina looked stricken. Her lips shaped his name.

Nico said loudly, "What of Pedro de Alvarado in Guatemala, my dear Andrés? Can one be certain that he will remain subordinate? One might suspect that Alvarado likes to govern better than to be governed." He set the triangular smile on his lips again, above his neat, triangular beard.

"Would you care to wager on the loyalty of Pedro de Alvarado, Nico?" he said. "Señor?" he said, turning to Fernando Rodríguez—"or on that of Gonzalo de Sandoval?"

"One would be a fool to wager against the loyalty of Sandoval," Fernando said, bowing. "Or that of Andrés Dorantes."

Caterina clapped her hands together and said, "Please let us speak of matters more interesting to ladies, hidalgos!"

Ignoring her, Luisa Vásquez said, "I have heard it said that the famous luck of Hernán Cortés was simply that he had with him these fine captains. Provided for him by Diego Velásquez. Is it not true, Don Andrés?"

And so, in the end, he fell to quarreling with them.

Later, when they were alone together, he told Caterina he was sorry he had let himself be drawn into contention by Nico and his friends.

"I cannot believe it is a bad thing to be loyal to one's commander," she said. "Even if he is—who he is." She looked frightened, having said too much.

"I am not always so quarrelsome, but it is difficult to remain silent when these hidalgos tell me the Conquest was nothing. I will tell you, Caterina, those jaguar knights and eagle knights in perfect array, advancing toward us in their thousands, were as fearful a sight as a man could see!"

She smiled politely, her face expressing interest. But she was not interested; probably she would not believe his tales, even if she listened to them, for latecomers to New Spain professed to believe that those proud knights had been no more than nursery toys against the steel of Toledo and Spanish infantry armored in breastplates and mail, that their fishbone spearheads and wooden clubs, and shields of wood and reed, were as nothing against protective steel and biting steel, and they were mowed like grain before a scythe by the artillery, and by the cannons of the brigantines. It was claimed that to the Aztecs the silence in which the Spaniards fought was more terrifying than their own constant din of whistling and screeching, that they were unmanned by the Spaniards' dogs of war, for their own dogs were very small and kept for the purposes of eating merely; and most of all they were terrified of the cavaliers, for at first they considered man and horse as all one manmonster. And it was claimed that, in the end, it was not Spanish arms that had defeated the emperor Cuauhtémoc, but the Spanish disease, the smallpox.

As a gift for Timultzin, he brought back from the capital a mirror with a silver back cunningly engraved in small squares with the fourteen Stations of the Cross. She had become somewhat vain of her pretty face and had asked for a mirror of her own. She held it to her breast with flushed cheeks, as she bowed her head in thanks.

He told her that he and Blas had together taken a fine house in

Tlatelolco in the City of Mexico, with a large garden and trees and flowers and many cages of birds, for her and Martín and Blas's concubine and son. He had settled upon Tlatelolco not because it was the Indian quarter, but because it was near the Convent of Santiago Tlatelolco, where Rufino now resided.

"That is very nice, Andrés," she said. She was slim in her embroidered dress, holding up the mirror to glance at her face in it. "But we are very happy here, and I can watch out for matters of the crops and the animals. Who will do that if you are gone to Honduras and I to Tlatelolco?"

He said that Miguel the overseer could be trusted. She disliked the man.

"He is very hard with the Nahua, my lord. It is possible there will be trouble. Some, when it has been too hard with them, have burned the crops."

"I have instructed him that he is not to be so hard." Because it seemed he had been criticized, he said, "He is hard in the way of the pipiltin with their peons, my pretty one."

She bowed her head to the rebuke, holding the mirror to her breast.

"It will be better for you in Tlatelolco where Rufino can look after you and Martín," he said. It was a decision he was to regret all the rest of his life.

His son appeared at the arched gate in the wall, with its cascade of purple bougainvillea, running to him in his white huipil and breeches. Martín jumped into his arms, pressing cheek against cheek.

"Father has come back from the city!"

"But must leave again tomorrow, my son."

"And goes far away?"

"Far away, I'm afraid." He realized again that he was, in fact, afraid; dread like a weight upon his heart; fear as well as reluctance. Timultzin stood with her straight back and proud, sleek head watching him. It seemed to him that she also felt what he did. He did not know how to reassure her, or himself.

"For long times?" Martín demanded, tugging at his face demanding his attention. "For how long, Father?"

"Well, for more than a week. For more than a month." He did not say, "I'm afraid," again.

"Oh, but that is too long!"

He laughed. "When I come back you will be a big boy."

"But I am a big boy now. Oh, I will miss you, Father!"

"And your pretty mother?"

"Very much, Donandrés," she said softly.

154

He indicated the mirror. "When you look at your face you are to think of Donandrés."

"I will think of you whether I look in this mirror or not, my lord," she said.

He put his free arm around her waist as they walked toward the flowered arch. He could not rid himself of the chill of dread. It seemed to him that the happiest time of his life was ending, and much more than that as well.

Chapter Six

On a warm October morning the army departed from the capital to punish the traitor Olid, to preempt Honduras from Pedro Arias de Ávila who was pushing north from Panama, and to investigate tales of fishermen who weighted their nets with gold nuggets. Cortés rode in the lead in his burnished breastplate, gold chain, and black feathered cap. With him were the captains Gonzalo de Sandoval and Juan de Jaramillo, and Doña Marina, her dark face and plain clothing contrasting with the fair skin and bright silks of the ladies who floated in barges alongside the causeway, fluttering their scarves and calling out farewells. Among them was Caterina, to whom Andrés waved his cap.

Also with the advance party were Cortés' master-of-the-household, butler, chamberlain, chaplain, doctor and surgeon, pages, grooms, musicians, and master-of-the-hounds with his pack of greyhounds. On their white horses, cloaks drawn around them, with feather crowns above their proud, dark faces, were the emperor Cuauhtémoc, his cousin the lord of Tacuba, and two other Aztec princes, whom Cortés did not dare leave behind for fear a rebellion would be launched in his absence.

The Spanish cavalry was a hundred and thirty strong. In the second rank Andrés rode between Blas and Bernal Díaz. Sumptuous new banners were carried that seemed to him cheap and gaudy compared to those precious, tattered ensigns of the Conquest.

Behind the cavalry marched the infantry, armed and armored, vizers raised on sweating, bearded faces, metallic clatter of their tread. Drumbeats echoed unevenly across the gray water. After the infantry came three thousand Indian allies in quilted armor, the captains wearing helmets and carrying swords, each division with its own proud banner, the flying crane of the Tlaxcalans, the mysterious red figure of the Cholulans; following them an enormous mass of native bearers, loads suspended from tumplines, last of all a herd of squealing pigs.

So they passed off the causeway onto the mainland, leaving behind the barges filled with admiring ladies, and the canoes of fishermen and birdcatchers who had paddled close to watch this grand departure.

Watching Cortés riding with Doña Marina, the captain-general and his linguist-mistress, the two Malintzins, he ached at this departure from Timultzin, left behind in Tlatelolco with Martín. Doña Marina was no longer the conqueror's bedmate, and her own Martín had also been left behind. It was rumored that Cortés had murdered his Castilian wife because she had complained of his newest favorite, one of the daughters of Montezuma.

In the hot, low province of Tehuantepec, the native land of Doña Marina, Cortés granted a vast encomienda to Juan de Jaramillo and married his former mistress to that captain.

"He would not have won Mexico without her," Bernal Díaz said. "And now he throws her off like an old shirt."

"Bad luck!" another veteran said. "Mark my words, we will all suffer for it!"

And soon enough the expedition that had set out so bravely began to fall into disarray. They plunged into swamps and tropical forests. The heat was terrible, the insects a torture. Dorantes' face was always swollen. Invisible insects burrowed beneath his toenails to lay their eggs, which had to be cleaned out with a knife tip. They mounted into chilly highlands, where they fought Chamulans. Indians deserted. There were violent rivers to cross, and men and horses were swept away in floods. Trees had to be cut down and bridges built—in one thirty-league stretch fifty of them. Arrows flew out of the jungle and Spaniards died. A pitched battle was fought, with the enemy fading into the jungle as the cavalry managed to charge through the thick underbrush. More arrows flew as the army buried its dead. The men's feet rotted from the constant damp; Dorantes' stunk so that he could not look at them without his mouth straining in distaste.

Beyond the hot lands they encountered chain after chain of mountains. In one pass in the Sierra de Pedernales seventy of the horses lost their footing and plunged to their death. There were brief, terrible encounters with invisible enemies. Moreover, the news from New Spain was alarming. The weaklings Cortés had left as acting governors had been deposed by his enemies, who now ruled in the capital. Cortés became morose and silent, and it was observed that Sandoval had assumed command of the army.

In a place called Izanzanac an informer among the Aztecs advised Cortés that Cuauhtémoc and the lord of Tacuba were plotting to murder him and return to Mexico to lead a great rebellion. They were sentenced to death.

"They say Cortés showed them a mariner's compass, which they had never seen before," Blas said. "He told them the needle never failed to point out the guilty one."

He laughed. Dorantes did not laugh, boot off as he picked beneath his toenails with the tip of his dagger. The flesh of his feet looked as though it was falling away from the bone.

"It is bad luck," Bernal Díaz said gloomily. "Once there was only good luck."

"It seems the compass points to guilty ones but not to the way out of these endless forests," Dorantes said.

The tattered, limping army stood in ranks to watch the execution. Cuauhtémoc faced Cortés with his filthy cloak drawn around his body. He had lost his feathered crown at the river crossing where the army's banners had also been lost. He spoke in Nahuatl.

"Malintzin! Now I find in what your false words and promises have ended—my death. Better that I had fallen by my own hand than trusted in your power in my City of Mexico. Why do you thus unjustly take my life? May God demand of you this innocent blood!"

Cortés signaled to the constable, who passed behind the emperor and tossed the end of his cord around the brown neck. He braced his knee against Cuauhtémoc's back as he jerked the garrote tight. The prince of Tacuba was similarly executed. Their bodies were suspended in a ceiba tree, in their tattered finery, with the pathetic bent necks of the hanged.

Afterwards Cortés walked among his soldiers pretending camaraderie, with a word for each man, but many had been shocked by this callous act and responded stiffly.

"Do you turn against me also, my Turk?" Cortés said to him.

"No, sire. But this is an evil day."

"For those who conspire against me!" Cortés said, and turned on his heel. From then on he was little with his soldiers and much alone, and his orders, through Sandoval, were more and more petty and unjust.

They were quartered in a ruined temple, a series of platforms in the jungle overgrown with vines and tree roots. Andrés was wakeful, feverish, as were all the soldiers, and sour in his mind. The moon was fractured by the branches of the ceiba tree beneath which he lay. Earlier the three dogs had taken turns barking at the moon or the rustle of the snake with angry soldiers shouting at them for silence. Now the silence was intense.

He heard a whisper: *"Help me!"*

He located the voice at the foot of the stone platform, where a man had evidently fallen. As he made his way down through the tough brush, a greyhound barked and there was a shout from the watch. *"Here!"* the man said.

It was Cortés, whispering, "Who is it?" He identified himself and half-dragged, half-carried the general out of the undergrowth, cursing and cursed when he tripped and fell. Cortés groaned continually, and in the moonlight his face gleamed pale as marble. His teeth were clenched in his beard, and one arm was gripped against his chest.

He eased his burden onto the lichened stone of the lower terrace. The barking had subsided. Cortés wore a soiled nightshirt and his bare legs and feet were hatched with bloody scratches. Andrés said he would fetch the physician.

"No!" Cortés groaned.

"But you are hurt, sire!"

Cortés was panting and shaking his head. The moon dodged among the branches above them. On the temple platform where the soldiers slept there was silence. "No one must know I am hurt!" Cortés whispered. "It is not possible that Cortés is hurt in such a stupid manner!" He managed a laugh that was half a groan. "You will never speak of it, do you understand, my good Turk?"

He asked what had happened.

A dog roused himself to another fit of barking. A soldier cursed. The rough stones made Andrés' knees ache. Groaning, Cortés moved his arm to straighten it out at his side.

"I could not sleep," he said. "I walked out here, where God knows what pagan horrors have taken place. Just then the moon vanished, and I fell." He halted, panting. "Pushed by a witch!" he whispered. "Malintsin!" he said, suddenly loudly, as though calling to Doña Marina. Andrés laid a hand on his shoulder, at which Cortés grimaced with pain again. "My God, why hast thou forsaken me!" Cortés said.

Then he said lucidly, "No one must know I have fallen. No one must know I am hurt." The moonlight blanched his face again. "Help me, Andrés."

He assisted the general to his feet, up the steps to the higher terrace, and into his chamber in the temple. Hung on the wall above the cot was a golden crucifix, which sparkled in the light when Andrés lit a candle. The general sank down on his bed with a groan and turned his face into the pillow.

"No one must know," he said in a muffled voice.

"Shall I blow out this candle, sire?"

"Leave it burning, my son. How one's sins crawl out of the corners in the dark!"

So it was that he became Cortés' confidante, along with Gonzalo de Sandoval. He protected Cortés' secret, as he had sworn to do. Whether the conqueror fell from grace because of the discarding of Doña Marina, the murder of the Aztec princes, or simply because heaven was no longer interested in Cortés, he could not know. But from that time Cortés' appearance changed. He, who had been slim and muscular in his black silk doublets, became swollen-bellied and shrunken-limbed. He walked stiffly with the effort not to limp and with his damaged arm clamped to his body. One of his eyes drooped, giving him a cynical and bitter expression. He was quick to anger, which often turned on the faithful Sandoval, who, however, never complained.

After more than a year the remnant of an army arrived at the little settlement of Triunfo de la Cruz, which Cristóbal de Olid had founded, to discover that the traitor was long dead, executed by loyal officers. A year of suffering had been for nothing, and Mexico traded for a flea-bitten mud village.

The news from the capital was that Cortés and his army had been officially declared dead. Gonzalo de Salazar, who had seized power, had expropriated the property of those declared dead, had executed Cortés' cousin and majordomo, Rodrigo de Paz, and arrested his chief justice, Alonso de Zuaso.

Worst of all, Cortés seemed to lack the will to return and set matters right. He lingered in Triunfo de la Cruz. Daily he rode his black stallion along the hard sand of the beach at a pounding gallop, clad in a dark robe like that of a Franciscan monk, in which, Sandoval had confided to Andrés, the general wished to be buried. He had also had a coffin constructed, which he kept in his quarters. In the evenings, with the two of them, he overindulged in wine, pounding a fist on the table as he recounted old triumphs, but also dwelling long upon wrongs he had suffered.

"He is certain that he is soon to die," Sandoval said to Dorantes after one of these unhappy evenings. "He believes that he has thrown away all that he has achieved in this stupidity."

From his window Andrés watched Cortés on El Arriero, galloping down the beach toward the cluster of gleaming black rocks far along. Very small there, he lingered for a time, finally returning with his black monk's habit bellying behind him. Gray and white seabirds flapped into flight before him and circled his passage. From this distance he might have been the Cortés of old.

Out to sea, past the low white lines of surf, congealing out of the mist, were the sails of a plump brigantine, a red and white pennon fluttering from the masthead.

The captain came ashore, to kiss Cortés' hands and present letters from his loyal friends in Mexico begging him to return.

That night, at dinner with the captain, Sandoval, and Andrés, Cortés still ignored the subject of Mexico, speaking as though his only decision was whether or not to build a capital of Honduras further inland and on higher ground, where the climate was more healthful. But finally, after much wine, he announced that he would tell the three of them a tale that would amuse them.

"There was a Moor who found the Gran Nopal," Cortés said, leaning on his elbows with his beard brushing his wine cup, "this mountain of jewels that gleamed so bright a man could look at it only from the west in the morning and the east in the afternoon. And one day this Moor saw a rabbit—a hare!—steal one of the smallest of his precious stones from the very edge of the mountain of them. Taking it in his teeth, you understand, and running off with it. In a great rage the Moor set out after the tiny beast, running for league after league, through jungles, over mountains. Until at last he found the hare fallen dead of exhaustion and reclaimed the stolen jewel. But he was never able to find the Gran Nopal again. Tell me, Gonzalito, is that not a fine story?"

"Very sad, sire."

"Andrés?"

"Sad, sire."

"And do you also agree that this is a sad story, Don Diego?" Cortés said to the captain, who cleared his throat to say that he did.

"By the Moor I meant only a fool, you understand, my sons," Cortés said, swinging his head to glance cunningly-drunkenly from one to the other of them. "Only a prideful fool who thought he could do no wrong."

"And he was only a Moor, after all," Sandoval said, close-set eyes peering down his nose at his general. "Had he been a good Castilian he would have been able to see the grand glitter of that mountain. And know it was his again as soon as he returned to it."

Cortés chuckled and nodded. He nodded for a long time. "Tell me, my son," he said to Sandoval, "if your general asked you to hold his sword like a good Roman soldier while he fell on it, would you do it?"

"No, sire," Sandoval said. "But I would fall upon my own if he ordered it."

Cortés continued to nod. His bloodshot eyes swung to Andrés. "And my good Turk?"

"No, sire," he answered. "But I beg you to return to Mexico, which many good men pray that you will do."

The general only smiled stiffly, and shrugged and refilled his cup, and presently dismissed them. Wakeful, Andrés saw that Cortés' candle burned most of the night, and the next morning he was summoned to the general's presence.

Today Cortés was not dressed in his monk's habit, but in his breast-plate and golden chain, and his drooping eyelid and cynical expression were not so evident. Before him were five documents, rolled, tied with ribbon, and sealed with red wax.

"My son, I have a mission to request of you."

"Yes, sire."

"You will return to New Spain on this ship the *Perla de las Antilles*. Don Diego will put you ashore at a place north of Villa Rica. You will make your way to the capital, with great care and under a false name so you will not be apprehended by the constables of my enemy Gonzalo de Salazar. You will deliver these letters to the loyal men to whom they are addressed, at the monastery of San Francisco where I am told some of them have taken refuge."

He asked if he was to bring back replies.

"There will be no replies. They are told to hold themselves in readiness for my return, which will be soon. You will proceed as swiftly as an arrow, my son, and I pray God that you will not fail me."

"I will not fail, sire."

The next morning there was a parade, Cortés, with Sandoval at his side, riding along the ranks of the soldiers; and afterwards a mass. With the tide the *Perla de las Antilles*, with Andrés Dorantes aboard, set sail for Mexico.

He was put ashore in a cove north of Villa Rica de Veracruz, and from there made his way to Jalapa, on the great highway to the capital. In Jalapa he bought a mule, and, in workman's clothing and under the name of Juan de Flechilla, the arrow of Cortés set out for the City of Mexico with the letters that were his mission in a leather pouch tied around his waist inside his blouse. He was often frightened, for the constables of Salazar, in pairs, were to be seen in every town along the route.

Chapter Seven

The light was failing as he led the mule through the cobbled streets of Tlatelolco. The quarter seemed strangely deserted. Few lights showed, and there was a pervasive stench that caught at his memory and brought on an oppression that must be only from exhaustion. At first he thought he had mistaken the street, for he could not find the house he and Blas had taken for their women and children. Then he found it, blue glazed tiles set into a cross on the wall beside the gate. The house appeared deserted, dark, the patio bristling with potted plants, shadowy reflection of the branches of the jacaranda tree in the little pool. He called out, and thought he heard a reply within.

Just then it came to him that this stench that stirred his memory was that of Tlatelolco on the day of victory, as though it had lingered all the years between. He pushed the door open. A tiny Indian woman met him there, her face shrouded by a shawl against the night air.

"Doña Juana!" he said, more loudly than he had intended. The woman stared at him uncomprehendingly. "Timultzin!" he said.

She led him through dark rooms filled with the inanimate shapes of furnishings. A barely discernible figure lay in a bed with a high carved head and foot. There was an abrasive whisper of flint, a sudden stir in the bed, a murmur in Nahuatl.

The candle flame caught and swelled. He gasped, his legs bearing him two steps back from the bed. In the instant before the flame was extinguished the face on the pillow showed, a swamp of smallpox pustules, unrecognizable except for half-open black eyes. Matted hair was spread on the pillow. Then the darkness shut it out.

He stood panting, willing himself to approach the bed. His legs would not carry him there, where his Nahua beauty was dying of the Spanish disease.

"Where is Martín?" a voice said loudly. He was not even aware of having spoken.

There was no sound from the bed. He swung toward the darker bulk of the serving woman, with her face shrouded not against the night air but the stench of death in Tlatelolco. He said, in Nahuatl, "Where is the boy?"

"Gone with the others, lord."

"Is he sick?"

"Not sick, lord. But all who have remained in this barrio are dead of the Spanish disease. All."

The leather pouch swung against his belly inside his blouse as he took another step back away from the bed. His mind seemed to tilt, slip, slide toward blackness; catch itself. "Holy Mother!" he whispered.

Did he hear it, or did the words only form themselves out of madness, the whisper: "Your Christian God has found me at last, my tuele." He fled the house of death.

In the Spanish quarter the windows were alight. There were men in wineshops and men afoot, a horseman, many soldiers. With a clatter of hoofs the watch passed him, cloaks slung over shoulders, glitter of light catching helmets and breastplates. He kept to the shadows, leading the mule. The house in Salamanca Street was lighted also. He let himself in the gate. Candles burned in the sala, and he could see Caterina seated in a chair that was too large for her. The pale oval of her face was pointed toward him, as though she had been waiting for him, whom he had last seen more than a year ago fluttering a scarf at him from a barge floating beside the causeway.

Still he waited, trying to control his breathing, which, from time to time, broke loose raggedly. As she turned her head to speak to someone within the room invisible to him, he saw that she was great with child in her brocaded dress as heavy as body armor.

He stepped inside. Nico was with her, staring at him with his mouth gaping open above the neat tricorn beard. He wore green velvet with yellow hose, a poniard slung from his belt, his hand on the hilt. Caterina whispered, "Andrés!" Nico cursed.

On spread legs he was not certain would support him he stood confronting his pregnant wife and her kinsman.

"But they said you were dead!" Caterina began to weep noisily. "You and all of them!"

"Not dead," he said.

"But they said—"

"Listen, my friend," Nico said in a shrill voice. "You are declared dead, understand? This house is now my house, for the properties of Hernán Cortés and all of his army have been confiscated. This is my house! And this is my wife! Do you understand?"

He did not understand.

Nico halted for breath, then continued, almost shouting. "And you, Andrés Dorantes, are under arrest by the order of Gonzalo de Salazar, who is governor of New Spain and chief justice also!"

When Nico drew his poniard Andrés flung himself upon Caterina's kinsman, smashing his knee into Nico's groin and seizing the naked steel with his right hand. Nico squealed with pain as they fell together, Caterina screaming. "*No! No! No!*" He wrested the poniard free, feeling the clean bite of the steel in his hand, and, reversing the blade, jammed it with all his strength into the green tunic of the man who had scorned the victories of the conquerors, whose contempt he had accepted for the sake of his wife. Nico squealed again as the Toledo steel pierced him.

Andrés scrambled to his feet and braced his foot on Nico's shoulder as he wrenched the blade free. A gout of blood gushed over the tricorn beard. Nico seemed to be chewing on the blood as he tried to speak. His slippered feet kicked out as though against some confinement. He died.

Andrés bent to wipe the blade clean on the green velvet, and straightened to point it silently at the dark face of Rafaelito, the majordomo, gaping at him from the far doorway. The face vanished. He turned the blade toward Caterina.

"Castilian whore!"

She leaned stiffly backward away from him, stiff hand clapped to her mouth, eyes fixed on his. She stammered, "They told us all were dead! They confiscated the property because you were dead. All the wives were told they must marry other men. So Nico— So—"

"How long has this been?"

"Months, Andrés! Many months!"

He pointed the tip of the blade at her belly. "This is many months also." Her pale eyes with their pale lashes stared into his with horror. Her hand strained to her mouth, her body strained back from the poniard. "Seek your peace with God," he said.

"*No!*"

But his rage had leaked away, as though in the scalding tears that wet his cheeks. He could not even see his pregnant wife through the tears and the vision of the destroyed beautiful face of Timultzin, like the magic city of Tenochtitlán destroyed for this gray city of ugly fortress-houses. His nostrils still breathed the stink of death. Whose fault? Whose fault? He felt the bulk of the leather pouch against his belly. He turned away from his wife. His cut hand dripped blood onto the tiles and he wrapped it in his handkerchief.

He kicked the body of Nicolás de Cuéllar before he left the house, concealing the poniard in his sleeve. Leading the mule, he went on through the night toward the monastery of San Francisco and the loyal friends of Hernán Cortés.

He braced his chin on his two hands as though without support his head would fall to the plank table from exhaustion, from grief, from remorse, from the bitter dregs of rage, as he sat with the five men who had taken sanctuary here. By candlelight their faces were pale, with black pits of eyes. Francisco de Tápia poured wine into his goblet. Andrés rewound the handkerchief around his bloody hand.

"The general names his kinsman, Francisco de las Casas, and my brother as acting governors," Jorge de Alvarado said, tapping the rolled parchment on the table top. He was a smaller, younger version of Pedro with a short-cut reddish beard and his brother's heavy jaw.

"Unfortunately Pedrito has remained in Guatemala and Francisco is in chains, bound for Spain," Alvarado said. "This pig Salazar would have executed Francisco, but for our efforts!

"The second choices are Rodrigo de Albornoz and Alonso de Estrada. Second choices indeed! Still, they are loyal to the true governor." Alvarado looked from face to face, grinning grimly. "So, friends, with this letter of authority we will pen the pig. There may be a good fight!"

"Salazar has made his house a fortress, they say," Tápia said. "He keeps a garrison inside!"

"I tell you, hidalgos," the younger Alvarado said, leaning forward, "his soldiers will drop away like leaves in autumn, while on our side all are sworn to the cause of Cortés!"

Andrés gazed from face to determined face, and it came to him that not only was he delivered of his duty, but he was finally done with the cause of Hernán Cortés. And he was done with New Spain also, after this night of nightmare. Tápia was speaking to him:

"Tell us, how fares Cortés in Honduras?"

"Not well," he said. "Better," he said. "He had been ill. He is still frail, and has been discouraged, but your letters have encouraged him to return." His voice echoed hollowly in the hollow of his skull.

"When we have dispatched this pig we will welcome Cortés back to the city with great festivities. Fifteen months!"

"Fifteen months," he said, nodding stupidly.

Wine was poured. The mood was grim, but optimistic. Was Hernán

Cortés frail, ill, and discouraged, still capable of imbuing these men with loyalty and optimism from four hundred leagues away? Why had he let himself be recruited to that doomed expedition? Every fiber of himself had been reluctant to go; yet he had faithfully gone. Why had he insisted that Timultzin and the child move from Xicomilpa, where they did very well, to Tlatelolco, where the Spanish disease awaited them? Why, even, had he killed poor Nicolás de Cuéllar, who, perhaps, had not deserved death for his silly bravado? Because Nico would have interfered with his delivering his messages, he thought, nodding as though to excuse himself, whom nothing could excuse. His last duty to his general. He wiped the back of his hand across his eyes, where the tears continued to flow at intervals.

He said, "I am sorry I cannot join your efforts on behalf of the governor. I have killed a man tonight, and must be gone from here tomorrow."

All stared at him, Jorge de Alvarado with the wine jug half-raised.

"One who claimed that he had married my wife, who had been declared a widow by Salazar," he continued. "Can this be true?"

One of them cleared his throat. Jorge was nodding. "Yes, it is true. All of you were declared to have died in a great battle on the route to Honduras."

"Many died, it is true," he said tiredly.

"All were declared dead, and such marriages ordered," Jorge said. "Juana de Mansilla was whipped through the streets because she declared her husband still lived and would not take another."

"Alonso Valiente lives," he said, nodding, "and is with the general in Triunfo de la Cruz."

"When Francisco de las Casas returned from Honduras to say that Cortés still lived, Salazar threw him into prison, and, as I say, would have executed him to still his mouth."

"Then I have acted hastily," he said.

"But this man you have killed was Nicolás de Cuéllar?"

When he nodded there was laughter, and a wine bottle was banged on the table. "But that was a blow well struck!" someone said.

"Cuéllar was a great friend to the pig," Jorge said, grinning.

"Still," his brother said, "it would be well if Andrés continues his disguise as Juan de Flechilla and leaves the capital tomorrow. If the constables are seeking him and our plan is delayed, he will be in danger here."

"I believe that is best," Jorge said, nodding.

He nodded silently also, head lowered; his eyes were leaking again. When next there was a lull in the excited talk of the foray against Salazar, he observed that smallpox had broken out in the city.

"It is a fearful thing!" Tápia said. "In Tlatelolco the indigenes die and die, and continue to die!"

"The stink of the dead is terrible," Jorge de Alvarado said, and all agreed with him that the stench of Tlatelolco was past bearing.

And so as Juan de Flechilla he made his way back to the coast and took ship for Santiago de Cuba. By the time he reached Havana the news had preceded him that the partisans of Cortés had captured Gonzalo de Salazar and imprisoned him in a cage of logs pending his shipment in chains to Spain. As time passed he came to realize that Doña Caterina had never accused him, Andrés Dorantes, of having murdered her new husband; and presently came the news that the Castiliana was dead in childbirth and the child of Nicolás de Cuéllar stillborn.

He purchased from a planter a Moor named Esteban, fulfilling an old resolution. He was recruited as a captain of infantry by his old commander, tall, gruff, one-eyed Pánfilo de Narváez, who appeared to hold no grudge against those who had deserted his cause for that of Cortés after the defeat at Cempoala. Soldiers and settlers were needed for the conquest and settlement of Florida, of which Narvaéz had been appointed governor. Among them were Álvar Núñez Cabeza de Vaca, the King's Treasurer, a thin, severe, uncompanionable man, and Alonso del Castillo, another captain, cheerful and well-liked by everyone.

It seemed to him that in some vast plan he was incapable of understanding, Heaven had arranged that all things come around again, like the slow revolutions of some celestial wheel. So once again he was a soldier of Narváez. But he had vowed that the path of his life would never again intersect that of Hernán Cortés.

Book Three

THE CITY OF MEXICO
(1536-1539)

⚙

Chapter One

The Children of the Sun approached the capital by the Tacuba Causeway, in cotton chemises instead of naked, and in sandals instead of
barefoot, preceded by their mounted escort. The causeway was
thronged with Indians, and their progress was slowed by a gilded
carriage drawn by four white horses, which made its way with difficulty through the crowds. Canoes plied the gray lake alongside.

Dorantes walked between Alonso and Álvar, matching his reluctant
steps to theirs, while Esteban strutted ahead. His black arms spilled out
of the shirt that was too small for him, his hair was decorated with red
feathers, and his ankle bangles clicked cheerfully. From the carriage
that creaked ahead of their escort, a small blackamoor in gay silks and a
jeweled cap descended to trot alongside, and Esteban never took his
eyes from this elegant little person; Dorantes had a sense of temptations awaiting his slave—of treacherous terrain ahead for them all, and
for himself in particular.

The city hulking up before them had grown immensely from the
four hundred houses ranging in sixteen blocks around the plaza mayor
that had been built upon the ruin of Tenochtitlán. But it was still the
city of Hernán Cortés, a fortress city, with the muzzles of cannon
gaping from the walls of purplish stone and little greenery showing.

They came through gates where Castilians had retreated, fighting
for their lives, and fought their way back again to the tolling of the
great drum that still seemed to ring dimly in his skull; and on into the
plaza where once the pyramid had stood, with its temple housing
the monstrous idols and its sacrificial stone. Now the cathedral squatted
there, to its left the palace Cortés had erected when the city had been
rebuilt, which now bore the viceroy's red and yellow banner. Opposite
it, another, larger palace was under construction, flourishing a more

magnificent banner. Upon this were depicted the black, double-headed eagle of the Holy Roman Empire, a golden lion, three gold crowns, and a grid ringed with seven crowned heads.

"Very grand," Dorantes said to one of the escort.

"Very grand indeed, though still the viceroy walks on the right," the soldier said, with a wink. He referred to Cortés as the marqués. The marqués was very rich, not only from the spoils of the Aztecs, but in Spain he had married a very rich and noble lady. Sometimes the marqués and marquesa were in residence in this grand, new palace, at others in Cortés' other palace, in Cuernavaca.

So Cortés had made a marriage both suitable and convenient, and, a grandee of Spain, would at least himself sleep through eternity beneath escutcheoned marble.

On scaffolding along one wing of the palace, Indians labored, two by two, lifting blocks of dressed stone to others on higher levels. Hammers and chisels rang. In the square, carriages and men on horseback breasted the crowds afoot, richly dressed men and women in silks and velvets, and many Negro slaves also fine-dressed, as well as the throngs of Indians. Young, ragged half-breeds lounged before the cathedral, watching the show, or ran through the square in bands—children of the Conquest, Dorantes realized, with a rush of emotion. Martín might have been one of the older ones. Now the din of Tenochtitlán was the racket of carriage wheels and hoofs on stone, the chinking of hammers, the cries of flower women, tamal venders, and beggars, and of the urchins. The plaza smelled of flowers and filth, and with every step he felt the presence of Hernán Cortés. If the governor of New Galicia had been obsessed with the idea of Cibola, what of the Marqués del Valle de Oaxaca? And what of the viceroy?

They passed through the viceregal gates, between two guards in their red and yellow uniforms, into a large paved area as busy, it seemed, as the plaza outside the wall, peopled with sumptuously dressed and uniformed horsemen and pedestrians; and on into dark cool corridors in a press of these elegant ladies and gentlemen, who turned from their conversations to gaze in astonishment on the Children of the Sun. And thus they came at last to the presence of the viceroy, Don Antonio de Mendoza, Conde de Tendilla, in a reception sala with his secretary and two more of the pikemen.

In his gold embroidered robe and wool cap the viceroy embraced Dorantes, Álvar Núñez, and Alonso del Castillo in turn, while Esteban stood by with his arms folded and white teeth gleaming. Mendoza smelled of rosewater, a dark-skinned, dark-bearded, sharp-eyed man of about fifty, with the face of a benevolent wolf.

"You are welcome, brave men, valiant ones!" the viceroy said.

"Welcome to New Spain! Come, seat yourselves, how weary you must be!" He crooked a beringed finger as they seated themselves, and sherry and sweet cakes were produced.

Mendoza peered from face to face with a curious little twisting of his head, as though screwing their features into his memory. "Tell us how you have accomplished this great thing. A thousand leagues, is it possible?"

"The grace of God was furnished us, Excellency," Álvar said.

"Of course, of course! And just how was this grace manifested, Álvar Núñez Cabeza de Vaca? A goodly and renowned name, if I may say so, señor!"

Álvar looked pleased at the compliment, and Dorantes thought that here was a man as remarkable in his way as Hernán Cortés and Beltrán Nuño de Guzmán; and this one was called "good."

"The power to heal, Señor Viceroy, was granted us," Álvar said.

"Not to all of us, Excellency," Alonso said. The viceroy turned to examine him with the little screwing motion. "The blackamoor and I were the heralds of these two, who were the healers."

"Of which I was much the lesser," Dorantes said. Sharp, dark eyes, whose force he could feel, examined him. "Álvar healed those truly ill and wounded, while I dealt with headaches and bellyaches."

"And translated when I preached the Holy Faith," Álvar added. "The slave is also a linguist—of the hands."

Esteban had seated himself on a cushion, grinning and nodding to the viceroy's examination. The secretary, who wore a starched white collar, stood with his hands clasped together at his waist, his attentive eyes blinking slow as a turtle's. Dorantes could feel the concentration of attention, but not the danger he had felt in Campostela.

"And how is it you are able to speak these many tongues, Andrés Dorantes de Carranza?"

"I learned Nahuatl in the Conquest, and the language called Han from our captors. Between these two I could make myself understood in many places."

There was a fraction of a moment of intense stillness before Mendoza murmured, "Imagine! And you were of the service of Hernán Cortés then?"

"In Tenochtitlán, the Panuco, and Honduras, Excellency."

Nodding, smiling, the viceroy said, "You will find many of your old comrades here in this city, Don Andrés." To Álvar he said, "Of this grace, my good healer: can you tell me just how this power to heal revealed itself to you? The sensation, can it be described to someone who has never known such a wonder?"

Álvar held up his hands in illustration, gazing at the viceroy serenely.

173

"It was a thing that might be grasped in the two hands and held like this." Dorantes found himself nodding as Álvar said, "As to sensation, it was as though a great warmth flowed down the arms, from the heart, and into these hands."

"Imagine!" the viceroy said. He screwed his head toward Alonso. "And your part, Alonso del Castillo Maldonado? You and this Moor preceded the others and told of their coming?"

"I was the trader and collector, Excellency. I have things in my pack that will be of interest."

"We will see them! We will see them in good time. But nothing of precious metals, I am given to understand? And no trace of the king-dom called Cibola that obsesses so many in New Spain?"

Esteban leaned back against Dorantes' leg. The viceroy glanced from face to face as there was no response.

"You would not understand this obsession, for you have been in the wilderness these many years," he continued. "But the reports of the wealth of Peru have truly driven men mad. And so Cibola seems to them the next Cuzco. There will be great interest in your journey, my friends."

"We will tell you our story," Dorantes said. "And you will draw your own conclusions about Cibola."

"Yes, I will hear your story now," Mendoza said. "And a narrative of your journey must be written, for the Audiencia and for His Cath-olic Majesty. Meanwhile I will do my best to protect you from atten-tions you would find obtrusive. You will have my full hospitality for your comfort! How will we arrange the responsibility for these narra-tives, please?"

It was decided that Álvar Núñez and Dorantes would write separate relations, which Alonso, who could not write, would then criticize. All would collaborate on a map of the lands they had traversed.

"Very good, very good," Mendoza said. "After I have heard your story you must rest from your privations, and after that we will see that you are properly attired to be presentable at my table, in this, I must say, very fashionable City of Mexico."

That evening, attired in a heavy doublet of green velvet, green hose, and uncomfortable shoes, he walked through the very fashionable city, along streets thronged with Spaniards and Indians, and more Negroes than, it seemed, whites; with beggars, cripples, terribly pockmarked indigenes, and the small bands of mixed-bloods; underfed, brazen, and pathetic, and perhaps vicious. He passed an Aztec cacique in his half-European and half-Indian finery, half-impressive and half-ridiculous in its extravagance, with his retinue of Indians as arrogant as he; two

Negroes in their finery and arrogance also, strutting arm in arm, with eye-rolling side glances at a black woman in Castilian dress with much naked bosom under a white shawl. He passed a man he recognized, whose name he could not remember—a soldier of Alvarado's division; velvet tunic, the heavy gold chain called a fanfarron burdening his shoulders, feathered cap, hand on the hilt of his poniard, and an arrogance that surpassed that of the cacique and the slaves, a sauntering contemptuous stride that all moved aside before—one of the conquerors. He caught Dorantes' eye, nodded once, looked troubled, but passed on without speaking.

In Salamanca Street he passed the house he had never liked. The gate was open and he could see through the greenery-filled patio into a lighted room, where a Castilian woman was railing at someone in a fishwife voice. He supposed there was some question of the ownership of this house, and of Xicomilpa also, which had been confiscated by the acting government of Salazar. One day he must find Rufino, who would know of these things. His heart, already troubled, beat harder at the memory of the heels of Nicolás de Cuéllar kicking his life away on the tiles, and of Caterina with her child's body too narrow for the birth of Nico's child.

He drove himself on to walk to Tlatelolco and find in the busy Indian barrio the house with its cross of blue tiles, almost invisible now, beneath the dense runners of a vine creeping along the wall. The gate was closed, and there was a sense of life within. He turned and retraced his steps to the Spanish quarter.

Many of the houses here were turreted now, and some had thrown second stories out over the street to become minor palaces. Here were fashionable people, horsemen, two together of the watch; a carriage rumbled toward him. He stepped into the dark mouth of an alley to watch it pass, aware of the quickening of his breath as he peered at the device on the hammer-cloth, which was not, however, the complicated arms of Cortés. Following along behind the sparking wheels, he passed a wineshop, within which dark shapes of men sat together at three tables. He hesitated, but did not go inside for fear of encountering someone he knew. He was not yet ready to face the questions, which, as the viceroy had put it, were certain to be obtrusive.

Chapter Two

He did not have to dread for long his first encounter with Cortés, for the work on the relations of the journey and the collaboration on a map were interrupted by the marqués' celebration of the Feast of St. James. In their new clothing, the Children of the Sun were summoned to become part of the viceregal cavalcade of grand carriages filled with ladies and gentlemen, and the mounted cavaliers of the court and of the guard riding alongside.

On grassy fields on filled land on the edge of the city, watched over by the serene white heads of Sleeping Woman and Smoking Mountain, amid gaily flapping banners, two sets of chairs had been assembled facing each other across the green turf. Here the carriages and horsemen halted, and all descended and dismounted in a milling group of servants and slaves, gentlemen armed with swords and poniards swaggering among the ladies in mantillas and layered silks, all of them casting glances to the other side of the field, where the banners of Cortés floated and another procession of horsemen and coaches was arriving.

He watched the Marqués del Valle de Oaxaca handed down from his coach in his black velvet and gold fanfarron, a portly, rather bowlegged middle-aged man, who, however, bounced lightly to the ground and swung around with a flurry of his cape to bow to his wife. She was a fair young woman in white and gold, with a proud little head. Cortés performed another bow aimed at the viceroy, sweeping his hat around excessively so that the salute seemed almost a parody. The new wife of the conqueror curtsied.

From one of the other carriages on Cortés' side of the field, a short, dark-skinned woman in elaborate Spanish dress was handed down by two young cavaliers. Dorantes' breath came short to realize that this was Doña Marina, with her husband, Juan de Jaramillo. They were ushered to a seat not far from Cortés and his marquesa.

The jousting began, bulls turned into an area behind barriers and horsemen spurring at them aiming long canes like lances. These splintered when the stroke was fair, the horse then wheeling away from the jabbing horns. Gold trim on the carriages winked in the brilliant sunlight, and women cried out when a fine Andalusian bay was gored in the haunch.

Esteban mingled with the other slaves of the viceroy's retinue. He had acquired a pale blue doublet from the viceregal wardrobes and high maroon boots that appeared a bit too small, for he managed to combine a limp with his swagger, a reminder that he had walked a thousand leagues with the Children of the Sun. He wore a cap with a golden ornament, red lips and white teeth grinning until his master caught his eye and jabbed a finger at him to remind him that he had been warned and threatened to keep his mouth shut on the subject of Cibola.

Seated between Dorantes and Álvar was a Judge of Examination, Diego Pérez de la Torre, and the viceroy's half-sister, María de Mendoza, whose milky skin was protected from the Mexican sun by a parasol held by a slim young black. The judge was a hard-lipped man speaking in brief spurts to Álvar, then listening, scowling, and firing another question; Guzmán seemed to be the subject. Dorantes thought Doña María beautiful, with an admirable bosom, a thin blade of nose, eyes set close together, and an enticing way of snapping her fan open to cover her face, all but the black eyes, when she spoke to him.

"What tales you must have to tell, señor!"

"Just now my companions and I are writing those tales into relations for your brother, Doña María."

"Surely one can hear them from the lips of a man who has experienced these adventures!"

"If His Excellency permits it, it would be my honor."

"I have had no adventures," the lady continued. She leaned forward with interest as a bull appeared to gore another horse, straightening when this proved not to be the case. "It is not permitted that ladies have adventures," she said.

"There is a lady who has had adventures," he said, indicating Doña Marina across the field, who was also shaded by a parasol.

"I see that the complexion becomes darker with adventure," his companion said. Her fan failed to conceal a smile of small white teeth. "Still, one would pay the cost!"

"Tell me, who is the marquesa?"

"Why, she is the Doña Juana de Aguilar y Zúñiga, niece of the Duke of Béjar."

His breath caught once more. "Daughter of the Conde de Aguilar."

"A great favorite at court," María de Mendoza said, nodding. "She has brought her husband favor there, and a great fortune besides."

He gazed across the field at the small, pale face beside the conqueror, the two of them seated in thronelike chairs. He remembered the beautiful child in that gay tiny company of the count's court, with her protective old greyhound. Timultzin had been baptized with that name. Doña Juana too had longed for adventure, and had married the most famous adventurer of the time.

"The rumors one hears of you, señor!" said María de Mendoza. "That you and your companions crossed rivers that flowed in banks of gold! That you discovered children playing their childish games with diamonds and pearls, and emeralds cast aside as of no interest. That you—"

She halted at his laughter. "Señorita, you will be disappointed in the truth. We passed through many mud villages, and many deserts, and saw no gold nor diamonds."

Her eyes studied him over her fan. "And they say you have found the fabulous seven cities of Cibola."

"No, my lady. No."

After the jousting, in which Cortés participated, acquitting himself well against a trumpeting, farting, black bull, food and wine were laid out on long tables protected by sunshades of blue-and-white striped cloth. Slaves swung long-handled whisks against the flies. Above the volcanoes clouds were mounting, illuminated by flashes of lightning, but over the city paler clouds merged with the pale blue of the sky.

Members of the viceroy's and the marqués' factions mingled in friendly fashion while the two leaders strolled arm in arm. Then he saw Cortés trotting toward him, one hand holding his sword to keep it from tripping him, the other hand raised. His belly bounced in his tight black doublet. "*Andrés Dorantes!*"

"Señor Marqués—"

Cortés embraced him, slapping him on the back, thrusting him out to grin into his face, and embracing him again. He smelled of sweat and perfume. "My good Turk! My Juan de Flechilla! But you disappeared; it was thought you were dead! I was unable to express my gratitude for the successful journey of the arrow!"

"I had good reason for leaving the capital, sire."

"Yes, I know, I know," Cortés said, rubbing his chin where the scar still showed through his beard. "But—to join that pudding fool Pánfilo de Narváez a second time!" He raised his hands in a gesture of incomprehension. "Come!" he said, taking Dorantes' arm.

He was introduced to the marquesa, slim and imperious in her white and gold. Her neck looked too slight to support the weight of the pearls and gold of her necklaces. A slave hovered behind her with a parasol. He was conscious of all the eyes of both companies upon him.

Bowing, he said it was the marquesa who had sent him to the New World, where he had joined her husband. Both stared at him in surprise. Cortés' left eye still drooped slightly, which made it appear smaller than the other and set at a different angle in his head. The marquesa had a band of pale freckles across her nose and cheeks.

"At the palace of your father, the Conde de Aguilar, Doña Juana," he said, "in whose service I was. A young crossbowman from Béjar. A gracious lady there advised me that one's fortune could be made across the seas."

Although she pretended to recall it, he saw that she did not. So many years had passed. He was no longer a young crossbowman, and she was no longer a child. Tiny parchment wrinkles showed at the corners of her eyes, and her hair had lost the luster of that child's fair hair. There was a hint of petulance in the tuck of her small mouth, and more than a hint of boredom.

Her expression changed when Cortés said, "My good Turk is one of those who have traversed the continent through the northern lands. These discoveries have excited this city as nothing has done since the news of Peru, Andrés!" he said, laughing, showing his teeth, scratching his chin. He had a way of standing, hands on hips and legs spread, an eagerness to the thrust of his head, and belly sucked in, that made him resemble the captain-general of old.

He managed to laugh also. "Ah, no, Señor Marqués—Doña Juana—we have only seen a great distance of land, and none of those marvels of which the gossips here seem to know more than we do!"

"Yes, this is a great place for gossip, old friend! Tell me, have you seen any of our old companions of the Conquest?"

He said he had not yet done so.

"A sore-headed, jealous, bickering, recriminating lot. All feel they have been treated with ingratitude for their great service. As perhaps I feel myself!" He laughed again, and the marquesa smiled thinly—who would have heard too many old soldiers' stories. He noticed that she glanced continually in the direction of the viceroy, but could not read her expression. "Believe me, I have done the best I could for them!" Cortés continued. "How we are all disliked by those more recently come from Spain! And so I can only preach that old comrades remain loyal to one another. It would have been well if you had come first to me on arriving here, my good Turk."

"It was not possible, sire."

Cortés, nodding, stalked up and down before his wife and his old comrade. "You must tell me of these exploits. Soon!"

He said that he and his companions had been given the task of writing narratives of their journey for the king and the Audiencia, and of drawing a map. Cortés halted before him, staring straight into his eyes with those hard, rather protruberant eyes of absolute ambition.

"I will see your relation and your map, my good Turk."

It was not a question, and he did not reply to it. He felt the net of conspiracy and secrecy settle upon him, weighted with old loyalty. To change the subject he asked of Gonzalo de Sandoval, that unquestioningly loyal captain. Cortés' face fell into sad lines.

"Dead! Gonzalito accompanied me to Spain, and fell ill before we had arrived. He died in Palos. I loved him like a son, Andrés."

"He was the most loyal of soldiers, sire. Who would have fallen on his sword, had his general demanded it."

"Others demurred from that unpleasant duty, as I recall," Cortés said, smiling. His wife's hand was on his arm; others were waiting to speak to him.

Dorantes disengaged himself, and he and Álvar walked apart, watching the spectacle of the lightning over the mountains. He felt a great oppression.

"This Judge of Examination wishes information about Beltrán Nuño de Guzmán," Álvar said. "I have told him all we have seen and learned. Pray God we can assist in his downfall."

"It would be well if we brought something of value to New Spain, and not merely tales of the riches of Cibola."

"We have brought no such tales!"

"We are accompanied by a cloud of them. Rivers flowing through banks of gold, children playing with precious stones. The same tales we heard of Apalachen!"

"I saw you speaking with the marqués."

"With him, and the sister of the viceroy also."

Álvar walked beside him in silence, hands clasped behind his back, face fallen into heavy lines. "Andrés, I am determined to go to Spain and petition the court for the governorship of those lands through which we passed. I believe it is not impossible that this should be granted. I trust I have your support in this."

He thought of those with whom Álvar, in his innocence and his faith, would be contending. Álvar wished to know if he had changed his mind, or found an ambition of his own toward the territories of their journey. He could truthfully say that he had none. Moreover, that his most fervent wish was that those lands and those people be left in peace.

"I have vowed it, Álvar," he said. "You need not ask it again."

"Good," Álvar said, in a voice of relief. "But—there may be great pressures to separate us in our wish, Andrés."

He had already seen that that would be the case.

That evening they met with Alonso to compare their first rough drawings of the collaborative map of their journey, and immediately burst into laughter at their differences.

The cathedral was heavy-walled as a fortress, built of mortared stones, some of which still bore the bas-reliefs of the razed Aztec buildings which had furnished these building blocks, squat and oppressive by night, with dense shadows and pale circles of light cast by lanterns. Loitering in these shadows was one of the gangs of mixed-blood boys which made way for him with sullen glances, ragged urchins light brown in color but darker with filth, bare feet pattering, and cries back and forth in their language, half-Castilian and half-Nahuatl and all but incomprehensible to him. One was a cripple, stumping out of his way on a stick for a crutch; several were badly pocked. One, guided by another, had ghastly eyeballs, like the blind of the Anaquas; fruit of the syphilitic loins of the conquerors. He passed on into the cathedral, white and gold alive with candle flames and thick with shadows. A cassocked priest stood, head bowed, before the sumptuous golden glitter of the altar. Another passed Dorantes with a rustle of garments. A ragged, long-haired boy with the face of an animal crouched beside the marble font, arms and legs tucked beneath him; he fled as the priest made threatening gestures.

Dorantes remained in the shadows, watching a few communicants being served; body and blood of the Redeemer. *You also eat your God,* Timultzin had said. *It was the same with us. But you sacrifice your God. I know it is the same and not the same; yet the same.*

He stood watching the glow of the altar. The child of impure blood had sneaked back to crouch again beside the font. He felt bloated with sin. Was it Timultzin who had taught him to doubt, the doubt learned with her tongue as she had learned his faith with his? *Your Christian God has found me at last!* In the upright coffins of the confessionals, priests listened to the sins of men, who were shriven and freed to partake of their God. In the high emptiness of the cathedral, steps echoed.

A tall man in dusty traveling clothes entered, cloak slung over his shoulder. He fell to his knees, rattle and scrape of his sword on the stones of the floor, and advanced toward the pale Christ on his cross, bleeding hands and feet, bleeding head from his crown, bleeding slit in his side like a dark vertical mouth. The man on his knees approached with arms raised high above his head in supplication and entreaty. A gold ornament on his cloak glinted in the candlelight. Something about that proud bare head was familiar as he scraped along toward the altar with his arms held out to the pale Christ.

It was Beltrán Nuño de Guzmán who made his way along the aisle on abraded knees, arms raised almost in surrender. Dorantes stood watching the governor of New Galicia until he rose to disappear into one of the booths, there to confess his sins and be absolved, and afterwards to kneel again before the rail and receive the host. The third powerful man interested in Cibola was come to the City of Mexico.

When Dorantes left the cathedral a few stars showed among a scudding of black clouds. A little rain splattered on his face and then passed. As he walked along the side of the cathedral in the dense darkness he was aware that he was followed—a padding and rustling, whispers.

With a shout for the watch he backed against the stone wall as they set upon him. He slashed back and forth with his dagger to keep them off, four of them, maybe more. A rock smashed against the wall beside his head. He grunted through his teeth as another bruised his shoulder. When he charged they scattered before him, but immediately he was pressed to the wall again. One of them had a stick, which first prodded him, then swung at his head. He fended it with his dagger. He summoned his breath to shout again.

There was a clatter of approaching hoofs. With a whispered sibilant the group of denser shadows before him dissolved. He leaped after one, caught his arm, swung around by the other's force but keeping his feet as his assailant stumbled and went down. He knelt on the boy's chest with his dagger point held just over the face.

By starlight the face glared back at him, teeth bared in fear and panting, dark-eyed, brown-skinned, pocked cheeks. The boy's panting seemed to tune itself to his own in an undercurrent to the sound of the approaching hoofs. He drew the dagger back, straightening.

Then he released his grip and rose. The boy scrambled away, lost instantly in the darkness, as the watch, with a lantern, trotted up, two horsemen looming against the night sky. Panting still, he identified himself and described what had happened.

"Mestizo bastards!" one of the watch said, stink of wine breath as he spoke. "Run in packs like dogs. Turning nastier every day."

Growing older every day, he thought, the mongrel children of the conquerors and the pretty girls of the conquered. "What did they want of me?"

"Just your purse. There's been a few that's had beatings from them. Nothing worse yet."

"We'll catch a couple one of these times," the other said. "Stretch their necks for them. Then the others'll tread light for a bit."

"Worse than dogs," the first said. They rode along beside him to the viceregal gates.

Lying awake in the dense blackness of his quarters, he heard the small creak of the door opening. With a rush of blood-warning he sat up to grope for his dagger. Then he heard the rustling of skirts. She came swiftly into his bed, warm breath on his cheek, swaddled face, bare warm slimness beneath her skirts. His manhood swarmed to its outpouring quickly, while she moaned once in her pleasure, feigned or genuine. It might be María de Mendoza, or the plump, widowed young niece of the judge, de la Torre, also María; or more likely the slender Beatriz de Escandón, who had sat near him at the viceroy's table for several meals, plying him with questions and disbelieving of his plain tales. It occurred to him that whichever Castiliana it was came at the behest of the viceroy, and soon the questions must begin: Cíbola with its rivers of gold, mountains of precious stones, and women who governed their men like masters and slaves—

Instead there were caresses, quickening breathing, and a second bout. After it the woman slipped from the bed and was gone, all in silence.

In his after-lovemaking sadness he lay awake grieving for his dead Nahua love, for his lost son; and all at once his heart swelled as though it would burst at the realization that the woman had had no scent—that gingery trace of perspiration under the flowery perfumes of the Spanish lady.

Chapter Three

"But everyone knows of this fantastic journey!" Gil de Herrera said. He leaned on the scarred planks of the wineshop table, fingers locked around his cup, sweating jowls gleaming in the candlelight. "You must tell us, my fellow Turk, what you have discovered. Great cities, eh?"

The three of them gazed at him intently, Gil and the two others, one short, one skinny, both younger, neither of them old conquerors but cronies of one. He thought they would believe whatever fantastic tale he chose to weave and disbelieve the truth.

"We heard rumors of some larger towns, not cities," he said. "We did not take these as important. It is not rich country."

"Cibola lies in that direction," the short one said, rolling his eyes.

"You must promise to take me along when you return," Gil said. "For old companions' sake! Ah, what this one and I have been through together!" he said, swinging drunkenly toward his friends. "The Night of Sorrows! And remember the hide of poor Juan Juste! Flayed alive, poor devil!" he said to the others, to whom Dorantes had taken a dislike. "They had hung his skin like an old coat in a temple there. What a thing! None of us could bear to touch this abomination to take it down but our brave Turk, here. Soft as the finest suede, he said of it. Eh, Andrés?"

The others clucked admiringly but condescendingly, bored with the repetitious tales of the conquerors.

"And the girls!" Gil said. "Where are all those pretty girls now, I would ask?" He stretched out his thumb and forefinger. "The Hook of Extremadura! Those pretty girls would run and leap like fish in a pool trying to escape us, until the Hook took them!" He laughed, hiccoughing, wiping his mouth, shaking his head at the potency of his memories.

Gil drank deep and slammed down his cup. "Ah, Andrés, how

ungrateful they are to us! Hungry, thirsty—desperately wounded! Carved up and eaten with chiles! And none of it counts shit anymore! Bunch of cock-a-hoops from Castile think they're better than we were. The viceroy plots against us, Andrés. He thwarts Cortés at every turn!"

"Careful, man!" the short one said, glancing toward the host, who was observing them from before his wall of wine barrels.

"Tell us more of Cibola, señor," the skinny one demanded.

"A fairy tale. For children to believe in."

Leaning toward him, grinning with yellow teeth, glassy-eyed with wine, Gil said, "Remember when Tenochtitlán was such a fairy tale, Andrés? A fairy city out of the romances, out of *Amadis of Gaul?* But it was true!"

The skinny one said, "Tell us of the cities of these lands. Surely there were cities."

"Mud villages, señor," he said.

"But there was gold!"

"We saw no gold, nor silver, nor precious stones."

The three gazed at him without meeting his eyes, as though embarrassed by his clumsy lies, and he was furious at the cool sweat on his forehead.

"What of the corporal?" he asked Gil.

"Caballo's blasphemies are a scandal, Andrés! His head has gone soft from wine and the women's disease. A gut like a barrel. He is a grand encomendero!"

He asked of Rufino.

"The fattest of us all, Andrés!" Gil said, banging his goblet down. "Fat as a capon!" He leaned forward to whisper, "They say he cut off his balls so as to become a better priest. Can anyone believe such a thing? There is a college in Tlatelolco where they teach indigene children what they have no need of knowing, and where Rufino and others study the ways of the Aztecs. Stupid!

"These things are the doing to the viceroy. He coddles the indigenes and ignores those who conquered them. Little by little Hernán Cortés is diminished. We are all diminished! We will all be reduced to beggars, and the captain-general to the captain of beggars! They set our enemies above us! This college of Rufino's, and the caciques who have been baptized! Have you seen them strutting in the plaza? Endonned: Don Pedro this and Don Rafael that. We should have destroyed all their foul race! They keep slaves in their thousands, harems of hundreds! Giving themselves airs in front of Castilians! Not a week ago I shoved one out of my way. I thought the dog would turn his lackeys on me! But they know one of their conquerors still! So the black-skinned bastard gave me the evil eye and slunk away. More wine here, fellow!" he called to the host, who brought another pitcher.

"What an enviable position you have, Andrés Dorantes," the skinny wine drinker said, squinting at him. "To possess knowledge such powerful men would give much to share. One can understand your carefulness, lest that knowledge become tarnished." He winked knowledgeably. "One has heard of Don Antonio's torture cellar. That, at least, is no tale of Cibola!"

He made no reply, thinking of Beltrán Nuño de Guzmán, in the capital now, who needed Cibola to save himself from the Judge of Examination, Diego Pérez de la Torre; and Hernán Cortés, who needed Cibola to keep from being diminished. And the viceroy, Don Antonio de Mendoza, into whose power the Children of the Sun had placed themselves? All of them seemed to believe in those *Amadis of Gaul* romances of the seven cities of Cibola. Esteban had been threatened and Alonso cautioned by Dorantes, for gossip of the golden heads of dolls, of golden sinkers for fishermen's nets, of rivers with banks of gold would destroy those gentle people—as Gil would have had the Aztecs destroyed.

He placed the flat of his hand over his cup as the short crony slopped wine into the others, and asked of Blas de Garay.

"Married," Gil said, nodding, eyelids twitching to remain open. His hands described large breasts. "He has a thousand indigenes at Chapititlan, he claims. He is very grand when he arrives in the city with his fat wife and brood of children. We will drink wine together, Andrés! But tell me," he said eagerly, leaning forward drunkenly again, "have you seen Cortés?"

Blas was as portly as Gil, elegantly clothed and perfumed, with a silk handkerchief tucked into his sleeve, seated in the same wineshop with Gil de Herrera. After more news of old friends had been exchanged— Pedro de Solís, an alcalde in a town whose name no one could remember, Bernal Díaz in Guatemala with Alvarado, this one dead of an illness, that one returned to Spain—Dorantes asked what had become of Blas's concubine Gualcoyotl.

Blas looked pained. "Ah, who knows, Andrés! The smallpox struck while we were in Honduras with Cortés. I believe all were dead in the quarter." He took the handkerchief from his sleeve and patted his forehead. Then he said, "But you returned—what, three months?— before I did! Did you find Timultzin?"

"Dying," he said, and hesitated to gain control of his voice. "All the others were gone. Gualcoyotl and the children. Did you never try to find if she lived?"

Blas shook his head. "They say Tlatelolco was a graveyard. What a terrible thing for the indigenes is the smallpox. And they say that every seven years it will return! Before long there will be no Indians to work our lands." He wadded his handkerchief back into his sleeve. "And now you must tell us of this great journey that is the newest marvel since Peru! They say that Cortés is bound to make an entrada. And you will guide him?"

He shook his head silently. His head felt stuffed and aching; he had become obsessed with the woman with the swaddled face who had come silently to his bed—for he was now convinced that it had been Timultzin.

He did not know why he had been reluctant to call upon Rufino in Tlatelolco, when almost every day he had walked the streets in that direction. Today he passed on by the house with its square of blue tiles almost concealed by the vine, headed for the great plaza of Tlatelolco.

The church of Santiago stood on one side, where the pyramid had been, and a vast Indian market flourished in the square before it, teeming with exotic colors and smells: flowers, fruits, a dozen varieties of red chiles, sunlight glinting on pyramids of glazed pottery and heaps of yellow baskets. He marveled at the extent of it as he made his way down the aisles among the crowds of indigenes, Franciscan friars, and Spanish sightseers. There was nothing like it in Spain, although those who had fought in Africa said that the souks of the Moorish cities rivaled it. There were streets of iron knives and tools, whose manufacture the Indians had quickly learned; an area of every kind of fabric imaginable; still others of vegetables, of hares, and of fowl, and the fat little dogs in cages, and an aisle of caged birds twittering and whistling. There were stalls where food was served, spicy smelling and thickly gravied, too rich for Castilian bellies, and, it was said, filled with such horrors of Aztec cuisine as cooked lice, snakes, and the intestines of toads. Further along were aisles of gold- and silversmiths, more cunning than their Spanish counterparts; a street of barbers, physicians, and dentists, who bent over their clients under striped canopies. Beyond this he wandered past the rough red stones of the ruined temples, where Cuauhtémoc had surrendered to the power of Cortés, and the church, hulking and ramparted, built of the same stones.

Next to the church was the College of Santa Cruz of the Franciscans, a long, low structure. The first friar he saw when he had passed inside was very fat, tonsured, garbed a little differently than the other friars—sandals on his feet, a belt instead of a rope at his waist. He was facing away as he spoke to three young Indians in smocks, then turning slightly until a smooth-shaven cheek was in profile; turning more with that familiar stagger on his left leg, wounded by a javelin on the Night of Sorrows.

He approached along the rosy tiles, in the high, open, clerestory-lighted space, crucifixes on the walls, white-clad students at a narrow table, the three indigene youths watching him with alert dark faces, Rufino gaping.

His fat cheeks shook as he spoke: "Andrés, can it be you?"

"It is, Rufino!"

The priest hugged him to his huge belly—the most grossly fat yet of his old comrades. "Andrés, one was so certain you were dead, that—that—"

An arm encircled him, urging him along. Rufino spoke in Nahuatl to the young Indians, who drifted away. They entered a white-walled cubicle filled with painful light through a high window. Rufino stepped away to face him; his fat cheeks were chalk white with emotion. He himself found it impossible to speak. "*You* are the Dorantes of the castaways, of whom everyone speaks!" Rufino said. He mopped his upper lip. "You must tell me all! Ah, and I all to you! Please, seat yourself."

He sat, tears burning on his cheeks as he watched Rufino limp across the room, rustle of his robe, slap of sandals. The friar removed a saucer that covered a green pitcher and poured chocolatl into two cups, one of which he handed to Dorantes.

In a loud, embarrassed voice, he said, "Once I overindulged in the plant of Noah. Now in chocolatl. A small indulgence that will be forgiven, surely."

More quietly he said, "Do you remember when you came to confess to me after the final battle? What sins were those? Who can even remember them?"

"I have come to confess again, Rufino."

"No, I!" the priest said. "*I!* But not just yet, my God! Things must be learned." His hand shook with his small cup, and he exclaimed in exasperation as brown fluid spilled on his robe. Brushing at the stain, he said, "You must know of this, Andrés. That it was reported that you were dead. All of you dead. By those dogs who ruled in the absence of Cortés. Francisco González—the crier, you remember— was set to tolling the news like the very hours. And your wife—"

"I know that."

"Married her kinsman, who was later murdered by robbers. And she, poor soul—"

"I know that, Rufino," he said impatiently. "But I must know of Timultzin. I thought she was dead also. But now—" He stopped.

Rufino stared at him with his face gleaming with sweat. He daubed at it with a handkerchief taken from his sleeve. "She did not die of the smallpox."

"I must find her," he whispered.

"Must you?"

He closed his eyes against that glimpse of her face that had haunted the years between, the swamp of pustules of the plague of the conquerors that had destroyed so many more indigenes than their steel weapons. Did he want to see her now, who had so cravenly fled that vision then? He listened to the hard rustle of his breathing.

"She would not want to be seen," Rufino said. "She had great pride in her beauty. Too much pride, perhaps. I know you have searched your soul, Andrés. But I wonder if she would want to be found."

"Could you help me find her? And the boy—perhaps he also lives!"

Rufino shrugged. "If her name is put out to ten that I know, and by each of those to ten more—it is the way these things are done, when so many have been scattered and lost. And have died."

"I must leave for Spain soon," he said.

Rufino stood before him in a long silence, mopping his dripping face. Dorantes asked what the others did in this place, in this school.

"We instruct the children of the Aztec nobility. All are bright, interested, quick to learn—yet always that remote, mysterious part. Do we rightly try to eradicate it? Come, you will see my work, which is a separate thing from that of the college."

Rufino led him into a sun-washed, vaulted space where Indians in white mantles worked at long tables, some standing, some seated. Rufino seemed a different person, genial and voluble as he pointed and explained.

"Another and I work together—Fray Bernardino—you will meet him. For me, these indigenes create a dictionary of Nahuatl. You must understand that they had libraries of histories, and calendars. All had to be drawn as pictures, as you will remember from those early days with Timultzin. Because their characters were insufficient, they could not set things down exactly, but only give the substance of their ideas. They were very accurate, however, in such things as astronomical records and tribute rolls. Still, we have had to devise means to transcribe Nahuatl into Castilian."

Dorantes was introduced to Fray Bernardino de Sahagún, a beaky-faced young man whose movements were quick and birdlike. Fray Bernardino led them into cubicles like Rufino's, where elder Aztecs painted depictions of their lives as they had been before the Conquest. The little squares showing men in action with various objects were exactly like those cartoons Timultzin had drawn.

A grey-headed artist with ropy-veined brown hands leaned back to examine his drawing. "See, a Mexica woman is instructing her daughter in the making of tortillas," Fray Bernardino said in his bright voice. "The curl means the mother is speaking. The girl kneads flour in the mortar. The circles are the baking pans. How do you call them, Fray Rufino?"

"Cumal," Rufino said.

"Cumal!" the artist said, grinning toothlessly, nodding and pointing.

In another cubicle a younger artist drew pyramids, and the temples atop them blazing, repetitively.

"Historical," Fray Bernardino said. "When the Mexica captured an enemy town they burnt the temples and destroyed the pyramids. This fellow is one of a group putting together a history of the Aztec conquests before the coming of the Christians."

"Just what we did to their temples and pyramids," Dorantes said. He felt ill, a weakness in his knees and a buzzing in his head, that last vision of Timultzin's face behind his eyelids.

"There are many similarities, as you remember, Andrés," Rufino said, mopping his forehead.

"We do not believe these similarities to have been coincidental," Fray Bernardino said. "It is the purpose of our investigations here to trace them to their roots."

Rufino said, "One may speculate that the god Quetzalcoatl was in fact Saint Thomas, you see. And that his teachings were corrupted after he was driven out of the Aztec pantheon."

Elsewhere, artists depicted the tribute delivered to Tenochtitlán by conquered states: the skins of animals, birds, maize, weapons. Another drew the plan of Montezuma's palace, still another scenes from Cortés' progress from the coast to Tenochtitlán.

"Doña Marina is always shown behind Cortés, hand out, curl of speech," Rufino commented.

"I see that often she is drawn larger than he."

"Yes," Rufino said. "One notices that."

Fray Bernardino led them to his own cell, which was crowded with tables supporting stacks of papers and leather-bound volumes.

"We are fortunate that the viceroy understands the importance of our task here," Fray Bernardino said. "The bishop also." He fixed his hard little eyes on Dorantes.

"The indigenes accept the True Faith too easily," he continued. "We have burned their temples and destroyed their pyramids. They accept the gods of their conquerors as they have historically done, but already we see them turning our depictions of the Christian saints into idols for their idolatry.

"These similarities I have mentioned chill one's blood as more and more are discovered. They had baptism, confession, fasting, celibacy of the priesthood, nuns dedicated to their gods, a kind of Lent. They burned incense, made beeswax candles to illuminate their temples. Their supreme god, Tezcatlipoca, is a hideous parody of Our Lord. Their bloody abomination Huitzilopochtli can only be Satan himself!"

He glared at Dorantes, while Rufino leaned against one of the tables with his handkerchief wadded in his hand. "Many of us believe their entire religion is a parody of the True Faith, that they were taught Christian rites by Lucifer in order to mock our Lord. Even to the worship of the cross—In the Mayan lands to the south I am told that crosses proliferate. In groups of three!

"We make this record of their history and religion and customs in order to uncover these similarities of which we have spoken. So that we will be armed against the return of their old, satanic faith. For those who have so easily accepted the faith of Christ the Redeemer will easily fall into the way of apostasy and idolatry. The great idols of Tenochtitlán are still undiscovered, despite the efforts of the bishop!"

This impassioned Franciscan reminded Dorantes of the apostates screaming in the embrace of the iron prophets in Seville, which had appalled him more than the horrors of the Aztecs. He did not like Fray Bernardino. *Your Christian God has found me at last,* Timultzin had said, dying; not dying.

"Bernardino concerns himself much with the works of Satan," Rufino said, mopping his forehead, when they had returned to his chamber. He started to take up the pitcher of chocolatl to refill the two cups, but changed his mind.

"Andrés—perhaps there are other reasons than the destruction of her beauty, that she would not wish to be found."

"What other reasons?"

"Many years have passed." Rufino gestured vaguely.

He demanded to know what Rufino knew of her, but the other professed ignorance and would speak no more of the matter, while continuing to blot the sweat that streamed from his face.

When he left his old friend and confessor he sat in the church tormented by his thoughts. How quickly she had been converted to the True Faith, how quickly, at his wish, baptized Juana; how quickly, then, become disappointed because her new God did not speak to her. At first she had been shocked by Christian hypocrisies; soon she no longer mentioned them. How far had she gone in questioning her new faith? Many years have passed, Rufino had said, sadness in his voice, sweating with knowledge he could or would not reveal.

Chapter Four

The viceroy's second audience with the Children of the Sun came after a month, when a compromise map that satisfied none of them had been agreed upon and Álvar's narrative was complete. Dorantes' was only half-finished. Each day he managed to produce a few pages before he locked the slowly growing stack into his red Morocco-leather box and went for a walk in the plaza or through familiar streets. His excuse to himself was that he was disused to the written word, and had none of Álvar's familiarity with official reports.

They waited upon the viceroy in an antechamber, watching the busy life of the palace pass outside their door, beautiful women and elegant young men, a bearded officer with his helmet under his arm, Judge de la Torre in his black robe, disdainful Christian caciques in feathers and bright cloaks, black slaves and Indian servants. Outside rain fell as though it would never stop, and the great plaza was awash, as it regularly became during the summer rains.

"It is different from social occasions among the Marímnes," Dorantes commented, "but not entirely different."

Alonso chuckled, and Álvar smiled. Esteban stood with arms folded watching the passing show with a disapproving scowl.

"These slaves are very proud, Masters," he said. "Estebánico thinks some of them need good beatings."

"The black maidens are attractive in their white silks," Alonso said. "Flies in milk, I hear them called."

"These ones are very bold, Masters. But pretty, yes, and smell better than Marímne girls for certain!"

"Has Estebánico been telling tales of Cibola to these bold black girls?" Dorantes asked. "I hope not."

"Oh, no, Master; Estebánico says nothing. Nothing!"

"Perhaps Estebánico would like to become one of these palace slaves with jewels in their hats making eyes at the black maidens?"

The Moor laughed with an excessive show of white teeth. "Ah, no, Masters! In truth this fellow was most happy on the great journey, with the gentle ignorants who took us from place to place and loved the Children of the Sun so much!"

Had they come to love those gentle ignorants of the north simply because of being loved by them? Was that how the trap had been woven—Álvar's determination, and his own vow?

"Tell me, Alonso," he said. "How do things develop with this pretty widow, Doña Isabel, with whom one often sees you in conversation?"

Alonso said gravely, "She is very grandee. She has encomiendas near Tuxtitlan of three thousand souls, perhaps more. She needs a competent man to deal with her affairs."

"She says this?"

"I am told this by others."

"What others?"

"The secretary Lope de Quevedo, who has been friendly to me."

"Alonso, you do not speak of matters of speculation in regard to Cibola because that is what Lope de Quevedo and Doña Isabel wish to hear?"

Alonso flushed. "No, Andrés, I do not. Nor to Don Beltrán, who has come to the capital and who frightens me very much."

"But what is this?" Álvar said, leaning forward with his serene blue eyes fixed on Alonso's face.

"Don Beltrán says it is well known that Álvar Núñez resides in the viceroy's pocket and Andrés Dorantes in that of the marqués. He seeks an occupant for his own pocket." Alonso flushed more darkly.

Dorantes felt the galvanizing flutter of danger, of potencies circling. "And what do you say to him, Alonso?"

"What I have said to you and Álvar, that I have had enough of journeying to last the rest of my life. And what do you say to Cortés, Andrés?"

"Nothing as yet, but I hope that Álvar and I are en route for Spain before he returns from the Marquesado, for he can be a very persuasive man. And you, Álvar, do you inhabit the pocket of Don Antonio?"

"I have spoken alone with the viceroy on several occasions," Álvar said. "And he frankly with me. If an entrada to the north is to be mounted, it must not be by Hernán Cortés. It is his part to ensure the Crown that Cortés has no more great triumphs, which would increase his power and give trouble to the Crown. As for Guzmán, I am assured that his time is running out."

"I would be very happy to believe it," Alonso said in a troubled voice.

"Things are more complicated in New Spain than in the great north, Masters," Estebánico said.

"And more complicated still in Old Spain, as I fear Álvar and I will discover there," Dorantes said.

"Listen, friends," he said, leaning forward toward the other three in his intensity. "I believe what we all feel is this: that we do not wish to see armed and armored conquerors marching to the lands of the Pímas or the Arbadaos. Or even of the Marímnes. For these would then be tortured to produce the gold they do not possess, and their women raped, and the chiefs burnt—" He halted to gain control of his voice. "I believe that the Children of the Sun do not wish to see the sword accompanying the cross into the north. And none of us would do anything to cause that to happen."

"Yes, that is my wish also. Just that," Alonso said, and Esteban said, "Yes, Master. That is well said. Estebánico will say nothing of Cibola and tall houses, nothing!"

"As for me," Álvar said, "I am not sure that the matter is so simple. It may be that certain things must be revealed in the right quarters if this entrada, which I believe to be a certainty, is to be that of the cross and not the sword, as Andrés has said."

He was looking worriedly at his friend when the secretary, Lope de Quevedo, bustled into the chamber in his white silk slippers to say that Don Antonio would see them now.

Again they were served sherry and little cakes by one of the blacks, who was very arch in presenting a glass and plate to Esteban, while the viceroy smiled and turned a ring upon his finger, glancing from face to face with his sharp eyes.

"I have read this narrative with the greatest interest," he said, fixing on Álvar with the screwing motion of his head, which mannerism, Dorantes thought, might have been snakelike but in fact was not unattractive.

"Very modest!" Mendoza said. "Which is not always a virtue of our race. You work more slowly than Don Álvar, Don Andrés. Perhaps there have been distractions?"

"The City of Mexico offers many distractions, Excellency."

"Of course you find many old comrades here."

"Yes, I have met old friends."

"The Marqués del Valle, of course!"

"I have seen Hernán Cortés only at the Fiesta of Saint James, along with Your Excellency."

The viceroy squinted at him speculatively before nodding. "The two relations should be sent to the Audiencia together," he said. "And a letter of agreement from Don Alonso would be helpful."

"Yes, Excellency," Alonso said.

"The Audiencia and the Crown will be most interested in what can be said of the 'tall houses,'" Mendoza said. "That would be of the greatest interest. The term is a provocative one."

"I will include everything that can truthfully be said, Excellency," Dorantes said. "One would not like to feel it necessary to tell the Audiencia merely what it wishes to hear."

Álvar looked troubled. He was no longer emaciated, as he had been on the journey, for the viceroy was generous with his viands and liquors, as with everything. Don Antonio's eyes had hardened, as though at an impertinence. Then he waved a hand, dismissing the matter.

"Not at all, not at all, Don Andrés. You must above all describe truthfully your great adventure, as I am certain Don Álvar has done. And as I am certain Don Alonso will certify!"

"One more thing, Excellency," he said. "I must ask how privy these relations are to be considered. Are they only for the eyes of the Audiencia and the Crown, through, of course, yourself?"

The viceroy's eyes hardened again, and his face darkened like a shadow sweeping up from his throat. "Only that, Don Andrés. Any irregularity in the matter you mention would be treason."

He nodded in acceptance. "And what of the maps we have drawn? One we have agreed upon together, and I would understand that it would be similarly privy. But what of those each of us has drawn individually? Would the same case obtain, or might one exercise one's own judgment?"

As the viceroy studied him with his head cocked to one side, he thought that Don Antonio understood exactly what he was asking.

"I believe I would trust your judgment in the matter, Don Andrés," he said, and rose, dismissing them.

The next day he spent the morning at his labors with pen and paper. He was less than proud of his spelling and penmanship, and the difficulties not so much of recalling what had happened day by day, but of setting it down exactly, oppressed him. He had never had the practice of penning love notes or poetry to young ladies. Once he had considered writing a letter from Tlaxcala to Doña Juana, to inform the daughter of the Conde de Aguilar of the adventure he had found in the New World. His disabilities had halted him, and he was ashamed to ask Rufino to script such a foolish missive for him.

He was strolling in one of the viceroy's sunny patios, resting his cramped fingers, when he encountered Doña María de Mendoza. The viceroy's half-sister, with whom he had spoken briefly once or twice since the Feast of St. James, waited, smiling, for him to join her. She was tall in her lace-covered mantilla, slippered feet like tiny silken animals showing beneath the hem of her gown.

Joining her steps to his, she said that she had heard from her brother that Don Andrés had been one of the conquerors. They strolled together around the patio, out of the sun and over mossy tiles in chill shade, and back into the sun again.

"You must tell me of those other adventures, señor. The battles. The terrible dangers."

She pleaded with a curious intensity, and he was pleased to be asked for once about his part in the Conquest rather than the great journey. He spoke lightly of the Battle of Otumba, when that wounded, aching, exhausted, and terrified little band of survivors of the Night of Sorrows had stood upon the ridge looking down upon an ocean of plumed warriors.

She took his arm. "And what did you do, Don Andrés?"

"We consigned our souls to God and followed Cortés." He laughed, but he remembered very well that exalted madness when all of them had possessed strength beyond their strength.

She insisted upon knowing what he, personally, had done there. Her cheeks were flushed, as, holding his arm, she raised her face expectantly. He told her of the charge of Caballo's square into that mass of warriors, so crowded together it was impossible to swing a sword, which they had been cautioned against anyhow, only to thrust, and they had thrust like machines until they broke through to where the cacique who was their quarry reclined on his litter, his guards scattering when he, Dorantes, slew one of them holding up the canopy, the striped cloth collapsing on the chieftain while Gil leaped upon him with a yell, all of them yelling their triumph. And during that time, which had seemed both half a minute and half a day, Cortés and the cavaliers had charged straight into the center of the horde to kill the Aztec prince. When he thought to finish she spurred him with questions.

"It is unsuitable that a lady hear of all this bloodshed."

"I am greatly interested, señor, and see no reason why I may not satisfy my interest," she said. Her eyes gazed levelly into his, and she tucked back a black curl from her cheek.

"You will please tell me more of the Miracle of Otumba," she commanded, as they strolled in the sun. "Ah, Don Andrés, you cannot know how boring it is listening to the gossip of ladies!"

He said, "I remember when it was over and those thousands of warriors had fled before our power. When we could hardly believe we were still alive and were free to march on Tlaxcala, I had to pry my fingers from the hilt of my sword. One by one." He illustrated, perhaps overdramatizing.

"Ah, my God!" whispered María de Mendoza. "Yes, tell me more of *that!*"

"Of hands?" he said, and told her of the hand of the eagle knight that had continued to grip Cortés' shoulder even after his arm had been severed.

She walked with him along the corridor to his apartment as casually as though she belonged there. Inside, she seated herself on the edge of the bed, removing her mantilla and shaking loose her head of glossy black hair.

"And did you possess many Indian maidens, señor—the fruits of these victories?"

"You would consider it many, Doña María. I was not so avid as some."

"But they had loathsome diseases, these women."

"Not so loathsome as those we brought to them."

She continued to gaze at him; it was not what her question had been. He bowed. "None that I knew were the possessers of diseases."

"These matters interest me very much," she said, as she continued her undressing. "It is maddening, señor, that a lady finds so many fascinating matters closed to her. Will you tell me of these maidens? Did they give themselves willingly, or had they to be forced?"

"They accepted what could not be avoided."

Her face twisted with irritation. "Will you please tell me, as you have told me of the fingers on the sword and the hand on the shoulder of Cortés?"

He moved to touch her white shoulder. Her flesh, cool to the eye, was warm to his fingers. She laid her hand upon his hand, gazing up into his face.

He told her of the harem of Gil de Herrera and Pedro de Solís in Coyoacán, and the girls dancing for their masters. He stroked her breast, caressing the hard nipple. There was a little shine of sweat on her face, and the tip of her tongue appeared to wet her lips.

Again she wanted to know of him, personally. "And the girls of your journey. Were there many maidens of the north for the Children of the Sun?"

"It was thought that as gods we should be celibate. My slave, Esteban, however, did not feel such a necessity."

She stared at him in demand, the twist of irritation again.

"There was one, however," he continued. "A girl of the Arbadaos in a rabbitskin skirt who danced very—prettily. I requested her and she was sent to me. They thought the Children of the Sun had brought them rain."

She lay back on his bed, a hand covering the delta of hair between her legs. Her flesh was so white, her nipples so rosy, that he had to remember to breathe.

"You are very beautiful, señorita."

"Come to me now."

He lay on her, seized as though by a hot mouth. His heart thudded against the cushion of her breast. She whispered, "You will not empty your seed into me, please."

He emptied himself upon her belly and then lay beside her. She sat up to smear the sticky stuff around on her flesh and brought her fingers to her nose to sniff, small nose-wrinkle of distaste. The tip of her tongue appeared to touch her finger.

"The seed of the conquerors is sour like any other's," she said. "Is there more, Andrés?"

He said there was more. She smiled at him as she wiped her fingers on the coverlet. "Tales of the Conquest," she said.

He said there was plenty of both, flattered that she would take this roundabout way of enquiring of the tall houses of Cibola.

He had known that Cortés' demand for his narrative would be made again, and he might have known that this would come from an unexpected quarter. A young Indian in livery brought him a message from Doña Marina, requesting that he call upon her in Coyoacán.

In a patio full of flowers and greenery, under a jacaranda tree, she sat with Juan de Jaramillo, a hulking, large-headed man with a shock of graying hair and food stains on his doublet. With him was a balding, quick-eyed fellow, whom Dorantes could not place, by the name of Don Luis.

Both men embraced him as an old comrade and hurled questions at him regarding the journey and Cibola, while a butler served them red Malaga wine. Doña Marina sat watching him, small, dark, stolid, and no longer young, with her black hair and black eyes as hard as those of Cortés, and no sign now of the greatness that had driven her, ambition perhaps not so much for herself as for her great lover.

The talk between the two old soldiers resumed, its subject Bartolomé de las Casas, who had the king's ear, claiming rights for the indigenes which would be the ruin of the encomenderos. The Dominican had even the effrontery to preach his doctrines in the City of Mexico!

"My God! My God!" Juan de Jaramillo spluttered. "The wrongs of the Indians, my God! What of the wrongs of the men who won this Mexico for the Crown with their own horses, arms, and lives! I say damn these noisy priests! Buggerers!"

"You would think the Aztecs had conquered us!" Don Luis said.

"They will bankrupt us all!" Jaramillo said. "Then who will furnish the food for New Spain?"

"We will not be bankrupted, Don Juan," Doña Marina said in her rather flat and inflectionless Castilian. "You and Don Luis overstate."

She rose and said, "Come, Don Andrés. I will show you the gardens. See how the rain and sun bring forth the flowers!"

They walked among flowerbeds. Down the aisles of greenery and color Juan de Jaramillo and Don Luis could be seen leaning toward each other in their chairs. Doña Marina walked close to him, and he shortened his steps to match hers.

"There is talk of nothing but your great journey, Don Andrés."

"The gossip in all the wineshops has us walking through treasures greater than those of Peru."

"When Cortés returns from the Marquesado, he will wish to hear more of your journey."

He did not reply, and she directed them further along, perhaps to be completely out of earshot of the other two.

"Your experience would be of the greatest aid to the marqués' plans," she said.

"I cannot aid him, Doña Marina."

She halted to face him, her dark hands with their jeweled fingers knitted together at her waist. Passionately she said, "He seeks to keep his head above water, señor! Many would push it under. That great man has enemies on every hand. Those who are his true friends must prove it now!"

It was easier to resist her pleas than it would have been those of Cortés himself, but he could feel her force. He said again that this time that aid was something he could not perform, and resisted the pressure to say why.

"Once all of us were able to perform whatever he asked of us!" she said. "And so we were victorious! Now if we cannot perform for him, all must be defeated in his defeat!"

"You are very loyal."

"Once you were also! You and Don Gonzalo. He spoke of the two of you as his beloved sons!" There was a kindling in her black eyes.

He bowed and said, "But you have remained the most loyal, Doña Marina. I had thought you a bitter woman, on the road to Honduras."

"I admit it! It was a failure in me! I should have known he had his good reasons for marrying me to my present lord. Always he had the best of reasons. Already he prepared to return to Spain, to find a wife of nobility and great wealth, as was a necessity to his high estate."

"No, an indigene wife would not have done."

Her nostrils flared at his obtuseness. "Of course not, señor!"

"He persuaded me also that such a wife would not do, and that I must marry a Castiliana. I have regretted that persuasion, señora."

She shrugged. "It did not matter, for you were not a great man. But there was greatness in our lives. It was Hernán Cortés! Without him I was nothing, a miserable slave—not even pretty. With him—"

"Some would say that without you he would have been nothing."

"Has he ever denied it?" she cried. "Was he ever less than loyal to those who were loyal to him? Our debt to him is great, for that greatness that has been in our lives. That rare, rare thing of greatness!"

"Perhaps it is fortunate for mankind it is so rare," he said.

She glared at him. He bowed again and said, "So much destruction because of greatness. So much death and sorrow."

Doña Marina, Malintzin, Malinche, drew herself up very straight. "I believe you were not here, señor, when Cortés returned from Spain. The roads were lined with people. From Villa Rica de Veracruz to the capital, they lined the road. His way was strewn with flowers. They cheered and sang and sought to touch him, or only to catch a glimpse of the conqueror returning. It was a thrilling sight. Tears poured from the eyes of those who observed it. And who were these people who waited all night long to see him pass? They were indigenes, señor. They were the very people he had conquered. They were the people he had freed from the tyranny of Tenochtitlán, but there were Mexica there also, whom he had freed from the tyranny of their priests! These were people who had been governed by other Castilians in his absence. The same people who now, when they flee the tyranny of the encomenderos—" She gestured contemptuously toward her husband and the other. "Do you know where they flee? To the Marquesado! To Cortés!"

She paused, breathing hard, before she said, "You owe the marqués your loyalty, Don Andrés. I understand that at least you have promised him the narrative of your journey."

"I have promised him nothing, Doña Marina, and cannot. I am forbidden to show him my relation. Perhaps I can give him a map, but I assure you it will show nothing that will interest him."

"Yet you give your narrative to that devil Don Antonio de Mendoza!" she hissed.

A young man in gray riding habit approached, a crop in his hand which he tapped against his leg. He was of a dark complexion with lighter hair, slim of figure and graceful, a handsome face that was half-Indian and half-Castilian, the mestizo and illegitimate get of the conqueror, but this was no mongrel like the abandoned street children of the plaza mayor. Martín Cortés was a year older than his own Martín would have been.

The mother introduced them. The boy had good manners, proffering little, but listening politely. When he had excused himself, saluting with his riding crop, he strode off through the gardens, veering away from the wine drinkers. Dorantes saw that Doña Marina's obsidian eyes had melted as she gazed after her son.

"He resembles both his mother and his father," he said.

"What will be his fate, do you think, among Castilians who put such a store in pure blood?"

"I believe that must change in Mexico, Doña Marina."

When she attacked his loyalty again, he tried to explain that he owed his loyalty to neither Cortés nor the viceroy, but to another principle entirely, which surely she should understand. She refused to understand, and, silent and offended, directed their steps back to rejoin her husband and his friend, further along in their cups now, and in their own grievances. Very soon he took his leave to ride back across the causeway to the Very Noble, Notable, and Most Loyal City of Mexico on the fine mule borrowed from the viceroy's stables.

Chapter Five

One of the haughty palace Negroes led Dorantes to a small, tiled patio at the rear of the palace, where an Indian waited for him. The man's lower lip had been destroyed by the G brand of the prisoners of war taken at Tlatelolco, so that his lower teeth were revealed in a kind of sneer. His stance was proud-backed, proud-headed. His hair was tied back with a twist of maguey, and he wore a filthy velvet shirt. Even filthier breeches fell to his calves, which were splashed with mud that had dried lighter than his skin. He stood with his skinny chest thrust out and his chin tucked in, like a soldier. When the servant had withdrawn, he said, in a guttural voice, "Timultzin?"

He said in Nahuatl that he sought Timultzin.

The other stood as though frozen for a moment. His black eyes smoldered. He said again, "Timultzin."

"Where is she?"

The Indian looked puzzled, finally shrugging and cupping a hand to his ear; and his voice had seemed the flat-toned voice of the deaf.

"Where is she?" he said again, loudly, but still the other did not respond, shrugging, cupping his ear, destroyed lip sneering. Dorantes pointed to himself and spoke his name, pointed to the other.

"Coyotl! Coyotl!"

"Who sent you?"

Again the shrugging. At the name "Fray Rufino" the black eyes only gazed at him uninterestedly. He was not certain whether the man was truly deaf, or only disturbed by the fact that he spoke Nahuatl.

"Timultzin!" the other said once more, and presented his palm and scratched in it with a finger.

Dorantes nodded, and the Indian made mime of riding a horse, jerking reins, and bobbing up and down. More interrogation elicited nothing but more shrugs and one guttural outburst from which it seemed that Coyotl did not himself know where Timultzin was, but could lead him to someone who did, for money. Since they were to proceed by horseback it must be some distance.

He thought it well to bring Esteban along, and to arm himself with his poniard. He, the Moor, and Coyotl were mounted on fine riding mules from the viceregal stables. Their guide bestrode his animal with confidence, gazing arrogantly down on his fellows as he led Dorantes and Esteban out across the causeway. Esteban looked ridiculous with his long legs dangling and black hands clamped on the pommel. He was sulking because he had been summoned from some activity that pleased him more than riding out into the Valley of Anahuac on a mission his master did not explain to him.

Beyond Atzcapotzalco they ascended low hills where there were terraced fields of maize, delicate green in the sun that flickered through clouds melting in the bowl of the sky; higher through stony ground and cactus patches, over a ridge that hovered above them, it seemed for hours, finally down into a narrow valley, and up another ridge. With the clouds dispersed the sun beat down and Esteban continually re-arranged himself in the saddle.

"Master, Estebánico is very *sore!*"

"Estebánico will be even sorer if his master gives him the good beating he deserves." Not since Florida had he beaten his slave out of his own frustration and anger. "Estebánico has been too much with those insolent palace slaves and the moscas-de-leche."

Esteban rolled his eyes and was silent, wincing as he changed position again. They descended into another valley, this one broad and green, with the geometrical fields and lines of crops of careful cultivation. Coyotl rode well ahead, out of range of questions. Before them were clumps of sheep and an Indian plowing behind a team of sleek oxen. Centered in the valley was a cluster of huts, smoke rising from a round oven like a brown turtle. On higher ground beyond were the walls and trees, and a single masonry turret, of a Spanish habitation. Esteban had dismounted to limp dramatically leading his mule.

In the village they watched Coyotl squatting questioning an ancient shriveled woman, who also sat on her heels, beside an oven. Her shawl was draped over her head and shoulders, and she shook her head as Coyotl harangued her. Coyotl cupped an ear and glanced sideways at Dorantes. His Nahuatl was more understandable now. He was saying they searched for a woman named Timultzin, illustrating her height, tall for an indigene, with an extended forefinger, and indicating on his own face that she was marked with the Spanish disease. The crone continued to shake her head.

Other women gazed from the doorways of the huts, a child or two in arms, others clutching their mothers' legs, whose faces seemed to consist of nothing but eyes; skinny, pot-bellied, sick-looking children. A crippled man slipped out of one of the huts to listen, skin and bones, one withered leg tucked under him, the other extended as he slid along, half-walking on gnarled fists like hoofs. Dorantes had remembered the Indians of New Spain as so much better fed, more prosperous, and more civilized than those of the north; not so these.

"Master!" Esteban whispered. "These do not have enough to eat!"

They were starving. "What place is this?" he asked the woman.

Her eyes moved, as though with a great effort, to squint at him. "Mezaculapan, lord."

As soon as she had spoken Coyotl slumped as though something of intensity had been accomplished. Dorantes asked who was the lord of this place.

The woman said something he did not understand. She looked frightened. "What did she say?" he said to Coyotl, who now seemed to understand well enough without cupping his ear.

"It is a Castilian lord," he said in his guttural voice. "She does not know the lord's name. He resides sometimes in the capital, sometimes in Mezaculapan." He jerked his head toward the turret showing through the trees, staring at Dorantes with smoldering eyes.

"This is his encomienda?"

To this Coyotl only shrugged. He thought of the plump oxen driven by the starving Indian, the herds of sheep cropping the grass to the roots, which would turn this green land into desert as had been done in Extremadura.

"What lord?" he demanded, but neither Coyotl nor the old woman responded. The crippled man scuttled further toward them, to call out, "Don Rodrigo!"

"What other name?" he asked, but the cripple knew no other name.

"Where is Timultzin?" he demanded. The villagers only looked puzzled. He took a coin from his purse and pressed the bit of metal into the old woman's claw. "Where is Timultzin?"

Her face contorted as though she would weep. Clutching the coin she shook her head once, twice. He thought to describe Timultzin, but Coyotl had already done so. She was pipiltin, niece of a lord of Atzcapotzalco, married to another uncle, a lord of Texcoco. He did not know either of their names. The woman only shook her head fearfully to his questions, the coin squeezed in her fist.

"Master, who is this that you seek?" Esteban called to him.

He drew his poniard and touched his tip to Coyotl's throat. "*Where is Timultzin!*"

The black eyes smoldered at him, the disfigured mouth sneered. Coyotl pushed the blade aside and rose. "There is another place we will look."

He resheathed the weapon, feeling Esteban's puzzled eye upon him. They remounted and left that sad, starving place, upon which Don Rodrigo's fortress-house looked down, the crone still crouched by the oven, the cripple sprawled in the dust, the women and children watching from the doorways with their enormous eyes. They rode on through the valley, passing one of the herds of sheep tended by men like brown skeletons. A dog yipped at the hoofs of his mule.

"Who sent you to me?" he demanded of the guide, but Coyotl only spurred further ahead.

"You must punish this filthy fellow who scorns you, Master," Esteban said, infuriatingly. Dorantes hastened forward on his mule, drawing his poniard again.

"Who sent you?" he shouted at the disfigured face turned toward him.

"It is said the lord seeks Timultzin and will pay."

"Do you know her?"

Coyotl shook his head.

"How do you know she is tall and her face marked?"

"It is said."

"Where do we go now? That old woman knew nothing!"

"To another place."

Teeth gritted, he thrust his poniard out, the point bobbing with the motion of the mule.

"Kill me, lord!" Coyotl said, and jerked at his shirt to reveal his skinny brown chest. He was laughing silently.

He dropped back, furious that he had let the Moor goad him into threatening Coyotl. He had no real reason to believe their guide was not genuinely trying to find Timultzin. In single file they mounted a rocky path. A mountain rose before the late sun, bathing them in cool shadow. Coyotl pointed ahead where buzzards planed.

Before nightfall they encountered a well-traveled road that wound back into the mountains, a mine road, Dorantes realized, as they passed a line of some twenty bearers staggering down the track carrying tall, square, heavy-laden leather buckets on their backs. There was a stink of rotting meat.

In a canyon that narrowed toward a cliff face meshed with the lines of tracks leading to the black holes of mines, the bodies lay. He had seen this before, in the Antilles. Vultures flapped off as they approached, sometimes so close he could feel the beating of their wings. The stench was overpowering. The slaves who were the miners crawled into the sunlight to die, and the buzzards disposed of the carcasses.

"This is very bad, Master," Esteban said. "This bad fellow only leads us here to make us ridiculous. You must punish him." He had his handkerchief pressed to his nose.

He called to Coyotl to halt. His own mule kept turning away from the stench. The flapping fat birds descended upon the corpses again. It was almost dark, and he couldn't see the Indian's face.

"What mines are these? Why have we come here?"

"Many mines. Many encomiendas. Many lords," Coyotl said. No doubt he was shrugging. Another line of bearers plodded down the track toward them.

"Timultzin is not here!"

"No, she is not here. Coyotl is mistaken." The guide's mule started back, and he and Esteban turned also, away from that familiar stench of the Conquest that during the siege of Tenochtitlán had seemed to infest their very hair, beards, and clothing.

They rode back along the mine road in the darkness, assuming that Coyotl was following; but when he summoned the indignation to turn on the guide again, he was gone. He cursed. Esteban complained, and he cursed his slave. They rode on until he could not be certain he still smelled that stench of Tlatelolco, or only remembered it, and the buzzards were no longer visible in the darkness.

"But Master, where can Don Andrés and Estebánico sleep?"

"Have you already forgotten how to sleep on the ground?"

They slept wrapped in their cloaks beneath a tree to which the two animals were tethered, stamping restlessly through the long night. He had also forgotten how to sleep on the ground. He lay awake staring up at the stars through the black fretting of branches, each in its appointed place and of its appointed intensity. He had become more and more certain that Timultzin had sent Coyotl to guide him to the encomienda of Don Rodrigo and to the mines. She had wanted him to see this destruction of her people. His remorse was not to be for her alone.

When he returned to his quarters after the expedition to Mezaculapan, he found that the red leather box in which he kept locked his almost completed relation and the map with which he had hoped to placate Cortés was gone.

Don Antonio de Mendoza gazed at him with eyes as hard as lead shot. "You will please explain this to me, Don Andrés," he said, very quietly. They were seated in a small chamber with a guard leaning on a pikestaff in the doorway, and the little secretary, Lope de Quevedo, seated past the viceroy, rolling his eyes at Dorantes.

"I was called away for two days' time, Excellency. When I returned the box was missing."

"And where had you been called away, please?"

He could feel the sweat on his forehead and the sensation of treading a very narrow path. The existence of the viceroy's torture cellar was well known, although whether it was employed in civil cases in addition to those of the Holy Office, he could not make out. María de Mendoza had once pointed out the torturer, a small man with a bald head, very ordinary looking.

"A messenger came with the name of someone I knew long ago and would give much to find again," he said. "I followed this man to the hills beyond Atzcapotzalco, but it proved a goose chase."

"Your belief is that you were led away so that the box could be stolen?"

"I believe that the two matters were separate, Excellency." Blotting his forehead he remembered Rufino sweating also in his discomposure.

The hard eyes remained fixed upon his. "There was a journey previous to this one, I believe."

"There was, Don Antonio. I was summoned to Coyoacán by Doña Marina. Her purpose was to impress upon me that Cortés must have my relation for his purposes. I said that this was impossible, but that he might have a copy of my map, although I assured her that he would find nothing of interest in it."

"Then you believe the marqués is responsible for the theft of your relation?"

He thought that there were at least three possibilities, one connected with bringing him to Mezaculapan, although for what motive he could not think. "Or someone of his persuasion, Excellency," he said. He blotted his forehead again. "You must know," he continued, "that there is a great loyalty among all those who served with Cortés— which is what Doña Marina sought to invoke. For my own part, once I vowed that my path would never cross Cortés' again. But now they have crossed again despite me."

The viceroy, in his courtesy or his guile, did not pursue the subject of his old connections with Cortés, and Dorantes suggested another possibility.

"I know that Alonso is very frightened of Don Beltrán who, as Your Excellency knows, is presently in the capital, and who is another obsessed with the idea of Cibola. I believe that Alonso is also pursued, but with threats and bribes instead of old comradeship."

The shadow of anger swept up into Mendoza's cheeks, and tiny points of fire kindled in his eyes. He leaned forward. "Tell me this, Don Andrés: by what means am I to determine that you tell me the truth? How am I to know that you have not simply given your relation to Doña Marina, or some other—for the marqués?"

"I could have had a copy made, Excellency. There has been time for that."

Quevedo snorted, and Mendoza said grimly, "Believe me, señor, I would have known of it. And I know that you did not." He sighed, and said, "Very well. My decision is to trust you. What now? You must begin again, eh?"

"I promise that it will proceed swiftly if I may dictate to a scribe. For I was almost finished and have it all in my head."

The viceroy squinted into his face again with the small twisting motion of his head and tented his beringed fingers together. "Will you tell me more of that goose chase past Atzcapotzalco? I am very interested."

"I was brought to the encomienda of Mezaculapan, Excellency. And was very disturbed by what I found there."

Mendoza glanced toward Quevedo, who said, "Don Rodrigo."

"The village is starving, Excellency."

"Ah, you have sympathy for these starving indigenes!"

"Once I was also starving. I had my faith to sustain me. We have taken away the faith of these and not replaced it with our own. And we have taken away their food, and their pride, everything—for the sake of these swollen encomenderos—" He stopped himself.

Mendoza tented his fingertips, "And who are these swollen encomenderos, señor? I will tell you who they are. They are the conquerors of Mexico who have been rewarded by Hernán Cortés with encomiendas. These encomenderos are accustomed to treating Indians as slaves, although that is forbidden."

"I have seen also the mines near Mezaculapan where the slaves crawl to the sun to die and the buzzards flock and the bearers die in their tracks."

The secretary said, "Don Lucas, Excellency."

"A kinsman of Cortés from Medellín," the viceroy said, gazing at him over the steeple of his fingertips. "What a city of kinsmen that is!"

Dorantes said, "I had thought the encomendero was entitled to tribute and labor from his indigenes, but in return was responsible for their welfare, as well as the propagation of the faith and military service."

"What would you have of me, Don Andrés?"

"Enforcement of the laws that would protect the indigenes," he said, but already his indignation was fading into discouragement.

"It will be of no consequence to your outraged conscience, señor," Mendoza said, "but it is well known that this particular encomendero is one of the most ruthless, along with Don Lucas of Las Minas. Others may not be so cruel to their charges. But I remind you that many of your former companions-at-arms are possessed of a hatred of their one-time enemies as though the Indian were a wolf or a viper."

"I hold the Indian to be a man, Excellency!" His voice sounded hollow even to himself.

"And so do the laws of Church and Crown! I can only assure you that as these encomenderos die, as each must do, their properties will revert to the Crown, from which they would never have been separated in the first place except for the powerful pleadings of Cortés!

"I am informed that you yourself once possessed a property of land and a house in the city that were improperly confiscated," Mendoza continued. "I assure you that the matter will be attended to, although it may be that other properties will prove more suitable."

"Thank you, Excellency."

"Put yourself in my position, Don Andrés," the other said, leaning forward. "Certainly these men deserve honor and privilege. The pressure to regulate them must never be so crudely exercised as to create the chaos in New Spain that exists in Peru."

With a deep breath, he said, "Excellency, a compassionate man would not wish to bring the cruelties of the Conquest and its aftermath to the indigenes of the northern realms. Perhaps Álvar Núñez has already spoken of this."

The viceroy's face became suddenly pinched. The secretary rubbed his nose nervously. "So he has," Mendoza said. "But this compassionate man should be certain his compassion does not work to the advantage of the most careless exercisers of that cruelty."

He could only bow his head in assent.

"There is an unhappy process that it seems must be followed," the viceroy continued. "Conquests are made by ruthless men who are not constrained by the laws of God and man. After them come those who serve those laws, and whose unhappy task it is to conquer the conquerors. But is it your belief, my good Don Andrés, that the northern realm can be conquered by men of moderation?"

"I believe it is possible, Excellency." He folded his arms on his chest to stop his shivering.

The viceroy glanced thoughtfully at Lope de Quevedo and back at Dorantes with the screwing motion of his head. "I will speak to Don Rodrigo in the matter of his transgressions against his Indians, Don

Andrés. He is an intemperate man, but perhaps a thoughtful caution can be engendered in him. You will understand that I would have little persuasion over Don Lucas."

When he left the viceroy's presence he thought he had accomplished nothing except to interest Mendoza in himself as a candidate for the captain of an expedition to find the cities of Cibola.

That evening he was sitting at supper with Álvar and Alonso in the great sala, in the cheerful clamor of the viceregal court at its evening meal, when Beltrán Nuño de Guzmán appeared between the columns of the doorway. The governor of New Galicia was clad in rose-colored velvet and pale hose, and he stood alone, imperious and handsome with high color in his cheeks as he glanced around for the viceroy, who had not yet made his evening's appearance.

The Judge of Examination, de la Torre, rose from his seat at Mendoza's table in his black robe, arm rising to point toward Guzmán. In a harsh voice like the squawl of a parrot he called out in the sudden silence: *"Arrest him!"*

On the far side of the room Dorantes saw a guard with a pike trot forward uncertainly; another appeared beside the governor, whose face now was paler than the judge's. Guzmán vanished between the guards, as though sucked back into the shadows beyond the columns.

The three of them were silent in the general silence. Dorantes heard someone whisper "El Grande," the name of the capital's prison.

As the noise of conversation swelled again, Alonso said in a dry voice, "How this judge acts swiftly when finally he acts."

"I believe it was Don Antonio who acted swiftly," Dorantes said. "I wonder if he will act similarly when our time comes."

"What time is that?" Álvar asked.

"In eight days I will have finished dictating my relation. Will we then be allowed to set sail for Spain?"

Both of them stared at him with their different expressions of alarm. "But he assured me—" Álvar started. Dorantes met the blue gaze. He had been cautious of snares set by Cortés, but now he had caught sight of the viceroy's hands manipulating this puppet show.

"But why would he interfere, Andrés?" Alonso said.

"Cibola," he said. "That obsesses men's minds."

"It would be best if the four of us went to court together," Álvar said. "For in the four of us is great strength."

"You are free of Don Beltrán, Alonso," he said, raising an eyebrow at the bald little man.

Alonso shook his head, muscles whitening at the joints of his jaw. "I tell you what I told him, Andrés. I have had my fill of journeying. I will marry Doña Isabel and be happy as an encomendero forever. It is well that Estebánico accompanies you to Spain, however."

"Why do you say that?"

"His character does not improve itself in the company of the conceited blacks of the capital," Alonso said.

Later he and Alonso walked to a wineshop, a dim, noisy place with a wall of piled casks with their varnished heads, the host in a leather apron, and the comforting sour stench of the wine.

"Yes, Estebánico has changed," Dorantes said. "His impertinences become intolerable."

Alonso leaned on the table, forehead wrinkled worriedly; his bald head was pale now, no longer sunburned by a northern sun. "Do you know his pursuits, Andrés? Do you question him upon them?"

"Are they not what they have always been?"

At a noisy table at the back of the shop a hugely fat man stood, back to them, swearing blasphemously as he pounded a fist on the tabletop. Other voices were raised in argument.

"Have you heard the rumor that the blacks of New Spain conspire to kill their masters and rule in their place?" Alonso said. "For they outnumber us. Of course Estebánico would not involve himself with such a wickedness, but has he the sense to stay away from troublemakers?"

He stared at Alonso in shock. He had accused Esteban of a flapping tongue in regard to the tall houses, but something so monstrous as this had not occurred to him. He didn't believe it. He grimaced in irritation at another outburst from the noisy table.

"What is that fat ranter trumpeting about?"

"He is indignant about the preachings of Bartolomé de las Casas. Have you heard of that Dominican?"

He had heard the indignation of Juan de Jaramillo and his friend on the subject of the "Apostle of the Indians."

"He preaches the 'Black Legend,' as it is called," Alonso continued. "How the indigenes, first of the Antilles, and now of New Spain, have been destroyed by Spanish greed. It is said that he possesses great influence at court—and so the Crown may indeed favor moderate men such as you and Álvar. But it is also said that he endangers his life by vilifying the conquerors. This fat one, for instance, suggests that his balls be cut off and stuffed down his throat!"

"And what does the encomendero-to-be think of the matter?"

Alonso grimaced and ran the palm of his hand back and forth over his head. "Once I was a great hater of Indians, as you know. On Malhado Island I hated our captors to the bottom of my soul. But on our great journey I changed. Perhaps one comes to love those to whom one gives of himself, perhaps that is written somewhere in the Holy Book.

"I am not the examiner of human nature that you are, Andrés. Still, one sees that he who has changed may change again, as we see our Estebánico has changed. As I believe that Álvar has changed, from one who loves the indigenes to one who loves the idea of the governorship of the north."

"Tell me, have I changed also?"

The bald little man stared at him steadily. He shook his head. "No, I do not think you have changed."

"How I will miss you, my good companion," he said, his voice thickening.

Tears started from Alonso's eyes, as though squirted, and he sat with eyes and mouth squeezed tight shut for a moment. "And I you, Andrés."

"It remains to be seen whether impediments will be found to our departure."

"Always you think in a complicated way. Taking note of the impediments that may occur." Alonso drank deep from his cup.

"I wish you great happiness, and no impediments, with your Doña Isabel."

"No doubt I will become fat and noisy like these other encomenderos," Alonso said, grinning and waving a hand toward the argumentative table. His expression sobered. "But we were speaking of Estebánico. He complains of terrible hardships on a journey you and he have recently made beyond Atzcapotzalco. Could it be that Don Antonio has offered you an encomienda for your services?"

He told of the journey, of what he had observed at Mezaculapan and Las Minas, repeating the name of the encomienda and encomendero at Alonso's request.

Down the room there was a silence, then the jarring of chair legs in the tile floor. The fat ranter swaggered toward them. "Who speaks of Don Rodrigo of Mezaculapan?" he said in a heavy voice.

Dorantes lurched from his chair to embrace him, crying, "Caballo!" as his old corporal shouted, "Whore of Jerusalem, it is Andrés!"

Even as he embraced the barrel body of the old corporal Caballo Botello, he knew that this was Don Rodrigo Botello, the encomendero of Mezaculapan.

That evening he and María de Mendoza supped together in his apartment, as they had done frequently recently, on chocolatl and sweet buns, and, after the servant had cleared away the dishes, a bottle of Malaga wine. María's leg pressed his beneath the table. Her smile of small teeth showing in her pink mouth promised a better night than this had been an evening.

Esteban sauntered into the room. Cap in hand, bowing, he said, "Master. Doña María. Don Andrés wishes to speak to Estebánico?"

Esteban's eyes would not meet his, and rolled toward María in a way he did not like. Perhaps because he had not challenged Caballo Botello on the shame of Mezaculapan, he challenged his slave before a lady.

"I hear you spend your time loitering in the plaza mayor. What do you do there?"

"Ah, Master, we make eyes at the pretty brown girls!"

"I do not think that is all of it."

"It is all, Don Andrés! We talk to these pretty ones, we make jokes, we—" Esteban stopped as he rose and went to the gilt-fronted secretary to take up the little quirt he had carried on the ride to Mezaculapan. He slashed it across Esteban's face.

The Moor staggered back, hands covering his face, crying, "Master! Why do you do such a thing? Why do you hurt Estebánico?" Puffing, he examined the palms of his hand for blood. María sat smiling with a kind of surprised interest. It was the expression of the avid listener to his tales of the Conquest.

He gripped the quirt between his two hands. A familiar sickness flowed in his veins, the violence that, once he uncapped it, was difficult to control—that had caused him to slaughter that poor fool Nicolás de Cuéllar.

"You will tell me where you go each afternoon!"

"Esteban goes with his friends to this place or that place; for pleasure merely, Master!"

"What friends?"

"These blackamoors, Master, as you have seen!"

"Who are they?"

"Stefano, of this place, and Torito of the household of Don Pablo— the stout one—"

He slapped the quirt into the palm of his hand, and Esteban stopped as though he had been struck again. He passed fingers gingerly over his lip. He pouted, but still his eyes avoided Dorantes'.

He slammed his whip against the Moor's shoulder, and the slave staggered, hands covering his face again. He began to snivel.

"Tell me what you do!"

Sobbing, mopping his eyes with his handkerchief, Esteban said, "They are bad fellows, Master! I only go with them to find out how bad they are."

"How, bad?"

"These fellows hate their masters, who are bad to them. They speak of how some day they will do evil things."

"What evil things?"

Esteban hunched his shoulders as though to make himself small. "Sometimes they boast that they will kill their masters and become masters themselves. But I think they are only puffing themselves."

Now María watched Esteban with the pleased expression.

"And what do you boast?" he demanded.

"Oh, Master, nothing of this! I only say that my master saved Estebánico's life three times." He held up three fingers. "Once in the barges, once on Malhado, and once on the journey!"

"Do you boast of the cities of tall houses you have never seen?"

"Oh, no, Master, for you have told me—"

He slashed the Moor again. "Master, only that we have heard there were tall houses!"

"With streets of gold and silver?"

"Oh, no!" Esteban smiled tremulously, shoulder raised to fend off the quirt. "What a foolishness, Don Andrés!"

"But it is strange that all in the capital know that we have found seven cities of Cibola, with streets of gold and silver. Is it you spreading these lies?"

"Estebánico swears it is not true on the gown of the Holy Virgin! No, no, no! These evil fellows ask me questions and questions, but Estebánico's lips do not open to any false thing!"

"Get out of here now, and stay away from evil fellows. Do you know what happens to blackamoors who gossip of murdering their masters?" He made a motion of jerking a rope tight around his neck. "Perhaps Don Álvar and I should leave you behind."

"Oh, no, Master. No, no! No more of those evil ones for Estebánico. Please, Master, you must take me with you to Spain!"

The Moor recovered his velvet cap from where it had fallen and slipped out the door. Dorantes slapped the quirt into his hand once more before replacing it. When he seated himself opposite María again, a black depression descended upon him. Esteban, who had been a companion on the great journey, had become a slave again in the company of slaves, acting the slave so that he, the master, treated him as one; so that he himself became something different also—the master of a slave. He yearned keenly for those days of marching across the high deserts, barefoot and naked, wooden cross tapping against his chest in rhythm with his stride, the bands of worshipful, innocent souls following them, sometimes singing in their high spirits, in their exaltation, in their nearness to Heaven.

"Does your brother know of these slaves?" he asked.

"He knows most things that occur in the City of Mexico. I will see that he knows, of course." She regarded him steadily, smiling. He thought her meaning was that all that took place here was relayed to her brother. Nothing had passed the other way.

"Of course he knows of us."

She squinted at him comically, as though in wonder that he might think otherwise.

"Tell me," he said, "will he let us go to Spain?"

She shrugged. "Why would he not, when one of you will accept advancement only from the emperor, and the other does not seek advancement at all?"

"Is that what he thinks of me?"

"That is what *I* think of you!" Smiling, she said, "Ah, dear one, you could be of great service to your emperor and his viceroy as well as yourself!"

"There are others I am sworn to serve," he said. "At least not to do them disservice."

"Ignorant, filthy savages shivering in their mud villages, as you tell us," she said. Her smile was half-cruel, half-affectionate. "Ah, Andrés, it is difficult not to believe you over your companions."

His mouth felt dry. "What do you mean?"

"You accuse your Moor of spreading rumors of cities of gold with streets of silver. At any rate, of cities of tall houses inhabited by artisans of worked metals. But he is not the only one."

He thought she meant Álvar. He did not want to know if she meant Alonso as well. Smiling, she shrugged one shoulder, exposing the breast.

"Come," she said. "And tell me once and for all the truth of Cíbola."

He told her exactly what there was to tell, and she laughed at him and made love to him with a wildness he found very exciting. It did not matter that he knew what he had always known, that she served her brother first of all and played deep-revolving games too complicated for him to fathom.

But once she murmured, "Ah, dear one, what if I tell him he must not let you go for *my* sake! How far we might go together!"

Chapter Six

The day he finished dictating his relation to Fray Leonardo, who promptly bore the signed document off to the viceroy, Dorantes set out for Tlatelolco again. He found Rufino in his chamber at the College of Santa Cruz, seated with Fray Bernardino and another Franciscan listening to an Indian who wore a short cloak over a European tunic. The Indian was clearly of the nobility, lean cheeks with high cheekbones, a coppery complexion, dark eyes that took Dorantes in as he halted in the doorway.

All glanced toward him, Fray Bernardino with an irritated expression, the other friar squinting, Rufino beckoning him to an empty chair.

"Continue, Miguel," the third friar said.

"The lord Huitzilopochtli had no father," the Indian said, in creditable Castilian. "There was no father, lords. Coatlicue conceived from a feather which fell from the sky, and the god was born."

"One moment," Fray Bernardino said sharply. "If there was no father, is not Tezcatlipoca implied? Invisible and omnipotent, and of the sky —from whence this feather dropped; is it not so?"

Choosing his words carefully, Miguel said, "It may be, Fray Bernardino. There were different beliefs. To the Mexica Huitzilopochtli was his own father, for he was their god. To the Texcocoans it was not the same."

"This one is Texcocan," Rufino whispered to him.

"Tell us how the Mexica celebrated their god," the other friar said. He had a tonsured, freckled head.

Miguel bowed in compliance. "On his feast day they made his figure from the dough of amaranth. They ground the seeds, from which all corrupt material had been sifted, pulverizing them into a powder. They mixed this with water and formed figures of the god. These they baked in ovens. After they had eaten of them, they said, 'The god is eaten,' and it was said of those who had eaten: 'They guard the god.' "

Rufino mopped his face with his handkerchief. "But the god of Tenochtitlán was not the god of Texcoco."

"Many of Texcoco worshiped the Lord of Near Proximity, Fray Rufino. Whom some called He of the With and the By. Tlaque Nahuaque."

Dorantes thought of Timultzin complaining that the Christian god did not come near her, with her, by her. He glanced at Rufino's damp face.

"Apparently very like Quetzalcoatl," the third friar said to Fray Bernardino. "He required no human sacrifice—only snakes and birds."

Like the god of Pímas, he thought, who had presented the hearts of deer to the Children of the Sun. The other Franciscan continued:

"Of course Huitzilopochtli was the most demanding. He was the sun at noon, and if he was not well satisfied would disdain to rise."

Fray Bernardino blew his breath out in a sigh.

"Yet they were all the same, lords," Miguel said, folding his arms. "Different, but the same."

"The three!" Rufino said.

"Yes, Fray Rufino. As some called them, the red Tezcatlipoca, the black Tezcatlipoca, and the blue—he who was the Huitzilopochtli of the Mexica."

"Three!" Fray Bernardino said.

"And your Texcocan god of the Near Proximity was also 'Smoking Mirror'?"

Miguel bowed his head in thought for a moment. Finally he nodded. "Yes, that also, for he was both one god and all gods."

The friars glanced at each other, Bernardino shaking his head. "Yet Quetzalcoatl was betrayed by Tezcatlipoca into drunkenness and incest, and so had to flee Mexico, although promising to return?"

"That was the belief of the Mexica, Fray Bernardino."

"So that at first it was thought that Cortés was Quetzalcoatl returning," Rufino said to Dorantes. He remained seated as the two other friars rose, Fray Bernardino with a curt nod to Dorantes. When they had gone, their heads together in consultation, Miguel remained gazing at Rufino, awaiting to be dismissed.

"Here is another who was at the canal at Tolteca on a certain rainy night, Andrés," Rufino said.

He stared at the Aztec, who stared back at him, a small man, half a head shorter than he, with close-cropped black hair. He tried to envision that face screeching within an eagle helmet.

"I was wounded there." He was surprised to hear himself speak. He touched his thigh.

"I also, lord," Miguel said, and laid a hand to his side, beneath the ribs.

"Tell this lord what you have told me."

"The Castilians were discovered on the Tacuba Causeway at midnight, making their escape," Miguel said. His voice took on a slight storyteller's sing-song, but his Spanish remained clear. "They carried a wooden platform which they placed across the canals, where we have removed the bridges. I was an ocelot knight—the knights of Tezcatlipoca, who was the lord of the young warriors." He paused as though expecting a challenge.

"But you were of Texcoco?" Dorantes said.

Miguel bowed. "When Texcoco fell we could do nothing but flee to Tenochtitlán, lord."

"Go on," Rufino said, leaning his bulk on his elbows on the table.

"After the second canal the foreigners were unable to carry their platform further," Miguel continued. "There all of the rear but Tonatio were cut off, and ran away down a street there. Later all were killed. We took a great toll also at the third canal, and the fourth, where the Tlatelolca came up in their canoes. The fifth was that of Tolteca. So many were fighting there that the thundertubes and crossbows of the foreigners were of no use. The water was very deep, and filled with men and canoes and swimming horses. We hacked them as they tried to cross the water. We pulled the men from the horses, separating them. Many were killed. Many were taken in the canoes. We tried to reach the lord Malintzin and the woman, and the lord Tonatio, who were there."

He had been speaking faster and he paused to control his voice, his face remaining impassive. "We thrust always for the legs," he said. "That was what we had been instructed to do. Many were lamed there."

"I was lamed there," Rufino said.

"I was a crossbowman," Dorantes said. The Aztec met his eyes again, the calm coppery, soldier's face like the reflection of his own face seen in a dark mirror, the two of them speaking of old battles with the passion gone. Once, after this recital, he would have killed this man.

"Many there of the Mexica were killed by the whistling darts of the crossbows," Miguel went on. "But there the thundertubes spoke no more." He paused again, before he said, "There I was pierced by the sword of one of those who surrounded the lord Malintzin."

Dorantes licked his dry lips, waiting for Miguel to continue, but the other only slumped, as though exhausted, and said, "May I leave you now, Fray Rufino?"

"Thank you, Miguel," Rufino said, and the Indian bowed and departed. Rufino sat leaning on his elbows, as though also exhausted by memories.

"Rufino, did you send an indigene named Coyotl to me?"

Rufino was shaking his head before the question was finished, fat face in profile. He mopped at his forehead.

"A man with a G-brand on his lip."

"I have told some to tell others—that Don Andrés at the viceregal palace seeks the woman Timultzin. That is all." He drew a deep breath before he said, "Tell me what has happened."

Rufino sat motionless, turned half away, as though listening to something else beside Dorantes' voice telling the story of the journey, and of the meeting with Rodrigo Botello. "Yes, they are the worst," he said finally. "Mezaculapan and Las Minas. Poor souls, poor souls. Timultzin would have wished you to see these infamous places."

"She never liked Caballo."

Almost Rufino said more, but only shook his head and mopped his face.

"I leave for Spain within a week. With Álvar Núñez."

"Will you return?"

"I do not know."

"Then this is farewell, Andrés?" the priest said in a voice of relief.

"Yes. Farewell," he said, and rose awkwardly. Rufino rose. They embraced. Rufino's back was damp, and he stank of sweat. It seemed they had nothing further to say to each other.

At the cathedral mestizo boys lounged in the sun against the cut stone facade, among the beggars who accosted all who entered or departed. He halted by a tiny Indian woman, holding an apparently dead infant swathed in her shawl, and a one-legged man with a crooked limb for a crutch. Behind him was a ragged, long-haired boy with a pocked face. Surely that was the face that had snarled up at him when the street boys had assaulted him that night, before the watch had come. He moved aside, caught the boy's eye, made a show of reaching in his purse. The boy approached with a queer dragging gait, as though pretending to be crippled, one shoulder lower than the other, and half turned, eyes fixed on him. He held out a coin.

The boy's hand shot out, but he closed his fist.

"Your name?" he said.

The boy's mouth was strained into something between a snarl and a grimace of anxiety. He muttered something.

"Is your name Martín?"

The boy scratched viciously under his arm and shook his head. "Pato," he said. "Name Pato." His voice was queerly reminiscent of Coyotl's. "Pato," the boy said, nodding.

He felt relief and disappointment. "Who is your mother?" he demanded.

"No mother," the boy said. No father either then, like Huitzilopochtli, the war god of the Aztecs. "Pato," the boy said, with what was meant to be a beguiling smile. "Maravedi, lord," he said, pushing at Dorantes' fist.

He opened it, and the boy snatched the coin and backed away, his smile changing to one of triumph. Others gathered around him. Dorantes turned way.

The day before they were to depart for Villa Rica de Veracruz, and, with the viceroy's blessing, take ship for Spain, he and Álvar strolled together in the lacy shade of the Alameda gardens. It seemed that luck held, and he would depart from the capital before Hernán Cortés returned from the Marquesado; but his heart sank, as though at an evil omen, when he encountered Rodrigo Botello again, Caballo with three others playing at bowls on a sunny patch of sward. One of them was shouting encouragement as his ball rolled down the turf. Hands on his knees, laughing, Caballo wore a fine doublet with the tunic open at the throat and a feathered cap like that Cortés had always worn. Two of the others Dorantes also recalled, Lorenzo Morón of Narváez' army, called "Silkcoat" even then for the elegance of his haberdashery, in violet silk now, with a hatband decorated with a rose of pearls and rubies; and an infantryman of Olid's division named Alamilla. The fourth was a short, bowlegged man he did not recognize.

"Hola, Andrés!" Caballo called, and immediately he and Álvar were surrounded by the three old soldiers, who shook his hand and peppered him with questions. He felt a wrench of conscience that he was not as glad to see them as they were him, and the complex of emotions that fixed upon Don Rodrigo of Mezaculapan.

When he introduced Álvar the bowlers looked at him with even more interest.

"The talk of Mexico!" Lorenzo said. "How one hears of you two famous travelers everywhere! Is it true that Don Antonio keeps you locked up so that no one may speak to you?"

"Yes, how have you escaped, friends?" Alamilla demanded. "Come, tell us of your adventures!"

"You won't get anything out of Andrés," Caballo said, grinning.

"Just as well ask questions of a wall! Maybe this other is more talkative."

Álvar only smiled. His leanness had filled out during their well-fed incarceration, but he was taller than any of them. Caballo was the stoutest: he resembled a sausage in his fine silks.

"You are sworn to silence then," Lorenzo said, nodding knowingly.

"They depart soon for Spain to fill the king's ear with their tales," Caballo said. "Not for hairy ears, these marvels."

He said that they had been guests of the viceroy while they completed the narratives of their journey, and felt there were already too many rumors of what they had found in the northern lands, all baseless.

Caballo winked at him fondly. "Yes, yes, the rumors of Cibola. Baseless, baseless; worth no one's troubles, those deserts of the great north."

He found himself avoiding Caballo's eyes as though he would see reflected in them the starving Indians of Mezaculapan, and the corpses and buzzards of the mines of the kinsman of Hernán Cortés. Caballo bent to pick up his bowling ball, fingers spread to reveal the gap where his middle finger had been lost on the Night of Sorrows.

"Indeed, we have found some things that have interested Don Antonio and will interest the court," Álvar said. Smiling, he said, "But of Cibola we ourselves heard only rumors."

Now Dorantes found it difficult also to look at his companion, who seemed more and more ready to accept those rumors of Cibola as he had fallen in love with the idea of the governorship of the north.

"They say," Alamilla said, "that as Peru is richer than Mexico, so Cibola is richer than Peru! For one, I will enlist for that entrada! Remember me, Andrés! Don Álvar!"

"And I, by the horns of Joseph!" Caballo said. "If only to rid me of this lard of peace!" He slapped his belly with his free hand. To Álvar he said, "And are you an old soldier also, señor?"

"I soldiered in Florida. I was King's Treasurer there."

Caballo grimaced. "We knew another King's Treasurer, did we not, Andrés? That shithead Alderete who lost us forty good men. I say we should have given those buggering priests Julián de Alderete! No offense, Don Álvar." He winked at Dorantes again.

"Soldiering in Florida was a month of sorrows," he said. "The Indians of Apalachen could send an arrow with such force as to drive it through the body of a horse and the boot and leg on the other side. There was no way to dispute with those arrows. We ran."

"An old soldier is one who ran when he was young," Caballo said. "How we ran on the Night of Sorrows! When those howling devils would let us! How Gonzalo de Sandoval gave us courage! Rallied us when we were all but lost. He is dead, you know, Andrés; dead in Spain, watching them steal his seventeen bars of gold as he died. Ah, that good fellow; the finest of soldiers!

"I remember those animals dragging off Bernardo Fuentes," he continued. "They had their hands on Andrés also!"

He said quickly that Caballo had saved his life at the Tolteca Canal before Caballo could say it.

Shaking his head grimly, Caballo said, "How the memory dwells on the fine things, and the sad things! It is long past now, but I will never forget those screeching devils of the Night of Sorrows. Ah, the *devils!*" He dropped his bowling ball and held up his maimed hand, scowling at it. "I have paid my due!"

"And I mine!" Federico Alamilla said, loosening his collar to trace a scar that ran from his ear to his windpipe.

"Was it worth it?" Dorantes asked suddenly.

There was a silence as the old conquerors and Álvar stared at him.

"Of course it was worth it, man!" Caballo said in an offended tone. "Did you not hear Federico say he would enlist for Cibola in an instant? And I also. By the great pocks of the mother of the holy bastard, it was worth it all! Not for the seventeen bars of gold not many of us ever saw, but killing those devils!" He shot his teeth out in a grin that was a snarl.

"Come, we will show your companion the classical crossbowman's defense. How to retreat with order—so long as the bolts hold out, eh, Andrés?"

He found himself posturing with Rodrigo Botello as though loading and firing, as he had been taught by old Agustín, master-at-arms of the Conde de Aguilar, and had perfected killing indigenes; reaching for a bolt, cranking to load, aiming and releasing while Caballo, employing his tunic as a shield, laughing and noisily instructing the others, slanted the fabric one way and the other to deflect the shafts of the javelins and wave off the flights of arrows, never blocking his aim. Caballo told them that two or three crossbowmen and their shieldmen could hold off a thousand filthy degenerate Indians—until the bolts were all shot and panic seized the army, as it had done at the Tolteca Canal where they had almost been overwhelmed by the Aztec Miguels.

Later the six of them repaired to the wineshop where he had first encountered Caballo, to sit at the plank table swilling sangría, Caballo beside him with a heavy hand on his shoulder.

"We speak of the old times, Andrés," he said quietly. "What times they were! It is to each other that we owe our debts. To those who were our comrades and our saviors, for each man was the savior of his comrades! And we owe the opposite debt to those painted, howling cannibals who were trying to kill us all. Andrés, can you favor this Antonio de Mendoza who seeks to dishonor and disinherit your old comrades? It is to Cortés that we owe our lives and fortunes, not that fop!"

"He has returned!" Lorenzo called down the table. "Cortés has returned to the capital!"

He saw that he had Álvar's eye before he said to Caballo, "There is a debt Álvar and I owe that you will not understand."

"And what might that be, my friend?"

"It is the same debt owed to comrades, who were one's saviors; and whose saviors one was. But our comrades of our journey were indigenes. And we would not see done to them the things that have been done to the indigenes in New Spain. The terrible wrongs," he said, in a lowered voice; but said it.

The honest, fierce, vengeful, and loyal red face gaped at him. Álvar leaned back in his chair; the others leaned forward.

"But Andrés—they were devils!" Caballo spluttered. "You *know!*"

"We were devils also! In war each side is devil to the other. I can name things we did as terrible as those they did."

"By God we did not cut them up to eat!"

"We cut them up. They did not burn us alive." He shrugged and said, "Nor do I feel the debt to Cortés that you feel. I have paid my due to him." He stopped, but he could not stop. He felt flushed with wine. "I was his Juan de Flechilla," he said. "His good Turk. But there was a girl I loved—" Why did he not stop now? "You remember her," he said to Caballo. "And a son I loved. But Cortés issued his order that all who wished land must marry Castilianas. I begged an exception, who had saved *his* life, and was refused it. And—" And what? "And so when I ask if the Conquest was worth its cost, for me it was not."

Álvar was gazing at him, frowning, no doubt at this drunken bluster. Caballo's hand squeezed his shoulder. "Andrés, if it is brown meat you favor—I can furnish you ten, twenty!"

"They are very scrawny, those you can furnish," he said, and this time stopped himself, calling himself a coward and a hypocrite that he had done so. He stared at Caballo's three-fingered hand wrapped around his wine cup.

"I have so many I can hardly service them," Caballo continued in a jovial voice. "And light-brown get in flocks. Fifty, sixty—"

He was grateful beyond measure when Lorenzo interrupted to propose a toast to these two who set out for Spain tomorrow. Success to them!

"Success to Cibola!" Federico Alamilla announced.

He joined them in their toast and noticed that Álvar did also. When the two of them took their leave he saw Caballo, whom he could no longer separate in his mind from Don Rodrigo, staring after them in puzzlement.

"I was afraid," Álvar said calmly, as they walked back toward the viceregal palace, "that you would bait him to a brawl, or even a duel, which would have interfered with our departure tomorrow."

"Yes," he said. "It was a good excuse for not doing that."

The message summoning him to the palace of the Marqués del Valle across the plaza he left upon the table, intending to give it to María to carry to her brother. But she did not come to him this last night. He thought this meant that she was certain she would see him again. That night, which he himself thought might be his last in the City of Mexico forever, he lay awake thinking not of her white body, but of the secret, silent, dark one that had come to this bed once long months ago.

※

Chapter Seven

They left the City of Mexico with a train of mules late on a Sunday morning, with the cathedral bells chiming farewell. The viceroy had received them for a few moments and blandly wished them good luck in the continuation of their great journey, while Lope de Quevedo stood by, tapping a finger on his appointment book. María de Mendoza had not appeared.

Esteban disdained to ride and strode ahead, tall-headed with red feathers again braided in his hair. Dorantes knew the Moor felt that old freedom of new realms opening before him from the spring of his stride and excessive swing of his arms. When they had topped the pass and started down the muddy highway toward the coast he grinned back with a brilliant show of white teeth.

"Ah, Masters, it is fine to be ourselves again!"

Dorantes felt dazed with relief that they had been allowed to depart from the city of Antonio de Mendoza and Hernán Cortés.

He and Álvar explored the beach at Villa Rica de Veracruz with Esteban following decorously behind: a bewildering clamor of Indians hawking fruit, the squawling of gulls, the cries of whores and the shouts of stevedores and sailors, the crack of caulking hammers in the stink of tar, garbage, and excrement. Small boats plied offshore, tending a couple of large carracks and a number of brigantines. There was a glint of the cloud-filtered sunlight on colored pennons, painted canvas, and gilded aftercastles. A brigantine had been beached for tarring. Flames licked under the tar pot and sailors with bare legs and bright scarves wound around their heads swabbed the black stuff on the planking.

Hidalgos, factors, and ships' officers strolled along with them. Beggars thrust palms out as they passed, and a cripple sat moaning and swaying on a pile of driftwood. Constables glanced into their faces, and he dreaded encountering these groups of functionaries.

The *Innocente* departed for Sanlucar in the morning with the tide, a three-master with upslanting lateen yards at the mizzens, brilliant strike of sun on the windows of the aftercastle. Water gushed from her plump side, below four sailors driving pump handles up and down. Aboard, Captain Diego de Grijalva showed them a tiny cabin at the waterline. It was filled with trunks and bales, which a sailor was directed to move out to make space for the travelers. After an exchange of money the three Children of the Sun returned ashore for their personal effects.

Standing with the mules and the frightened muleteer were two constables, one short and stout, one tall and stout, the short one armed with a pike, the taller scowling at his warrant as he read from it. The slave Esteban Dorantes was under arrest, indicted as one conspiring to rebellion and murder.

Esteban looked as though he would faint as they clasped the irons upon his wrists. "Masters!" he gasped.

Dorantes drew Álvar aside, who stared in consternation at the constables.

"It is a treachery!" Álvar said. "That spider has caught Estebánico!"

"He has caught me also," he said. He wondered if it were María who had caught him, for she had threatened it; and he himself had stupidly set the trap.

"Masters!" Esteban said, in a strangled voice. The constables were leading him away, the high, black, sweat-shining face twisting back imploringly.

He made no sign to his slave, but took Álvar's arm: "Come."

They sat at a table beneath the bright shade of a triangle of filthy sail that flapped alive with gusts of wind off the sea. A lame man brought them wine and cups. "Would you desert me, Andrés?" Álvar said, leaning toward him.

"The Moor will die of fright if I desert him. You need me less than he does. I am of no value to you at court."

"This trumped up business—"

"It is not entirely trumped up. Don Antonio has only played his trump."

"He will have you to lead his own entrada!" Álvar said fiercely. "I have known it was in his mind. And so he is rid of me! You must come with me to court. You have vowed it!"

"I said I would be of no value to you at court. In truth, I would be of less than no value."

"What do you mean?" Álvar whispered. Gazing into Álvar's no

longer serene face, damp with sweat in this hot place, puffy and twisted with anger, his heart turned with sympathy for his friend, whose grace had deserted him.

"If you are to claim more than we saw, or know, I would not support you."

"You *vowed*—" Álvar whispered, hunching over the table and the winecups.

"Not to that! I know you believe that if you are to gain the ear of the court it must be through Cibola. The tall houses. The workmanship of metals, and what that denotes. Even precious metals. And the rest of it, Álvar."

The blue eyes closed for a moment, and Álvar's lips were drawn into a line like a scar. "I have prayed for guidance," he said. "For of course what you say is true. So be it, then! The first thing is that the court be interested, yes. Then that I am appointed governor, with you as my captain. Then we are in control! Then—"

"No, Álvar, then Cibola is in control."

Álvar hunched over his clenched fists, with his scar of a mouth and his swollen eyes. " I *vow* to you—"

"Old friend, I know it as well as I know my life."

"You desert me," the other whispered again. "That spider has—has *bought* you? Through his harlot sister? Through—"

"I vow I will be the captain of no one else. Will that suffice you?"

Álvar covered his face with his hands, fingers kneading his features. In a muffled voice he said, "Our strength runs out. First Alonso, then Estebánico and you. *He* has done it. I am afraid!"

"You must have faith, Álvar."

Álvar uncovered his face, lips crumpling into the semblance of a smile. "Of course, I understand that you must remain here with Estebánico," he said. "We must not forget that we are the Children of the Sun."

"Nor our great objective. Nor will I forget my vow to you. My heart goes with you, Álvar."

"And mine remains with you and Estebánico! You shall hear of my success as soon as I know of it myself!" They rose and embraced. Then Álvar was gone, his tall figure disappearing up the cluttered beach that was dull now, with the sun hidden behind yellow-gray clouds.

In the plaza mayor more soldiers and steel were displayed than he had seen there since Cortés' grand departure for Honduras, mounted soldiers in breastplates and morions picking their way through the laden mules and carts, the Castilians and Indians, that filled the paved expanse between the palaces of the viceroy and the Marqués del Valle, before the cathedral. Esteban's eyes, which had been rolling right and left as he jounced along slumped on his mule between the two constables on the long five days ride from the coast, suddenly fixed straight ahead.

From four poles hung four crates formed of iron strapping. Birds perched there, rising in flights when one of the horsemen rode close by. As they approached the first of these, Dorantes could make out a blackened leg inside the cage. A gray hand, fingers half-open, was thrust out. A picked-clean skull impaled on a spike gleamed on one corner of the top of the box, which contained the four quarters of what had been a man. Further along another skull surmounted another box, this one crowned with an iron coronet. The quartered corpses were black. Birds settled on the skulls, and fluttered and fed within the boxes.

Esteban seemed to have contrived to make himself physically smaller, huddled on his mule as they progressed across the square. No other Negroes were to be seen. The constables rode close on either side of him, the one named Bustamente raising a hand in salute to one of the helmeted soldiers. Dorantes rode behind them, through the gate of the viceregal palace, where the red-and-yellow banner bellied on its pole.

In the cellar room Dorantes' eyes smarted from the smoke of the charcoal fire beneath a grill, and he breathed the stink of smoke, fear, and sweat. The instruments of torture were displayed. On the grill were a brick and an iron bar, beside it the complicated pulley of the strappado, the boot-shaped iron strapping of the tabillas. He had only heard of these things. The two constables had to support the Moor facing them, and his own legs felt weak enough. Through a far door the bald-headed little man appeared in a leather apron, to seat himself on the stool beside the strappado. Esteban leaned dramatically against Bustamente, arms pulled down by the weight of his chained wrists.

All present ignored Dorantes, and yet it seemed to him that this display was a puppet show for his benefit. He watched Esteban's eyes flicker to the iron boot, the iron-rod with its smoking tip, the bald-headed little man who stared back at him steadily. The Moor's pale tongue appeared to swipe at his lips.

Lope de Quevedo stepped into the room, in blue velvet with darker blue flashings. He pressed a handkerchief delicately to his nose. "If you will accompany me, Don Andrés—"

"Master!" Esteban whispered.

In the simplified Nahuatl called Primahaitu, he told the Moor that all here was for show; he would not be harmed. Esteban's eyes were glazed with incomprehension.

Mendoza, in his red robe and wool cap, was seated in the small chamber in which, after their first reception, he had always interviewed the Children of the Sun. Pikemen guarded the doorway. The viceroy greeted the bowing Dorantes and dismissed the secretary. His expression was severe.

"Have you been advised what has transpired here in the City of Mexico, Don Andrés Dorantes?"

"I see that some blackamoors have been executed, Excellency. The smell is very foul."

"It is planned that the smell will have a salutary effect," Mendoza said, beckoning him to a chair.

"My slave has been arrested in connection with the same business."

"Yes, your tall fellow has been implicated," Mendoza said. "Information came to us that a rebellion was planned by the blacks of New Spain. They would murder their masters. They had elected a king, one who was called Gatito. The indigenes were to join their rebellion. This king and his ministers would rule New Spain when the rebellion had succeeded."

"These are the ones on view in the plaza mayor, Excellency?"

Mendoza nodded, hands steepled together. "The evil creatures were arrested and brought to the torture, where they implicated many others. You understand that these confessions are difficult to assess, for the mere sight of the instruments will cause certain ones to babble like brooks. Do they tell the truth, or only what their interrogators wish to know? Many names have been recorded, and so some of the Negroes of New Spain will be branded and a few lose their right hands, but in most cases their masters are only apprised of the matter." He gazed at Dorantes with an eyebrow hooked up—a spider, Álvar had called him, with his sister his informant.

"It is a serious case, señor," Mendoza said.

"I believe that it is my case that is the serious one, Excellency."

Immediately Mendoza leaned back in his chair and assumed a milder expression.

"I confess I was mystified that Álvar Núñez and I were permitted to leave the capital in the first place."

"It was your own choice to return, Don Andrés."

He tried to shake off the stink of charcoal smoke and the sight of the instruments of torture, which blurred his thinking in this chess game with the viceroy. He said, "Nevertheless, Excellency, Don Álvar has my promise that I will be captain of his entrada, if his appeal to the court is successful."

"And if it is not?" the viceroy said, fingertips angled together before his nose.

It occurred to him that the viceroy knew that Álvar's appeal would fail, that he had already ensured that failure, who surely had more influence at court than the relatives of Álvar Núñez Cabeza de Vaca.

"Why, then," Mendoza continued, smiling for the first time, "you would be free of this fine promise, would you not?"

"Please hear me out, Excellency," he said. "On our journey we learned many things. Perhaps I should have learned more of the fabulous cities of Cibola, but instead I learned things of the heart. These concerned myself as a Christian and a Castilian, who had once been a violent man and a violent hater of the Aztecs like my comrades of the Conquest—perhaps of all the brown-skinned race. If not so much as Don Rodrigo Botello hates, still as much as I was capable of hating. But curing these Indians who called us the Children of the Sun, we learned to love them. In their gentleness and their dependence upon us, and ours upon them, they made me ashamed of my countrymen in our violence and our greed, and our hatred of those we oppress.

"My promise to Don Álvar is part of an agreement in this matter of the heart I mention. Surely it is possible to bring the True Faith and the service of His Majesty to these people without murdering and starving them, without raping their women and burning the chiefs alive to make them produce more treasure, or to punish them for sins they do not understand. Surely these are not the roles Christians should play. I have seen these pagans more Christian in their behavior than we were. Generous with their food when they were starving, gentle when fear might have made them savage. Not, of course, all; but after we had become their healers, and objects of their faith, then all. Excellency, when I wept upon our journey it was when we encountered the soldiers of Guzmán in Sinaloa, and it was not with joy but with shame."

"You speak very eloquently, Don Andrés," Mendoza said, leaning back in his chair with the severe expression again. "And you would have me believe that you and Don Álvar are capable of such a gentle conquest?"

Once, certainly, he had believed it; but little by little, over these months in the capital— He said carefully, "I have believed it, Excellency."

"Could you not then believe that without Don Álvar you could lead such an entrada yourself, under our banner?"

It seemed to him that the wings of danger fluttered near as he shook his head. The viceroy sucked on a tooth, tented his beringed fingers, and squinted at him with the small red flares of anger in his eyes.

"Then, Don Andrés, I put it to you that such an entrada as you and Don Álvar dream of is impossible by the very definition of conquest. The best that can be done is to be certain that the achievement is worthy of the means necessary to it. And those means controlled insofar as it is within the power of a good commander to do so."

"With all respect, Excellency, what can be said of the means that confine my slave to a place of torture during this conversation?"

The viceroy squinted at him again, but without the flares of anger. He raised his hands, to drop them flat upon the arms of his chair. "Surely, Don Andrés, a man of your intelligence must realize that your Moor, who is a linguist in the tongues of the New Lands, is too valuable to be badly used. Let us return to our previous discussion, please. Tell me, freed of your promise to Don Álvar, might you be persuaded to the cause of your old commander? He will already know of your return to the capital and is famous for his powers of persuasion."

"No, Excellency."

Mendoza nodded once. "There is another interested in a northern entrada. I do not refer to Don Beltrán, who is en route to Spain in chains, but to the governor of Guatemala. Pedro de Alvarado has received a commission to explore the islands of the Southern Sea, and is assembling ships and an army. There is no doubt that he will sail north, drawn like an arrow to its target by these rumors you deplore. Is Don Pedro the man of restraint you seek?"

"Of less restraint than Hernán Cortés, Excellency."

The news of Alvarado, the viceroy continued, had galvanized Cortés into moving to Acapulco to rebuild his own fleet in order to forestall his old captain. Cortés' fleet, however, came under the direct authority of the viceroy, and he had been forbidden to sail north. "Expressly forbidden," Mendoza said, tenting his fingers and staring at him over them with angry eyes. "If he sets sail, he is in rebellion against the emperor."

"I promise you that I will not serve Cortés in this enterprise," he said. "Will that suffice you, Excellency?"

Mendoza jerked his head in a terse negative. "I will speak frankly. Your Moor will accompany you on this entrada under my banner, or he will accompany another. With this news of Don Pedro there comes a press of time, and already I have begun gathering the horses for an expedition. We will await the results of Don Álvar's appeal to the court, but meanwhile you and the Moor will continue to partake of my hospitality. Do we understand each other, Don Andrés?"

"I understand, Excellency."

· · ·

When Esteban had been freed from the torture-cellar and his arrest, and, dazed and excessively grateful, had repaired to his quarters, his master obtained a mule from the stables, and set out for Tepeyac, on the mainland at the end of the northern causeway. Rufino had told him some weeks before of the Sanctuary of Guadalupe—the shrine of the so-called Dark Virgin—and he found himself impelled there by something more than curiosity.

From the causeway the lake gleamed like pewter. A few canoes floated in the middle distance, and once there was the white flash of a fishing net. Beyond, barren mountains rose against the sky. Tepeyac was a village of low buildings and narrow streets, a hill looming behind it. Here, according to Rufino, an Indian had encountered an apparition of Our Lady, who had told him to urge the bishop to build a sanctuary for her in this place. The bishop had bargained for a sign, and the summit of the hill had blossomed with roses. The Indian had gathered some of these in his cloak to show the bishop, and the imprint of the dark-complexioned Virgin had been found when the cloak was emptied of the flowers. The sanctuary had been erected on the hill where the roses had bloomed. The Franciscans disapproved of the haste and indignity of the whole affair, and because the hill had also once been sacred to the worship of an Aztec goddess.

Above Tepeyac zopilotes wheeled, those buzzards that had never been out of sight during the Conquest. At the foot of the hill was a market area, where stalls displayed trinkets, candles, and foodstuffs to sell to the worshipers of the Virgin of Guadalupe, or of the goddess Tonantzin.

The line of Indians, men and women on their knees, inched up the rutted track that mounted the hill of Tepeyac, some with hands flattened together in prayer, others with forearms crossed upon their breasts. Slowly they ascended the hill, with blood from their abraded knees mingling with the dust of the track—the Aztec love of blood mingled with Christian attitudes of piety. As he walked along beside the line of kneeling Indians he recalled Beltrán Nuño de Guzmán on his knees, with his arms raised demanding forgiveness.

On the top of the hill the sanctuary was a small building with a tile roof and low-browed doorway to which the line of supplicants led. The interior flickered with candlelight.

In a scent of flowers and burning wax, the cloak of Juan Diego hung upon the wall. On the woven raffia was the image, in muted colors, of a woman enclosed in a kind of cocoon, tongues of flame springing from it as though driving back darkness. She was dark-haired and dark of countenance, wearing a blue cowled robe decorated with golden stars.

The sweet, forgiving face was simplified so that the worshiper might fill in such likeness as he chose to adore. Her hands were pressed together in prayer.

Indians knelt motionless before her, heads bowed and hands joined in reflection of hers. He knelt. He joined his own hands. He prayed for peace, for illumination, for wisdom. He prayed for Timultzin and for his son. The inside of his head buzzed with emptiness. Eyes closed, he smelled the wax and flowers, the sweat and dust of the others who worshiped. In the dense emptiness of his skull he perceived a little Indian woman like the image on the cloak, kneeling in blowing snow with her child presented in her arms. In that old powerful dream, his aching arms draped around her his coat of marten fur. Had it then become marked as this poor cloak was marked? Had his God spoken and he had failed to hear, or understand? He prayed for the deliverance of the Indians from conquest as he had known it, and from the enslavement that had followed.

An image formed in his mind's eye, preternaturally vivid, sharp-edged, and bright-colored; Timultzin in the exact pose of the dark, flame-encircled Mother, in her purple huipil, serene honey-colored face turned down in tenderness, in love, not upon her child but upon him as he knelt before her. Tears burned. Through his open eyes he saw her fuzzy-edged and runny-colored, standing facing him across the roomful of tongues of flame, an Indian woman in voluminous skirts, white shawl covering her shoulders and cowled around her head, one dark hand holding the edges of cloth together beneath her chin. When his eyes encountered hers immediately she began to drift backwards through the Indians who filled the space before the cloak of Juan Diego.

He started to his feet. She disappeared. Outside, under the staring eyes of the queue of worshipers, he was blind in the sunlight. Had he even seen her at all, or only the haunted mirage of his prayers? Panting with his emotion he circled the stuccoed structure, with its sound of low humming from within. From the stony hilltop was visible the gray bulk of the island cities, connected to the mainland by the narrow strips of causeway. *Timultzin!*

He prodded the sulky mule faster than it wished to go back across the causeway as the sun sank toward the western mountains. In the thick dark of his room he waited in his bed, shivering. Once or twice he slept to jerk awake at some sound real or imagined in the power of his anticipation, to shiver until his body ached. But no visitor came to his bed.

· · ·

"So you have made a great vow, Andrés," María de Mendoza said, as they sat with sherry and fruit in the garden adjoining her apartments, with its brilliant margins of flowers.

He was wary of her today, for she seemed both coy and imperious, as though their relationship had changed with his return.

"I made a vow once as a silly girl," she continued. "Which may mean that I can never marry. So I consult my good little confessor Don Arnulfo as to whether the vow is forever binding. The bishop himself must decide! And so you see it is well to be careful of one's vows."

It occurred to him that she smiled at him possessively. Something was required of him. He had thought he had escaped the viceroy's spiderweb. Now other filaments entangled him.

"I am surprised you have not heard this gossip of me," she said.

"I have been so careful avoiding gossip of Cíbola that perhaps I have listened to no other."

A ray of sunlight slanted against her cheek, and she motioned the pretty black mosca-de-leche, Caterina, to adjust her parasol. She leaned forward. "I know it is whispered that I am my brother's creature," she said. "That I inform him of everything. Do you believe this to be true?"

"You have hinted much of it to me yourself," he said uncomfortably.

"Now I act in my own interest. With Antonio's permission, of course," she said, and smiled brilliantly.

"I don't understand what you are saying to me."

She drained the remaining sherry in her glass, the white column of her throat straining back. He thought she was a little tipsy. The flower scent she exuded was cloying today.

"I say that my brother believes you to be an honest and a competent man, as I have often told him. And not a dreamer like your Don Álvar. And my brother searches for competent men."

She beckoned Caterina to fill their glasses again. Damp of perspiration shone in the fine hairs of her upper lip. "For one, Diego Pérez de la Torre, who replaced his victim Beltrán Nuño de Guzmán, is dead of a fever in Campostela. Who will now be named governor of New Galicia? I think Francisco Vásquez de Coronado. He is a favorite of my brother's: young, very rich, very grandee. And for two, he seeks a captain-general of this great entrada—" She stopped herself with a finger laid to her lips, and winked at him.

"I have told Don Antonio I would not do it, María," he said.

"Oh, not for the treasures of Cíbola, which we know to be only the fantasies of greedy men," she said roguishly. "But there are other treasures to be plucked, are there not?"

Again he did not know what she meant; or did not want to know.

She waved to the black girl, dismissing her. She said to him. "I say that Don Francisco is very rich, very grandee. But the captain of my brother's entrada may also become a grandee of Spain. As Hernán Cortés has become the Marqués del Valle de Oaxaca. Marqués of Cibola! Then one might marry who one would!"

In his embarrassment he remembered his dream of returning from the New World, a planter of fantastic wealth, to marry Doña Juana de Aguilar y Zúñiga. He no longer had such dreams. "You mock me," he said. "Both of us know I could never aspire to marry such a highborn lady as yourself."

"You mistake me, señor," she said with a wave of her hand. "Have I not told you I am prevented from marriage by silly old vows? Beware of old vows, I say, which prevent honest aspirations!"

She laughed at his confusion—too long, he thought—her face reddening with her amusement, pearls of perspiration beaded on her upper lip. Then she said, imperiously, "Come!" She took his hand and led him into the cool dimness of her apartments.

Bartolomé de las Casas was the fiery Dominican who preached "The Black Legend" of the destruction of the Indies by Spanish greed and cruelty. It was his great influence at court that Álvar counted on to aid his suit for the governorship of the New Lands. Don Arnulfo, María de Mendoza's confessor, spoke with admiration of the Dominican, and told of three others of the order who had made a peaceful entrada in the province of Vera Cruz in Guatemala, subduing savage tribes there by persuasion, by preaching the faith, and by example, rather than by war. One of these friars, Pedro de Angulo, had been preaching in the capital to the fury of the secular clergy and the encomenderos, who had threatened the preacher with violence for his views.

In these long weeks of waiting for Álvar to reach Spain, for the decision of the court, and for the news of his success or failure, he went one Sunday to Santiago Tlatelolco to hear Fray Pedro preach.

The church with its soaring walls smelled of the mint leaves with which the aisles were strewn. The altar was illuminated by a hundred candles, whose flames trembled against sumptuous gold and silver, and the pale and bloody crucifixion. In the nave a choir of Indians in their white cotton dress chanted in plainsong, their clear, emotional voices rising in contrast to their stolid faces. He found Rufino there, who seemed dazed to see him. After he had explained his return, they sat together watching the singers.

"They love music, these little ones," Rufino said, mopping his perspiring face. "It is a route we have found to their hearts. Fray Marcos plays the rebec, and an indigene made a copy of it and in three lessons absorbed all that Fray Marcos could teach him. Within two weeks he was playing his instrument along with the flutes and executing counterpoint with them."

The church filled: Franciscans in their brown robes, Dominicans in black, secular priests elegantly gowned despite the sumptuary laws; Castilians in doublets and hose, poniards and daggers slung from belts, the aging conquerors identifiable by their paunches. There were also a few of the baptized Aztec nobility, dark, small, proud men in their finery. Dark-faced masses crowded into the rear. The choir chanted.

He told Rufino he had visited the sanctuary at Guadalupe, but not that he thought he had glimpsed Timultzin there.

"You have seen this famous cloak, then," Rufino said, frowning. "It has been examined by experts, who have determined that it is the depiction of an Aztec princess by some indigene painter. The whole affair has been badly handled. Worship of this image has spread like wildfire. Do they worship the cloak itself rather than Our Lady whom it represents? Idolatry! Or do they worship the image of their own Tonantzin? Who can say, Andrés?"

Fray Pedro de Angulo, who had ascended to the high pulpit, was a wispy-bearded young man with a voice that was shaky at first, but gathered strength as he described the successful mission in which he and another friar had aided Bishop de las Casas, the "Apostle of the Indians." After three years of preaching and instruction among the tribes of the most rebellious province of Guatemala, a treaty had been negotiated between the chiefs and the governor, Pedro de Alvarado. The province had been renamed Vera Paz, for it had been peacefully pacified for the Crown and the True Faith.

He was aware that Rufino was very nervous, presenting a puffy, sweating profile as he glanced toward the rear of the church, where there was muttering, and once a scornful laugh. Fray Pedro gazed out over the congregation, gripping the pulpit railing. His voice had strengthened.

"By the Laws of Burgos, we hold these truths!" He raised a forefinger, not quite pointing at the grumbling Spaniards in the rear. "That unbelief does not preclude the ownership of land!" He extended a second finger: "That our Holy Caesarian Majesty is not the lord of the world. Nor is the pope its temporal lord—who has no such power unless it serve the spiritual realm.

"Therefore, the refusal of the Indians to recognize the power of the emperor or the pope is not a reason for making war upon them and taking away their lands!

"Hear me, fellow Christians!" he cried, as the tumult from the rear rose to a roar of protest. He held both hands up, palms out, until the angry voices subsided.

Fray Pedro pointed a finger again. "Christians do have the right to go to the lands of the Indians, to dwell there and carry on trade, and above all to preach the gospel. If the Indians interfere with the preaching, then and only then can they be made war on—for this falls within the spiritual realm. And only then may they be despoiled of their lands and goods, through just war—for that is the law of nations.

"But!" he said, leaning dramatically out over the railing of the pulpit, "we hold that if the Indians do not hinder the preaching of the gospel, whether they accept its truths or not, they may not be subjugated! And if they have been lawfully subjugated, then they become the wards of the emperor and the pope and they may be not enslaved!"

His voice was drowned in pandemonium. Spaniards trampled down the aisle in a reek of crushed mint, shouting, "Pull him down! *Liar!*"

"Violence!" Rufino said in a stifled voice, as the gang of encomenderos and their sympathizers bulled their way to the foot of the pulpit. "Sacrilege!" another friar cried. Fray Pedro dropped from sight in the pulpit, scrambling down the ladder.

"Balderas!" someone shouted. Others among the encomendero party took up the name, and there was laughter at the flight of the Dominican. "Balderas!" Dorantes knew of this abbott, a popular figure in the Spanish quarter.

"A great wine-swiller!" Rufino said in his ear, as, in his white robe, clutching the beads of his rosary, Balderas was thrust forward and lifted to the ladder. His bald head appeared above the pulpit railing. He stood holding out beringed fingers for silence.

"Fellow Christians! Can it be that a poor secular must instruct a regular in the laws of the Holy Church? Is not the pope 'lord, king, and superior of the universe' by virtue of the inheritance of Peter? And has not a portion of this power been ceded to our Holy Catholic monarch, who has been granted sovereignty in the New World? Therefore all peoples therein must accept the Spanish Crown and its Holy Faith or there *is* just cause for war. Private ownership and sovereignty become *res nullius* in the course of just war. *That*, my friends—and my Dominican friend—is the law of nations!"

He beamed, pink-faced, holding out his glittering hands to the shouts of approval.

"Fellow Christians! Can it be that the benefits we have brought to this land have already been forgotten? And are the bringers of these benefits to be slandered as rascals and brutes? Is it forgotten that the rulers of this unhappy land were cannibals? Their capital exceeding Sodom and Gomorrah in its perversions? Their gods bloodthirsty abominations? Brave men, my friends, brought the gospel to this place, threw down the bloody idols, and slaughtered the filthy priests!

"We have taught these people the True Faith, fellow Christians. Taught them to till the fields of grain grown from seed we have brought them—and with an ox and plow instead of a pointed stick. Brought them beasts of burden, brought them fruit trees and silkworms. Taught them to weave silk and a thousand other useful crafts!"

"What of all this, Rufino?" Dorantes asked.

"So true, and so false. True in its particulars, but false in—" He stopped as Balderas continued.

"And why has so much needed to be taught, fellow Christians? Nay, not because these indigenes are animals, as some have claimed. And others that they are worse than animals!" Laughing, he pushed out his plump white hands to silence the cries of approval and laughter at his wit.

"Not animals, friends, but not people of reason either. They are but children. And those who claim to love them, as do the learned brothers of the regular orders, love them because they are but children. For they are children truly, as any priest who has heard their confessions knows. For children love untruth. Children cannot learn numbers above one and two." Balderas leaned out over the railing. "Friends, what can be said of a people who cannot count as high as the Holy Trinity, much less conceive its meaning?"

Rufino's face was wreathed in a scowl as the cheers and laughter rang out again. Dorantes saw that all the dark-robed friars had shrunk away from the violent faction of the encomenderos.

"Yes, my fellow Christians," Balderas said. "Mere children. And surely the regular orders will come to see that these children must be cared for, and watched over, and instructed—by those who are lawfully authorized to perform the responsibilities of parents to such children!"

The young Dominican, Fray Pedro, scrambled up on the seat of a pew, raising himself above all but the abbot in the pulpit, and cried out:

"Fellow Christians, what can be said of parents who sin so grievously against their children? What hyprocrisy is it to call those they exploit and debase merely children? For what good Christian would treat his true children in such a manner?"

With a bellow of indignation the encomenderos surged against the ring of black and brown robes that had surrounded Fray Pedro. Rufino was crying, "Stop this, Joaquín! Antonio, this is a holy church! This sacrilege must cease for your immortal souls! *Rodrigo!*"

Dorantes had already glimpsed him, red-faced and as corpulent as Rufino, lumbering down the aisle to join the shouting pack surrounding the Dominican. Rufino's hand caught his arm. He detached it as in a dream, watching Andrés Dorantes, the moderate man, advocate of the gentle entrada, trotting in his anger after Rodrigo Botello, who had saved his life over that of Bernardo Fuentes' on the Night of Sorrows.

Fray Pedro had stepped down from the pew to stand stiffly facing the encomenderos, wrists crossed and hands flattened to his breast, his face pale and Christ-like.

"Sodomite!" a man with a pocked face shouted at him.

"Spawn of the whore of Nazareth!" Caballo shouted. "I spit on you!" He spat, prodigiously.

While the circle of Spaniards laughed, Fray Pedro wiped his face with his hand, his hand on his robe. "May God forgive you!"

An encomendero with a grizzled beard slapped him. His head jerked and he staggered. A thread of blood appeared at the corner of his lips.

"This sacrilege must cease!" a friar cried.

"We were never met with violence in Vera Paz!" Fray Pedro said. "I repeat myself, fellow Christians! We hold that Indians are as beloved of God as any other man!"

Another encomendero slapped him, harder. "Let me at him!" Caballo bellowed, surging forward. Dorantes grasped his fat shoulder and jerked him around.

Caballo glared at him insanely.

"You restrain me, Andrés!" he said in a thick voice.

"Unless you restrain yourself."

"You take the part of this pisspants priest against your comrades?"

"I do, Caballo!"

The old corporal lurched at him with a speed that took him off guard. A fist grazed his nose, and tears sprang to his eyes as he jerked back. Rufino cried out, "Rodrigo!"

"Traitor!" Botello rasped. "Betrayer of Hernán Cortés!"

"Monster!" he said, gritting his teeth at the gross bulk that confronted him among the other gross remnants of conquerors. "You have become worse than what we once fought. I have seen your victims!"

When the wad of spit struck his cheek he found his hand on his poniard and the blade half drawn.

"You display your steel!" Caballo shouted, and laid a hand to his dagger.

"Sacrilege!" someone cried. Others took it up. Caballo resheathed his blade at the same instant that he did, straightening into a military posture to glare at him from above the red velvet barrel of his belly.

"So, Andrés, will you then pay me back for the life I saved for you? Tomorrow, in the very place where we played at shield-and-crossbow not two weeks ago?"

Anger he had not felt since Malhado Island gripped him by the throat and stifled his voice, but he felt a lightness also, a relief from the constriction of reasonable conduct, from the prudence that had bound him since the journey; and from the hypocrisies of his old friendship with Caballo Botello.

"With pleasure," he said. Rufino was staring at him in dismay.

"At matins, then, buggerer of Indians. You may make your apologies to our old commander through me!"

"At matins, dead man." He was pleased to see that strike like a wad of spit in the scarlet face before him. "For I will kill you before you starve any more of the children who were given to your care."

Caballo spat again, not so prodigiously. "What, so little moisture this time?" he said, wiping his face with his handkerchief. Two of the others restrained Caballo, and he stood facing the corporal a moment longer. The anger had drained away but the lightness remained. At last there was relief from his fears and frustrations as to how the Indians of the north might be protected from the ambitions of Cortés, the cunning of Mendoza, the ravage of conquest. Now at least he could act against cruelty and Indian-hatred. With a gesture of salute he turned away under the silent shocked stares of the friars and the glowering contempt of the encomenderos and their sycophants. He moved along the aisle and into the nave, through the close-packed crowd of Indians there.

Outside, in the blinding sunlight, Rufino caught up with him. "Andrés, this must not be! He was your friend. You must pray for wisdom!"

He shook his head and said, "My prayers are already answered, for there was no other way I could honorably kill that monster. And when I have killed him many lives will have been saved and the achievement will have been worthy of the means to it." It amused him to find himself parroting the viceroy.

Others were pouring from the church now, and Rufino drew him away. In the College of Santa Cruz they passed rooms filled with the white-clad Aztec boys at their studies, chatter of Spanish and Nahuatl. He seated himself in Rufino's whitewashed cubicle, table stacked with books and manuscript pages in folders, crucifix on the wall. Rufino, his face gleaming like butter, poured chocolatl into two cups and offered him one. His own hand was shaking this time, with the ashes of passion. He thought it was not fear.

He said, "It was not a robber who killed Nicolás de Cuéllar. It was I. I was sent by Cortés with letters for his supporters—dressed as a workingman and using a different name. I found him in my house, with my wife. He drew his weapon and I killed him with it."

Confessing it made his breath come short. He sat across the table from Rufino with his right hand enclosing the little cup of chocolatl.

"I saw Timultzin," he continued. "I thought she was dying. I think I became mad. From there I went to Caterina—" He stopped himself, bowed his head, and tried to laugh. "It will not be the first time I have confessed to you before a battle, Rufino!"

"First I must confess to you," the friar said in a muffled voice. "I must have your forgiveness, Andrés."

He didn't understand. Rufino was shaking his head, face still hidden in his hands.

"I cannot excuse myself, but you must remember that it was thought that you were dead. All of you had been declared dead."

"I know that."

"Let me explain a little." Rufino uncovered his face, but still sat with his head bowed. "There is a tale of ancient Greece. The sculptor Pygmalion hewed a lovely woman from stone only to fall in love with his handiwork. Timultzin was my Galatea. I do not know what I was to her. Yes, I do know. She sought our God, and since I served Him I must know Him as she could not. Indeed, I believe she thought I must be a part of Him.

"Let me explain myself," he said again. "I taught her Latin, history, the sacraments, the lives of the saints. Her hunger for knowledge expanded until I could no longer satisfy it. Her Castilian was excellent. She could write a hand as fine as a scribe's. How swiftly she learned you know as well as I. But their minds are not as ours are. That terrible religion haunts them still. I say, she connected me with the Godhead."

"What are you saying, Rufino?" He could feel the sweat on his own face as he watched the fat priest blotting his cheeks with his handkerchief.

"Listen, please, a little longer. The lusts of the Conquest had been very difficult for me. When you and the others were chasing and catching those pretty maidens, I was praying for my immortal soul. My dreams were terrible. Sometimes I would prop my eyelids with splinters so I would not sleep and dream temptations I could not withstand. And at last there was real temptation, and I did not withstand it."

The legs of his chair jarred back as he started to his feet, and for the second time that day displayed the naked blade of his poniard. "*Rufino!*" he whispered.

The other crossed himself. The gray, red-rimmed eyes in the fat face looked into his. "I have made my peace with my God and with myself, Andrés. Now I must make it with you on whatever terms you demand."

He jerked the blade free of its scabbard. Esteban had said on the great journey, that there was absolutely nothing like having a woman beneath him who thought the man surmounting her was a god. Timultzin had connected Rufino with the Godhead. Why would she not? And why would she not accept a god into her bed, surmounting her, when her terrible religion had considered the victim of sacrifice already a part of the god? And what had he, her tuele, her Donandrés, been to her anyway, who had been declared dead; who had first raped her, then possessed her as a concubine, and could not marry her, if that had even mattered to her, because he must keep his blood clean for the impractical reason of the vow to his father, and the practical one of land and slaves?

"*Dog priest!*" he whispered. But he closed his eyes against Rufino's steady gaze.

Of course he had never understood her mind. He had only loved it as part of her body. His own mind slipped like quicksilver over the functions of that religion that of course had haunted her, the mangled bodies, the stinking priests with their torn earlobes and obsidian knives, the skulls on the racks before the cu, the stench of rotting flesh mingled with the fragrance of flowers. Out of those visions, and that faith, how quickly she had entwined herself with the idea of the tortured Christ upon his own rack. And how quickly she had been disillusioned, for that God had never spoken to her, never found her until she and Rufino had found each other, and until the smallpox had found her, that he had thought had killed her but that had only destroyed that beautiful face of which she had been too proud.

"I will tell you one more thing," Rufino said, "that will perhaps allow you to spare me. I am a joke. The capon priest."

He had heard that, but had not understood. Rufino's face was wreathed in a smile that was not a smile.

"It had almost happened, by a javelin on the Night of Sorrows, and I had thought it perhaps a message from my God. So I relieved myself of what had tortured me into mortal sin. It was not very painful. All of us have seen it done to animals, who squeal once or twice and then seem to have forgotten their loss."

"Ah, my God, Rufino!" He sheathed his weapon and sank back onto his chair. Rufino's plump pillow of a hand carried the tiny cup of chocolatl to his lips.

"How you have suffered," he said in a voice so thick he could hardly understand his own words. "Rufino, if only by forgiving you this thing I could make you intact again. And bring back her—" Her what? Her beauty? Or just her presence.

"I do not wish to be intact again, my friend," Rufino said. "For I am at peace, which I find preferable. And as for her—Andrés, I am very fearful. Of course she told you of dancing for her god. Of knowing that her god was conscious of her. It even spoke to her. How often does a Christian experience this? Andrés, I am fearful that if she lives she has gone back to that terrible god!"

"Apostasy!" he whispered.

"What meaningless labels the Holy Church sometimes puts to things," Rufino said, and poured himself more chocolatl with a shaking hand.

And so he went again to the Shrine of Guadalupe, and in these close, dim quarters with the stench of unwashed bodies, darkness shivering with candle flames, he prayed before the famous cloak with its depiction of a Mexica princess by some Indian painter, that was either worshipped of itself in idolatry, or as the Aztec goddess Tonantzin in apostasy by those who had been baptized. He prayed for forgiveness for himself, and for Rufino and Timultzin; he prayed for Timultzin and Martín, and the soul of Rodrigo Botello. He prayed for the grace to forgive those who had sinned against him, writhing to think of Timultzin celebrating her union with the Christian God beneath the lusts of a depraved priest, like Esteban in his multitude of seductions. *But she had thought he was dead!* And how many others, after? But when he had returned to Mexico she had crept into his bed. His! He grimaced until his eyes ached to think of her covered by that gross, sweating bulk. Who had castrated himself for his sins.

This time the image that gathered substance in his mind's eye was Timultzin with Martín. The child's hand was streaming blood, and Timultzin, white-faced, staunched the blood with a white cloth. Blood stained the cloth. Martín had cut his finger pulling from its scabbard his father's sword of the Conquest, regarding his blood without tears but with great eyes and a tightlipped mouth. Later there had been the weal of white scar wrapped half around that tiny finger. The whiteness of the scar on the brown flesh hung in his mind's eye.

Then the scabbard of his poniard scraped on the stone floor, the image disappeared, and his thoughts flew out like water skittering in a hot pan. He himself had no sword for his meeting at matins.

The sun was low when he trudged back over the causeway into Tlatelolco. There in the great native market, he found a stall of weapons; poniards, a broad-bladed cinqueada, a half dozen rapiers held erect in a hollowed section of log. One of these he drew out to examine. The steel cup was perforated and damascened, with a triangle torn away as though it had been lopped with an ax. The gray-haired little Indian proprietor pointed out where rust had been scraped away to reveal the stamp of Toledo. He paid the asking price and, with the narrow blade slung through his belt with his poniard, started on back toward the viceregal palace. This evening he was better prepared for an assault by the half-breed wild boys who lurked around the plaza mayor.

He saw a group of them in the shadows before the cathedral. As he approached they evaporated before him, except the one on crutches, whom he cornered. The mestizo hunched, panting with fear, fangs bared like a dog. He offered a coin. "Pato," he said.

The other made off, plock of his crutch on the paving stones. He waited in the shadows. Suddenly Pato was sidling toward him, filthy face half-fearful, half-cunning, hand out. He seized the hand and brought the fingers close to his eyes, while the boy cursed shrilly, trying to jerk away, stinking of fear. Smallpox scars made coin-shaped shadows on his neck and cheek. There was no white weal on the index finger. He grasped the other hand, that flailed at him, freeing the first. This finger had been scarred by the Spanish disease merely. The boy squealed and pummeled him. He released the hand, and fumbled in his purse for another coin. Pato snatched it and fled.

Chapter Eight

In the Alameda gardens, on the patch of sward upon which he and Caballo had played at shield-and-crossbowman, he waited with a terrified Esteban, who whispered, "But Master, what will poor Estebánico *do*?" Gray dawn spread behind the eastern volcanoes, their white heads visible now. "But Master—" Esteban whispered, and managed to stop himself.

Rodrigo Botello arrived with two companions, one with a towel over his arm, the other carrying a leather sword case, both heavy men in doublets and high boots. He noticed that Caballo, for all his purposeful stride, walked with the perceptible heel-and-toe rocking of a man far along with paresis. The three of them whispered together, the two seconds scowling in disapproval at the Moor. Caballo stripped off his jacket, huge in his white shirt that gleamed like a pearl in the first light. He drew a blade from the case and whipped it flexing before him.

Dorantes handed his own jacket to the slave and stood facing his enemy with his own blade pointed to the ground. An edge of sun blazed over a snowy peak, turning the thick figure before him black as a cinder. He raised his own sword as Caballo swept his back and forth with its sound of angry bees. The cathedral bells began their chiming and Caballo advanced a step, a booted foot extending, the other brought up behind. A gleam of sun ran along the blade of his rapier.

The blades made contact in salute. He felt the strength of the other's wrist. He tried to make out Caballo's features in the silhouette looming against the sun.

Caballo halted as though he had been struck. He stood swaying, blade slanting downward. In an almost unintelligible voice he grunted, "Tell Gonzalito—"

One of the seconds called, "What is that, Caballo?"

Caballo stood swaying to the chiming of the bells. He dropped his sword. He clasped one hand in the other. He dropped to his knees. Then he fell straight forward, making no effort to break his fall.

The seconds hurried to turn him on his back. Dorantes handed his rapier to Esteban, and knelt beside the fat man also. Caballo's face was bloody from his fall. His eyes were wide open. His lips moved.

"Tell Gonzalito—"

"Tell him what, Caballo?" one of his friends said in a shrill voice, but there was no answer.

Dorantes thought that Caballo had wanted Gonzalo de Sandoval to know that his old corporal was coming to join him. He knelt beside the man whose heart had stopped, taking the wrist beneath its lace cuff between his thumb and forefinger. There was no flicker of pulse. The bells of matins ceased.

One of the seconds moved to elbow him away, muttering, "Witch!"

"Betrayer of your comrades!" the other said, rising.

"Come, Master!" Esteban said. "It is done, Master!"

He remained in his apartments all that day, frightened by the death that had taken Caballo, whom he had been determined to kill, and examining the sins of his life. "Witch!" one of the seconds had said. Álvar Núñez, at least for those months of their journey, had been blessed with the power of life, while he had possessed the opposite. The Cuchendádos and Aguénes had perceived it. The Marímne nick-named Shitface perhaps had died of it. He rubbed his arms where he could remember the warmth of healing and wondered if ever again he would feel that sensation of faith made tangible. He prayed for the soul of Rodrigo Botello. When Esteban knocked softly he sent the Moor for food. He was relieved that María did not come.

But when in the night he heard the whisper of the door opening it did not occur to him that it could be anyone else. A figure cowled like the Virgin of Guadalupe showed for a moment against the lesser dark outside. When the door closed the shape vanished. A voice whispered in Nahuatl.

"Who is it?" he said, sitting up.

"It is I, my tuele."

He reached out for her. His hand encountered nothing. It was as though a weight crushed his chest so he could not breathe. He fumbled on the taboret beside the bed for flint, steel, and the candle, but her hand immobilized his. Her remembered scent filled his nostrils. Her denser shape congealed in the darkness.

"My heart, you have seen Rufino, I know. We were told all were dead on the road to Honduras. I died then. And when it seemed that I was truly dying of the disease, you came—"

"And fled, and died in my own self." He carried her hand to his face, as once when he had been used to caressing her beneath her dress she would bring his hand to her cheek instead. "It was you who sent me to Mezaculapan, I know."

"I believe that you bared your sword again for me!"

"It was God who took him, for his sins."

"I saw you at Tepeyac," she said breathlessly, when he kissed the palm of her hand.

"And I you! I should have known you would pray—"

"No, I must tell you!" she interrupted. "I have returned to my own gods. I serve them completely. I cannot tell you more!"

Had he not known that already? What meaningless labels the Holy Church put to things, Rufino had said. But he felt a swift flutter of danger. Her fingers touched his lips, so lightly. His fingers caressed her smooth arm. His need was acute and painful. He whispered, "Please come into this bed."

"If you want me, my heart. Oh, if you should want me!"

He reached out to grasp and pull her to him, shivering as though he would break apart. He found her bare slimness under the swaddling of her clothing, and his hands found and remembered every part except for her face. There her hands drew his away. As their groins joined she breathed in Nahuatl, with that frankness that had sometimes shocked him, the name of the organ which she had possessed along with his heart, and which now possessed her. When he exploded inside her with a violence he thought must have hurt her, she babbled, "Ah, my lord, my master, my heart, my tuele, my beloved—"

Surmounting her now, he managed to loosen the facebands from her cheeks, gleam of her eyes gazing up at him. Carefully he drew the cloths away; gently he touched the shocking roughness of the flesh. He kissed her scars. Panting, he kissed her tear-wet destroyed features that once had been so beautiful they haunted his memory.

When he lay still covering her, with his face laid beside hers, he said, "The viceroy has promised me Xicomilpa or another place. We will return to live there. As we once lived. Where is Martín?"

Her hands stroked the small of his back. "I do not know. I have not found him. Gualcoyotl took him with her when she fled with her own Antonio, but then she was also stricken. I prayed, my heart! To your God, and to mine. But he is lost. He is gone. I believe in my own heart that he is dead, and it is said that a mother knows these things."

He turned over on her arm, pinioning it as once he had in the garden of the palace at Texcoco, until Caballo had approached panting.

Her whisper was warm in his ear. "Andrés—I did not tell you. How could I tell you? When the priest looked into the tonalamatl the auguries were very bad for the day of his birth. There were influences of Tlaloc, of the rain; of tears, you understand. Also of Tlazolteotl, of excrement and evil. Of Xolotl, of the evening star, of death. It could not have been worse for a child. And so you remember we changed the day of his birth to One-reed. But it was not properly done. Priests should have come, in numbers, with heads painted blue. There should have been gifts. I knew that you could not allow that, and almost I myself felt that it was unnecessary. But I believe that he died of water, my heart, for so it was prophesied."

She wept. He stroked her scarred face.

"And you believe—all that," he said.

"I did, and did not, for I was a Christian then. But now I believe all that again. And serve what you may not know."

"Nevertheless, we must search for him. Remember the scar on his finger?"

"I remember, my heart."

"And we will return to Xicomilpa, you and I. And there—"

"My lord," she whispered urgently. "My good tuele, my brave one, who bares his sword for Timultzin—" She brought her lips to his as though to stop his speech.

When he awakened she was gone. For a despairing moment he thought she might have been a dream.

The next day he strolled in the plaza between the two palaces. Stocks, newly imported from Spain as a punishment for drunkenness, had been set up before the cathedral, and the whipping block and gibbet were fixtures. Today two Indians were being flogged across the square.

Over the heads of the shorter Indians, he marked the approach of Gil de Herrera and another familiar face. Gil stared at him and spoke to his companion; both stared at him, hard-eyed and sneering, as they passed each other. Gil spat. He saw that it would be difficult to avoid another challenge out of the death of Caballo.

He was oppressed also by Timultzin's intimations that she had not only relinquished her Christian baptism, but actively served her old gods, for this was the very offense of the Indians who were being punished.

The two had been stripped to the waist, and there was vicious red crosshatching on their backs. They moaned and cried out as the constables whipped them along, and one jumped in a way that amused the spectators. A crier and a donkey laden with heavy sacks followed them.

The crier shouted, "This is the punishment for apostasy! This is the punishment for idolatry! This is the punishment for opposition to the evangel!"

Following the painful progress, he encountered María de Mendoza and her confessor, Don Arnulfo, before the cathedral. She smiled at him over her fan, while Don Arnulfo stood slightly apart, frowning judiciously at the guilty ones. The comic squealed and hopped at his stripes, to guffaws and calls of encouragement.

María laid a hand on his arm, as tall as he in her peach-colored silks. "Tell me, what are the sensations of a duelist as he faces a man who will try to kill him?"

"In this case I could not see his face, as he stood with his back to the rising sun."

"Yes, yes. Continue, please."

"You may sometimes read a man's next move in his eyes. Also, the sun in my eyes would be troublesome. Therefore I would have to maneuver him to one side."

María laughed delightedly, patting his hand with her gloved one. "How well you explain things to one who has had no adventures! But were you not frightened?"

"Not very frightened, for he was heavy with good living and unsteady with the pox. Though his wrist was strong."

"I would have you more careful, Andrés," she said. "If the affair had ended differently, you would be dead, or en route to Cibola."

He asked what her brother had had to say.

She flipped her fan to cover her face as a Castilian standing nearby glanced at her. "He spoke with sadness of the reputation for moderation of Andrés Dorantes, and said he hoped the rivers of compassion did not merely run north."

"The river of compassion had dried up at Mezaculapan," he said grimly. "And the river of old comradeship at Las Minas."

Her eyes turned serious over the edge of her fan. In a momentary lull of the groans of the Indians and the laughter of the spectators, the sickening whack of leather thongs upon flesh was audible.

The two were flogged to the steps of the cathedral, where they knelt with bleeding backs. A constable unfastened one of the sacks from the donkey's packsaddle and let it drop with a crockery crash. He dropped the second bulky sack also, the donkey scampering sideways on frail legs.

"This is the punishment for apostasy! This is the punishment for idolatry!" the crier intoned.

While the Indians knelt with arms flung up for mercy, the constable took clay idols from the sacks and smashed them on the stone steps before the penitents. The other wielded his whip with vigor. Dorantes felt his face twisting with anxiety. He had the sensation that this exhibition was contrived for his elucidation, the other side of the coin from the exhibition of Mezaculapan, for of course Timultzin's intimations had been of idolatry as well as apostasy.

Don Arnulfo observed the whipping and smashing of idols with a severe expression, sometimes nodding his approval. He was a plump, befrocked little man with a chin-fringe of beard. He moved to join María and Dorantes.

"What will happen to them, Don Arnulfo?" María enquired.

"It is the law that indigenes may not be relaxed to the secular authority for punishment," the little priest said in a pompous voice. "Therefore they will not be burned, richly as these apostates deserve it. Most probably they will be imprisoned in El Grande."

They listened to the whacking of the whips and the cries of the Indians.

"The good bishop is much occupied with idolatry," María said.

"It is the chief concern of the Holy Office just now," Don Arnulfo said. "They find these pottery abominations everywhere, and the idol of their rain god has been dug up in the mountains and destroyed. But the other great idol still eludes us, although the Holy Office searches everywhere."

"Don Andrés has seen those idols in their oratories," María said, mischievous eyes glancing over her fan.

"What is this?" the priest exclaimed.

He described what he had seen when, with Cortés, he had fought his way to the top of the pyramid—years ago. The other stared at him, finally turning to observe the flogging again, scowling. "I believe it was a mistake to give power to the old Aztec nobility," he said. "They conspire against us. Some are said actually to preach faith in Satan rather than God the Father. They revel in drunkenness. They have the morals of monkeys! One is known to have raped two virgins in church. And during Lent! The bishop is right to concern the Inquisition in these matters."

The penitents were rousted to their feet and whipped staggering back to the center of the plaza, with the crowd retreating from their path. They knelt again, the whips were folded at last, and shears produced. A barber roughly scissored black locks of hair from their scalps.

"So you have actually set eyes upon the great idols," the little priest said.

They left him still watching the punishment of the idolators and made their way on across the plaza, avoiding the beggars and the tag-playing urchins.

"It amuses me to think of those horrid idols in their oratories in this very place," María said. With her fan she indicated the palace of Cortés, with her gloved hand that of the viceroy: "Like the housings of these two great men who are not used to being balked in their courses. Do you not sometimes feel hot breath upon your back?"

"Often," he said.

"There is crisis between them now. My brother strives always to avoid a direct confrontation, but he has drawn an edict that Cortés' fleet may not sail north from Acapulco. Will the marqués obey this?"

"I believe that he must, señorita."

They walked on through the thinning crowd toward where the banner of Don Antonio de Mendoza flourished in a breeze. "Coronado drags his heels in proceeding to Compostela to take up his duties as governor," María said, grasping his arm. Her stance seemed now to be that if he became a great captain in the coming entrada to Cíbola, they might marry. He did not know whether she mocked him or baited him. Always it seemed she must hide her true feelings behind derision and ridicule.

"It is clear he is your brother's great favorite," he said.

"All the world is fascinated by the idea of Cíbola," María continued. "The emperor enquires, in his letters. And now there is a press of hurry. It will be such a grand entrada I believe that only one of great wealth and noble family can be chosen to lead it."

Now her meaning was clear. He wondered if the tightness in his chest was disappointment as well as relief. "So it will be Coronado."

"With captains under his command," she said quickly. She flipped up her fan as she turned toward him. There was something in her eyes he did not recognize.

"I will not be one of those captains, señorita."

She laughed merrily, the momentary seriousness dissolving. "We will arrange a wager as to that, señor! For had Don Rodrigo died of a sword through the heart instead of natural causes, you would be one of those captains or you would be in El Grande. And something else will transpire!"

He told her that he would be very careful, and she withdrew her hand from his arm, although she continued to walk close beside him toward the viceregal palace, her fan kept raised to conceal the lower part of her face.

In a small audience room with its dark wooden cross and silver figure of the Savior, and high windows casting slanting squares of sunlight upon the tiles, he was introduced to the Bishop of the Diocese of Mexico, the Apostolic Inquisitor and Protector of the Indians, the

Franciscan Fray Juan de Zumárraga, a short, white-haired Basque with a nose like a swollen parrot's beak. He sat beside Mendoza in his plain brown robe, impatiently swinging the rope end of his girdle.

As Dorantes knelt to kiss the bishop's hand, Mendoza said, "Don Andrés was one of the party of Don Álvar Núñez Cabeza de Vaca, who traversed the continent through the northern realms, Your Grace. He was also present at the Siege of Tenochtitlán."

"Where he has seen the great abominations, as Don Arnulfo has reported to me. Yes, yes," the bishop said in his harsh voice.

Dorantes rose to stand facing him. On a higher step Coronado watched with an arrogant blue eye, fair-haired, slender, and straight-backed in his slashed blue velvet. Also present were Lope de Quevedo and a Franciscan underling.

The bishop leaned forward, elbow braced on his knee. "Is it true, my son, that you viewed these satanic idols with your own eyes?"

"I saw one of them, Your Grace."

"Will you describe this abomination for me, please?"

"It was in the style of those things, the size of an ox, but more square in shape, with glaring eyes and a belt of golden serpents." He summoned as much from his memory as he could, from his own observation and the gossip among his comrades afterwards. The bishop prodded him with questions.

"I would have observed more if I had not been so frightened," he said. "The place stunk of blood to turn the stomach, and we were in great danger there."

He saw from Coronado's expression that the young nobleman would not have been frightened. He had often enjoyed describing the terrible fears of the Conquest to newcomers to the New World, taking pleasure in observing their contempt for the faint-hearted conquerors.

The bishop leaned toward him again. "And what was the disposition of these abominations when Tenochtitlán fell, my son?"

He racked his memory for the answer. Mendoza was leaning back in his chair, eyes fixed upon him, as were those of all in the chamber. All he could recall were the depictions of ruined and burning temples in the pictographs that had been produced for Rufino and Fray Bernardino at the College of Santa Cruz.

"It may be that the Tlaxcalans destroyed them or carried them away. I believe it was common practice to destroy the pyramids and the idols of the enemy."

"The idol of Tlaloc has been found hidden in a cave in the mountains and destroyed, Don Andrés," Mendoza said. "But that of Huitzilopochtli has not been found."

"It is a conspiracy," the bishop said wearily, spreading his hands wide apart to shape the enormity of it. "Surely this conspiracy emanates from Satan himself. We must track down this abomination and destroy it, Don Andrés! As long as this idol exists the sovereignty of the Holy Church in this land is in the very gravest danger!"

When he allowed himself to think of Timultzin—who had returned to her own gods, she had said, who served them completely—his breath came short and he felt transparent under the unblinking stare of the bishop. Wings of danger, of connections, hovered over him in close proximity—those words he recalled as the curious name of a different kind of Aztec deity, He of the With and the By.

The bishop cocked a finger and the friar stepped around his chair to unroll a rectangle of woven raffia, the same substance upon which the miraculous image of the Virgin of Guadalupe had appeared. Depicted upon this, in the familiar Aztec style, were four bundles bound with ropes, squat, squarish masses swathed in fabric, two large, two smaller. Surrounding them were Aztec heads with the curls of detached tongues which signified speech, and written words of Nahuatl phoneticized into Castilian. There were symbols he did not understand: a large bird's head, a sheaf of maize, a rattlesnake. Lines connected the heads, the bundles, and the other symbols. One of the large bundles had been labeled, and he recognized the word. In the upper corner were lines of tightly knit cursive.

"Do you understand Nahuatl, my son?" the bishop asked.

He nodded, and sounded the words out: " 'yn axcan ninococotica huel mococohua ynonacayo amo pactica yece yn notlamachiliz pactica yn iuhqui nechmomaquili yn toteo dios amo nitlapolohua—' He says he is sick—not healthy—but his understanding is well enough. The Lord God gave it to him and has not taken it away. If he is now to die—"

"It is correct, Your Grace," the friar said.

"And what is the name given to the bundle on the left, my son?" Zumárraga asked.

"It is Huitzilopochtli."

The bishop hunkered back in his chair, breathing heavily.

"Don Andrés and Don Francisco would be interested in the tale, I am certain, Your Grace," the viceroy said, and the old man vigorously massaged his nose and flipped a hand at the friar.

"The tale is this," the friar said. "When it became clear that the City of Tenochtitlán was doomed, the great idols were placed in the safe-keeping of the Prince of Texcoco, Tlatolatl, who hid them in Atzcapotzalco. Anahuacaca became prince-of-the-house upon the death of Cuauhtémoc, and the idols came into the charge of his sons upon his death. These sons, however, were baptized in the Holy Faith, and one of them, Don Mateos, on becoming close to death—it is his words you have translated, Don Andrés—has come forward to advise the Holy Office of the existence of the abominations. They were taken from the control of him and his brother, and brought into this city by one named Don Miguel—"

"Who was not then baptized and so did not have a Christian name," the bishop snapped.

"His indigene name, Fray Junípero?" Mendoza asked.

"Puxtecatl Tlayotla, Excellency."

Dorantes recognized the name. Puxtecatl Tlayotla was the uncle in whose household in Atzcapotzalco Timultzin had been raised. Miguel had been the name of the ocelot knight of the Night of Sorrows, whom he had met at the College of Santa Cruz at Tlatelolco. Miguel was a common Christian name, and surely he was too young to be Timultzin's uncle. He scraped his memory for the features of the younger Aztec who had accompanied Timultzin's husband that day he had drawn his sword against Gonzalo de Sandoval.

"Don Mateos and his brother, Don Pedro, claim not to know the whereabouts of the great idol," the friar continued. "They were told it had been removed again, but not where. Back to Atzcapotzalco, Don Mateos thinks. Possibly to Tula. Don Pedro believes the image of Huitzilopochtli may have been removed to the north, so that rebellion may be carried out there in its name. Both brothers have been shown the instruments of torture, but do not change their stories. Nor is there reason to doubt them, for Don Mateos, at least, came to the Holy Office of his own free will."

"But what of this Don Miguel, Your Grace?" Coronado asked, standing with his legs in his high, soft leather boots braced apart, arms still folded on his chest.

Zumárraga shifted his shoulders restlessly in his brown robe. He said in his harsh voice, "He claims the idols left his keeping before his baptism, thus he cannot be accused of idolatry. He also has been confronted with the rack. All he will say is that perhaps Huitzilopochtli has returned to Atzlan, the ancient home of the Mexica, in the north." He waved a hand toward the north. An old, furious, and exhausted man, Dorantes thought—with this burning mission.

"Atzcapotzalco and Tula are near," the viceroy said. "And can be torn apart house by house. But the north is far and very large, eh, Don Andrés?"

"This abomination will be found if it has been hidden in New Galicia, Your Grace," Coronado said, with a set jaw of determination.

Zumárraga bowed his head slightly in acknowledgment, while the viceroy smiled approvingly.

"I believe that rebellion may indeed occur in the north, if that is what the idol is sent to incite," Mendoza said. "In the lands that Beltrán Nuño de Guzmán savaged and enslaved, but never truly subdued."

"We will be prepared, sire, if such a time is to come," Coronado said confidently, uncrossing his arms to rest a hand on the hilt of his poniard.

"There is a great north beyond New Galicia," the viceroy said, smiling. "Perhaps Fray Marcos de Niza, who is a walker of distances almost as renowned as yourself, Don Andrés, will investigate rumors of the presence of the idol when he goes forth to investigate the other rumors of those lands."

This Franciscan friar, in a tattered brown robe proudly worn, who had walked barefoot from Guatemala City to the capital, was the latest novelty in the viceregal court. He had accompanied Alvarado on that governor's expedition to Peru, when Alvarado had sold out his rights to Peruvian conquest to Diego de Almagro. He had been present also at the death of the Inca emperor. It was known that this missionary had been recommended to the viceroy as a man skilled in cosmography and exploration as well as theology.

Esteban was indignant at the pretensions of the newcomer, striding up and down before Dorantes in his extravagant manner, in his fine clothes. His conceit had recovered from the terror of his journey back from Villa Rica to the torture chamber. Flower scents wafted from him.

"This Fray Marcos is a great braggart, Master! He has walked so far—from Niza to Seville, from Guatemala City to the City of Mexico! He will walk to Cibola! He will find the seven cities! He will walk there alone, if need be!"

"Barefoot!"

"Yes! Barefoot!" Esteban squinted at him to see if he were being mocked. "Master, how much longer must we wait in this place?"

"We wait to hear news of Don Álvar's success in Spain."

"But when will that be, Master?"

"It should be soon."

"And then we will return to the north? Estebánico thinks so often of those beautiful days of the four Children of the Sun. And think of it! To return with what one has learned since, it is to become again a young man with the wisdom of the old."

"Don Alonso has become a wealthy encomendero and would not

accompany us," he said. "And Don Álvar may fail in Spain, and not return. And I have made a wager with Doña María that I will never return. You would be the only Child of the Sun upon this second journey. Would you care to accompany this barefoot Franciscan?"

The Moor pulled a long face. "Pooh! Such a braggart. He would not be able to keep up with the walking of Estebánico!"

"Don Antonio has told me that you and I will go together or you will go without me. He keeps a fine golden noose lightly around my neck, from evidence given him by that fine friend of yours, Gatito, the King of the Slaves." And in the matter of properties in the Valley of Anahuac, and the City of Mexico, he thought; perhaps also a duel almost fought in the Alameda gardens; and something else would transpire, María de Mendoza had said.

Esteban swiped at his lips with a pink tongue. "But do you not wish to come back with Estebánico, Master?"

He shook his head. "Nor with anyone, although I have sworn to accompany Don Álvar. But the time grows long. He may have failed."

Esteban looked suitably saddened at the thought. Then he executed a dance step and swept his feathered cap around him at arm's length. "There is to be a grand feast!" he said excitedly. "The Marqués del Valle honors the viceroy and his household with a feast, exhibitions, jousts, music—everything! It will help to pass the time, Master!"

He could not play truant from this grand occasion of the Marqués del Valle's. Once there, he would not be able to avoid the unwanted confrontation with Cortés. And there would be other old soldiers of the Conquest there, more loyal to their commander than he had been, whose hatred since the death of Caballo he must face. He must face all these things, enduring vilification and insult as far as his honor permitted. After which he became caught even more securely in the web of Mendoza.

That wakeful night he was convinced by the intensity of his longing that Timultzin would come to him again, again to be bitterly disappointed. Instead, in a waking dream, he had a visitation from Álvar Núñez. The healer was in court finery, white satin with gold embroidery, imposing in his height as he backed, bowing, from the presence of majesty. Surely his posture was one of gratitude! But his expression seemed to share triumph and disappointment. He called out to his friend, who ignored him for the attention of the more powerful personages of the court as he bowed and backed, bowed and backed. He could not make out whether Álvar had been successful or not. "Álvar—" he said again, but it seemed the old, almost unspoken, communication of the great journey, and after, was gone. And yet a kind of intimation had passed over the countless leagues between Old Spain and New and he knew a decision had been made.

Seated beside María de Mendoza in the dining sala, he watched the lean, sunburnt Franciscan beside Mendoza at the head of the table. He could not hear what Fray Marcos was saying, but his gestures, expressions, and postures were expressive of the kind of swaggering braggadocio so common among his countrymen. This friar, with his burning eyes and tales of wonders encountered in his travels, both filled him with contempt and seemed a reproach to his own prudence. No doubt Fray Marcos, who would soon leave for the north on a scouting expedition, would bring back proper tales of Cibola.

When the uniformed Indian musicians on their bough-and-flower-draped stand struck up some music, he said to María, "You are very quiet tonight."

"My dear one neglects me," she said. Her eyes flashed at him, and her pink lips formed the pout that seemed to him sometimes cruel and at others captivating.

He asked what she meant.

"He has changed. He is less avid. I do not enquire if there is another."

"Your brother has another for Cibola," he said. "Perhaps this man you mention is aware that he has been a disappointment."

She shrugged. "Don Francisco has fifty thousand reales which he will invest in the entrada," she said. "Money speaks with a strong voice in these delicate matters."

"The reales will not be well spent," he said. "They will be disappointed." He hoped it had not sounded bitter.

María bit into one of the honey cakes with her white teeth. "Is it not always so?" she asked. "In conquest as in love?"

On a bay stallion from the viceroy's stables, in the unfamiliar stricture of breastplate and helmet and with the unfamiliar weight of a sword slung from his belt, amid the glitter and metallic chinking of other helmets and armor, he rode among the cavaliers of the viceroy's household, following Mendoza in his splendid gold-chased armor. He calculated that this was a larger troop than had charged the Aztec horde at Otumba.

They crossed the plaza, with its crowds of Indians, Spaniards in fiesta dress, sullen mestizo youths and the Negro slaves who were beginning to show themselves again among the beggars, cripples, and vendors of foodstuffs.

On the far side of the plaza mayor they were met by Cortés' troop, also larger than the army at Otumba, and many of the cavaliers soldiers who had fought there, generally older than Mendoza's retainers, stout, red-faced men of whom Caballo had only been the heaviest and ruddiest, encomenderos and men of the city who had no honorable occupation but war and no income but its spoils, who considered themselves hard up and put-upon while they lived in luxury in a land where most of the population existed on the barest necessities of life. There were younger cavaliers of wealth and good family in attendance upon the marqués as well, and the conqueror himself rode at their head, a gauntleted hand raised in greeting. His gold-chased armor matched in splendor that of the viceroy, and he wore his heavy gold chain, which had so impressed the soldiers of Narváez after he had beaten them at Cempoala and solicited their enlistment in his cause. The viceroy and the marqués greeted each other in a horseback embrace, their mounts shifting and turning until the leaders had reversed direction, and Dorantes could see Mendoza's dark-bearded narrow face with its fixed smile, encased in the gleaming cowl of helmet. The two companies rode on together into the grounds of Cortés' vast, uncompleted palace, with the stacks of timber, tiles, and cut stones concealed beneath drapes of embroidered cloth.

In the marqués' plaza a forest of young evergreens was arrayed in huge clay pots. Beyond was a miniature jousting field, with a grandstand and covered viewing stand in which the faces of ladies could be seen, as well as those of the notables of the church and the City of Mexico. Cortés and Mendoza dismounted to join these, while the two companies surrendered their horses to grooms and took their places in the grandstand.

The first event of the afternoon was a horse race, with women of the town as jockeys, mounted astraddle with long skirts caught up to reveal colored stockings, and long hair flying free. There was spirited betting despite the viceroy's edict against gambling in the capital, as, in a milling confusion, the mounted whores were lined up and sent flying in a circuit of the city.

The race was won by a plump woman with a sweating red face, who, clutching her purse of silver reales, curtsied to the viewing stand. A rose was flung to her, the stem of which she clamped between her teeth as she executed a caracole and was swept away before the next event.

This was a mock battle between Castilians and blackface Moors with elegant turbans and curved scimitars, the two sides slashing with their swords and advancing and retreating to the cheers of the spectators. The Christian knights had the worst of it, forced back and back with the cheers dying away, until, on the battlements of the palace, the

Virgin appeared, all in white and gold, a cross held up in one hand, a sword in the other. With a twist of his heart Dorantes recognized the face of the marquesa, who, at this distance, still resembled the child he had seen among the dwarfs of her father's court. Her dress was that of the Virgin of the Remedies to whom the survivors of the Night of Sorrows had prayed beneath the tree at the end of the Tacuba Causeway.

The Christians attacked with renewed vigor and cries of "Santiago!" The Moors soon surrendered, and kneeling, received baptism from the priests who circulated among them, while a choir of Indian boys chanted a hymn in their shrill, flatted voices that chased chills up his spine.

Stewards passed among the spectators with cups and an urn of spiced wine. Now there was jousting with poles for lances, the horsemen confronting each other in gallop and counter-gallop, with little contact until Cortés and a burly cavalier of Mendoza's household rushed furiously together. Both lances shattered, the horses slamming breast to breast, one falling to his knees while the other staggered off riderless. Cortés and his antagonist lay on the ground as though dead.

Dorantes was jerked to his feet in a queer rush of nausea to see the conqueror supine in a huddle of metal and scarlet velvet. First there was utter silence, with all the other horsemen reined to a halt. Then, with a shout, men dismounted to run to the aid of the marqués. The other had risen, tottering and holding his head. Then Cortés was also up, shaking off a helping hand and waving to the occupants of the viewing stand. Wincing at Cortés' efforts not to limp, he remembered that same effort after the fall on the route to Honduras; Cortés strode to his horse and mounted. He refused the new pole that was proffered him and rode out of the lists waving and smiling.

Cortés presided over the banquet, seated at the head of the table with the viceroy on his right and the bishop, the marquesa, and the other notables close by. Servants trotted to the long tables with steaming platters of pork, mutton, fowl, and vegetables. There were cycles of toasts and arguments between the older men and the younger. In a funk of depression Dorantes was reminded of the great feast at Coyoacán after the surrender of Cuauhtémoc.

He was strolling outside among the ranked pines in their clay tubs, light-headed with relief that there had been no scrapes with Cortés' old soldiers, when a young hidalgo trotted up to him. The marqués wished to speak to Don Andrés Dorantes.

He accompanied the messenger back through the banquet hall with its stink of grease and sour wine where many still sat, some leaning together in argument or reminiscence, a group singing drunkenly and banging goblets on the table. Indian servants were clearing away the dishes. In a private apartment Cortés sat with a bare leg stretched out on a footstool. An Indian woman bent over the abraded white calf, daubing with a damp cloth while her patient sat with a set face. He smiled when he saw Dorantes.

"You will pardon me if I do not rise to embrace you, my good Turk! This body seems not to be so young as it once was. Please, come to me!"

He bent awkwardly to embrace Cortés where he sat: vinous smell of breath and a mixture of dried sweat and the aromatic emollient the servant was rubbing into the bruised leg. He was conscious again of that body heat the conqueror radiated, as though he burned at a higher temperature than ordinary mortals. He calculated that Cortés, who had been thirty-six at the fall of Tenochtitlán, was fifty-two; as he, who had been twenty, was now thirty-six.

"You have been witness to another fall of mine, Andrés," Cortés said, with his infectious laugh.

"I was sorry for this one also, sire."

"My shaft snapped." Cortés reached for a golden goblet, shoving the servant aside with his foot to dismiss her. "In this life, my old friend, one is constantly at the mercy of flaws in the instruments on which one must place his trust." He crowed with pleasure at the cleverness of his aphorism.

Dorantes seated himself in the chair Cortés motioned him to, remembering that good humor in the face of adversity they had all admired. Cortés had rarely shown anger. The only mark of it that he could recall was a low whistling through his teeth. But he was as shocked as he had been by the crashing fall to notice that the conqueror's beard no longer contained gray hairs, which had been plentiful in Honduras. The offending hairs had been plucked or dyed.

"So you continue to ride in Don Antonio's company," Cortés said, smiling.

"I accept his hospitality, and have been summoned to swell his entourage."

"My hospitality has always stood ready, old friend."

He raised his hands helplessly. "Sire, you are acquainted with His Excellency. Having lighted on his branch the bird finds his feet caught in birdlime."

Cortés chuckled. "And looking up perhaps detects the net settling over him as well. Yes, yes, yes, perhaps he and I must share you, as we share the pillow upon which we kneel to pray together at the cathedral. He, of course, always on the right hand. And as we share the head of the table at banquets such as this one, he also on the right. And also when we ride together, neither of us daring to precede the other. Such a business of spurring and reining as cannot be imagined! And what a business it was, one day, when at some function my servant dared to advance my chair a finger's breadth before his. The sky darkened, thunder rolled, and lightning flashed in the heavens!"

They laughed together. He was aware of the great charm focused on him, but he remembered disturbing matters: that pervasive gossip about the sudden deaths that had surrounded Hernán Cortés; the demise of his first wife so soon after she had inconveniently joined him in Coyoacán, the death of Francisco de Garay, rival for the conquest of the Panuco, after an intimate breakfast; that of Luis Ponce de León, sent to replace the conqueror as governor of New Spain; even the death of the faithful Gonzalo de Sandoval who had accompanied Cortés in his triumph to Spain. And he remembered the disputed division of the spoils of Tenochtitlán: after the king's fifth, which had been lost to a French corsair en route to Spain, and Cortés' fifth, and, it was rumored, a second fifth, and the share of the captains, there had remained sixty gold pesos apiece for the horsemen and fifty for the foot—just the cost of the crossbow he had lost on the Night of Sorrows.

Cortés indicated a pitcher and cup with which he was to refresh himself, and watched so intently as he poured and lifted the cup to his lips that he only gingerly touched his tongue to the sweet wine.

"I have news from Spain which perhaps has come to you also," Cortés said. "It concerns your companion Álvar Núñez Cabeza de Vaca."

He said that he had heard nothing and sat with his full cup steadied in his two hands.

"Hernando de Soto is commissioned governor of the province of Florida," Cortés said, watching him. "That is a great part of the country you have traversed, I believe."

He listened to the beating of his heart and felt something of the emotion that had suffused him when he had found no scar on the finger of the street boy before the cathedral. He said, "I believe I have heard his name before."

"He was with Dávila in Darien. Later he supported Francisco Pizarro in the civil wars in Peru and returned to Spain with a great fortune. Thus he is well able to support an expedition to Florida, and has powerful friends at court besides. Álvar Núñez has been appointed governor of Río de la Plata province." He paused. "This is a disappointment to you, Andrés?"

He did not know how to answer. Cortés raised an eyebrow and continued: "You should know, old friend, that Don Álvar has made a great boasting at court of what has been discovered on your journey from Florida."

Cortés reached for a peach in the bowl full of them on the table beside him and began stripping the peel with the point of his dagger. "He claims that seven great cities of the north were often spoken of by the indigenes you met along your way. Cities greater than Tenochtitlán and of course seven times as numerous." He laughed, showing his teeth.

"Streets of silver and walls of gold studded with jewels," he continued, in a sarcastic tone. "How often have we heard these tales of wonders beyond belief, eh, Andrés?"

Pity for Álvar ached in his throat. He said carefully, "We heard of no such wonders, sire."

Cortés shrugged. "In any case those wonders have ensured that a better connected and a wealthier soldier will explore Florida, and west from there. It seems that your companion has also made much of the idea of peaceable conquest, of persuading the indigenes to the Holy Faith and the Royal Estate by healing and faith—which methods Bartolomé de las Casas has also been preaching." He pulled a long, disbelieving face. "Therefore he will go to Paraguay to practice this upon Indians there who are known to chew rocks and spit out arrowheads."

Cortés took a bite from his golden peach and mopped at the juice that ran into his beard with the back of his hand. "And what now of your case, Andrés? It is speculated that you wait for these storms to blow over so as to return to those realms whose secrets you know. To become the new Cortés of new Tenochtitláns. Can this be true of my faithful Juan de Flechilla?"

"Do you think it true, sire?"

Cortés shook his head, gobbling his peach down to the stone, which he dropped to the floor. He mopped again at the juice in his beard, stretched indolently, then winced and reached down to touch his bruised leg. His eyes fixed on a spot in the exact center of Dorantes' forehead.

"What an adventure we had, eh, Andrés? Who could have asked more from his life? That first sight of Tenochtitlán from the pass! Like a magical kingdom! A kingdom of true wonders!"

"The memory remains magical, sire."

"When a man has had such an adventure, what more can he ask of his life? And yet more is required, for otherwise all turns to ashes. The fuller the past the emptier the present, and so more fullness must be demanded of the future. Moreover, as you know, others do not even honor that past with its exploits, and so anger is always festering. When one has risked all, when to fail was to be baked into a pie— surely this is not to be snickered at by pimple-faced boys!"

"You yourself are greatly honored, sire. Is it not enough?"

Cortés shook his head again, grinning. "And what of you? Are you content?"

"Remember that I have had two great adventures. One as great as the other. And where in the first the indigenes were my enemies and wished to bake me into a pie, in the second they were my friends and saviors. In whose conquest I do not wish to participate."

"Andrés, in that magical city we glimpsed from the pass, a few people lived well, with great pleasure and distinction. The rest lived in misery. At any moment they might be snatched away to the sacrificial stone and their hearts torn from them. Or their children snatched away to the same purpose, or to the harems of the lords—boys and girls alike. You will say that we have brought these people many evils, and that is true. But we have brought great good also. The sacrificial stone is demolished! We have brought them the Holy Faith, a forgiving Lady instead of cruel priests. Certainly their old lords preferred the old ways, and certainly some of our own comrades—like our friend Caballo Botello, may his soul rest in peace—are little better than those old lords. But I tell you we have brought better times to this land, painful birth though it was!"

With difficulty he said it: "Sire, perhaps you have not visited Las Minas of your kinsman Don Lucas. Where the buzzards gather in hundreds to devour the dead. It is worse than the mines of the Antilles, there."

Cortés' eyes widened dangerously for a moment. "Ah, my Turk— can that be it? But if you will forgive me my greedy kinsman, I will forgive you your poor fat corporal—and see that others forgive also!"

He found no reply. Cortés rose and limped on one bare foot and one leather slipper across to the window, where he leaned on the sill in a beam of sunlight. Back turned, he said, "So many things are held against Hernán Cortés. Even his successes are his damnation. Guzmán interfered with my every move by land or sea. De la Torre, before he died, proved as bad; and this pretty young man of Don Antonio's will be no better. Because they act upon the instructions of my enemy, your host! Now Pedro de Alvarado forms an expedition that should have been mine, and Don Antonio *expressly* forbids my fleet to sail. I am forbidden, Andrés!"

He swung around, half-crouching in his intensity. "I do not say you lie deliberately. I do not even say you are blind or misguided, but there cannot be so much smoke without fire! So many legends of tall cities, of seven cities. There must be some basis. You yourself admit to hearing of the cities of tall houses!"

"Sire, I believe they are only mud villages. There was only one Tenochtitlán."

"There was Cuzco!" Cortés straightened, to stand laughing at the window. "Is one woman enough for a man?" he said. "Besides, think of this, my Turk. It is not the end that one desires beyond all else, but the achieving of the end. Not the stink of Tlatelolco, and the gold, or the lack of it. *But the getting there!*

"Listen to me," he continued, in a grave voice. "Let me speak again of our great adventure. How did we succeed against such odds? First, they thought we were gods, with our white skins—come to reclaim what was ours, according to their legends. It was the same with Francisco Pizarro in Peru. And consider, again it is the same with the indigenes of the north—to whom *you* were gods!"

He ticked a second finger. "The next thing. The tongues. In Cozumel, when we had freed Jerónimo de Aguilar, we possessed one who knew the Mayan tongue. And in Tabasco we liberated Doña Marina, who spoke both Mayan and Nahuatl—and soon enough Castilian as well. So first we had the belief that we were gods, and next the tongues by which to hold parley. Both of these elements you possess, Andrés. With them we could conquer again, you and I!"

He found himself shaking his head, but felt as though the sweet wine he had been sipping had been laced with pity for the conqueror. Cortés glared at him, as though to force him to submit by sheer power of will.

"Your captain-general, Andrés! Your comrade of the march to Honduras! Of that vision of the Lake of Texcoco and its magical cities! Your Turk of Turks, of the Night of Sorrows, of Otumba, of Tenochtitlán!"

"Sire, I have vowed to Don Antonio that I would never again be a part of a conquest like that conquest."

"And so another lance proves its flaw. An arrow in this case," Cortés said, and managed a laugh. He snapped his fingers loudly, and a servant in a tight white uniform appeared.

"Bring the red box from the shelves of documents." When the servant vanished, Cortés said, "What of your slave? Who is also a god, though a black one, and also adept at tongues? Will you roll dice with me, your slave against his weight in silver?"

His pity for the conqueror, which was flavored with fear, did not prevent him from remembering that Cortés was famed for his luck at dice. He tried to explain the web Mendoza had woven around Esteban, but Cortés was clearly not listening, whistling once through his teeth. The servant reappeared with his red Moroccan leather box.

"Give it to this lord," Cortés said, "whose property it is."

"I am sorry for this, sire," he said, as he took the box and tested its weight.

"It is a sorry document, brought me by an overzealous friend, but a loyal one. Tell me, was it a trap? Surely this is not the same dry-as-dust relation you presented to your friend Don Antonio."

"The same, sire. Perhaps the second one was even drier."

"Yes, I have always thought you a simple fool and not a clever one." Cortés glared at him with his drooping left eye, and rose. "I would like never to see you again, my one-time Turk," he said, and hobbled from the chamber.

When he returned that evening to the viceroy's palace, a letter from Álvar Núñez awaited him, tied with white ribbon and sealed with red wax. It told him no more than Cortés had, although Álvar professed to be flattered by his commission as governor of the province of Río de la Plata, in Paraguay, and was enthusiastic at the prospects of a peaceable settlement of that place. There was no mention of a part for Andrés Dorantes in the expedition, and so that, he thought, as he rolled the document and retied the ribbon, was that.

In the small hours of the night he wakened to the certainty that Timultzin had come again. He held his breath to listen and thought he heard the small rustle of her breathing. He put out a hand that encountered nothing. Then her nakedness touched his hand, and she was in bed beside him, her swaddled face pressed into his shoulder. She would not let him touch the bands that bound her cheeks.

"It is the last time, my tuele," she whispered.

"Why, my heart?"

"It is too dangerous. For you, for me, and for others."

"What is it that is dangerous? Is it the service of your god?"

"You may not know of it. It is unimportant, probably. There is a chance that it is important, and that is what is dangerous. It is not only you and I who are concerned."

Again he began to speak of the viceroy's promise to restore to him Xicomilpa, or another property in the valley, but she stopped his lips with her hand, gasping once as he eased into her warmth.

"It cannot be, my tuele. We are past dreams. You would not be content in daylight hours with a woman whose face you could not look upon, nor would I be content to be concubine to an encomendero, however kind he might be. We are past dreams and youth, and there are serious matters for each of us. Listen, I have thought of you—much. Every moment sometimes. But this is the last time we will be with each other. You must promise me that you will not try to find me."

"Could I find you if I tried?"

"I could make certain that you could not, and I will do that if I do not have your promise. But you must promise."

"Please—"

"It is I who say please."

They moved together in sweetness. He whispered, "He whom you serve; is it the Lord of Close Proximity?"

There was a small, laden silence before he felt her warm breath start again. "You know of him."

"The man Miguel—is he your uncle?"

"A kinsman merely. But already you know too much. It is very dangerous for us all! You must promise me, Andrés—but first we will have this night of lovemaking. We will do all the lovemaking in this one night!" She moved with sure enticement beneath him. Once she giggled, which seemed to be some kind of release of tension, for when he kissed her eyes they swam with tears.

"You must marry another Castiliana, Andrés," she whispered, patting the small of his back when he had spent. "Be happy, my tuele. Be happy with another, for this is the end of Timultzin and Andrés. For you must promise me."

In the end she extracted the promise from him. It seemed to him that in his life he had suffered from too many promises that must be kept. Still he assured himself that she must come again: surely she would come again. He tried not to sleep in his satiation, knowing she would be gone when he awakened, but failed.

"Yes, there is something," Rufino said, leaning on his elbows on his table, the little cup of chocolatl held in his two plump hands. "A cult. One must know the history of these people. It is not very long! Once Texcoco was dominant in the Triple Alliance, and their king was Nezahualcoyotl. His god, Tloque Nahuaque, was this one of whom you enquire. He was referred to in different ways that perhaps mean the same thing: The Lord of Close Proximity, of the With and the By, He By Whom We Live; the Creator. He required no sacrifice, unlike Huitzilopochtli of Tenochtitlán. That god with his bloody requirements was also a late-comer! The two contended. It is fascinating, and very sad. For the bloody god became dominant along with the Mexica, and Tloque Nahuaque is hardly remembered."

"But Tezcatlipoca is god over all?"

"It is difficult for us to understand," Rufino said, sipping chocolatl. "But perhaps no more difficult than the Trinity is for them."

"Is it the same idea, Rufino?" He looked down at his scarred hands, resting on the table also. When he thought about these things his mind shied away. There was too much he did not understand of his own religion, too many things it frightened him to question.

"I will tell you, Andrés," Rufino said. "Some of us who study these things think all are manifestations of Satan, but others think differently. Nezahualcoyotl is a prince one can understand. He was a poet as well as a warrior, a founder of libraries and a great builder, a stern lawgiver but a man who changed much in his lifetime. He reminds us of Hebrews before the coming of the Savior, a monotheist in a land of a thousand gods. Some of us think the religion of Tloque Nahuaque was not that of Satan at all, but the opposite."

He leaned back in his chair trying to understand. "Is Miguel a leader of this cult of the Close Proximity?"

Rufino sighed and said, "I do not know. Nor wish to know. Certain things I surmise. I am often told I am full of error. But you know that Timultzin is part of it?"

"She said that she serves her god, and that there is danger."

"The Inquisition," Rufino said, with tight lips. His face gleamed palely. He gazed down at his cup. "Is she—terribly disfigured?"

When he thought of Rufino in his great sin, of Timultzin with what perhaps had seemed to her a manifestation of the Christian God, his brain seemed to kindle like coals under a bellows. He closed his eyes for a moment. "She conceals her face."

"How does she seem?"

"Herself. And not herself."

"And she serves a different god from Him we know," Rufino said. "Perhaps the service is more important than the name." He gripped his cup in his hands. "And the seeking of a god is always the seeking of Him. But you must never breathe a word that I have said such a thing! What of your son?"

"In her superstitions she thinks he is dead by water."

"And you will see her no more. I believe that means they will leave the capital. I believe it is a requirement of their cult that they follow the life of Nezahualcoyotl, who wandered a refugee in the wilderness for some years before he returned to claim his heritage."

He told Rufino that it was the idea of the Holy Office that the great idol may have been spirited away to the north to furnish inspiration for a great rebellion there.

"Ah, the north, the north!" Rufino said tiredly. "The never-ending rumors of the great north!"

Chapter Nine

He was walking with María de Mendoza in one of the patios where a fountain sprayed its coolness into the dry air, when they encountered Francisco Vásquez de Coronado, in a white doublet, with his trim golden beard, and fair hair combed straight back from his high forehead. He bowed in greeting to them.

"Good day, Don Francisco," María said, fan raised.

Standing so erect that he seemed to be leaning backwards, one hand on the hilt of his poniard and the other stroking his beard, the young governor of New Galicia said, "Ah, Don Andrés, if you could answer a question or two? If you will pardon this interruption, Doña María?"

"But certainly, Don Francisco!" María said. Her gloved hand pressed Dorantes' arm.

Coronado gazed at him with frowning concentration. "In these lands to the north of the town you have named Corazones, there is a great valley sweeping north to limestone cliffs. Then there is desert for many leagues?"

"That is what we have shown on our map."

"But I have been told there was some disagreement among the makers of the map."

"The further west the less disagreement."

Coronado bowed again. "And the peoples of these deserts—in their paganism they worship the sun?"

"Other things as well. Some were only fearful of a devil they called Bad Thing. I believe they would readily accept our Christian faith, Don Francisco."

Coronado nodded solemnly, paraded a few steps to the right, and turned, presenting the aspect of a serious man deep in thought. "Yes, surely it is our Castilian duty to bring the Holy Faith to these benighted ones. Now, señor, these sun-worshipers—they considered men of white skin to be children of the sun?"

"In fact, Excellency, it was not the color of our skins that caused them to call us Children of the Sun, for that color was not much different from theirs and one of us was black; but because we insisted always on traveling in the direction of the setting sun."

"Ah!" Coronado said, with a jerk of his head, but not as though he were convinced. "And these sun-worshipers; is it true that their women are the notables among them?"

"Why, these are sensible people, then!" María said.

"Not of those among whom we passed, Excellency," Dorantes said. "We had heard that this was true elsewhere, but did not see it."

"Might these then be Amazons in the cities of the tall houses?" the governor asked. "Fray Marcos is convinced that this is the case, but one is not anxious to form conclusions before one has seen for oneself."

María's hand exerted its pressure again, a signal for caution or a reflex of affection or amusement.

"It was not a conclusion that came to us, Excellency, since in fact we heard so little of the places of tall houses."

Coronado nodded knowingly again. "These narratives do not mention sodomy among these peoples, Don Andrés. Were these peoples not great sodomites like the Aztecs of Tenochtitlán?"

He said that they had observed no sodomy among the people of the north.

"And when is this great entrada to set out, please, Don Francisco?" María asked.

"Ah, that cannot be said, Doña María. Many questions must still be settled. Experienced cosmographers must be sent ahead, reports received, soldiers recruited—so many things!" He spread his hands.

"This Moor of yours, Don Andrés. The narratives speak of a magic gourd-rattle of his possession. This had great potency with these peoples?"

"They were gourds painted and inscribed in certain ways, which were considered holy. Once, however, one was taken as evil, and Esteban found himself in great danger. It seemed that the gourds that had been made by enemies were to be considered Bad Things."

"Yes, yes; but this slave—you would be willing to part with him for a good figure?" Coronado gazed at him with such intensity that his eyes seemed to cross. The grip on his arm had tightened meaningfully again.

He shook his head. "I have already been offered a good figure, Excellency. By Beltrán Nuño de Guzmán and by Hernán Cortés. And to each of these I have said that he is not for sale."

The governor bowed again.

"Please tell me, Don Francisco," María said, "what will you do if these northern peoples resist the Holy Faith and the Royal Estate?"

Coronado grinned suddenly boyishly. "Why then, señorita, we will see how they resist Spanish steel!" Immediately his face took on its solemn set again, and he bowed in farewell, hand on the hilt of his poniard, left leg in its white stocking and foot in Morocco leather slipper extended.

"Good day, Doña María, Don Andrés," he said, and took himself off in his careful, backward-inclining strut.

Watching the young governor disappear among the arches, he felt a strain as though he had been endeavoring to hold shut a door that must be forced open despite his strength. With another pressure on his arm, María said, "Come, my dear Andrés, I have been too long in the sun. I feel myself becoming the color of the notable women of the north."

Her skirts rustled as she lengthened her stride to match his. "Just when I begin to think you a dolt," she said, "for what you keep to yourself, and do not keep to yourself, you understand—just then you show me again that you are more true to yourself than any other I have known. I think I have become overused to devious men. Come! We must be alone so I can give you good advice."

In his apartment she pushed him into a chair and stood over him, tapping her folded fan on her gloved hand. Her small, half-cruel mouth was smiling, but her eyes were pink with emotion and there were round spots of color in her cheeks.

"How could you know of all the grand strategies and tactics of which you have been the center, my dear one?" she said. "Some of it you know. That I was set to find out what you were made of and what deviousness was in you. And found much! And none! Well, well, and then womanly feelings came to possess me, and I hoped to convince you of the grand prize to be had if you would only grasp your possibilities. But no. And now the grand entrada has passed you by, and that pompous boy is to be captain-general. I had thought Andrés Dorantes might be another Hernán Cortés!"

"There is only one Hernán Cortés," he said, with difficulty.

"Praise God!" María said, crossing herself and laughing. "Ah, dear one, I am a silly and romantic woman overused to deviousness, and you have been good for me. In truth, my own case drags on. When will I know if I can marry at all, from my silly vow? And when I do it must be someone of noble blood, so my brother assures me. And for your part, I see I interest you less and less. Who can she be? I cannot imagine! My spies fail me! But in any case, you are relieved of me along with other things."

"I'm sorry," he said. "There is another, but that is an impossibility also."

Her eyes had reddened still more as she smiled down at him. "Now I will give you my advice. It is that you present the Moor to my brother as a loan. If you do not give him freely he will be taken from you. And there is much to be gained by the first move."

"It is good advice," he said.

"You will do it?"

He nodded. At least he would not have sold Esteban, who would be well enough pleased with the arrangement.

"Praise God," María said again. "I have won something from you!"

"You had only to ask." They laughed together, he uncomfortably, she producing a handkerchief to dab at her eyes.

"You will be well rewarded," she said. "For my brother will give you the encomienda of Don Roderigo and the four thousand souls he also possessed, to whom you will make amends for his cruel treatment."

He stared at her and did not know whether to laugh or weep.

"And now I have another piece of advice for you," she continued. "There is another María whom you must marry. You know her, María de la Torre. She is the niece of the judge Diego Pérez de la Torre, who is dead and was a wealthy man, and the widow of Alonso de Benevides, who is four months dead and was also a rich man. She possesses very large rents in the towns of Asala and Jalazintzo. She is, besides, pretty, plump, and devout, and she will not make jokes at your expense as sometimes this other María has done, for I think she does not recognize jokes."

She reached out to touch his shoulder with her fan. "Come," she said in a throaty voice, "let us take our fill of one another one last time. Then I may assure my confessor that this sinning is finished."

She was the third to say to him that this was an ending between them, and this ending was a pleasant one. After their fill had been taken, he reminded María de Mendoza, as a joke, of their wager that he would not be a part of the expedition to Cíbola.

"But it has not set out yet, dear one," she said. "How will we know until that very day?"

Chapter Ten

FROM A LETTER FROM HIS EXCELLENCY, DON ANTONIO DE
MENDOZA, VICEROY OF NEW SPAIN, TO HIS MAJESTY, THE
EMPEROR, 1539

"—having here with me Andrés Dorantes, one of those who went
in the expedition of Pánfilo de Narváez, I consulted with him many
times. It seems to me that he could render great service to Your
Majesty if he were sent with forty or fifty horsemen to lay bare the
mysteries of that region. On that account I spent considerable money in
providing what was necessary for his journey, and I do not know how
it was that the plan fell through and the undertaking was abandoned.

"Of the arrangements made for this plan, I retain a Negro who had
come with Dorantes, some slaves whom I bought, and a few native
Indians of the region whom I gathered. I sent them with Fray Marcos
de Niza and a companion of his, a friar of the Order of St. Francis,
men long trained in the hardships of this region, experienced in the
affairs of the Indies, earnest persons of exemplary lives. They accompanied Francisco Vásquez de Coronado, governor of New Galicia, to
the town of San Miguel de Culiacán, the last outpost of the Spaniards
in that region, two hundred leagues from this city—"

INSTRUCTIONS OF THE VICEROY TO FRAY MARCOS DE NIZA, 1539

First: Upon arriving at the province of Culiacán, you are to exhort
and urge the Spaniards residing in the town of San Miguel to treat the
peaceful Indians well and not to employ them in excessive tasks, assur-

ing them by so doing they will be granted favors and rewarded by His Majesty for the hardships they have endured there, and that they will find in me a good supporter for their claims. If they do the opposite they will incur punishment and disfavor.

You shall make clear to the Indians that I am sending you in the name of His Majesty to tell them that the Spaniards shall treat them well, to let them know he regrets the abuses and harm they have suffered, and that from now on they shall be well treated and those who may mistreat them will be punished.

Likewise you are to assure them that no more slaves shall be taken from among them and that they are not to be taken away from their lands; on the contrary, they shall be left alone as free people, without suffering any harm. Tell them that they should not be afraid, but acknowledge God, Our Lord, Who is in heaven, and the emperor, as he has been placed on earth by His hand to rule and govern it.

Since Francisco Vásquez de Coronado, whom His Majesty has appointed governor of that province, will go with you as far as the town of San Miguel de Culiacán, you shall inform me of how he provides for the affairs of the town in matters pertaining to the service of God, Our Lord, and the conversion and good treatment of the natives of that province.

If with the aid of God, Our Lord, and the grace of the Holy Spirit, you should find a way to go on and penetrate the land of the interior, you shall take along Esteban Dorantes as guide. I command him to obey you in whatever you may order him, as he would obey me in person. If he should not do so, he will be at fault and incur the penalties falling on those who disobey the persons empowered by His Majesty to command them.

Likewise the said governor Francisco Vásquez is taking along the Indians who came with Dorantes and others from those regions who could be brought together, so that if he and you consider it advisable that some of them should go along, you may employ them in the service of our Lord as you deem fitting.

You are always to endeavor to travel the safest way possible, informing yourself first as to whether the Indians are at peace or at war among themselves, so that they may not do any violence to your person that would give cause to taking up arms against them and punishing them, because, in this case, instead of helping and enlightening them, this would do just the opposite.

You shall be very careful to observe the number of people that there are, whether they are few or many, and whether they are scattered or living together. Note also the nature, fertility, and climate of the land; the trees and plants and domestic and wild animals there may be; the character of the country, whether it is broken or flat; the rivers, whether they are large or small; the stones and metals which there are; and of all things that can be sent or brought, send or bring samples of them in order that His Majesty may be informed of everything.

Try always to send reports telling how you are faring, how you are received, and particularly what you may find.

If God, our Lord, should will it that you find some large settlement which you think would be a good place for establishing a monastery and for sending friars who would devote themselves to conversions, you are to send a report by Indians, or return, yourself, to Culiacán. Send back reports with the utmost secrecy so that appropriate steps may be taken without disturbing anything, because in the pacification of what is discovered the services of Our Lord and the welfare of the natives shall be taken into consideration.

Although the whole land belongs to the emperor, you shall take possession of it for His Majesty in my name and draw up the documents and set the markers that you feel are required for this purpose. You must explain to the natives of the land that there is only one God in heaven, and the emperor on earth to rule and govern it, whose subjects they must all become, and whom they must serve.

DON ANTONIO DE MENDOZA

Book Four

CIBOLA!

(1539-1541)

Chapter One

A RELATION OF THE REVEREND FATHER FRIAR MARCOS DE NIZA, TOUCHING THE DISCOVERY OF THE KINGDOM OF CIBOLA, SITUATED ABOUT 30 DEGREES OF LATITUDE TO THE NORTH OF NEW SPAIN.

(abridged from the actual document)

I

I, Friar Marcos de Niza of the order of St. Francis, for the execution of the instruction of the right honorable lord Don Antonio de Mendoza, Viceroy for the Emperor in New Spain, departed from San Miguel de Culiacán on Friday the 7th of March, in the year 1539, having with me Esteban, a Negro belonging to Andrés Dorantes, and certain Indians who came to the valley of Culiacán, showing themselves to be exceeding glad, because they had been set free, and Francisco Vásquez de Coronado had sent before to advertize them of their liberty, that none of them thenceforth should be made slaves; signifying unto them that the emperor had commanded that it be so.

With the foresaid company and according to my said instruction, I followed my journey as the Holy Ghost did lead me, and many of the people of the country gave me great welcome in all places where I came. In all this way, I saw nothing worth the noting save that there came to seek me certain Indians from the island where Hernán Cortés, the Marqués del Valle, had been. These Indians had about their necks many great shells which were mother-of-pearl. I showed them pearls which I carried with me to show, and they told me that there were in the islands great store of them, and those very great; howbeit I saw none of them.

I followed my journey through a desert of four days, having in my company both the Indians of the islands and those of the mountains which I passed, and at the end of this desert I found other Indians which marveled to see me and sought to touch my garments and called me Hagota, which in their language signifies a man from heaven. To these Indians I advertised by my interpreter, according to my instructions, the knowledge of the Lord God in heaven, and of the emperor, and I sought information where any countries were of more cities and people of civility and understanding than those which I had found. They told me that four or five days journey, at the foot of the mountains, there is a large and mighty plain, wherein they told me that there were many great towns, and when I showed them certain metals which I carried with me, to learn which rich metals were in the land, they took the mineral of gold and told me that thereof were vessels among the people of the plain, and that they have certain thin plates of that gold, wherewith they scrape off their sweat, and that the walls of their temples are covered therewith, and that they use it in all their household vessels.

Thus I traveled three days through towns inhabited by the said people, and came into a town of reasonable bigness called Vacupa. And because it being two days before Passion Sunday, I determined to stay there until Easter. And I sent Esteban Dorantes the Negro to go directly northward fifty or threescore leagues to see if by that way he might learn news of any notable thing which we ought to discover, and that if he found any knowledge of any peopled and rich country which were of great importance, that he should send me certain Indians with that token which we were agreed upon, to wit, that if it were but a mean thing he should send me a white cross of one handful long; and if it were a country greater and better than New Spain he should send me a great cross. So the said Esteban departed from me on Passion Sunday after dinner: and within four days after the messengers of Esteban returned unto me with a cross as high as a man, and they brought me word from Esteban that I should forthwith come away after him, for he had found a people which gave him information of a very mighty province, and he sent me a certain Indian which had been in the province. This Indian told me that it was thirty days' journey from the town where Esteban was to the first city of the said province, which is called Cibola. He affirmed that there are seven great cities in the province, all under one lord, the houses thereof are made of lime and stone, and are very great, and the least of them with one loft overhead, and some two and three lofts, and the house of the lord of

*the province of four, and that all of them join one another in good
order, and that in the gates of the principal houses there are many
turquoise stones cunningly wrought, whereof he said they have there
great plenty; also that all the people of this city go very well ap-
pareled; and that beyond this there are other provinces, all of which
are much greater than the seven cities. I gave credit to his speech
because I found him to be a man of good understanding.*

II

*The same day came three Indians of those which I called Pintádos,
because I saw their faces, breasts, and arms painted. These dwell farther up into the country towards the east, and some of them border
upon the seven cities; and among other things they gave me information of the seven cities, and of the other provinces, which the Indian
that Esteban Dorantes sent had told me of, almost in the very same
manner that Esteban sent me word.*

*So with the three Pintádos above mentioned, I departed from
Vacupa upon Easter Tuesday, the same way that Esteban went, from
whom I received new messengers with a cross of the bigness of the
first which he sent me, which hastened me forward and assured me
that the land which I sought for was the greatest and best country of
all those parts. The said messengers told me without failing in any one
point all that which the first messenger had told me. So I traveled that
day and two days more, the very same way that Esteban had gone; at
the end of which they told me that from that place a man might travel
in thirty days to the City of Cibola, which is the first of the seven.
Neither did one only tell me thus much, but very many; who told me
very particularly of the greatness of the houses, and of the fashion of
them. Also they told me that besides these seven cities there are three
other kingdoms which are called Marata, Acus and Totonteac. And
they told me that the people of the city of Cibola wear very fine
turquoises hanging from their ears and at their nostrils. They say also
that of these turquoises they make fine works upon the principal gates
of the houses of this city. They told me that the apparel which the
inhabitants of Cibola wear is a gown of cotton down to the foot, with
a button at the neck, and a long string hanging down at the same, and
they girdle themselves with girdles of turquoises, and over these some
wear hides of kine very well dressed. These Indians gave me very good
entertainment and brought certain sick folk before me, that I might
heal them.*

The next day I followed my journey, and carrying with me the

Pintádos I came to another village where I was well received; where they told me that from that place certain people were gone with Esteban Dorantes, four or five days' journey. And here I found a great cross which Esteban had left for me for a sign, that the news of the very good country increased, and that he would stay for me at the end of the first desert that he met with. Here I set up two crosses, and took possession according to mine instruction, because the country seemed better unto me than that which I had passed, and that I thought it meet to make an act of possession so far as that place.

In this manner I traveled five days, always finding inhabited places with great hospitality and many turquoises and ox hides. Here I understood that after two days journey I should find a desert where there is no food for me; whereupon I hastened my way, hoping to find Esteban at the end thereof.

Before I came to the desert I met with a very pleasant town, by reason of a great store of water conveyed thither to water the same. All of the people in this village go in caconados, that is to say turquoises hanging at their nostrils and ears, which turquoises they call cacona. And having my garment of gray cloth, which in Spain is called zaragoza, the lord of the village and the other Indians touched my gown with their hands, and told me that of such cloth there was a great store in Tontonteac, for in that place there was certain little beasts, from whom they take the thing wherewith this apparel is made. And they told me said beasts were about the bigness of the two bitch spaniels which Esteban carried with him.

III

The next day I entered into the desert, and at the end of four days I entered into a valley very well inhabited with people. Here there was a great knowledge of Cibola, as in New Spain of Tenochtitlán, and in Peru of Cuzco; and they told us particularly the manner of their houses, lodgings, streets, and marketplaces. I told them it was impossible that the houses should be made in such sort as they informed me, and they for my better understanding took earth and poured water thereon, and showed me how they laid stones upon it, and how the building grew up. I asked them whether the men of that country had wings to mount up into the lofts; whereat they laughed and showed me a ladder.

Through the foresaid valley I traveled five days' journey, and in all these villages I found ample report of Cibola. Here I found a man born in that place, who told me that Cibola is a great city, inhabited with great store of people, and having many streets and marketplaces; and that in some parts of this city there are certain very great houses of five stories high. He said that the houses are of lime and stone, and that the gates and small pillars of the principal houses are of turquoises, and all the vessels wherein they are served, and the other ornaments of their houses, are of gold; and that the other six cities are built the same, whereof some are bigger; and that Ahacus is the chiefest of them. He said that toward the southeast there is a kingdom called Marata, and those great cities do wage war with the lord of the seven cities, through which war the Kingdom of Marata is for the most part wasted.

Likewise he said that the kingdom called Totonteac lies toward the west, which is a very mighty province, replenished with infinite store of people and riches. He told me also that the inhabitants of Cibola lie upon beds raised a good height from the ground with quilts and canopies over them. The like relation was given unto me in the town by many others, but not so particularly. I traveled three days' journey through this valley, where I saw above a thousand ox hides most excellently dressed. And here I saw far greater store of turquoises and chains made thereof, than in all the places I had passed; and they say all comes from the city of Cibola.

IV

Here they showed me a hide half as big again as the hide of a great ox, and told me that it was the skin of a beast which had but one horn upon his forehead, and that this horn bent toward his breast, and that out of the same goes a point right forward, wherein he has so great strength that it will break anything how strong so ever it be, if he run against it, and that there are great store of these beasts in that country. Here I had messengers from Esteban which brought me word that by this time he was come to the farthest part of the desert, and that the farther he went the more perfect knowledge he had of the greatness of the country, and that since his departure from me he never had found the Indians in any lie; for even unto that very place he had found all in such manner as they had informed him.

I set up crosses and used those acts and ceremonies which were to be done according to my instructions. The inhabitants told me that from that place there were four days' journey unto the desert, and from the first entrance into the same desert unto the city of Cibola are fifteen days' journey. Likewise they told me that with Esteban the Negro were gone above three hundred men to bear him company, and to carry victuals for him, and that in like sort many of them would go with me to serve me, because they hoped to return home rich.

Thus I entered into the second desert on the 9th of May, and traveled the first day by a very broad and beaten way. In this sort I traveled twelve days' journey, and here met us an Indian the son of the chief man that accompanied me, which had gone before with Esteban, who came in great fright, having his face and body all covered with sweat, and showing exceeding sadness in his countenance; and he told me that a day's journey before Esteban came to Cibola he sent his great gourd by his messengers, as he was always wont to send them before him, that he might know in what sort he came upon them, which gourd has a string of bells upon it, and two feathers one white and another red, in token that he demanded safe conduct, and that he came peaceably. And when they came to Cibola before the magistrate, which the lord of the city had placed there for his lieutenant, they delivered him the said great gourd, who took the same in his hands; and in a great rage and fury he cast it to the ground, and willed the messengers to get them packing with speed, for he knew well enough what people they were, and they should in no case to enter into the city, for if they did he would put them all to death. The messengers returned and told Esteban how things had passed, who answered them that it made no great matter, and he would proceed until he came to the city of Cibola; where he found men that would not let him into the town, but shut him into a great house that stood without the city, and took all things from him which he carried to truck and barter with them, and certain turquoises, and other things which he had received of the Indians by the way, and they kept him there all that night without giving him meat or drink, and the next day in the morning this Indian was thirsty, and went out of the house to drink at a river that was there at hand, and within a little while he saw Esteban running away, and the people followed him, and slew certain of the Indians which went in his company. And when this Indian saw these things, he hid himself on the banks of the river, and afterward crossed the straight track of the desert. The Indians that went with me hearing this news began incontinently to lament, and I thought this heavy and bad news would cost me my life, neither did I fear so much the loss of mine own life, as that I would not be able to return to give information of the greatnesses of the country, where our Lord God might be glorified; and I cut the cords of my bundles which I carried with me full of merchandise for traffic, which I would not do till then, nor give anything to any man, and began to divide all that I carried with me among the principal men, willing them not to be afraid but to go forward with me, and so they did.

And going on our way, within a day's journey of Cibola we met two other Indians of those which went with Esteban, which were bloody and wounded in many places; and as soon as they came to us, they which were with me began to make great lamentation. These wounded Indians I asked for Esteban, and they agreeing in all points with which the first Indian said, that after they had put him in the foresaid great house, without giving him meat or drink all that day and all that night, they took from Esteban all the things which he carried with him. The next day when the sun was a lance high, Esteban went out of the house, and some of the chief men with him, and suddenly came a store of people from the city, whom as soon as he saw he began to run away and the others likewise, and forthwith they shot at them with arrows and wounded them, and certain men fell dead, and others beneath them dared not stir, and so they lay all night, and heard great rumors in the city, and saw many men and women keeping watch and ward upon the walls thereof, and after that could not see Esteban any more, and they thought they had killed him, as they had done with all the rest which went with him, and that none others had escaped but them only.

V

Having considered the former report of the Indians, I thought it not good willfully to lose my life as Esteban did; and so told them that God would punish those of Cibola, and that the viceroy would send many Christians to chastise them; but they would not believe me, for they said that no man was able to withstand the power of Cibola. Then again I divided among them certain other things which I had, and requested some of them to go to Cibola, to see if any other Indians escaped, with intent that they might learn some news of Esteban. I said unto them that I purposed to see the city of Cibola, whatsoever came of it. They said that none of them would go with me. At last when they saw me resolute, two of the chiefs of them said they would go with me; with whom with mine own Indians and interpreters I followed my way, till I came within sight of Cibola, which is situated on a plain at the foot of a round hill, and made show to be a fair city, and is better seated than any I have seen in those parts. The houses are builded in order, according as the Indians told me, all made of stone with several stories, and flat roofs, as far as I could discern from a mountain, whither I ascended to view the city. The people are somewhat white, they wear apparel and lie in beds, their weapons are bows, and they have emeralds and other jewels, although they esteem none so much as turquoises wherewith they adorn the walls of the porches of their houses, and their apparel and vessels, they use them instead of money through all that country. They use vessels of gold and silver, for they have no other metal, whereof there is greater use and more abundance than in Peru.

I was tempted to go to see the other kingdoms, for I knew I could but hazard my life, and that I had offered unto God the first day I began my journey; but in the end I began to be afraid, considering in what danger I would put myself, and that if I should die the knowledge of this country would be lost, which in my judgment is the greatest and best that hitherto has been discovered; and when I told the chief men what a goodly city Cibola seemed unto me, they answered me that it was the least of the seven cities, and that Totonteac is the greatest and best of them, because it has so many houses and people, and there is no end to them. Having seen the disposition and situation of the place, I thought good to name that country El Nuevo Reyno de San Francisco; in which place I made a great heap of stones by the help of the Indians, and on the top thereof I set up a small cross because I lacked means to make a greater, and said that I set up that cross and heap in the name of the most honorable Lord Don Antonio de Mendoza, Viceroy of New Spain, for the emperor our lord, in token of possession, according to mine instruction. Which possession said that I took in that place of all the seven cities, and of the kingdoms of Totonteac, of Ahacus, and of Marata. Thus I returned with much more fear than victuals, and went until I found the people which I had left behind me, with all the speed that I could make.

I write not here many other particularities, because they are impertinent to this matter: I only report that which I have seen, and which was told me concerning the countries through which I traveled, and of those of which I had information.

Chapter Two

The millers were the age Dorantes' own Martín would have been, one tall, one short and broad-shouldered, both pocked about the neck and cheeks, the scars showing as disks of white from the dusting of flour that covered their faces and arms. They stood facing him and his guest, Melchor Díaz, the alcalde of Culiacán who, three years ago, had been the first honest Spaniard the Children of the Sun had encountered. The big wooden gears rumbled against the slosh of water from the great wheel. The stone turned slowly, groaning. Melchor sneezed and crossed himself.

"The finest flour in Mexico," Dorantes said, taking up a handful from one of the huge jars and letting it run through his fingers. The tall miller smiled nervously.

"The encomendero is proud of his flour, eh?" Melchor said. He gripped his gauntlets and soft cap in his left hand, from time to time slapping them against his thigh. His freckled, balding head gleamed in the light from the high, flour-misted window. They passed on outside. Dorantes never spent much time in the mill, for his presence seemed to paralyze the millers.

"Those two are mestizos, are they not, Andrés? It is not simply the coating of the fine flour of Mezaculapan that causes them to appear light in color?"

"I brought fifty of them here off the streets of the capital so they could learn the skills of farming, milling, harness-making—a hundred different things. Along with me!" He laughed as they mounted their horses.

"And is this successful?" Melchor asked.

"Some disappear back to the city again, bored to distraction in the country. They would rather starve in the city than eat well out here."

"It appears that the country life agrees with you, my friend," Melchor said. The hoofs resounded on the plank bridge across the stream below the mill.

"An encomendero's life is very complicated, Melchor." He watched the movement of the haunches of the fine dun stallion the captain from New Galicia rode, clearly from the viceroy's stables. "But tell me why Don Antonio summoned you to the capital."

"I am not certain entirely, Andrés. He is very deep, and his purposes are not always those that appear to the eye." Melchor slapped the bundled gauntlets against his thigh. "But clearly he is not satisfied with this report of the grand visions of Cibola of Fray Marcos. It is unfortunate the good friar was unable to obtain any of these golden cooking vessels and sweat scrapers."

"He wished your opinion of Fray Marcos' relation?"

Melchor nodded. "Matters do not proceed rapidly enough to suit Don Antonio. Coronado drags his heels in Compostela. Another party is to follow Fray Marcos' route, and make certain of what he claims to have observed from his mountain top. And of what caused your unfortunate Moor to send back the very large crosses indicating very large discoveries."

"And you are to lead this party?"

"Yes, Andrés. But I must tell you what Don Antonio said of you. He said if you had written this report of Fray Marcos' he would have no difficulty of credulity."

"I see why I have been honored by this visit. Please do not ask it. I cannot go."

"Very well, Andrés," Melchor said with a sigh.

"Perhaps you have seen enough of Mezaculapan for one day. Let us go partake of some wine and cakes."

"With pleasure, my friend," Melchor said.

His wife, María de la Torre, thick with their second child, accompanied them into the patio with its green shade and neat lines of moss growing in the interstices between the tiles. The wet nurse brought Caspar to be admired, and the soldier chucked him under the chin and laughed at the sunny child's giggles. When the women withdrew he and Melchor sat facing each other over cups of wine.

"Your own wine, encomendero?"

"We trade our flour for it." He offered Melchor the plate of cakes, and the captain sampled one and nodded judiciously, then burst into laughter.

"Ah, Andrés, what a very different person you have become from the naked, long-haired healer of Indians one encountered so long ago!"

He smiled also, but asked, "What more can you tell me of the fate of

Esteban? Is it entirely certain he is dead? Perhaps Fray Marcos is not to be trusted in that report as well."

"It is certain that Fray Marcos believes him to be dead," Melchor said. "After he had retreated from Cibola he was told that the black man was cut into pieces, which were sent to each of the seven cities. To show he was not a god, but a man of flesh and blood, you see."

He leaned back in his chair, Melchor watching him sympathetically. "I am sorry, my friend. Although he was black and a slave, I know he was your good companion and much valued."

"Once before we encountered indigenes to whom his gourds were not sacred, but the opposite."

"The skinny friar thinks it was not merely gourds, but scandalous conduct with women."

He sighed and nodded silently.

"Many girls, says the Franciscan, who had it from the Pímas. Multitudes of girls. The Moor would come to the gates of a place, rattle his gourds and demand that pretty girls be produced. Also turquoises. These girls joined a harem that accompanied him, along with two fine sleek spaniels, that it is said were eaten at Cibola by indigenes who had never seen their like before. The Moor had become arrogant past all reason, says Fray Marcos."

"Tell me, Melchor, are you convinced by Fray Marcos of the golden glitter of Cibola?"

The other shrugged hugely. "It is admitted that this city is not called Cibola by the indigenes, but Hawíkuh."

"Hawíkuh!" He knew that name.

"Let me tell you why perhaps the viceroy does not hurry Coronado to this entrada," Melchor said, leaning toward him confidentially. "There is another great quarrel with Cortés. He has continued to send his ships to the northern gulf of California against the express command of Don Antonio. For this they say Don Antonio may be able finally to clip his wings. On his part Cortés issues warnings: the entrada will strip New Galicia of its soldiery—the province Guzmán never truly conquered, but only scoured for slaves. The Indians will join in a rebellion that will sweep all before it. Because of these warnings Coronado lingers in Compostela."

"Do you think this rebellion is a danger?"

Melchor scratched his fingers in his clipped beard, frowning. "One dislikes agreeing with the great schemer, but yes!" He leaned back in his chair, and, with one eye closed, squinted around at the pleasant patio that Don Rodrigo Botello had built, with its greenery and flowers.

"And so, Andrés, this life of ease—making fine flour and babies—it contents you?"

"I understand that the other great schemer continues to devise schemes that will take me back to the north. I do not wish to go, Melchor."

They took supper at the long table in the dining sala, which reminded him of a dungeon, with its arrow ports for windows and crude vaulting: he, Melchor Díaz, María de la Torre, and Padre Bernardo, her confessor. He had come to detest the padre more each day during this last six months of María's sickness-of-the-spirit that accompanied her second pregnancy: the thickness of his waist, the waxy plumpness of his face with nose and chin inclining toward each other over his disapproving mouth, and his habitual stance, bent backward from the waist with thumbs hooked into his belt, and his expression of censorious contempt. His hands appeared formed of mutton fat, the backs covered with knitted black hair.

He watched the fat hand reach out for its goblet of wine, the dark, thin little mouth convulsed with chewing. Padre Bernardo wiped his mouth with his napkin and addressed Melchor.

"Tell me, my good Captain, is there a great deal of idolatry in Culiacán?"

"You do see a good number of those clay idols about, that's for certain, Padre."

"Idols!" Padre Bernardo said with satisfaction. María's eye caught Dorantes'. The eye was pleading, her face luminously beautiful as it became in her pregnancies. She had begged him not to quarrel with Padre Bernardo. She had wept when he had told her he himself would rather confess to one of the hogs in the swineyard.

"I can tell you the Tarascans enjoy a fine mass," Melchor said heartily. "Pímas too. A whole congregation of those fellows followed the Children of the Sun down from the north, to settle in the Valley of Culiacán. Love a good Mass. Sing like birds. And dance!"

"Idolators!" Padre Bernardo said heavily. "The Holy Office has much work to do. One can only hope the good bishop's shoulders are broad enough to sustain his labors. He grows old!"

"It seems the good bishop could find better work for the Holy Office than smashing clay pots," he said, and María's eye flicked pleadingly at him again. He said, "The Holy Office should pay more attention to these local caciques who are despots in their pueblos, and undo any good work the church might do."

He knew these petty despots, especially Don Pedro Tlaxemetla in the nearby pueblo of Asala, from which María had an income, an Aztec noble as poisonous and arrogant as Padre Bernardo, and indeed he had a good reason to believe the two conspired against him. Don

Pedro was corrupt, sycophantic, cruel, and sexually profligate, and used his Christianity as a weapon. Many of the members of the old Aztec nobility who had been favored by the Spaniards were filled with contempt for their inferiors and for their conquerors alike. Padre Bernardo considered Don Pedro of Asala a good Christian.

Now he was pleased to understand that the padre, avoiding his eye, was seeking a quarrel with him by criticizing the popularity of the Virgin of Guadalupe. His waxy fist banged gently upon the table for emphasis.

"These people should be studying the meaning of the Trinity rather than climbing a rocky hill to worship a pagan goddess and a painted cloak!"

He heard María whisper his name, but he could not stop himself. "It is difficult to adore the Trinity, Padre. They seek to worship one who loves the poorest peon as much as a grandee of Spain."

The padre glared, but not at him directly.

"They seek mercy," he continued, "and the Holy Trinity is not notable for the quality of its mercy."

All stared at him. It pleased him to go too far. He had come to love the dark Virgin, who herself went too far, caring nothing for social distinctions and little for human or even divine law. None of those poor Indians on their knees need fear approaching her. Nor did he, one of their conquerors. Humility was her grace. Her pity was infinite. As all his life he had found the Redeemer too sublime, too terrible, too just, for his most intimate prayers, so now he found even the Virgin of the Remedies, who had healed their wounds, exhaustion, and great fear after the Night of Sorrows, too perfect, too Castilian in her doll-like, painted, gold-and-white beauty. She was to be appealed to for strength, but not for mercy or compassion.

"Yes, it is known that you also worship at Tepeyac, Don Andrés," Padre Bernardo said, as though his guilty secret had been laid bare.

"Among those who will never understand the meaning of the Trinity," he said, looking steadily at the priest. "At the feet of Our Lady, who does not understand it herself."

"Be careful, Don Andrés!" the priest exclaimed. Melchor was staring at him with mock wide eyes, María with real ones, her napkin pressed to her lips.

"And who will fill her heaven with those despised by fat priests and elegant abbots," he said, "despite the Trinity."

Padre Bernardo jarred the table, rising. "I warn you to have care, señor. This is blasphemy!"

"I knew a priest who was a great sinner," he said, "a fornicator, although he understood well the meaning of the Trinity. But that good

man cut off his own balls, and so at last he was no longer a hypocrite."
He rose also. "Will you warn me of blasphemy, priest? In my house,
with my food and drink greasy on your lips?"

Padre Bernardo shoved his chair aside and stamped out of the sala.

María followed the priest, calling his name, trotting with one arm
clasped over her swollen belly. He slumped back into his chair.

"Please forgive me, Melchor. Such scenes in front of friends are
inexcusable."

"It is not many soldiers who are pained at the discomfiture of priests.
But I see that truly an encomendero's life is a complicated one."

"Wives are a complication that one must put up with, but I am very
tired of the judgments of this fat father confessor." But his quick
angers were not all due to Padre Bernardo. Often he found himself
longing for that second time of felicity in his life, during the great
journey, when each day's complications could be solved each day.

He managed to say lightly, "My child is a complication one can do
with more of. María calculates that a brother is due in November."

"At which time I will be far north of Culiacán. How often I will
wish you were riding beside me, to guide us!"

"I know the way on foot only."

"Yes, yes! I do not urge you, of course."

Old Abel entered with a plate of sweets and surveyed the empty
chairs with dismay. In Nahuatl Dorantes told the little Indian that the
señora and the padre had departed early for their quarters, and the
sweets should be served to them there.

"Tell me how you learned the language of the indigenes so well,
Andrés," Melchor said.

"I lived for some years with a Nahua woman. From her I learned
their tongue. And from a priest she learned Castilian until she spoke
better than you or I. And some Latin as well."

"But why would a priest teach her such things?" Melchor inquired,
puzzled. But the conversation had already gone further than he wished,
and he turned it to other matters.

María lay on the canopied bed in yellow candlelight, fat black
psalter beside her hand. The lace of her nightdress covered her blue-
veined bosom, and the lace of her glossy brown hair was spread upon
her pillow. Her expression was tremulous and reproachful. She regarded him as a violent man and a great and unredeemed sinner—
though not so great a one as she herself. He seated himself facing
her.

"The child rides well, María?"

She tented her hands over the mound of her belly with a gripe of her features that signified pain and anxiety. "Oh, Andrés, I am frightened when you become angry like that! I know it is bad for him!" She patted herself. She had been married at seventeen to a man almost three times her age; now, at twenty-eight, pregnant with her second child, it seemed to him that she was reverting to her girlhood that had been cut off by her marriage to Alonso de Benevides.

"I am frightened, my husband," she whispered. "They say a child in the womb absorbs the bad things of the life outside the mother's body, and these will become his imperfections."

"He will become a fat priest, then," he said, and immediately regretted it, for she flinched as though he had struck her.

"It is improper for you to be so blasphemous with Padre Bernardo. It is a vice in you, my husband."

"It is because he seems to me a blasphemy in his very person."

"He is a holy father of the church!"

"He is a blasphemy all the same. He concerns himself with the drunkenness of the indigenes but gives them no faith to replace their own which we have destroyed. He concerns himself with smashing clay idols instead of preaching the faith. He would train a child by breaking his toys instead of listening to his catechism."

It was useless to say these things. He watched her pale hand trace the sign of the cross on her belly. Still he continued.

"He calls them stupid because they cannot understand the meaning of the Trinity, and idolators because they worship the cloak of Juan Diego. The Lady of Guadalupe is the only one who can give them comfort, except for the god of drunkenness through whom they forget their misery."

"He is a holy father of the church and must know best. You know I would not speak against my husband in anything, but what can I do when he himself speaks against the Holy Church?"

"I do not speak against the church but against hypocrite priests. Listen, once I knew a man who was truly holy for a little while. If you had known him then you would know this priest for what he is. He loved those to whom he tended. He cared nothing for his appetites, as our Savior cared nothing. He was as thin as this one is fat. He—"

"Is this the one of whom you spoke so grossly at table, Andrés?"

He shook his head and did not continue, watching her fingers picking at the lace of her bodice.

"Andrés, if you bear me love—you will be gentler with him. You will drive him away, and I need him very much."

He rose to stand facing the door, with his back turned to his wife. "I know that is true," he said. "Why is it?"

"My soul is troubled. It is very stained."

"Because you slept with men in adultery. When you were married to an old fart who visited your bed once a year until he did not visit it at all."

"There is terrible sin upon my soul, Andrés," she whispered.

"For which forgiveness is continuous. Does not your confessor tell you that?"

He listened to the quickened rustle of her breath. "I know one who would forgive your sins. She offers comfort to all who come to her, whether they suffer foolishly or not."

"But she is only a pagan goddess, Padre Bernardo says!"

He bade her good night and went to his own room, where, on his knees, he prayed to his Lady for the health of his wife.

In the morning he rode with Melchor Díaz through the wheat fields, vegetable gardens, and orchards, where the Indian souls of his responsibility, if not sleek and plump, were at least not the starvelings of Mezaculapan when Don Rodrigo had been its patron. Melchor was interested in the tiny dots of buzzards circling over the northern hills, where one day Dorantes had followed the guide who had been sent to him by Timultzin.

"Las Minas," he said. "The mines are worked by a cousin of Cortés'. His indigenes toil until they die. They are allowed their extremity in the open air, where buzzards pick their bones clean."

Melchor gave him a troubled glance, leaning on the pommel of his saddle. "I see you are bitter toward our fellow Christians in many cases, my friend."

He nodded. No doubt his lack of forgiveness of his fellow Christians was a vice, like his blasphemies to the priest. He watched the slow circling of those high dots beyond the tan fields—the mark of the Castilian in New Spain. It had been the mark of the Aztec before them. Why did he love this blood-stained land so much? Was it only pity?

"Once I thought the Conquest could not be worth the misery it caused," he said. "Now I believe it would have been worth it if these people could have been relieved of their nobles, whom we have returned to power. Don Pedro of Asala is a vile animal. What would you say of a man whose habit it was to force eight-year-old girls? And what of a priest who would condone such a matter while demanding that peons be flogged for drunkenness?"

"I thought the breaking of clay idols was his abiding interest," Melchor said, laughing.

"These two activities are his great service to the Holy Church."

They rode back through the fields, and his eye was pleased by the aspect of high Spanish walls, the dark branches of the oaks spreading above them, and the narrow spires of the pines. He showed Melchor the outdoor chapel, with its crudely carved Stations of the Cross, and pointed out the blind wall behind which had been kept Rodrigo Botello's harem.

"The first day I came here they lined up for me, as no doubt they were used to doing," he said. "They lifted their shifts for me. These were girls of thirteen, fifteen at the most, a dozen of them. Elsewhere were the older and pregnant ones, and mothers with children. There were more than fifty of these. Many of the children were diseased. There were idiots, lame, and blind. It was like a village we came to once on the great journey, where there were many blind. Álvar thought we could cure them, but I said we must go on quickly. Their eyes were white."

He stopped to gain control of his breathing. "I suppose something can be said for him that he kept them here. He could have sent the diseased ones away. And the concubines were well-fed enough. Maybe it pleased him to see the ruin he had caused."

"And you keep them here also?"

"Yes, they are here, though it is painful for me to see them. When I brought my mestizo youths from the capital, I thought they might marry some of the young girls who were not diseased. I thought I would be helping—both. But they are uninterested in one another. Several of the girls still make eyes at me when I come there."

"This seems very hard, encomendero," Melchor said.

"And yet the people of the household say my predecessor was not altogether an evil man," he went on, for again he could not stop himself. "They say he was only harsh to them sometimes. He kept these—blind children. Even though he fed his livestock better than his Indians and was a truly blasphemous man, he took to heart his responsibilities for the conversion of the indigenes. In that he did better than I have done."

"With this same sour padre?"

"This priest is my wife's confessor from the capital. He is here because he is no longer welcome at Don Antonio's palace."

"I think you must not blame yourself for things that cannot be different, my friend," Melchor said.

Dorantes summoned Abel and sent him for the seventeen who were training as soldiers, and led Melchor Díaz to the target butts beyond the stables. Soon the mestizos appeared: Santiago, the corporal, and the groom, José, the two millers, the carpenter, carters, harness-maker, and household servants. While Melchor watched with his cap pulled down to shade his eyes, the little army brought the crossbows and shields from the shed and formed themselves into groups of two, with Santiago, who was the most intelligent of them, directing his orders to the crossbowmen and shieldmen. At his signal they began to shoot at the targets, while Dorantes and Melchor Díaz peppered them with small stones. These the shieldmen neatly deflected. All put down their weapons and trooped off to the butts to collect their bolts. Pánfilo's cheek was bleeding where a stone had struck him.

"In Cuba there were dogs trained to retrieve the bolts," Melchor said. "But this is very well done, Andrés! That one in the white jacket looks like a real soldier."

"My predecessor, who was a godless blasphemer, trained his Indians well in their catechisms, while I, a lover of peace, train my mestizos in the arts of war. Come, you will give instruction in swordplay, for we have lacked an expert swordsman."

The soldier went at it with great energy, thrust and parry with the short sword, shrinking himself behind his shield, from which the blade leaped out. With the rapier he seemed taller and more slender, as, with bent knees, he shuffled forward, closed with his rear foot, feinted, thrust, and mimed a wound, which brought smiles to the circle of tan faces.

Afterwards he and Melchor sat in the sala drinking cool sangría and laughing with the excitement that came from swords and wine. Melchor complimented him again on his troop, which it was his duty to furnish the viceroy in time of rebellion.

"Ah, but Andrés, it is clear from the color of their skin that Mexico was conquered not with the sword but another weapon. What memories you must have! The girls!"

Attended by Santiago, he rode with Melchor Díaz as far as San Blas, on the coach road back to the capital. He watched the captain jog on with his pack animals, half-obscured by the tan dust raised by the hoofs of the animals, en route back to the City of Mexico, and thence to Compostela, Culiacán, and Hawíkuh.

The alcalde of San Blas was a lame old soldier named Luis Rodríguez, with whom he always took a cup of wine on his visits to the dusty little town, in a patio outside the inn.

"It is all the talk in the capital," Rodríguez said, leaning over the table toward him, grizzled close-cropped hair and beard, scarred brown hand gripping his cup. "The Franciscan saw the golden walls with his own eyes. From a mountain some leagues away, it is said; but the glitter was powerful even there. He was afraid to proceed closer because of the death of the Moor. Have you heard this?"

He had heard it. Santiago squatted with his back against the mud

wall nearby, the mules hitched beyond him, cavalry crossbow slung
from the saddle of the gray one.

"What one would give to be one of the soldiers of this grand entrada
that forms in Compostela," the alcade said, and sighed. "But no one
wants a crippled fellow."

Dorantes saw Santiago craning his neck to gaze down the road. With
a padding and creaking a team of mules appeared, drawing a heavy
coach. He felt the beat of anger to recognize that coach. Indians in
outlandish livery were perched all over it, on the box, on the roof, and
clinging to the rear. The coach drew up in a choking cloud of dust,
and dark-complected servants scurried to open the door and place a
gold-and-blue painted box before it as a step. Girls' faces showed
in the window, and Don Pedro Tlaxemetla bent forward to pass
through the door, wearing a rainbow-dyed crown of feathers, a white
cloak fastened at the throat with a golden ornament, peach colored
doublet decorated with designs of colored feathers, green, soft leather
boots.

"This pig is very grand," Rodríguez said loudly. The coach seemed
filled with girls, peering out the door and window. Some of the liv-
eried servants knelt before their lord, while others swarmed around
him with feather whisks, brushing dust from his costume as Don Pedro
turned one way in profile, then the other, extending his boots one by
one to the whisks. When one of the servants knocked his crown
askew, he slapped the offender, whispering viciously in Nahuatl.

Dorantes began to laugh. It came first as an irresistible tickling in his
throat, then surged up in long guffaws that purged him of bitterness.
The Aztec stood facing him from before the crowd of faces in the
door of the coach, three of his servants kneeling before him frozen.
Don Pedro's hawk features had darkened.

He whispered again in Nahuatl and one of the footmen reached
inside the coach door, while the others grouped together menacingly,
some with hands on daggers. The one produced a painted bow and
arrow. But Santiago had also moved swiftly, to snatch the crossbow
from the saddle, cranking and raising it.

Rodríguez, red-faced, knocked his chair over backward stumbling to
his feet and jerking his poniard free. He pointed it at the footman, who
did not nock his arrow but let the hand holding the bow drop to his
side, his eyes rolling to his master. The others looked uncertain also.

"If that man draws his bow I'll have his hand lopped off," Rodríguez
said in a stifled voice. "And that goes for any pig who shows his
steel."

Don Pedro glanced once at Santiago's crossbow, then drew his cloak around himself. "Why do you laugh, please?" he said in his flat, peremptory voice like a parrot's call.

"I laugh at something funny."

"You think it is funny? Then perhaps I will show you that it is not funny."

Dorantes managed another chuckle, but he was beginning to dislike himself again. "I don't think you're funny when you're raping ten-year-old girls," he said. "And the church does not think it is funny when its converts maintain harems." He jerked his chin at the faces of the girls peering out of the coach.

"These ones are my nieces," Don Pedro said with dignity.

This time he and the alcalde laughed together, and Don Pedro Tlaxemetla glared at them with a face black with fury.

He rode hard following the messenger on his black horse to the estate of Juan de Jaramilo, in Coyoacán across the lake. Doña Marina waited for him in the patio. He strode toward her slapping the dust from his clothing with his hat. Her head was cowled in her shawl, hands clasped at her waist.

"The physician can do nothing," she said in her flat voice. "There is no one I can turn to but you, who have been a healer. Come!" she said.

The boy Martín Cortés, no longer a boy, eighteen, he calculated, lay in the center of a large bed in a dim room. A servant had been wiping his face with a damp cloth, and now she drew back and retreated to stand with two others in the far corner. He could feel the sweat on his own face remembering Timultzin lying like this in what he thought was her deathbed. The boy's forehead was very hot, and he moved his head restlessly, glint of open eyes.

"Two days past he was well. Yesterday there was this," Doña Marina said in a muffled voice. "Don Andrés has come to make you well, my treasure," she whispered.

The boy muttered unintelligibly.

Leaning awkwardly over the bed he placed the fingertips of both hands on the boy's burning forehead. He prayed to his dark Lady for that unforgotten sensation of warmth flushing through his forearms. He could only feel heat where his fingers touched fevered flesh. He prayed for Martín Cortés as though this were his own son. His arms shook with the strain of his position. He could hear the servants whispering in the corner, and he tried to blot the sound from his consciousness, concentrating on his prayers.

But the warmth did not come. He seated himself on the bed. He could feel the heat of the boy's body through the coverlet. He kept his fingers pressed to the forehead, his own head bowed, eyes closed. His head ached and he could feel the trickle of sweat on his cheeks. "Dear Lady, give me this power one last time, for thine own Son's sake."

It seemed to him that hours must be passing. He was almost weeping with disappointment for that remembered sensation that continued to elude him. And yet it seemed that the fever was not so strong as it had been. He sat erect, shoulders aching.

"Doña Marina, see if the heat is not less. I can no longer tell."

She was beside him swiftly, hand to her son's brow. "Yes!" she breathed.

"Not gone, but less!"

"Yes!"

He rose and staggered with exhaustion. He shook his arms to loosen the tight muscles. The sensation had not come, and yet the boy was better. Tears burned his cheeks.

Back in the sala he seated himself to rest, head in hands. Doña Marina came to stand beside him. She put a hand on his shoulder.

"Thank you, Don Andrés."

"I think I did nothing. The fever broke as fevers will do."

"Perhaps yes, perhaps no. I cannot ask you to stay long, Don Andrés. My husband will return from the city this evening, and he is very bitter against you for reasons you will understand."

He nodded silently.

"There is an inn at the end of the road. It is a pleasant place."

He rose and looked down into her dark face within the shawl. "What of Cortés?"

"He returns to Spain. His wife and the two Martíns accompany him, this one and the son of the marquesa. He goes to plead his cause against the viceroy, for their quarrel has become very deep. The entrada to Cibola should be his, Don Andrés."

He did not respond, hoping that his legs would support him until he had left here. He felt drained. "Farewell, Doña Marina."

"Farewell, Don Andrés. Be certain Cortés will know of this great service."

"It is unnecessary," he said, and left her there.

Chapter Three

He was wakened by Abel, who stood over him with a candle, his wizened face frightened. His breath reeked of pulque.

"Don Andrés, there is a woman, a Nahua—" He lapsed into Nahuatl in his fright. "She must see you, lord! You must come to her. Oh, she may be a ghost. She may be a witch! She is very powerful, lord! She is wrapped in cloths so no one may see her face, and she speaks like a tuele lord. She must see my Don Andrés!"

"Is she a witch of pulque, Abel?"

Shadows danced from the little Indian's agitation. "No, lord, she is a real witch or perhaps a ghost!"

Rising, he said, "You must not speak to Padre Bernardo of these ghosts and witches when you stink so strongly of pulque." Then his heart swelled as though it would burst, with realization.

Hurriedly he exchanged his nightgown for shirt, breeches, and slippers, and followed Abel outside and to the gate in the wall under a sky of stars brilliant as jewels. Timultzin was a denser figure against the vines. He sent the servant away.

"I have come for a favor, Andrés," she said, moving to meet him. The glimmer of her eyes was visible in her shrouded face.

"Tell me," he said. His hand encountered hers, but she seemed to hold him off. Her voice was tense and tired.

"We carry a thing that must be concealed. Morning light is coming, and we are far from any place to hide. A cave—a mine that is unused."

His heart had swollen differently. "There are caves in the hills."

"How far?"

"Half a league, a little more."

"We can trust no one but you."

"Wait here." He hurried to his chamber to dress in dark clothing and

2 9 8

heavy boots, halting once in a start of fright at glimmering motion. It was only his reflection in the looking glass.

Timultzin led him down the road, along a bank, and, sliding and stumbling, into a ravine. In pit darkness there he had a sense of a crowd of men in a frozen stillness. Timultzin spoke to someone so softly he did not catch her words. Immediately there was movement.

They were out of the ravine in the starlight before he was able to distinguish the burden of the bearers—an object large as a bull, shrouded with white cloth and bound with ropes. It was supported by two poles, ten men to each one. In addition to these were three other men in pipiltin robes. Walking ahead with Timultzin, in dread he told himself that he must not do this. She asked too much. She asked him to risk his soul.

"It is very slow," she said in the tired voice. "Much slower than we thought. They cannot walk far without resting. There are no strong men anymore, except Castilians."

He crossed himself. "Is it Huitzilopochtli?"

"Yes, Andrés."

It was the idol of the bishop's obsession. "I thought you were of the cult of Tloque Nahuaque."

"It is the same."

Once the bearers began to chant in low voices. A curt command silenced them. The path they followed was white as pipeclay in the starlight. Hills loomed like shapes carved from darkness.

"Where do you take it?" he asked.

"To the north."

One of the leaders hissed at her, and she said haughtily, "Do I not know this lord? Do we not depend upon him?"

"To the north so there will be rebellion there?" he asked.

She did not reply. They halted as the bearers lowered their poles to rest, some curling up on the ground in exhaustion, one with his cloth shoulder-cushion draped over his face, small, bare-legged, barefoot men. The three pipiltin stood apart in those postures of Aztec arrogance Dorantes could discern even in the darkness. While the bearers rested he scouted ahead for a fork in the trail that he recalled, leaving Timultzin conferring with the other leaders.

When they started on, the darkness seemed more intense, the starlight more frail, as though the stars were dimming in preparation for dawn. Timultzin walked beside him on the narrow path toward the black masses of the hills, occasionally touching his arm in some communication of trust or gratitude. Irritatingly soon the bearers halted to rest again.

"The bishop and the Holy Office seek this idol," he said.

"He was not safe where he was hidden."

"In Atzcapotzalco?"

"The less you know of him the better. Is it not true?"

"Do you know what you risk here, my heart? You and the others who are baptized Christians."

"And ask you to risk," she said, her hand on his arm. "Yes, Andrés, we know we are apostates and idolators. And we know that Don Carlos Ometochtzin was burned at the stake for just such offenses. But these gods are our gods. They are what we are, as yours are what you are."

"This one stinks of blood!"

"My heart, blood is his food as the blood of your god is your food. It is the same thing, for blood is what life is."

He shook off her hand to cross himself. "There is but one God!"

"No, Andrés," she murmured. "Whatever Rufino and the other good fathers of the church would have us understand of the meaning of the Trinity, there is a Father, and His Son, and the Holy Spirit. There is also the Mother of the Son, and the numerous saints. It is the same with our many gods, who are also one. We hope to preserve the forms of our gods from those who seek to destroy them, for in so doing we save a part of ourselves that is worth preserving, before that also is destroyed by you who have conquered us. Rufino understands, and I believe you do also, but in a different way."

"If you seek rebellion in the north with this idol, there will only be more blood shed for nothing."

She was silent, skirts rustling as she moved beside him. Finally she said, "No, I do not seek that. I do not say others do not. But it may be that men's spirits must live by vain hopes."

He remembered the viceroy saying the achievement must be worth the means that were necessary to it. In the lightening darkness he saw that one of the leaders was Coyotl, his guide to Mezaculapan, by the G-scar on his lip, and another Miguel, the ocelot knight of the Night of Sorrows, who wore a band of cloth around his forehead. Miguel gave him a nod of acknowledgment.

"If I am called to fight, I must fight," he said hoarsely. "This. You."

"I would understand that, my heart," Timultzin said. "But this god came to Mexico from the north. Now he returns, for a little while; or long."

Miguel approached them. "Surely it is not far now, señor," he said in Castilian. "Morning light comes very soon."

"It is not far now."

The bearers rested in their different postures, one on his back with an arm flung over his face, two others seated back to back. Timultzin and her cousin paced among them. Her bandaged face was invisible within the cowl of her shawl. When the bearers rose again to take up their burden they began to chant. This time they were not silenced.

In gray light they climbed more steeply into a canyon through which he had ridden once or twice, where he remembered a cave. Thick brush scraped white weals on the legs of the bearers. Some of whom were groaning now as they hoisted their burden upward. With relief he marked the black patch of the hole in the cliff face, just as the first brightening of the sun appeared over the eastern hills. He noticed that the three pipiltin never aided the bearers in their efforts. Slowly, the huge, cloth-bound idol was borne upward. Coyotl caught his eye, and, with his sneering, disfigured grin, made a saluting gesture.

As the leaders supervised the raising of the idol, with ropes, to the lip of the cave, he and Timultzin wandered away to seat themselves on a sandy ledge.

"It is said that your Castiliana carries another child," Timultzin said. "And is very beautiful. Does she know of me?"

"Yes and no."

"I leave your life now forever. Will you forget me?"

"You know I will not."

"Nor I you, my heart of hearts," she whispered.

"There is a thought I have had. That in time to come it is not your race or mine who will be the people of Mexico. But the children of your flesh and mine."

In a muffled voice she said, "Will they be content with their two parts?"

He could only shrug. "There is one god they can worship that belongs to each. She of Tepeyac."

They sat in silence, her shoulder touching his, as the sunlight crept toward them. He asked if he should bring food for the bearers.

"Food can be found now that the god is safe," she said. The pressure on his shoulder was removed. "We owe you much. Goodbye, my heart."

He bade her goodbye. When he had risen Miguel approached, to stand silently before him, head bowed. Timultzin assumed the same posture. He left them, starting back along the trail with the sun driving down the hillsides into his eyes.

A week later he rode back up the trail they had followed that night, and into the broken lands and canyons of the first hills. Tying the reins to a bush, he scrambled up the steep bank to the cave. It was low-ceilinged, not very deep. One wall was blackened, with the charred ends of old fires at its base. There was no sign of the idol, no marks on the earth floor where marks must have been left, nor was there scuffing on the bank where the bearers had raised the idol with ropes; no sign of anything.

One day he returned from his journey to the capital earlier than he had expected, to find no one in the patio or the sala. In María de la Torre's chambers he found the wet nurse with Caspar. She cowered as though afraid of him.

"Where is Doña María?"

"In the chapel, I believe, lord." Caspar was making the small huffing sound of beginning to cry, and with a deft shrug she produced the round brown breast he sought.

As Dorantes padded in his soft boots over the tiles toward the chapel, he heard a yelp of pain. He broke into a trot. When he turned the corner he had to halt abruptly to keep from running into the backs of the household servants. They were watching a tableau within the open air chapel. A cross of the peeled rounds of saplings had been propped upright there, and lashed to it was a man, with bare bloody back exposed. In his black robe, sleeves turned up on his fat white arms, Padre Bernardo held the whip at his side, long brown snake of it curved over the tiles. Beyond him stood María, arms folded over her breasts, head capped with a mantilla of black lace, her mouth so red in her white face it appeared to be bleeding. With her stood Rafael, the mestizo steward, and Angel, the field overseer. It was old Abel on the rack of the cross. On the wall behind him were the Stations, directly behind him the crudely carved depiction of Christ fallen, a helmeted Roman standing over him with the lash.

Panting, Padre Bernardo cried, "Drunkenness will not be tolerated! This man has fallen for the third time! After a warning, and a second warning! Drunkenness will not be tolerated!" His hand holding the whip jerked up. Abel blubbered, his voice rising to a shriek as the padre swung his arm and another stripe appeared on the brown flesh.

Dorantes thrust two of the servants aside and sprang across the tiles to snatch the whip from the padre, who clung to it until the two of them were locked face to face. He jammed his knee into the priest's groin, and wrung the whip free as the other groaned, and bowed, and swung aside. The handle was damp with priestly sweat. He saw Santiago's face.

"Cut him loose!" he said, and Santiago hurried to do it. He encountered his wife's wide eyes, in her shocked stiff face, and said, "This should not have been permitted, señora!" Then he swung around to face Padre Bernardo's mask of pain and hatred.

Santiago had loosened Abel's bonds, and the old Indian hobbled away, bent with his own pain. A wall of brown faces stared at the patron of Mezaculapan and the priest.

"The whipping of my servants will not be tolerated," he said. He swung the whip. He had not meant to strike the padre very hard, but some inner fury controlled his hand and powered the blow. The priest screamed like a woman, and turned to flee.

Dorantes danced to intercept him, swinging the whip again. "I will not tolerate priests whipping those they should be teaching the Holy Faith!"

Padre Bernardo covered his head with his hands and forearms, which were infuriatingly white. Dorantes exulted to see a savage red stripe mar the whiteness.

"These people are given to my care!" he panted. "I will not have them stupidly injured! Gluttons will not whip drunkards in this place!"

Then the priest was rolling on the tiles, feet kicking, hands shielding his face. Dorantes saw his wife's open mouth crying out to him as though through a mist of blood. He saw from Santiago's face that he went too far. He flung down the whip.

"Help him up," he said to Rafael.

When Padre Bernardo was erect and leaning on the steward's arm, his face dead gray, Dorantes said, "You will leave here immediately. Angel will furnish you with a mule. I wish never to see you again."

"You will regret this!" the priest panted. "I say you will regret this!"

He nodded to Rafael, who turned Padre Bernardo away from him. The priest shook off the supporting arm to swing back.

"You will suffer for these insults and injuries you have visited upon a father of the church!" he cried. "Blasphemer!" He thrust his head out like a snake striking. "And worse! Your sins and treachery are known. Will be known! Betrayer of the evangel, on your knees and beg forgiveness while you can!"

"Take him along, Rafael. Santiago! Angel!"

The overseer came reluctantly forward, but the priest swung away again, and, with dignity, stalked through the crowd of Indians who silently gave way before him.

In his chambers he sat naked and shivering in the wooden armchair. Teodora brought steaming jugs of water to dump into the pottery tub that raised a mist before the open casement. He soaked in water so hot he could barely stand it. His arm ached, pulled muscles from his violence. Whipping a priest! On your knees and beg forgiveness while you can! Even his bathing every day had seemed to Padre Bernardo a matter for condemnation. *Betrayer of the evangel!* He soaped himself as though to wash off the evil of the priest. His anger had turned to a dull headache.

He had toweled himself dry and was seated naked in the wooden chair again when his wife came into the room, still wearing her mantilla. She stood before him with hands clasped together at her breast.

He said, "Will you follow your father confessor to the city? Away from the blasphemer and worse?"

Her red mouth fumbled at the words. "No, Andrés, my duty is with my husband."

"Would you that your husband relieved you of that duty?"

She shook her head. "I know you are a good man, Andrés."

"For all my blasphemies and anger? And violence?"

"For all that. I know it does no good to whip Abel, but I did not know how to stop it."

"What did he mean, my treacheries are known? Betrayer of the evangel. Is this some new thing he has found against me?"

"He speaks with Don Pedro in the village, and with Angel. There is something. I pay no attention. Please do not ask me to understand things that drive me mad."

She gazed at him beseechingly. She knelt before him. He made a move to stop her, but she resisted it, the black lace of her mantilla tipping forward. Her hair brushed his thighs. He was surprised that his flesh responded, for he was frightened. He closed his eyes. It seemed that in some imponderable way he had made his wife proud of him.

Chapter Four

In the cellar chamber of the viceregal palace that Dorantes had visited once before, he sat in a cluster of chairs with Mendoza, Lope de Quevedo, and Agustín Guerrero, the captain of the household guard, in breastplate and soft cap. Beyond the viceroy was Bishop Zumárraga and the Franciscan friar, his secretary.

The bald-headed man in the leather apron squatted to poke at the little fire. This time, along with the strappado and the tabillas, leaning against the wall was a rack of woven iron straps, man-shaped but larger than a man, like the iron prophets of Seville. Gazing at the instruments of torture he could feel every muscle of his composed face, and his belly knotted like a fist. Agustín sat stiffly beside him. This bishop was wiping his forehead with a handkerchief. It was stifling in the torture chamber.

After a silent wait, the door was swung open by a pikeman with a red face, who maneuvered his weapon inside with difficulty, to stand by the door as others filed inside. These, Agustín whispered to Dorantes, were the prosecutor, the chief constable, and the secretary of the Holy Office. With them was a Dominican, the interpreter; and, in chains, naked except for a filthy loincloth, with a shaven head, and his delicate-featured, exhausted proud face, Miguel. He stood straight-backed as his chains were unlocked. His eyes flickered once at Dorantes, and then did not look his way again. A second pikeman brought up the rear.

When this company had arranged itself, some remaining standing by the door, and others taking empty chairs, the prosecutor, a small graying man in black doublet and white collar, confronted the Aztec.

"You will tell the whole truth!" he intoned, in Castilian. The Dominican repeated the exhortation in Nahuatl.

Now the prosecutor read from a scroll: "You have stated that before

305

you were baptized in the Holy Faith you were in possession of the idols. These, we know, have been brought to you in Atzcapotzalco after they were removed from the care of Don Mateos in this City of Mexico—by Coyoca, the Lord of Tula.

"You swear the idols were removed from your palace before your baptism, you know not where, and you hold that since you were not a Christian when they were in your possession, you cannot be held responsible. Coyoca has been questioned, but has never converted, and claims he knows nothing."

The prosecutor turned to face the bishop, who was blotting his face again, and the secretary of the Holy Office, seated on his right, as though awaiting some signal. Apparently receiving it, he bowed and turned back to Timultzin's kinsman again.

"You will tell the whole truth!"

The Indian did not respond, standing calmly before him, although his body gleamed with sweat. Dorantes' hands ached on the arms of his chair.

"When did you first notice the idols were gone?" the prosecutor demanded, the Dominican translating. Miguel said nothing, and the prosecutor continued: "Who removed the idols from your palace? Where were they taken?"

Still Miguel did not speak. The prosecutor signaled to the torturer, who rose from his chair to tip the man-shaped rack toward him, and lay it flat on blocks that raised it from the floor.

"You will tell the whole truth!" the prosecutor said once more.

The torturer grasped Miguel's arm and forced him down on his back on the rack, bending over him there to knot cords around his forehead, arms, and legs.

For the third time the prosecutor intoned his demand. Dorantes could feel the sweat running down his sides inside his shirt. His eyes stung from the smoke of the fire. The bishop was wiping his face again.

The torturer twisted the cords, one by one, until they bit into the flesh. Miguel's teeth showed. Someone hissed in sympathy.

The torturer passed a funnel to the constable, who forced it between the Indian's teeth, holding it there while the torturer poured water from a jar into the funnel. Miguel writhed. Again Dorantes heard the hiss of breath. The sound had come from his own throat. When the funnel was removed he could hear Miguel panting.

Once more the prosecutor demanded the whole truth, to no response. The torturer twisted the cords tighter. Miguel's teeth showed again. The constable forced the funnel between them, and the torturer poured water, part of it splashing on the contorted face.

The prosecutor leaned forward to repeat his demand, then straightened suddenly. "This man has lost consciousness!"

"Enough!" the bishop cried hoarsely. "Cut him loose!" The constable and the torturer hurried to obey. They raised Miguel to a sitting position, then lifted him to his feet, one supporting him from either side. Zumárraga was standing, gray-faced, grasping the shoulder of his secretary. Mendoza rose also. His eyes caught Dorantes', and he raised one eyebrow.

"He is to be taken to El Grande!" the bishop said in the hoarse voice. "He is never to leave there without my permission!"

The prosecutor's company half-dragged, half-carried the Aztec from the chamber, with the pikemen maneuvering out behind them. Mendoza and the bishop followed. Dorantes felt as though he himself had been freed from the rack as the others rose to leave. Agustín was mopping his face and neck.

"Cursed hot," he grumbled.

Lope de Quevedo approached. "You will await His Excellency in the east chamber, Captain Dorantes."

He waited upon the viceroy in the small room where they had conversed on previous occasions, and, after what seemed hours, Mendoza swept in past his bow, the secretary following him and a pikeman taking up a post at the door. Seating himself, the viceroy smiled at him with thin lips.

"A disappointing day for the good bishop, Don Andrés! Who pursues the abominable idol that continues to elude him. Have you wondered why you have been asked to attend this distasteful function?"

"I considered that it must be for the same reason that I viewed that chamber once before, Excellency."

Mendoza sat gazing at him with a stillness that seemed to congeal in the room. Lope de Quevedo stood frozen with his eyes moving from his master to Dorantes.

"Yes, there have been more denunciations and implications," the viceroy said, after a time. "Grave accusations have been made, having to do with this very abomination sought by the Holy Office. I hesitate to remand these to the Holy Office; indeed I have taken steps to ensure that they go no further at this time. And why do I hesitate, Don Andrés?"

He bowed his head, and, remembering the silence of Miguel, said nothing.

"Because I grieve with you for your good Moor Esteban. It was an unhappy loss for both of us. There are a number of other considerations. The bishop, as you saw today, is a soft-hearted man who cannot bear suffering. Moreover, my good Don Andrés, I believe you would show the same fortitude this Indian has displayed. Yet, as you have suspected, we would approach your conscience in other ways—as once through your slave, for whom it was clear you bore great affection. Similarly in this present case with an old comrade of yours, well beloved also it is reported, a friar at the College of Santa Cruz whom there is reason to believe may be implicated in this same unfortunate business. Oh, I tell you, señor, we will get to the bottom of these mysterious happenings at Mezaculapan if we are forced to it!"

He cursed the cool beading of sweat on his forehead. "What is it you would have of me, Excellency?" he asked.

"Do you not know, Don Andrés? Have you not always known? I cannot believe there is any question in your mind."

"You have a captain already, Excellency. Better qualified then I am. Nor do I believe in any golden cities."

Mendoza's expression of an anxious wolf took on a tinge of ironic amusement. "In truth what I would have of you has changed complexion, Captain. When I compared the narrative of a certain Franciscan friar with your own, my mind was made up. I must have eyes. I have sent Captain Melchor Díaz ahead, to find what he will in those lands. But the entrada must be made. There is too much at stake. Someone must accompany it who will serve as my eyes, my chronicler; who will serve me, and not himself or his dreams. Do you understand?"

Still he hesitated. He knew that he was caught, but he felt a lightness.

Mendoza sighed, and said, "Don Francisco and his army depart from Campostela within a month. Will you please read from my instructions those that will interest Don Andrés, my good Lopito?"

The secretary seemed to have committed these to memory. It was to be a Christian conquest. Francisco Vásquez de Coronado was held responsible in all matters pertaining to the service of God and the conversion and good treatment of the indigenes of the New Lands. No slaves were to be taken, by the specific command of the emperor. All natives were to be treated as free men, and they were to be taught to trust in God, Who is in Heaven, and the emperor who has been placed on earth by His hand, to rule and govern it. Indigenes were not to be employed in excessive tasks and were to be well rewarded for their labors. No bearers were to be impressed, but were to be voluntarily recruited and given just compensation, or else Castilians would carry their own weapons, goods, and supplies. There were to be no abuses or harm done to the Indians of the New Lands, and those who mistreated them were to be punished.

"Those who do not obey these orders will be at fault and incur the

308

penalties falling upon those who disobey the persons empowered by His Majesty to command them," Lope de Quevedo finished, and took a step backward with hands clasped behind him.

The viceroy bent his gaze upon Dorantes with the screwing motion of his head. "And what do you say to that, Don Andrés?"

He said that it was commendable.

Nodding, smiling, Mendoza said, "And who shall accompany Don Francisco to see that these instructions are followed? As well as these other services I have mentioned?"

He said that it seemed a position for a good friar.

Shaking his head, smiling, pointing his finger, the viceroy said, "No, señor, it is a position for *you*."

He marveled at the strange lightness—light-hearted, light-footed—as he went to find María de Mendoza, to tell her that she had won their wager after all.

Chapter Five

With his two mestizos he traveled the Great Western Road bound for Campostela, where he was to join the departure of the army of Coronado for the New Lands. In the hills above Campostela was a heap of volcanic rock overgrown with brush and grasses, a landmark where, he had heard along the road, dwelt the hermit and his followers—a holy man named Castillo Maldonado.

As he, Santiago, and José rode into the clearing, a naked creature scampered toward them—emaciated, clad in a loincloth, matted black hair and beard, a crude wooden cross swinging from a thong around his neck. Another appeared behind him, similarly clad, similarly skeletal, but older and moving more slowly.

"Hail, brothers!" this one called, signing his bare chest. The younger hermit smiled blankly up at Dorantes from beside his stirrup. "God's blessing on you, brothers!"

The two mestizos bestrode their mules close together, with the pack animals strung out behind them, José with an alarmed glance at a third hermit squatting among the rocks, Santiago with his expression of solemn concentration. The third hermit was waving an arm in greeting. Dorantes saw that he was black.

"Where may I find your master?" he asked.

"There are no masters here, brother," the old hermit said, limping closer. "All are brothers here."

"One called Castillo Maldonado, then."

"Summon the brother, brother!" the old one called to the blackamoor, who disappeared springing off among the jagged rocks.

"How do you call yourselves?" Dorantes asked. The simple-minded one continued to smile up at him, gripping his stirrup.

"The Brotherhood of the Sun, brother," the old one said. He gestured and shaded his eyes as he gazed up at the emblem of the sect, whose rays drove in long slants among the trees. A fourth hermit appeared, this one bald-headed, bearded, and lank as the others. He trotted in and out among the rocks and across the clearing, halting to hold up his arms in blessing. It was truly Alonso, and Dorantes swung off his mule to embrace his shriveled nakedness.

"Welcome, brother!" Alonso said in his ear. His breath was sweet as a milk cow's. Above the graying beard Alonso's eyes were pale brown, opaque. There were sun sores on his shoulders and his bald brown head. He wore the same simple smile as the first hermit; and Dorantes saw that his old companion did not recognize him. The Moor still crouched watching among the rocks. José was rolling his eyes at these apparitions, Santiago leaning woodenly on his pommel.

"Alonso, it is Andrés Dorantes," he said gently, but the other only smiled and bobbed his head.

"Welcome, brother, welcome! Come and sup with us in this holy place!"

"Alonso—" he said again, but gave it up as the Brother of the Sun peered at him with his impregnable unworldliness. Alonso summoned the old hermit to show Dorantes and Santiago into the cave, José preferring to remain guarding the mules.

The cave was high-ceilinged and broad, the rock floor covered with sweet-smelling herbs. Further back were beds of heaped pine needles, and a fire flickered against one wall beneath a clay pot in which something boiled with a vegetable odor. It appeared that the repast was ready, and it was served to him and Santiago in bowls like large cups, stewed weeds or herbs, very watery but with a mustard taste that griped at the back of his throat; no nourishment to it. Alonso and the other brothers, including the negro, six in all, squatted in a circle noisily sucking down the soup. When he had finished, Alonso rose to speak, hands clasped together, eyes raised to the roof of the cave:

"We thank thee, Father, for this good food we have eaten, and for the company of these brother travelers whom we have fed. We celebrate the brotherhood of all men under the sun, Father, white and brown and black alike, and pray that you bless us and keep us holy, in your name."

Having celebrated the brotherhood of man and the especial needs of travelers, Alonso's sermon became more conventional. Stiffly erect in the same stance, as though addressing the deity in the rocks above his head, he spoke of the Son of God sacrificed to expunge the sins of man, his blood, drop by drop, canceling sin by sin, his suffering in its enormity the enormity of evil in the world. He spoke in simple language that seemed very familiar, until with an aching heart Dorantes realized that these simple words were Álvar Núñez', which he himself had so often translated into Primahaitu. Alonso, right hand grasping his cross, was not only parroting Álvar's words, but his gestures and the very intonation of his voice, and had starved himself so that he resembled Álvar in those days of the journey. His disciples listened to him with reverence.

When it was over Alonso seemed in a trance. He tottered over to recline on one of the pine-needle couches, where he lay on his back with bare horny feet spread apart and his hands clasping the wooden cross.

Dorantes went to kneel beside the hermit, to thank him for the meal and the sermon. Alonso gazed at him with a brighter eye.

"Is it you, Andrés?"

"Yes, Alonso."

"Many have come by here, many soldiers and others. Sometimes—I cannot tell one from another. Do you return?"

The hermit sat up swiftly, a hand grasping his arm with astonishing strength. "Does Álvar go also?"

"He has gone to Paraguay."

"Oh—I knew that!" The grip relaxed, then tightened again. "And our Estebánico?"

"They say he is dead at Hawíkuh."

"Dead!" the hermit said. "Hawíkuh?" he said, uncomprehendingly. He lay back on the couch, eyes fixed on the cave ceiling again. The pulse of his heart was visible through the thin flesh of his chest.

"You are starving, man!" Dorantes whispered. "You have starved yourself! How have you come to this, old friend?"

He watched the thin lips tilt within the tangled beard. "Once I was a fine encomendero, Andrés. So many varas of land, so many souls who were in my care and made me rich. But there were so many complications, so many matters, so many more *things* than we were used to. Everyone needed something that only I could supply, and it seemed I could please no one trying to please all. If I had the gray hog killed, it should have been the brown one. If I sent reapers to the west field, it should have been to the east field. And I became a hard and quarrelsome man. I had Indians flogged! Who were my brothers! I beat my wife, whose sweet flesh I had reveled in. And all I could dream of was the old days. The great journey! The Children of the Sun! Ah, Andrés, of course I remember that it was hard. But what was hard to endure is sweet to recall! When there were no complications but our daily bread, and shelter or the lack of it, and walking to the sunset with our brothers, whom we loved. You, Andrés, and Álvar, and our Estebánico, but our other brothers as well. And the healing, even though I was no healer. The good that can be done when one is purified! The purity of prayer when one can shut out the aches of the body and the craving of the belly! Then the goodness. Then! I seek it here. But I believe you return to the north to find it again, Andrés!"

"Perhaps, Alonso," he said.

"But do you go with the soldiers? Can this be true?"

"It is true. To what they call the New Lands." His knees ached on the rock floor beside his friend's pallet. "Alonso, Alonso, you must eat. You are starving. We never starved!"

The bony hand sought his and clutched it. "We take enough to keep body and soul together, no more. And we pray. Will you not stay for the evening prayers?"

"I must go, Alonso."

"We will pray for you and the soldiers, and our friends, Andrés. Farewell, brother."

"Farewell, Alonso."

Riding beside him as they left the clearing, Santiago said in a low voice, "That one is a madman, is he not, patron?"

"A madman, but a gentle one."

"And more holy in his nature than Padre Bernardo, I believe."

He sighed and said, "Where the padre is too gross, this one is only bones and spirit. He pursues a felicity that is past and gone."

"The spirit is very strong, however, patron."

Pursuing his own thought, he said, "It may be, Santiago, that it is a mistake to look back to some better time, or ahead to a better one. For thus the time one has passes unnoticed in dissatisfactions."

Once Esteban had given them all just that same advice, in his own terms.

Chapter Six

The last great entrada of the Spanish Empire in the New World assembled in Campostela, capital of New Galicia. It was a larger force than that with which Hernán Cortés had first entered Tenochtitlán: two hundred and thirty horsemen and sixty-two foot soldiers, including nineteen crossbowmen and twenty-seven arquebusiers. The Spaniards, with their pennons unfurled and a thousand Indian allies swarming behind them, marched in companies past the viceroy and their general, Francisco Vásquez de Coronado. They were young men for the most part, new arrivals from Cuba, Santo Domingo, and Spain, eager for glory and gold. Many of them had been hangers-on in the viceregal household, and it was rumored that Don Antonio de Mendoza was doubly pleased to see them headed northward. A few veterans accompanied the army but more attended the review in the viceroy's company, men in their forties and fifties, gray in their beards, heavy bellied in their fine slashed silks, and memory in their eyes. Hernán Cortés, their old commander, was not among them. He was en route to Spain to plead his many causes and grievances, never to return to the New World alive.

After the army had knelt and prayed for the success of the expedition, they swore an oath of fidelity to their emperor and to their leader, resplendent in his white plume and gilded armor. They then set out following him, the companies of horsemen and foot, the throngs of indigenes, and the campfollowers, porters, and drovers, the baggage train and the herds of cattle, sheep, and swine.

Second in command was the army-master, García López de Cárdenas. The companies of cavalry were each led by a captain: Diego Guttiérez, Diego López, Rodrigo Maldonado, Tristán de Arellano, Diego de Guevara. In command of the artillery was the youngest of the Alvarado brothers, Hernando; of the infantry, Pablo de Melgoza. The chaplains were Fray Antonio de Victoria, Fray Juan de Padilla, Fray Juan de la Cruz, Fray Daniel, and the guide and inspiration of the expedition, the Father Provincial, Fray Marcos de Niza.

The viceroy rode with the army two days' march toward Culiacán, where he announced his regret that he could travel no farther on the great quest. His instructions to his general as to the treatment of the Indians to be encountered were specific. They were not to be molested, nor were their food or belongings to be taken without compensation, and for this purpose cargos of glass beads, glass plates, knives, and gewgaws were carried. Nor were native bearers to be impressed. For the first time in the New World Spaniards carried their own burdens.

As a warden of these instructions, although without specific powers or rank, listed upon the army's rolls as chronicler, was Andrés Dorantes; unofficially a linguist, but inferior in this role to the notary's translators, as he was inferior as a guide to Fray Marcos, and even inferior as protector of the Indians to the friars. He was well aware that he was viewed as the viceroy's spy, uneasy with the captains as they were uneasy with him, although he was treated with cool correctness by the general.

The homesick mestizo, José, had been sent back to Mezaculapan, but Santiago accompanied his patron, as did the Negro, Mariano, whom Dorantes had purchased from a planter in Campostela in what he had known was the foolish hope that Estebánico could be replaced. Also with the army were Natsá and a dozen Pímas, some of whom had escorted Fray Marcos to Hawíkuh.

He kept his daily journal and sent formal reports along with Coronado's frequent letters to the viceroy. The morale of the army remained good. There was some straggling, and the Indian allies began to drift away. It seemed to him, however, that the general and his captains enforced good discipline in the army's dealings with the Indians.

The army rested at Chichilticalli, at the edge of the uninhabited vastness called the Despoblado. For the first time there was clear evidence of the Father Provincial's tendency to exaggeration. His narrative had described this tumbledown roofless structure of red mud as a grand ruin from a lost civilization.

One night his old friend Melchor Díaz and his scouting party rode into camp, and Dorantes had a few moments with the sunburnt little soldier, who squatted on his heels just inside the tent.

"My friend, I am ordered to secrecy," he said in his rapid voice. "But I tell you that ahead there is nothing, for fifty leagues, nothing! The general sends us off so that the army will not hear of it. I go to meet Hernando de Alarcón at the River of Firebrands, to bring back supplies. Food! According to the Father Provincial it is no more than five days. We will see! But I believe you were correct, Andrés, there are no golden cities awaiting us. And for fifty leagues not even mud villages!"

In the morning Díaz' fast-moving little force was gone to meet the viceroy's supply ships, but it was clear to the army that his report to the general had not been encouraging. They started on, into the Despoblado. Soon they were reduced to half-rations. Tempers began to fray. One night there was a fierce little encounter with Cibolan warriors, and the action cheered the soldiers as evidence that habitations must lie ahead in this high wilderness. Signal fires now burned along their route, columns of smoke marking their progress on either side by day. The tired and hungry army marched on more eagerly.

His own spirits had lifted for different reasons. These great distances, the cool clear air, the pine forests, the far off mountains with their snowy flags that never seemed to grow any larger, were an old tonic to him. He had friends now: Fray Daniel; the worried, incompetent little physician; a couple of the captains. The Negro Mariano had proven himself an inveterate sulker, but Santiago, although silent and awed by his surroundings, was a valued companion.

The army viewed Hawíkuh from the hill which Fray Marcos had described as a mountain. Dorantes stood with Fray Daniel, Pablo de Melgoza, three soldiers, and Santiago, gazing at the collection of mud structures that appeared to have crumpled together for support. These were the "tall houses" at last, a mud village arranged vertically, no doubt for protection against enemies, rather than horizontally; hardly a city. Soldiers were pointing.

"The city of gold!" one said.

"See how the sun on the mud walls appears golden in color," Melgoza said. "It is clear that our good Franciscan viewed this grand city in this same light."

Dorantes folded his arms on his chest and felt his body shaking as he tried to stifle his laughter. Tears burned on his cheeks.

"Come!" Melgoza said. "It seems we have lingered in our admiration long enough. Now we must proceed to plunder this new Cuzco."

The army had started forward again, Coronado at the head in his white plume and gilded armor. As the Spaniards plodded across the plain toward the tall houses, indigenes poured out of the town, three or four hundred warriors forming themselves into ranks, armed with bows and arrows and war clubs, and leather shields. Their faces were striped with ocher paint. Coronado halted the army, and, with the notary and the army-master, rode forward to greet the men of Hawíkuh.

One of the warriors danced backwards pouring a line of reddish powder between the advancing Spaniards and the ranks of warriors. His fur skirt bobbed like a rabbit's tail.

"What is this, patron?" Santiago whispered.

"I believe that no one is to advance beyond that line or they will fight." He stared at the ocher-painted men who had murdered Estebánico and must be the same ones who had attacked the army two weeks ago. The Hawíkuh were more warlike than any of the western indigenes they had met on the great journey. Did that signify, with their stacked houses, a more civilized state?

The weary cavalrymen rested on their horses, hunched over pommels, infantry squatting or leaning on their weapons, while the notary made his speech, translated sentence by sentence. The Spaniards had not come to harm the people of Cibola, but to protect them from their enemies, in the name of the emperor who lived beyond the eastern sea. Fray Juan de Padilla also came forward, to harangue the Hawíkuh on the True Faith and its blessings.

When Cárdenas, on his heavy-footed sorrel, rode across the red line, however, there was a chorus of shouts from the indigenes, and they advanced in clumps of three and four, loosing arrows. The army-master spurred around and into retreat—he, Coronado, Fray Juan, the notary, and the linguist galloping back to the ranks of the Spaniards.

The Cibolans continued to advance, crouching and dancing, and letting fly their arrows in clouds. Dorantes felt again those old emotions of Otumba and the Reconquest, but frayed and worn as old battle flags. Santiago had unstrapped the light cavalry crossbow from his saddle. The brown-skinned, fur-clouted warriors pressed closer when the Spaniards did not counterattack. The arrows did little damage, deflected by shields, but the soldiers grumbled as they held their ground. Coronado was surrounded by his captains and the chaplains. Dorantes was summoned.

Coronado and Cárdenas sat their horses side by side, the army-master's face flushed dark within the enclosure of his helmet. "I believe we must repulse these warriors before they do us harm," Coronado said, in his stately way.

"They do us harm already!" Cárdenas shouted.

"We must attack!" said Fray Juan, who had been a soldier before becoming a friar.

"What say you, Fray Marcos?" Coronado said calmly. Arrows flicked past. Horses reared under the control of their riders.

"Yes, yes, attack!" the Father Provincial said. "You have done all you can, Don Francisco!" Coronado glanced at Fray Daniel, controlling his horse with difficulty, then at Dorantes.

"We must defend ourselves, Don Francisco," he said.

Coronado nodded to Cárdenas. The army-master jerked a clenched fist at Tristán de Arellano, who spurred off with a gauntlet raised above his head. Horsemen wheeled out of the Spanish ranks, individual riders with the long, gleaming spikes of their lances at a quickening walk, joining together and leaning forward at the same angle beneath the curved steel shine of their helmets, breaking into a trot with lances first leveled, then all dipping at the same instant, no longer individual horsemen but a troop of cavalry on the charge. The warriors of Hawíkuh scattered before them, fleeing back to their tall houses, leaving half a dozen bloody bundles crumpled on the ground.

The army was also advancing, each man with his individual imperatives of honor or greed, of lust or advancement, of imperial or Catholic zeal, but all fused into the master imperative of the army in its surge forward, so that Dorantes had the breathless picture of the general, the army-master, and the captains not so much leading the troops as propelled by them. And it was at that moment that he had to accept the realization that this conquest was as implacably bound for tragedy as any other.

Still there was something in him that was pleased to see the awed expression on Santíago's face, who had played at this all-exciting game only in the provincial exercises at Mezaculapan—holding the crossbow before him with white-knuckled hands as he watched the splendor of Spanish arms advancing, and Spanish banners flying as though in the wind this very force of arms had generated, forging ahead in that metallic silence that had affrighted the Aztecs. He was pleased also to see the sulky upper lip of the Negro wrinkled up over white teeth in amazement or anxiety, and Fray Daniel's expression of proper clerical sadness mixed with excitement. And he regarded in his own self that familiar exaltation at the hecatombs of enemies falling before Castilian swords.

The army poured in among the blind lower stories of the town, where the ladders had been jerked up, shields overhead as the Hawíkuh warriors swarmed on the high terraces, screeching taunts as they showered down stones and arrows. Then unbelievingly the Spaniards were in retreat, and out of their ranks came four soldiers stumbling under the weight of their general, white plume of his helmet knocked askew, blood on his white face. He had been felled, Dorantes learned, by heavy stones flung down from the balconies, and saved by the army-master and Alvarado, who had shielded him from the continuing bombardment and seen him borne away from the fight.

They were gathered by lamplight in the general's tent, Coronado with his bandaged forehead lying on his cot in a white, open-necked shirt, slim torso raised on pillows. The physician squatted beside him, a young man with squinting eyes and a fringe of beard. The light made brutish shadows in the eyes and mouths of the captains, grouped around the cot in their corselets. Cárdenas gazed down at the general with his hands on his hips, his florid face scowling. Behind the captains were Fray Juan, the Father Provincial, the notary, and Dorantes.

"We must smoke them out!" the army-master said in his harsh voice. "Smoke them off those terraces and out where the cavaliers can get at them."

"Tomorrow we cut wood, eh?" Arellano said.

"We were to have come peaceably to these new lands, friends," Coronado said.

"Their doing, sire, not ours!"

"I think we must make still another effort—"

"Surely it is to our disadvantage if it is known these barbarians have defeated us here," Alvarado interrupted. "If we crush this cursed village, the others will fall to us like ripe fruit."

"The other golden cities, yes, yes," Fray Marcos de Niza said, and the captains' gaze turned to the dark, sardonic face of the Father Provincial, who had wrapped himself in his cloak.

"The soldiers are hungry, sire," Cárdenas said. "Surely there are stores of corn here, if not gold."

"This, then," Coronado said. A lick of fair hair had fallen over his bandage, which he brushed back with a boyish gesture. "At first light men will begin foraging for dry wood, but we will also hold parley with these indigenes. Surely means can be found of convincing them of our intentions. See to the wood-cutting, army-master. Notary, you and I and your linguists must contrive more persuasive arguments. Fray Juan, what say you?"

"I hold with Don García, sire—that arguments prove more persuasive with a whiff of smoke."

Dorantes watched the general glance from face to face, counting the agreement of his captains. The blue eyes came to rest on his face. "Perhaps you know these northern peoples better than anyone else, Don Andrés. Had you heard that these of the tall houses were so aggressive in war?"

Now all eyes turned to him, most neutral, some unfriendly, a few friendly. He said, "I would venture this guess, Don Francisco. That before they killed him the Moor, Esteban, made threats that he would be avenged by white men from the south. So these of Hawíkuh do not believe we come in peace, but to punish them. This would explain their attack of two weeks ago, and the signal fires by which they have marked our progress toward them."

There was silence. Coronado raised himself to lean on one elbow. "What say you to that Fray Marcos?"

The Father Provincial nodded curtly. "Certainly Don Andrés would know his own slave."

"You knew him also, Fray Marcos," he said, and the other glanced at him briefly. These were unfriendly eyes; the Father Provincial had taken no notice of him until this time.

"I knew him as a disobedient and untruthful wretch," Fray Marcos said, hitching his cloak more tightly around his body. "But yes, I believe he would have blustered in just that way."

"What is your counsel, Don Andrés?" Coronado asked.

"That I be allowed to try to persuade them that we come in peace, sire. I believe they may know of me and my companions, who passed through these lands not far to the south and were known as men of peace."

"That is the proper course, then," Coronado said with a decisive nod.

"But we will collect dry wood all the same," García López de Cárdenas said.

The next morning, however, it was discovered that the inhabitants of Hawíkuh had fled their tall houses for the hills to the north, leaving behind them only a few old people, two frightened women far along in their pregnancies, and a warrior dying of his lance wound. Stores of corn had also been left, enough to feed a hungry army.

In a cellar, with a dusty sun ray slanting down from an overhead entrance, Dorantes questioned one of the old men who had been left behind. With him were Santiago, standing beside the ladder, Mariano resting on one knee beside him, and Fray Daniel still wearing a breast-plate over his black robe, tonsured head bowed. The old man squatted against a stack of fat, cotton sacks. His face was slashed with long wrinkles like scars, in which stains of ocher paint still clung.

"Why did they kill him?"

The Hawíkuh's eyes slanted toward Mariano. "They did not believe the black man, lord. He said white men followed behind him, and these were sent by a very great lord. These ones knew all the things of the sky, and came to instruct us in these things. It was not believed that white men would send a black man before them. Also the black man possessed a red gourd of our enemies, which he rattled loudly, and demanded turquoises and women. The people did not wish to give him turquoises and women, and it was thought he was sent by our enemies to spy. So it was decided to kill him, lord."

The old man's truthfulness reminded him of the Huastéco chieftains of Panuco, who had answered truthfully when Gonzalo de Sandoval demanded to know if they had killed Spaniards. "You saw this, old man?" he asked.

The other nodded vigorously. "He was kept in a house outside the gate while this was decided. We all watched them shoot him with arrows. It was then that the sorcerors warned us that many white men would come to destroy Hawíkuh."

He asked if anything of the black man remained. The old man rose painfully, but mounted the ladder quick as a monkey. As they waited they could hear outside the shouts of the soldiers searching the houses, and once a raucous snatch of song:

> *"Oh, Father Prevaricator,*
> *Tell us of the gold of Cibola!"*

"They call him Father Prevaricator to his face," Fray Daniel said unhappily. He was a clean-shaven young Franciscan with a sallow complexion, considerably pocked, who looked too frail to have walked these hundreds of leagues.

"Soldiers make threats to him," Santiago said. "They say they will cut him with their swords."

"Yes, cut him with swords!" the Negro said, his face convulsing in his sneering guffaw.

The Indian reappeared descending the ladder, carrying a bundle. He squatted on the hardpacked earth floor to open this. Wrapped in filthy green velvet were two bones, glowing white in the beam of sun, a jointed section of backbone, and a long bone knobbed at either end.

His gorge lurched, and somewhere between nausea and tears he gazed upon the remains of Esteban Dorantes.

They buried the bones outside the town gate, where Estebánico had been killed with arrows, Santiago scratching the shallow hole in the hard ground, Mariano useless as always, Fray Daniel offering prayers. Kneeling, Dorantes gestured angrily for the Negro to kneel also, as Santiago shoveled the loose earth to cover the green bundle.

As he watched Mariano's face twitch in and out of its sneer, his arm ached to beat this parody of a beloved friend, whose color, posturings, and extravagances had tricked him into thinking Estebánico could be replaced.

He said, "There is a legend in this place that if a bad black man is ground up in a meatgrinder and the forcemeat scattered upon the grave of a good black man, that good black man will rise up as fresh and new as he ever was."

It pleased him to see Mariano's eyes widen and whiten before he began to pout again.

Quartered in Hawíkuh, the army explored the other cities of Cibola, which offered no resistance but no wealth of precious metals and jewels either, except for a few turquoises. There proved to be only five of these, stacked mud villages much like Hawíkuh: Kechipáuan, Kwákima, Halóna, Mátsaki, and Kiákima. Detachments were sent on wider sweeps, Pedro de Tovar to the north to a land called Hopi, Cárdenas to the northwest to explore rumors of a vast and impassable canyon, Alvarado to the east. In his reports to the viceroy, Dorantes found little of which to complain of the army's dealings with the Cibolans.

One morning he was summoned to the general's quarters, on the second story of one of the deserted houses, just off a broad terrace. Coronado requested a favor of him.

The general, recovered from his wounds and bruises, sat at his many-drawered field desk in a white cotton shirt and breeches. "You have your chronicles to send to Don Antonio, I presume, Don Andrés?"

"I have, sire."

"I have letters also," Coronado said, nodding in his way that now seemed deliberate and careful rather than pompous. "Also cargos of the things of these places—pots and baskets, some of their painted dolls, the hides of the great hairy cows of the eastern plains, painted rattles, turquoises. One could wish these cargos would give Don Antonio more pleasure," he said, almost with humor. "I am also determined to send back the Father Provincial, who will also give little pleasure."

"One would give much to observe that reception," he said, and Coronado grinned swiftly and boyishly.

"I ask that you accompany this column as far as Chichilticalli, Don Andrés, and then that you travel west in search of Melchor Díaz. It has been two months since he left for the River of Firebrands. Winter is upon us, and we are in need of the supplies he is to bring us. Food, yes, and arms—but most of all warm clothing. I believe your knowledge of tongues will be helpful in finding him. Still, if you feel your duties require your continued presence with the army, I will respect that."

"I will go, sire," he said to this young man ten years his junior, whom, almost against his will, he had come to respect and trust.

And so it was that, with a detachment of soldiers under the command of a tough veteran named Juan Gallegos, Natsá and the Pímas, the Father Provincial, Mariano, and Santiago, he recrossed the Despoblado to Chichilticalli, where he saw a second black slave off in the company of the Father Prevaricator. He was pleased to be rid of both of them, for Fray Marcos in his bitterness was as poor company as Mariano.

With Santiago and the Pímas he set out west, following the traces they could find of the route of Melchor Díaz.

Chapter Seven

Far ahead on a barren ridge Dorantes glimpsed a glint of sunlight on a helmet, and two horsemen seemed to rise out of the earth, one helmeted, one bareheaded. More Spaniards appeared, a string of pack animals, and a crowd of brown figures bearing something upon their shoulders. He waited with Santiago, Natsá, and the eight Pímas while the others dropped into a draw, then showed themselves again, closer, the blurred gleam of the helmet as the two leaders came into sight, heads of their horses tossing in their ascent, the other horsemen behind, the pack string, and the half-naked bearers of their burden—a litter, he made out now. A little breeze came up to cool his face as he watched the approach, dust trailing off to the west. The helmeted leader raised a hand in greeting.

On the litter was Melchor Díaz. He stank of urine and rotting flesh. His body looked no larger than that of a child beneath a filthy cloth, eyes closed, bearded, balding head turning ceaselessly from side to side beneath a palm-leaf shade fixed to the rail of the litter. The Opatá squatted with the soldiers of Díaz' troop on one side of the litter, the Pímas in their buckskin shirts on the other. Santiago's nostrils were straining and narrowing at the stench. The two lieutenants were Hernando de Orduña and Pedro de Castro, bearded faces caked with dust. Orduña removed his helmet and held it in the crook of his arm as he told of the accident.

They had failed to encounter the ships of Alarcón on the River of Firebrands, although they had marched up and down that deep-sided river for weeks. Their route returning from their failure they called the Camino del Diablo, for it led around beds of burning lava, where cinders were boiling and the ground resounded like kettledrums under the hoofs of the horses. In the desert beyond they encountered giant

Indians, the Yumans, who were friendly. In their village Díaz' grey-hound bitch attacked an Indian boy for no reason, the boy screaming, the bitch snarling, women shrieking, the men hurling stones. The captain spurred his horse after the dog and the boy, and, failing to distract the bitch, hurled his lance. The lance rebounded, end for end, and, unable to stop, Díaz rode over it. The point pierced his groin and ruptured his bladder. He was not even unhorsed, riding back to join the other Spaniards. Castro dismounted in time to catch him as he fainted.

"There is water and shade not far back," Dorantes said. "We will go there." He cleared his throat, watching Melchor's head switching from side to side in his agony. "He is suffering."

"He has suffered much," Orduña said in his deep voice. "Sometimes he is awake."

"How long has it been?"

"Fifteen days. If he can live until San Gerónimo—"

At San Gerónimo there was a small garrison. The alcalde there was Diego de Alcaráz, who had been Guzmán's lieutenant in New Galicia.

They returned half a league to the spring and pond beneath a circle of trees, with a moving lace of shadows. He squatted beside Melchor, sponging his face with cool water. His friend's head continued its twisting motion. Sometimes his eyelids wrinkled as though he tried to open them.

He peeled the filthy cloth from the naked, shrunken body, mat of black hair between the paps, another around the penis. He groaned to see the wound, a swollen red mouth from which yellow liquid dripped.

He was panting as though he had been running as he touched flesh so hot it seemed to sear his fingertips; one hand on one side of the wound, one on the other. He closed his eyes. "Father in heaven—" He concentrated upon his prayers until black spots swam before his eyes. He prayed to the Virgin of Guadalupe for Melchor Díaz, a good man deserving of her intercession. But no faith would come. Had he ever cured anyone who had not had the faith to cure himself? The curing of Martín Cortés had been mere coincidence. On the other hand he had prayed then that he be granted the power one last time. He prayed until his head ached.

When he opened his eyes Melchor's eyes were also open, and Melchor's scabbed lips twisted into a grin. "Andrés, is it *you*?"

He laid a hand on the hot forehead, nodding. "Your fever is not so bad as it was, Melchor."

"Then it must be near sundown. At sundown the heat is less. Ah, Andrés, what a greenhorn trick it was! I have given myself a second asshole when one was sufficient!" He began to laugh, wiping a hand over his mouth as though to stifle the laughter, and made a sound half a sob and half a snort. "One fears he must piss like a woman for the rest of his life!"

The soldiers had butchered one of the sheep they had driven along with them, and its carcass turned on a spit over the fire. Blackened pots had been set on rocks around the fire, and one of the Opatá was stirring with a stick. The smell of cooking meat mingled with Melchor's stink.

"It was all your fault, my friend," Melchor said.

"Tell me what you mean."

"One knows you are tender toward the indigenes of the New Lands, and have some power over Don Antonio. Through his sister, it is rumored. And so these orders have been issued against the mistreatment of the indigenes. And so I spurred too fast to the aid of a filthy child my good bitch had attacked." Melchor laughed silently for a long time, eyes closed. Then he slept again, or feigned it, head lolling from side to side.

"This one is very bad, patron?" Santiago whispered, coming to squat beside him.

"Very bad," he said.

"I remember this captain when you played at swords with him at Mezaculapan. He pretended to be wounded then. It was very droll."

"The wound must not be allowed to heal," Castro said, coming up. "If it heals he cannot piss, and he begins to swell. And the pain—" He threw a greasy hand upward. "We have had to keep it open with a knife!"

"There are poultices I know—" Santiago ventured.

"I say it must not be allowed to heal!" Castro said.

These lieutenants of Melchor's, like other soldiers, were uncertain of how to comport themselves with the mestizo he chose to treat as a subordinate rather than a servant. In their hierarchy, the mixed blood might set Santiago above the simple Indians of their contempt, but their contempt for impure blood was also profound.

"As our unfortunate captain has said," Orduña growled, "if he had a silver tube he could survive. But in these bad lands there is neither silver nor anyone to fashion it."

In the night he lay awake listening to Melchor's groans, recalling those nights listening to Álvar Núñez' ecstasies of communion with his God, whose gift had been great faith. Melchor also mumbled words, sometimes praying, and more than once he cried out in pain. The night was very long.

He prayed for Melchor. He prayed for faith and for enlightenment.

He remembered Fray Cristóbal pointing out the stars in the summer sky of Béjar, insisting that each one had its particular reason for being, God-given, and that God had placed each one in the heavens like the notes of a musical composition, so that celestial melodies were formed wherein earth, sky, and mankind combined their strains in worship of Him who had arranged all things for the greatest good. What note, then, Melchor Díaz, in his agony? What Timultzin, once baptized Juana, with her destroyed face, whom he knew now he would never see again? What the son who was lost? And María de la Torre, and Caspar, and the new child? What note now Andrés Dorantes?

This morning Melchor did not waken, but slowly twisted his head, breath rustling between caked lips. Natsá came to join him beside the dying man, eagle feather in his headband and decorated shirt, serene old-young face gazing down at the wound.

"Will he live, brother?"

He closed his eyes and sought for faith, like some small vital object mislaid in darkness. He could only think of the lack of a silver tube. He found himself shaking his head.

"Once you healed, brother," Natsá said gently. "You and the other brother of the Children of the Sun."

"It seems that the power is gone." He tried to explain in Primahaitu that the healing had been a great gift, but that such gifts might be for only the little while of their necessity.

The young chief nodded. "I have seen such a thing in the healers of my people. When it comes it is a great gift, but when it is gone there is relief, as from great weight."

He nodded also. "Yes, it is true."

He rode beside the pallet borne on the shoulders of the Opatá as they moved through desert country, sliding down the banks of dry washes and toiling up the other side, with frequent halts to rest. Ranged against the eastern horizon were mountains the color of chocolatl, and, at the southern end of the range, was the Valley of Suya and San Gerónimo.

That evening he prayed over the wound again. The stink was unsupportable. Melchor lay panting in his cocoon of pain, head jerking, eyes closed. "Sing!" he commanded.

Dorantes began an old hymn. Orduña and Castro joined in, and the other soldiers as well. He had never heard a more tuneless voice than Orduña's; worse than Álvar Núñez'. Santiago did not sing. He knew no hymns. In the capital the sons of the Aztecs were instructed in hymns and prayers, rituals and sacraments; not so the sons, by brown women, of the conquerors.

Melchor died two days from San Gerónimo. One moment he was breathing, head still turning weakly from side to side. The next the motion had stopped, his breathing ceased. The Opatá put down their burden and, holding his breath against the stench, Dorantes bent his ear to the little captain's chest. There was no heartbeat. Kneeling, he gave thanks for the end of suffering, the other Christians kneeling with him, one of the soldiers with a handkerchief to his nose.

They carried the body on to San Gerónimo for burial. By the time they reached the outpost the stench that he had considered unsupportable days before was much worse.

San Gerónimo consisted of a dozen adobe cubes of huts, and half again as many shacks constructed of woven mats fastened to frames of branches. Cultivated fields slanted toward a rocky buttress of the dark mountains. A twist of trail led between the huts. At the other end of town was a crowd of Indians, dusty-legged men in breechclouts, women in long soiled skirts, babies on their hips. Dust was rising, and there was a sound of snarling dogs. A man shouted. Leading the company of horsemen and Indians, the Opatá still with their stinking burden, Dorantes rode on between the huts. Over the heads of the crowd he could see into a corral, where two greyhounds were harrying two Indians. Naked and smeared with blood, these stood back to back, the dogs circling them, heads down, one snarling, one silent. A man kicked out. Instantly a dog had caught his leg, jerking him staggering until he fell. Both dogs swarmed over him, and the other Indian ran kicking after the struggling, snarling group. Soldiers slouched at intervals, watching the action, armed with arquebuses and lances. Alcaráz, the alcalde, was seated with an Indian woman on either side of him, one very pregnant. He was grinning as he viewed the spectacle.

The two Indians recovered themselves to stand back to back again, the dogs circling as before, dust rising and blowing east. Dorantes snapped his fingers and gestured for Santiago's crossbow. The mestizo's eyes flashed white as he passed it over. Dorantes cranked the windlass until the bow curved taut, laid in the bolt Santiago handed him, aimed, and released the nut.

The dog screamed, tumbling end over end in a whirl of dust. The other trotted after him, stopping and turning back toward the bloodied Indians. Dorantes cranked the windlass again, the bow jammed against the pommel. He accepted the bolt Santiago held out to him. Alcaráz had risen from his chair to gape at them.

Holding the crossbow at the ready he urged his horse through the crowd of Indians, who gave way before him. The gate was forced open against a press of bodies. One of the ragged soldiers had his arquebus half-aimed. The dying dog lay in a puddle of blood, moving his head weakly. The other slunk away as Dorantes rode into the corral, followed by Santiago, Orduña, and Castro.

He rode straight across to where Alcaráz stood, a head taller than his dark-faced, tattooed women, hand on the hilt of his dagger. "So!" the alcalde cried. "What is this, please?"

"I demand to know what is *this* illegality!"

"These swine are rebels! Rebels! And who are you, please, to interfere here?"

"My name is Dorantes, and I have instructions from the viceroy which you are violating. We have met before, lieutenant."

Alcaráz glared past him. "Pedro de Castro! Where is Melchor?"

"Dead, Diego!"

"And who is this interferer, please, before I have him shot down like my good Peleas he has destroyed?"

"He has come from the army searching for Melchor, Diego. He claims he is the viceroy's chronicler."

"Whose order it is, Señor Alcalde," Dorantes said, "that these Indians, our allies, are not to be molested."

"I tell you these two are rebels! Listen: to the southeast all is in rebellion. So many soldiers have gone with the army to Cibola! Now rebellion also infects those of this region. These swine preach against the emperor and the Holy Church. They are possessed by Satan! I will have information from them!"

"You were having sport of them, Señor Alcalde. I remind you of the fate of your master, Beltrán Nuño de Guzmán. Perhaps you served your governor too long and too well."

Alcaráz spat, wiped a hand over his lips, and squinted up at him speculatively. "Come, we will discuss this matter and others over a cup of wine, Señor Chronicler," he said in a mollified tone. He signaled to the arquebusier to lower his weapon, and Dorantes handed the crossbow back to Santiago. The two bloody Indians had disappeared. From the log barriers of the corral dark faces watched as the alcalde strode beside Dorantes' horse, the two Indian women hastening after him.

Outside the corral Alcaráz drew a breath with a grimace of distaste. "By the odor I understand that Melchor did not die recently, poor fellow."

In the largest of the huts were several chairs made of deerskin and wooden slats and a large carved chair in which the alcalde seated himself. The two Opatá women knelt on either side of him like attendant angels. Their lips and chins were intricately tattooed. Plates of cakes and small, dark green, very sweet fruit were passed, and there

THE CHILDREN OF THE SUN

was red wine in clay cups. Lounging in his chair, Alcaráz listened to Castro's story of the failure of Melchor Díaz' mission.

"Such is a soldier's life," he commented, and turned his attention to Dorantes. "So, you are the castaway one encountered long ago. And now a chronicler with Don Francisco! Tell me of the gold of Cibola!"

He said no gold had been found.

Nodding, Alcaráz said, "Yes, that is the rumor we have heard." He seemed unable to look at Dorantes without squinting. "And you are the protector of the indigenes on the viceroy's order. These of the Valley of Suya are not worthy of your protection. They are great sodomites. They drink a wine made from the fruit of the thistle that makes them stupid. They tattoo their women." He flipped a languid hand toward one of his concubines. Castro laughed obsequiously.

Alcaráz grinned and leaned forward. "Tell me, Señor Chronicler, what are your powers if no attention is paid to your efforts to protect these sodomites? Have you the authority to arrest good soldiers and send them back to New Spain in chains? As my governor was sent back to mother Spain?" He leaned back, grinning and flexing his shoulders cockily for the benefit of Melchor's lieutenants.

"I have no such authority, Señor Alcalde," Dorantes said. "My part will come later, when a Judge of Investigation is appointed to enquire into this entrada to the New Lands. Then I will be summoned for my testimony as to whether the viceroy's orders as to the treatment of the indigenes have been properly obeyed."

There was a silence of some intensity. One of the women passed among them, refilling their cups. Alcaráz' face had turned sour.

"I should think, señor, that a man with such a task might not live to perform it."

He shrugged. "Tell us of this rebellion of which you have spoken."

"Yes, what of this, Señor Alcalde?" Orduña said.

Alcaráz' crop-bearded face hardened. He held his cup out to the pregnant woman, who refilled it from the wine jar. "Listen!" he said. "There are reports of rebellion as far south as Zacatecas!"

"What peoples?" Dorantes asked.

"Cascané mostly, but Zacatécos also. Perhaps the Tonalá." The alcalde hesitated dramatically. "And perhaps the Opatá as well! This might have been determined, had there not been interference. Listen! Reports come to me that these tribes rebel, they occupy their peñoles. From these heights they raid the encomiendas. They kill Spaniards, they kill Negroes, they kill the holy fathers! They are worshipers of Satan! They claim they have a god more powerful than the Holy Trinity. They are very fierce!" He raised both hands dramatically. "They poison their arrows!"

Castro whistled.

"And some of these idolators had been baptized!" Alcaráz added.

"Are there reports of a great idol?" Dorantes asked, and was relieved when the alcalde said he had not heard of such a thing.

"And when do you depart with this unhappy news for Don Francisco?" Alcaráz enquired.

"Tomorrow," he said. "These others will rest here for some days, for they have traveled very far." He rose. "But now we must bury Melchor Díaz."

After the burial, when they were alone, he told Santiago that he would send Natsá back to Corazones with the letter to the viceroy he must now write, telling of Melchor Díaz' failure to meet Alarcón's supply ships and the captain's death; also of Alcaráz' reports of insurrection. In Corazones a messenger could be found to take the letter on to the capital. The Pímas were now anxious to return to their homes.

"Would you like also to return?" he asked. "I do not wish you to accompany me back to Hawíkuh against your will. You are a free man."

"I will come with you, patron," Santiago said. He smiled his rare smile, which illuminated his face. "No, I am not a free person, for I have promised the patrona that I will bring Don Andrés safely home."

The mestizo danced mistily in his eyes. Piercingly he missed his wife, and his son's sunny laugh and warm, heavy little body. And the new child nine months old! Time clamped him in a cold grip. He was forty-one, gray strands in his beard. In damp weather his knees ached, and after a day's ride his legs hurt so that he could hardly walk. Now there were more than fifty leagues to ride to rejoin the army, still more if Coronado had moved on from Hawíkuh. He longed for home: two hundred leagues to Culiacán, two hundred more to the capital, and then those last few leagues to Mezaculapan.

"I am very pleased that you will accompany me back to Cibola and bring me safely home, Santiago," he said.

Chapter Eight

After Chichilticalli the wilderness of red earth and pine forests rose steadily, league after league, snow mountains floating on the horizons like islands. Sometimes they saw herds of sheep with massive curved horns, flocks that scattered before them, to disappear with one old buck left to observe their progress from a rock crag: he and Santiago with their pack animals.

In this high country the cold was intense. During the days a thin sun warmed them, but as soon as it had disappeared in the afternoon, their breath and that of the animals began to smoke, and at night they huddled close to their fire, wrapped in their blankets.

"There are many stars in these lands," Santiago said one night.

"I believe there are always the same number of stars, but one can see them more easily in this cold air."

Santiago silently absorbed that. Later he said, "And what are the stars made of, patron?"

"Some say they are the souls of the saved, shining in goodness in heaven. Others that they are little atomies catching the light of the moon like mirror glass. But there was a good padre in the place where I was born who said they were the will of God made manifest for all to see at night. And I know it was thought in ancient time that His will could be discerned by counting and measuring the movements of the stars."

In a low voice the mestizo said, "That is very difficult, Don Andrés."

"You will find as you grow older that the will of God becomes more important to your reflections than you feel now."

"Do you feel that now in your life?"

"I feel that now. When I was your age I thought only of staying alive through many battles and I did not think of such things."

"I do not think much of such things," Santiago said. "Only on nights like this one, of the bright stars."

The next day there was no sun, only sodden gray clouds. Snowflakes drifted down to settle softly on his skin with no sensation of cold, for the temperature had risen when the snow began to fall.

His spirits had curiously also risen with the snow, and he realized it was because four years ago he had encountered snow in this same half-magical land, snow that did not accumulate on the ground but floated in drifting veils of varying densities, to disappear when it touched the ground. He began walking more and more, leading his horse. His legs no longer ached, and he recovered that effortless, almost floating stride that had carried him across the continent. Although he had grieved for Melchor Díaz, as Natsá had said the relief at no longer having to consider himself endowed with healing power was immense. New doors stood open, as though now in these same realms he was intended for greater service than alleviating bellyaches or lancing boils. With physical well-being came hopefulness: the viceroy's insistence on a peaceful conquest, Coronado's steadfastness to Don Antonio's instructions, his own part. He and Álvar Nuñez had often assured each other of the great good that Spain and the church could bring to these lands. If the people had been exalted by Álvar's crude sermons, surely they could be brought to the True Faith by ordained preachers. And these impoverished fields had much to gain from Castilian knowledge of agriculture and animal husbandry. But still beneath his optimism a deep dread slept.

Near Hawíkuh they were joined by two stragglers, one limping, who reported that the army had marched east a fortnight ago, and that the indigenes had returned from the hills as soon as the Spaniards left. It was during one of the windless, curiously warm snowstorms that he glimpsed again the first of the cities of Cibola, passing by at a distance for he had no wish to see again the place where Esteban had died.

Beyond Hawíkuh snow continued to obscure and soften the landscape. On foot, leading his horse, he followed Santiago and the two stragglers, Luis and Manuel. So often these vistas seemed familiar, as clouds parted to reveal a rocky height or grove of evergreens; or, from a rim, he gazed down upon a river valley, where a script of leafless trees traced the watercourses. The villages were different from those in the other lands he had traversed—all of the houses of two, three, and four stories, with their ladders—but indigenes they encountered made the sign of the cross to signify peace. It was encouraging to think that sign had been adopted from the army, but might it have been passed along from the years-past journey of the Children of the Sun?

They rested for a day at a place called Tusayan, a town deserted except for a small garrison of Spaniards. At supper nine men lounged and squatted around a fire in a smoky room, eating greasy mutton with their fingers and sipping a thick, sweet, corn drink: Dorantes, Santiago, Luis, Manuel, and the five of the garrison. The corporal spoke glowingly of the girls of these villages—as Dorantes remembered the talk of the pretty girls of the Valley of Anahuac.

"They cover their parts with cloths like table napkins," the corporal said. "Tassels at the corners that they tie over their hips." He kissed his fingertips. "So quick to unfasten! And they wear their hair long and gathered over their ears—to frame their pretty faces. I tell you, señores, these virgins, with their little breasts and their pretty faces, are a great temptation to a man!"

"And how have you resisted these temptations?" Luis said.

"Not because of the preaching of the good friars so much as the general's order that anyone raping one will be shot by crossbowmen."

The corporal laughed, wiping his greasy lips on his wrist. Some of his men laughed with him, and Manuel. Dorantes remembered also those throaty laughs of sexual tension. The corporal leaned forward, showing the outside of a pressed-together thumb and forefinger.

"Like that, señores," he said. "Not a hair on them. Sometimes just a line around, like eyelashes." He blew his breath out in a dramatic sigh.

"How is it you know this if rape is prohibited?" Dorantes asked. His eyes were watering in the smoky room.

There was laughter. "No need to break the door down if you have the key!" the corporal said. "There is hunger about. These pretty things will untie their napkins for a bowlful of corn flour!"

" 'Ohi-yeh' is the word for it," another soldier said, and there was argument as to whether the word referred to the part of the anatomy or the activity that took place there.

The army was known to be encamped in the Valley of Tiguex, forty leagues further on, and they continued east under gray skies with occasional snow flurries. They passed the town of Ácoma atop its great rock, stately women carrying water jugs on their heads, climbing steps cut into the stone. Luis and Manuel called out, "Ohi-yeh!" laughing and repeating the call, although the women of Ácoma were too distant to hear, until Dorantes shouted at them to be silent, after which they sulked.

The Valley of Tiguex was bisected by a broad, frozen river. There was a deserted camp of the army on the rim, scattered charred wood-ends and the blackened stones of cookfires, shards of brown pottery, bones picked clean by animals, sharpened sticks that had been used as tentpegs, a carpeting of patties of excrement where the animals had been penned. Beyond this stood a tree of spreading, leafless branches, within which bundles were suspended.

"Holy Mother!" Luis whispered, just as Santiago called out, "*Patron!*" The three brown bodies hung with their necks cocked by the ropes that had strangled them, hands tied behind. It was like the horrors of first coming into Guzmán's New Galicia; like the ceiba tree on the road to Honduras, except that these Indians were naked and not garbed in the pathetic finery of Aztec princes. Their faces had been destroyed by birds. He stood staring at them for only a moment, with all the optimism he had felt for the peaceful conquest draining away, before he stumbled on with his horse's hoofs clopping hollowly behind him.

In the valley they passed onto the frozen riverbed, easier footing than the rocky ground, following the tracks of the army, of which the hanged Indians had been a part. Dorantes could feel the cold of the ice seeping into his boots.

The horse of Manuel, a heavy-haunched gray, broke through first— a sharp report with a duller echo, a whinney of fear and Manuel's shout. The gray settled head down, hindquarters still raised, then collapsed to roll onto the ice on his side. Luis spurred for the shore as the ice cracked in racing spider lines. Dorantes was nearest the shore and reached it quickly. All seemed safe, Manuel treading with exaggerated lightfootedness away from the gray, who kept flinging his head up, Santiago on foot also, leading his mule.

Both he and the mule vanished in an instant in a triangular patch of black water. A corner of ice reared up, then slipped down to disappear also.

Heavyfooted in his boots, he sprinted downriver to where they had passed the open water of a rapids. He saw the mule first, head breaking out of the white water, then legs stretched stiff as lances slowly revolving. At first Santiago looked like a water-battered log, buckskin coat soaked dark, caught between a jagged rock and an edge of ice.

He ran into the freezing water to pull the boy to the bank. The boots had been washed off, and the bare feet were bluish gray. The battered face was gray also, scraped flesh still oozing blood, open mouth, closed eyes, brown sodden hair. As he bent to cross the hands on the breast he examined both index fingers for the white weal of scar he knew was not there, although, like Martín, the boy must have been born under the influence of Tlaloc, the god of rain, god of tears also; to die of water.

He saw now that the rapids must run all up this side of the river, the ice thinner in consequence; he had not noticed it in his despair. As the two soldiers came up, Luis riding, Manuel limping, he dropped heavily to the ground, took the boy's cold, wet head in his lap, and bent over it, weeping.

After they had buried Santiago in a shallow grave scraped in the frozen ground, rocks heaped on top of it, they continued on for another day, the two soldiers riding, Dorantes afoot, to join the army before the town of Arenál.

While he awaited his appointment with the general, he walked along the bank with Fray Daniel, looking across the frozen river toward Arenál, the familiar high mud structures surrounded by a palisade of logs, with a gate through which men and women passed. Smoke from many fires rose from the rooftops, to mingle with the smoke from the fires of the Spanish camp across the river. A troop of horsemen was approaching from the east along the river ice. Soldiers wore long cloaks of black or white woven cotten that bellied in the icy wind, and Fray Daniel's black gown flapped as he walked with his hands tucked inside the fabric.

"He is ill again," he said, shaking his head. "It is of the lungs. He coughs. He lacks the strength to command his captains. The mood is bad. Nothing has been found, except for these fellows Hernando de Alvarado has brought back, who claim there is gold in a place called Quivíra—far to the east. Of course, I know these men are more interested in finding gold than bringing the True Faith." He freed his hands, reddened with cold, to gesture discouragedly.

"Why were the three Indians hanged?"

"They tried to steal horses. The army-master said it was necessary or we would be overwhelmed with thievery. I did not hear all the discussions."

They walked together silently. "I think the talk of gold in Quivíra has changed the mood," Fray Daniel continued. "There is—expectation, instead of anger. Do you understand me, Andrés?"

He nodded. He said, "I was sent to find Melchor Díaz, who was to have brought the warm clothing from the supply ships. But I see the soldiers have cloaks."

Fray Daniel tucked his hands inside his gown again, and they turned to walk back toward the tents of the army. The wind teared Dorantes' eyes and glazed his cheeks. "And the indigenes of Arenál have no cloaks," Fray Daniel said sadly.

In the general's great tent, Francisco Vásquez de Coronado lounged on his cot. He coughed into a handkerchief and studied the sputum. Dorantes sat in a chair beside the cot.

"So poor Captain Díaz is dead," Coronado said. "Success does not accompany us upon this entrada, Don Andrés."

"I was very sorry to see the three indigenes who were hanged, sire."

"I have written Don Antonio of the deed and the necessity for it. You must also." He coughed in a kind of damp bark and cleared his throat. "That goes without saying, Don Andrés."

"I must write also of the cloaks that were taken by force, Don Francisco."

"They were given trade goods in exchange, you understand."

"With respect, glass beads have not been a fair exchange for warm cloaks in the coldest winter for many years."

The general braced himself on one arm to take a cup from the bench beside the cot and sip from it. He reclined again. "I believe the cloaks were more of a necessity than the hanging of the thieves. These men have been terribly disappointed. They have known hunger and cold. I cannot blame my captains for taking the part of their men against indigenes more warmly dressed than they are. Nor do I believe it is a tragedy for the people of Arenál. Their women can weave more cloth for cloaks. We have no women to weave. I have written Don Antonio of this also, Don Andrés." He coughed into his handkerchief and scowled at what he saw there.

"At least there is news of precious metals to the east of here. Hernando has brought us this strange fellow—well, you will see him. There will be an assembly here later in the day. But, come, tell me what have you learned on your journey. There have been reports of trouble among the indigenes in New Galicia."

He told the general what he had learned from Diego de Alcaráz.

Tension charged the air as an interpreter questioned one of the three Indians. This one was called "the Toad," Fray Daniel whispered to Dorantes. He was a squat, heavyset fellow with bulging eyes, coarse features, and thick black hair, which he batted back from his eyes from time to time. The other two, crouched together in chains, were Cicúye chiefs—an old man, silent and watchful, whom the captains called "Cacique," for chief, and a younger man nicknamed "Bigotes" for his mustache.

Present, all standing, were the army-master, García López de Cárdenas, the captains Hernando de Alvarado, Pedro de Tovar, Tristán de Arellano; the chaplains Fray Juan, Fray Luis, and Fray Daniel; the physician, the little translator, the chronicler.

The Toad made a half-circle of his fingers around his wrist, then held up his thumb, squeezing it. Grinning around at the Spaniards, he said, "Acochis!"

The interpreter said, "He says that when he became a prisoner he possessed two bracelets of gold. These were as thick around as his thumb. They were taken from him by these of the Cicúye."

"Acochis! Acochis!" the Toad said in his guttural voice, grinning from face to face.

Fray Daniel said behind his hand, "Do you understand this tongue, Andrés?"

It was unfamiliar to him, although "acochis" clearly meant gold. Bigotes and the old chief watched the Toad expressionlessly. The physician, a chinless young Castillian named Portillo, squatted beside the general, who was clearing his throat and coughing.

Coronado raised himself on one elbow. "Ask him about the quantities of acochis in his province."

The interpreter put the question, and the Toad answered lengthily, with expansive gestures, signs, spurts of words. Pacing up and down before his audience, he encircled one wrist and then the other with his fingers, circled his neck with both hands, reached above his head as though plucking fruit, cast an arch glance at the two Cicúye, batted his hair back from his eyes, and spoke again.

After a pause the interpreter said, "He says there is much gold in Quivíra. All wear gold bracelets there. The chiefs also wear a neck bracelet of gold. The high chief sits in a chair that is covered with gold."

There was absolute silence. Alvarado leaned against one of the tent poles, rubbing his big jaw. Cárdenas was scowling, a thin, florid, stoop-shouldered soldier who appeared constructed from taut wires. The other captains and chaplains gazed at the Toad as though listening to a sermon. Dorantes watched the expressions of the two Cicúye as they watched the other Indian.

"How far is Quivíra?" Tovar said.

"Seventy leagues to Quivíra," Alvarado said. The youngest Alvarado, except for the big jaw, was a pale reflection of his conqueror brother. It was he who had discovered this prodigy on a scouting expedition to Cicúye, and he had taken prisoner the two chiefs on the basis of their prisoner's story of the gold bracelets. "Half again as far as Cicúye."

There was a groan at the distance. Cárdenas was massaging his knuckles into his black-bearded cheek, grimacing, Coronado inspecting the product of his last coughing fit.

"Acochis! Acochis!" the Toad said, as though to regain the attention of his auditors. He grinned at the Cicúye chiefs.

"What else did this ugly rascal say?" Cárdenas demanded. "He told you more than you told us, linguist!"

From the interpreter's expression, Dorantes guessed that he was relaying information that seemed questionable. "He says that Quivíra is on the bank of a river. This river is traversed by great canoes, one hundred men rowing each one. The chiefs sit behind, under an awning of gold, and thus pass back and forth across the river. In this river are fish as big as horses."

Again the silence fell, and Dorantes observed dissatisfied expressions.

"Ask him how big is Quivíra compared with these towns of Tiguex," Coronado said.

There was an exchange. The Toad made spreading gestures with his hands. Dorantes was beginning to understand some words, spoken in a hurried, guttural voice. Quivíra was bigger than all of Tiguex together.

"Ask him about silver," Tovar said, displaying his crucifix.

Again the expansive gestures and assuring grins. Much silver; more catalao than acochis. Dorantes perceived that the man was a liar, who thoroughly enjoyed his lies, the credulity of the Spaniards, and the humiliation of the Cicúye. He thought that the words "acochis" and "catalao" had been coined on the spur of the moment, and that no more of the precious metals occurred in Quivíra than in Cibola, if there were even such a place. Fray Daniel had closed one eye and was squinting at the Quivíran.

Dorantes said, "Ask him if, in Quivíra, the acochis or the catalao is the heavier substance."

The eyes of the captains turned on him disapprovingly. When the question was put the Toad stood as though frozen for the fraction of a second, hand forking hair back from his forehead. Then, arms hanging as though heavily weighted, he spoke in a rush; both were heavy, because so large. The interpreter translated, to some relieved expressions, other worried ones.

Dorantes said in Primahaitu, "In Quivíra, which is the harder substance?"

The bugged eyes regarded him with hostility. The Toad pumped his shoulders up and down and said he did not understand.

The interpreter said, "Don Andrés has asked which is the harder substance. This man does not understand the words."

"But you did?" Fray Daniel said, and the interpreter nodded. There was another silence. But Dorantes saw that the captains wished to believe. It was a kind of faith.

The general raised himself again. "Ask these others about the bracelets of acochis."

The little interpreter, who was daubing his forehead with his handkerchief, addressed himself to the old chief. The response was that there were no such bracelets. Bigotes joined in to say that this one was a great liar, and was not to be believed.

"Ask him how the Toad became their slave."

Bigotes said that the Toad and two others of Quivíra had been taken in a war. Of the others, one had died, and the other had been traded to the north.

The Toad spoke again, at length, making faces and waving his arms. He flicked a contemptuous hand at the Cicúye, and turned his back on them to stand set-jawed with arms folded on his chest.

"He says he was taken by treachery. These are treacherous men and great liars, and never to be believed." As the interpreter spoke, the Toad accompanied his words with gestures and postures, crossing his wrists on his chest, making a gesture very like the sign of the cross that signified peace, and stooping to make the plucking-at-the-ground and kissed fingers greeting the Aztecs had also employed, which the Castilians had called "eating dirt." Then he resumed his folded-arms stance.

While the Spaniards conferred among themselves, Dorantes considered his duties. The Cicúye were certainly molested, but clues to gold and silver would be pursued regardless of the orders of the viceroy, or the protests of the chaplains—though he had heard no protest from that quarter.

Arellano said loudly, "Let us warm the feet of Cacique as we ask about these bracelets of gold."

Tovar seconded it, and Alvarado nodded. Cárdenas stood in a stance exactly like that of the Toad's, arms locked on his chest. Coronado glanced from face to face with his pale eyes. Fray Daniel licked his lips.

Dorantes said, "I was present when they burned the feet of the emperor Cuauhtémoc after the fall of Tenochtitlán. They sought the gold that had been lost on the Night of Sorrows. They did not find the gold, but they lamed a noble prince, whom later Cortés hanged on the road to Honduras. It is such obscenities that Don Antonio's instructions to the general prohibit."

"Don Antonio will be more pleased to hear of the gold of Quivíra than obscenities against the Cicúye," Arellano said.

"Don Antonio is many leagues away, chronicler," Tovar said.

"Don Antonio is no further than pen and paper may reach."

"Do you threaten us then?" the army-master said. Coronado was coughing into his handkerchief.

He met Cárdenas' black furious eyes. "No, Don García. I inform you. I will write to Don Antonio of Indians hanged and cloaks taken by force. Which letter Don Francisco has already written, he tells me. And if there is torture, I will write Don Antonio of torture."

"Enough of this, friends!" Coronado said, risen to one elbow again. "There will be no foot burning here. Ask him to tell us more of Quivíra," he said to the translator. He lay back on his cot as though exhausted by his intercession, and the physician pulled the cotton coverlet over his legs.

Chapter Nine

Under a gray sky a muster of the army had been called, and the soldiers were drawn up in their companies. One of them had been accused of raping a woman of Arenál. The soldier had apparently seen this pretty woman on a rooftop and had asked an Indian, who, as it happened, was her husband, to hold his horse while he climbed the ladders. It was not until the Spaniard had come down and ridden back to camp that the husband discovered what had happened. Now he came with the village chiefs to identify the culprit and demand punishment.

Dorantes watched the army-master walking with the four Indians, Cárdenas in breastplate and helmet and a white Indian cloak, the indigenes, a head shorter, also in black or white cloaks, all flapping in the gusts of wind blowing down from the mountains. The Arenáles peered into the faces of the soldiers drawn up into lines on the rising ground between their tents and the frozen river. Cárdenas wore an expression as of a toothache. Dorantes stood apart with Fray Daniel and Portillo, but they were also inspected by the glowering husband.

"How Don García hates this," Fray Daniel whispered.

"It is the order of the general!" Portillo said pompously.

"Who endeavours to maintain the peaceful conquest," Dorantes said. Since his return to the army he had been feeling both oppressed and depressed, although this muster was certainly a sign of Coronado's good intentions. But yesterday Castro, Orduña, and the others of Melchor Díaz' little force had arrived with more and disturbing reports of the insurrections in New Galicia, that had now spread south from Zacatecas into Michoacan and Jalisco.

"Today the general is better," Portillo said. "The cough is better today."

"Restraints such as this bring powder kegs like Don García close to exploding," Fray Daniel said. "The general gave in to the captains in the matter of the cloaks, but the army-master must give in to the general in the matter of the execution of the guilty man, God rest his soul. Look, it snows again! Surely these are frozen tears."

"That is very poetical, Fray Daniel," the physician said, wringing his hands together to warm them.

Dorantes discerned from a slackening of tension that the guilty man had not been identified. There was a prolonged conference, Cárdenas, the interpreter, the notary, and the four Arenáles, all in their ballooning cloaks. The army-master's toothache appeared to have worsened. He shouted a wind-blown command, and, after interminable waiting and more angry orders, the horses and mules of the army were paraded before the Indians. The information was passed that although the husband had not identified the guilty man, he would know the horse he had held. The wife would not appear, in her shame. In these tense, impatient, and boring delays, Dorantes had an intuition of catastrophe impending.

The snow obscured the close-set buildings of the town and collected on the helmets and shoulders of the soldiers as the horses were paraded past the four Arenáles. He felt removed from the scene, drawn upward and away to a coign of vantage from which he watched in small the soldiers, the horses, the dark clots of the inhabitants of Arenál on their terraces and rooftops. He saw the inevitable identification of a chestnut horse, the husband, the three elders, and the three Spaniards stamping and gesticulating around the animal, presently its master and the soldier's captain, Tristán de Arellano, joining the argument. Angry words of accusation and denial rose against the drifting snowflakes that were sometimes blown horizontal in gusts of wind. He stood watching the scene with Fray Daniel and the physician, as though watching a staged tragedy.

The husband's accusations were denied. It could not be held that identification of a horse was an identification of his master. Cárdenas stood with his arms folded and his cloak drawn tight around his body, shaking his head. Abruptly the Indians turned away and hurried back across the frozen river. There was scattered laughter among the soldiers until the army-master turned a face of fury on them. The horses were led back to the corrals.

"Did you understand what was said, Andrés?" Fray Daniel asked.

"They say that the Christians do not keep their word."

Now, as the snow lightened momentarily, he could see the Indians watching from across the river. The husband and the chiefs scurried up the far bank, all bent forward at exactly the same angle in their haste. The sense of imminent calamity was very strong.

"The army-master is a good soldier," Portillo said. "He obeys when he must, but he protects his soldiers also. Clearly a man is not to be executed because his horse is identified."

"One fears this is not the end of the matter," Fray Daniel said sadly.

They stood conversing as the soldiers dispersed to their tents or their duties, Dorantes trying to think where his own lay. Snow drifted in scarves across the Valley of Tiguex in the fading light and blew in sharp bits into their faces. It was nearly dark when they saw the indigenes driving horses, with tossing heads and manes, across the river to Arenál, and heard the alarm given.

The tragedy continued to unfold. Most of the horses were recovered, but many had disappeared inside the log palisade, including several of the general's mules. In the morning, Cárdenas and two of the captains, with interpreters, went to parley, but were driven back by arrows. They reported a great noise within the palisade, where the captured horses were being punished with arrows: like a bull fight, they said. There was a conference among the captains as to how the Indians might be induced to come out on the plains to fight, for the walls of the town were very strong. Neither Dorantes nor any of the chaplains, except for Fray Juan, were consulted.

Coronado ordered the army-master to surround Arenál, and the captains Diego López and Pablo de Melgoza, with some soldiers, broke into the town from the rear, surprising the defenders and making their way to a rooftop. There they found themselves in danger from the stones and arrows from the higher roofs, and it was impossible to supply them with bolts or powder and shot, until the army had breeched the palisade. Even then the Arenáles continued to fight from within their houses. Fires were built to smoke them out. They were to be slaughtered if they did not surrender.

"Will you help me?" Dorantes said to Fray Daniel. "This must not continue."

"But what can we do, Andrés?"

"I think the Arenáles will listen to me, and Don García will listen to two of us more than to one."

The army-master stared at him, smoke-stained sweating face encased in his helmet. With his breastplate, mail neckpiece, and sleeves, sword in hand, he looked like a depiction of the Cid.

"I believe they will listen to me and Fray Daniel. They will not listen to you after yesterday."

Cárdenas scowled ferociously. Fray Juan, helmeted and corseleted also, leaned on his sword. "Tell them to send out the horse killers! Then we will talk!"

"We should pray for them, Fray Juan," Fray Daniel said.

"Time enough for that later, boy!"

"You speak their tongue well enough?" Cárdenas demanded.

"Well enough. And I know the sign." He crossed himself.

"They are not Christian!"

"They know the sign, I promise you!"

Cárdenas squinted up at the smoke billowing past the blank mud walls. They stood together, Dorantes, the army-master, the two friars, the captains Rodrigo Maldonado and Tristán de Arellano, and four musketeers. Arrows snicked past them and rattled and bounded off the hard-packed ground.

"Nothing will be gained if they are all broiled alive, Don García," Fray Daniel said, and, scowling, Cárdenas contrived to shrug and nod at the same time.

"Go to it, then!"

Dorantes trotted to the ladder, halting at the bottom to knot the chin-strap of his helmet and peer upward through the smoke. He climbed the rungs that were bound with rawhide to the poles of the uprights. An arrow whirred past his helmet. He was panting when Melgoza pulled him over the top onto the rooftop. Soldiers had flattened themselves against the wall of the next story. Diego López leaned on his crossbow, grinning in greeting. Melgoza helped Fray Daniel from the ladder, and they stumbled across the roof through the flung-down stones. From all around smoke blew out of doorways and window openings, to rise swirling against the leaden sky, sometimes flattening and blowing west.

"Hola, friends!" Melgoza said. "See how we have captured this place! What do you do here?"

Dorantes told him. Dark faces gazed down on them from parapet on parapet, where all the ladders had been drawn up. He moved away from the soldiers, beckoning to Fray Daniel to follow. With broad, slow gestures, facing upward, he made the sign of the cross. The friar followed suit. Dorantes stood looking from the Spaniards' upturned faces below to the down-turned ones above. He found the words.

"You must trust the Christians! You are angry because your cloaks were taken, and the woman molested, but the Christians are angry because of the killing of the horses. These angers must answer each other or many will die. The Christians do not wish to kill you. You will be well treated. You will not be harmed. Throw down your weapons and come down before it is too late!"

The silence was intense. Smoke billowed. A white-haired man ap-

3 4 5

peared on a higher rooftop, brown cheeks sagging as he peered down. He wore a white robe with his right arm free, a white feather in his headband.

"We cannot trust the Christians, who have broken their promises many times!"

His own voice scraped raw in his throat. "Do you know of the Children of the Sun?"

The brown face stared down at him. Within the silence was a rustling stirring. The chief said, "Why do you speak of the healers?"

He removed his helmet under the concentration of eyes staring down at him. "I was one of the healers," he said. "You may trust me."

The chief made the sign of the cross. Others did also. He and Fray Daniel crossed themselves again, fingers passed over steel breastplates.

"We will trust you," the chief said, and from all sides the Arenáles, men, women, and children, appeared on the edges of their rooftops, hazily seen through the smoke. The men began to throw down their weapons.

The file of the men of Arenál, more than two hundred of them, moved across the frozen river away from the smoking town, guarded by horsemen with lances and foot-soldiers with crossbows and arquebuses. Dorantes and Fray Daniel led the way.

They brought them to the great tent of the army-master, where the Indians edged inside past the two of them, eyes rolling white-rimmed at them for reassurance, in smoke-grimed faces. A sound of wood-chopping echoed from across the river, and Dorantes saw two soldiers carrying a peeled sapling taken from the palisade, and thought only that they had been set to dismantling the town's wall. One of the palings had been sunk in the ground before the gate, and soldiers were at work digging other holes. Snow and smoke swirled together.

The Indians were jammed inside the tent, surrounded by soldiers, all facing Cárdenas, whose helmet had been removed to reveal spikes of sweated black hair. With him were three captains. The blows of the axes continued to echo. The tent stank of sweat, smoke, fear, and, Dorantes realized, betrayal. There were rustles of whispering, a muffled exclamation, pushing movements. Dorantes saw two soldiers, one with hanks of cord clamped underarm, seizing one of the Indians.

The army-master caught his eye and beckoned. "Tell them they will have their hands tied! It is nothing. A precaution." His teeth glinted in his beard.

The silence was broken only by the arrhythmic chinking of the axes.

Fray Daniel's frightened eyes met his. He thrust his way forward to stand beside Cárdenas, facing the Arenál men who had trusted the Child of the Sun.

He shouted, "*It is a trap! They will burn you! Flee them!*"

The tent exploded as the Indians in a great surge burst out through the canvas walls. In a moment, except for the few the soldiers had already seized, all were gone, the soldiers running outside in pursuit. Cárdenas was bellowing.

Outside the Arenáles had scattered, running toward the plain, for they were deflected from the town by the horsemen on the other side of the ice. He saw horsemen galloping, lances slanting. He saw the first flower-burst of blood on a white cloak.

He ran panting to the general's tent. A guard tried to detain him, but he burst on inside and through to Coronado's chamber. The general reclined on his cot with a cup in his hand, Portillo standing beside him glancing back over his shoulder.

"They are killing the Indians who surrendered!"

Coronado made the sign of the cross left-handed. "Ah, Don Andrés, it cannot be helped. An example must be made—"

"They trusted me!" he panted. "They trusted Christians!"

"One understands your sympathies—"

"I am made a liar as well as you!"

Coronado closed his eyes in exhaustion or patience. Portillo shook a finger. He felt as though he were stifling. He plunged back outside.

Under the blowing snow the lancers ranged, driving the scattered Indians toward the town. One of the horses slipped and went down on the ice, and he felt an instant of elation to think it had broken through. Indians lay dead on the thin layer of snow that spangled the ground, bloody white and black bundles or half-naked bodies. Others were herded back toward Arenál, where a dozen stakes had been sunk before the walls. Already men had been bound to three of these. Others, prodded by lances, were forced to them. His heated brain summoned up the memory of white-skinned Castilians prodded up the steps of the great cu to the sacrificial stone; also of the betrayed Huasteco chieftains bound to stakes such as these on the order of Gonzalo de Sandoval, the good and obedient soldier of Hernán Cortés. He shouted hoarsely as he saw flames lick up toward a writhing brown body. He heard the screaming begin. He saw Cárdenas watching, standing with boots set apart and hands joined behind his back, within the group of captains.

He stooped to pick up one of the heavy tent stakes that had been knocked free of the ground by the flight of the Arenál men. He burst through the group toward the army-master, the club raised above his head. Cárdenas dodged the blow, shouting. Hands caught at him but could not hold him. He flung himself upon the army-master again, knocked suddenly to his knees by a blow on the back of his head. A second blow sent him face down to earth, spinning into darkness.

It had been for this then, the inexorable process that had brought him back to the north of the great journey, the Cíbola of disappointment, the Arenál of massacre.

Chapter Ten

In another snowstorm he led his horse along a stream half-crusted over with a film of ice among the bare trees of winter. He did not know where he was other than in a broad river valley, where miniature forests of pine appeared in the distance whenever the snow lifted, and some cultivated fields, although he had encountered no habitations or indigenes here. He must be somewhere between Chichilticalli and Corazones in the Valley of Sonora, that town that had received its name because there the Children of the Sun—himself, Álvar Nuñez Cabeza de Vaca, Alonso del Castillo, and the good black man Esteban, —had been given the hearts of deer to eat.

His horse, laden with his few belongings, stumbled footsore behind him. The snow drove across the valley in thin clouds. It caught in his beard. This must be the last snow of winter, for frail green already decorated the limbs of the white-trunked trees along the streams, and green shoots pushed through the earth in the fields he crossed. He breathed deep of the scent of spring and brushed the melting snow from his face.

The figure of the woman awaited him, dimly seen through the drifting veils. He halted for a moment, starting on with a jerk of the reins in his hand, steady clop of hoofs behind him. The sensation of warmth increased. Here the ground was clear of snow, and the field where she stood was spangled with flowers, red and yellow and white native blooms, not the Castilian roses of Juan Diego. She wore her starred cloak, with its tongues of light invisible from here as she patiently waited for him to approach, cowled dark face, a bundle held in her arms. It was the Child! He dropped the reins to kneel among the flowers before her. Her sweet face gazed down upon him, full of pity.

"My Lady," he said. "If only I could have brought back the warm clothing in time—" Emotion choked him.

"My Lady," he said again, when he had regained control of himself. "Everything I have done to try to please you has turned into the opposite of my intention. I have tried to save your own, only to destroy them. I am most heartily sorry."

"There is no offense, Captain Dorantes." She spoke in Castilian, better than his, her voice as sweet as her face. She lifted the bundle of the Infant higher against her breast. "When you have sought to serve, there can be no offense."

He tried once more to voice it, but she extended two fingers of her brown hand to stop his lips.

"I tell you there has been no fault. These matters are arranged by powers you may not understand. You must have faith that all is done for the greater good and the glory of God. *Look!*"

She unwrapped the Child, gurgling and sucking his fingers, little legs hinged up beneath his diaper. He gasped to see, upon the tiny, perfect feet, the bleeding wounds; upon the hands also; and the horror of the gaping mouth of a wound above the diaper. But the Child smiled sunnily, and exercised his bleeding extremities, and pressed himself to his Mother's body.

"Oh, my God, my God!" he whispered.

"But was this not done to the greater good?"

"Yes, my Lady."

Her face inclined as she wrapped the Child in her shawl again. "Perhaps I have understood no better than you," she said, "and my faith tested as well."

"And did you *accept?*" he managed.

She seemed not to have heard, her face still averted.

"I beg one favor, my Lady!"

She moved slightly, and her face, which she now raised, seemed remote, as though she had retreated from him, although she had not moved.

"I ask a penance for my offenses, whose weight I can no longer support."

Small white teeth glinted in her face, perhaps in amusement for those who suffered unnecessarily. She raised the two fingers of her free hand over his head. "My Andrés, I tell you again: only be what you are and there can be no offense."

"My Lady, a penance!" he cried.

"Well, then, one day you will build a chapel to the wounds of my Son!"

She gestured for him to rise, and he felt as though he had been bodily lifted. At the same time she receded from him, becoming once again the cloaked and misty figure he had first discerned, continuing to diminish until she had vanished.

He plucked up the reins and started on, plock of hoofs following him, through the fields of flowers that had not vanished with her.

Epilogue 1

As Cortés had warned, the Coronado expedition drained the Spanish power from New Galicia, and tribes that had been savaged by Guzmán, but never truly conquered, rebelled. What is called the Mixtón War was the only really dangerous native rebellion Spain faced in the New World. These tribes were chiefly Cascané, sometimes called Chichimecs, or barbarians, very fierce. They were joined by the Christianized Zacatécos. The rebels were incited by priests called Messengers of the Devil, who bragged of themselves as the Anti-Christ, and preached a new and terrible religion, which, however, incorporated the old blood rites. From fortified heights of land called peñoles, at Tepestistaque, Nochistlán, and Mixtón, the warriors swarmed to attack the Christians, who were everywhere defeated. One of their weapons was poisoned arrows, and men died in agony, with a pestilential stink, from only a scratch. Among the victims was Diego de Alcaráz, alcalde of San Gerónimo, who was stabbed with such an arrow by a mistress.

Pedro de Alvarado put in at Colima with his north-bound fleet to beg supplies from the viceroy. Mendoza prevailed upon Alvarado for military assistance, and the old conqueror marched to the relief of the Spaniards at Guadalajara. In the Spanish rout at the penol of Nochistlán, Alvarado was mortally wounded.

Bishop Zumárraga was appalled at the sweeping apostasy of the baptized tribes, for it seemed to him that his decision to baptize indigenes who had not been thoroughly inculcated in the Catholic faith had been tragically in error. As the idolators continued to gain strength, the viceroy was faced with the loss of New Spain and, if the uprisings spread, all the New World.

Antonio de Mendoza took the field in person, marching on Jalisco with an army of three hundred horse and one hundred and fifty foot, all the Spanish soldiers who could be scraped together. With them were fifty thousand Indian allies, including Tlaxcalans, Texcocans, Cholulans, and even Tarascans. The Indian lords were furnished with mounts and arms from the viceregal stables and armories, and, as the power of the encomenderos, who had failed to provide much military support, declined, that of the caciques increased. Once again Indians destroyed each other for the salvation of the Spaniards. The rebellious tribes were crushed, and the priests and war chiefs executed.

The Coronado expedition returned in failure in the spring of 1542. The general was carried on a litter, for he had fallen from a horse and been kicked in the head in Quivíra. His generalship came under severe investigation, for too much money and too many dreams had been wasted. It was clear, however, that his senses were impaired, and he was ultimately exonerated. Not so his second-in-command, the army-master García López de Cárdenas, who had been responsible for violent events at a time when legality and civilization had caught up with the conquerors. He was convicted, fined, and exiled from the New World.

The Mixtón War, which had threatened the rule of Spain in New Spain, the Crown believed to be directly due to conquistadorial oppression, specifically the savagery of Beltrán Nuño de Guzmán. This, combined with the revelations of the horrors of Pizarro's Conquest of Peru, resulted in the New Laws of 1542. The indigenes were given the rights of free vassals of the Crown. The granting of encomiendas and the Indians to work them was halted, and those existing were to be abolished upon the deaths of the incumbents.

There were by Mendoza's count 1,385 heads of families in New Spain, of whom 577 held encomiendas. This influential elite made such an outcry at the New Laws that violence and disorder became a strong possibility. The Crown did not relent, but Spanish lawyers devised compromises through "exceptions." Sons of the conquerors were granted these for one or more lifetimes, a few to the sixth generation; but all must expire with the direct line.

Meanwhile the Indians became more valuable because they were becoming scarce. Smallpox recurred about every seven years. As late as 1779 an epidemic killed 20% of the population of Mexico City. Measles, also a Spanish import, was almost as fatal.

Plagues like malaria and yellow fever, which had been imported from Africa along with Negro slaves, made the east coast almost uninhabitable, but most lethal was a virus that was either a form of typhus, or influenza, which struck above 3,000 feet of altitude, where the bulk of the Indians lived. In 1545 almost a million died of it, in 1576 almost two million. This bloodless destruction continued until, by 1650, only about a million Indians—of the population of perhaps eleven million which had inhabited Mexico at the time of the coming of Cortés—still lived.

After that date the population began to increase again, but now it was mestizo.

Epilogue II
The Children of the Sun

ALONSO DEL CASTILLO MALDONADO:
married a wealthy widow and embarked upon a life of comfort on the rents granted him by the viceroy from the town of Tehuacán. Nothing is known of his later years.

ESTEBAN DORANTES:
dead at Hawíkuh.

Or was he? An old report has it that he lived on in the country of the Mayos, marrying four or five women as was the custom there, and fathering many children. There is also a Zuni legend that the black white man with lips as red as chiles became a great chief among them. However, there is a Zuni song of the death of Esteban:

> *There by the river*
> *The black man was killed.*
> *Our grandfathers killed him*
> *There by the river.*
>
> *Then the white men came*
> *With their thundersticks.*
> *They seized the life-trails*
> *Of our grandfathers.*

He is also remembered by the Pueblo Indians, where dancers wear the black mask of Esteban el negro, and dolls are carved and painted in his image.

ÁLVAR NÚÑEZ CABEZA DE VACA:
appointed adelantado of the Province of Río de la Plata and set sail with an expedition in 1540. With a hundred and fifty men he marched

from Buenos Aires to Asunción, where he relieved the remnant of an earlier expedition, which was beseiged by the warlike Indians of Paraguay. The leader of this group was Martínez de Irala, who then became second in command to Cabeza de Vaca. The two leaders were immediately at odds, for Cabeza de Vaca was interested in civilizing the province by gentle means, and Irala sought conquest and the opening of an overland route to Peru. In violent conflict, finally Cabeza de Vaca was seized by the adherents of Irala on the pretext of conspiracy against the Crown and shipped back to Spain in chains.

He spent the next eight years in exile in Africa, trying to clear his name. He was finally recalled and appointed to a judgeship in Seville, where he died in 1564.

In 1542 his relation of his first great journey was published in Spain, entitled, *Naufragios—The Castaways*.

ANDRÉS DORANTES DE CARRANZA:
after serving the viceroy with great distinction in the reconquest of Jalisco, lived long in affluence and comfort, with extensive properties and large rents in the towns of Asala and Jalazintzo, "un caballero muy principal." He sired eleven children by his wife, María de la Torre, including three sons named Caspar, Melchor, and Baltasar—named perhaps for three who also made a journey to the west, although following the star that led them by night, rather than the sun by day.

Andrés Dorantes' own relation of the great journey has been lost, although references to such a document exist in the records of the Audiencia.

Author's Note

The journey of Álvar Núñez Cabeza de Vaca, Andrés Dorantes, Alonso del Castillo, and the slave Esteban across the continent in the years 1535–1536 is, of course, a matter of history. It has been considerably fictionalized here. It is a fact that Dorantes was first marked by the viceroy to lead an expedition to Cibola. Probably this project was abandoned because the great interest in Cibola aroused by the claims of Fray Marcos de Niza, and others, called for a much grander entrada, and as its general a noble and a wealthy man. Dorantes did unwillingly lend his slave to accompany Fray Marcos on his scouting expedition. The stories of Melchor Díaz and Diego de Alcaráz are also based upon fact. History records that Andrés Dorantes was of great assistance to the viceroy in the campaigns in Jalisco, and that he lived out a long life as a wealthy encomendero and citizen of the City of Mexico, where his descendants live today.

Cortés' emissary from Honduras to his friends in Mexico, his "Juan de Flechilla," was a Dorantes, but Martín rather than Andrés. All the rest of Dorantes' story herein is fiction.

The great idol of Huitzilopochtli, which was removed from its housing on the pyramid shortly before the Siege of Tenochtitlán began, has never been found.

Oakley Hall was born in San Diego and spent his youth there and in Hawaii. He took his B.A. at the University of California at Berkeley and his M.F.A. at the University of Iowa. He served in the Marine Corps in the Second World War. He is married to the photographer Barbara Hall, and they have four children. He divides his time between Squaw Valley in northern California and Irvine in the south, where he is a member of the staff of the Writing Program at the University of California. Two of his seventeen novels, Warlock *and* The Downhill Racers, *have been made into films, and he wrote the libretto for the opera* Angle of Repose, *which was presented by the San Francisco Opera Company as San Francisco's Bicentennial offering. He is a skier, tennis player, trekker, and Sunday painter.*